The
SLENDER
REED

By

H. H. LYNDE

CROWN PUBLISHERS

New York

PS
3515
U643
S5

To G. L. H. in appreciation of the
understanding and encouragement
so generously given for so
many years

Contents

Part One

Chapter One

AT THIS HOUR, AND THIS SEASON, DELEPHANT SQUARE WAS LIKE AN empty pool, with all the life drained out of it. No late strollers, no left-over couples on the park benches, no sleepy workers stumbling forth to an early job. Not yet. Even the breeze had dropped, so that the small new leaves on the trees were stiff and motionless. It was a hollow square, and the house fronts closing it in seemed only walls now, without their separate daylight characters. The Haskell Arms Apartments—the narrow old Delephant house—the corner drugstore with its faintly lighted glass front—even the Fairlie mansion, with its elaborate curve of reddish sandstone steps. . . People still called it the Fairlie mansion, sometimes in awe and sometimes in faintly envious derision, the fact being simply that they couldn't ignore it in 1928 any more than they could throughout the twenty-one years it had stood there. It was still the most imposing house on the Square. But at this hour it was only a shadow, a little larger and possibly a little blacker than the others.

Inside the house, the lower rooms were blacker still and vacantly quiet, except for the small one at the rear, the servants' dining room, where the dog Brute slept and snored. But on the second floor, there were people. More of the rooms were empty than were lived in, but there was a small one which opened into the passage between front and back halls, occupied by the upstairs maid (the young one with the red hair and the white skin). And across the front of the house, there were two big bedrooms with a small sitting room and a large bathroom between. The southeast one was Margaret's, and she lay there now, as deep in sleep as though day were still a matter of the indifferent, far-off future.

In the other bedroom however, someone—or something—was

3

moving. It paused at the door leading from the bathroom and listened, and took shape in the faint light coming in the open window. There was no daylight yet, just the diffusion from the street lamps which always lay in that room at night. In it, the shape became a man's, a tall man's, dressed in a long satin dressing gown with shadowy pajama legs showing beneath it. He didn't pause or listen long, only a couple of seconds, as he had paused an instant earlier when he entered the bathroom from the hallway. It occurred to him now that he might have turned on the water for a moment, to get himself a drink—to lend himself a sort of authenticity; but it really wasn't necessary. Madge hadn't so much as stirred.

He crossed the room softly and stood for another moment as he slid out of the dressing gown, looking down at the blurred shape on the other side of the enormous bed. His observation was detached, however, merely observation without thought. And without thought also, he climbed into his own side of the bed, shivered slightly at the cold place he found there, stretched out, and relaxed for a few more hours of sleep. Madge was still turned the other way, and she still didn't move—except for her eyelids, which opened, not sleepily but attentively. She looked at the wall opposite her, which had grown no lighter, and then she shut her eyes again, and gave a faint sigh. She wished she could sleep too for a while, if it only wouldn't start getting light too quickly now before she could drop off.

It was the third floor which caught the first light, when it came. When the first stab of sun came over the buildings at the corner of the Square and struck her window, Sarah knew it, and groaned slightly even before she opened her eyes. But she didn't lie there waiting to feel better about it. She knew her bones would ache just as much in ten minutes or half an hour as they did now. She put the covers back and sat up, groaning quietly again, and put her bare feet on the floor and went across to shut the window.

She shut it as blindly as though her eyes were still closed, not caring that the sun was bright, or that there was a froth of bright green leaves on the trees in the Square, which reached almost even with the third story level. Her business was to dress quietly, without disturbing Miss Margaret on the floor below, to wash expeditiously in the small bathroom between Ellen's room and hers, and rap on Ellen's door to wake her when she finished; to comb her thin white hair into its usual precise little bun, put on her spectacles and apron, and go down the narrow back stairs, past the second floor, without creaking unduly. (She wondered sometimes, dryly, whether her bones didn't creak louder than the stairs ever did.) And then on down into the maids' dining room, without falling over That Dog.

Sarah might have had a more sympathetic feeling for Brute, a very old collie whose name belied him, for his bones were as stiff as hers, or stiffer. But Sarah didn't hold with keeping any dog alive just because he was in a way the only thing left of young Ronnie Fairlie. She might have felt differently of course, if she'd been there herself when Ronnie was alive, but she'd only been with the family for seven years. Or she might have felt exactly the same; not having known the boy, she couldn't say.

She and Brute were always the first ones up and around the house. She let him out the front door when she went to take in the morning paper; it was supposed to be all right as long as there was still no traffic about. And presently she heard Sims rattling at the furnace down below, and was glad to feel a little heat seep through the house as she worked. She heard Ellen's slow heavy step in the kitchen too, after a bit, but she didn't go out there until she'd finished the dusting in her resentful but thorough way. By that time the other girl—that red-haired Nellie—was down too, and the three had their breakfast in the small back dining room where Brute had slept. They didn't say much. It wasn't until they'd begun to hear faint sounds above and the rush of the Mister's bath water in the pipes, that Ellen began wondering aloud what kind of eggs he'd be wanting this morning.

"Leastways, he always knows what he wants," said Sarah dryly. There was no reply to this, but the other knew what she meant. It wasn't so much a direct comment on the Mister, as it was a roundabout one on the Missis, who was felt not to have much of a mind of her own, or at least not to know her own mind, whatever it was. And yet privately, Sarah was inclined to think that Missis was the only one in the house with the beginnings of a sense of humor; and in the same way, it had come all over Ellen once or twice that Mrs. F. was the only one around there with real feelings—and Ellen in her emotional way put a high value on feelings. As for what Nellie thought, she hadn't been there long enough to count. She'd made a couple of fresh remarks at first about Her or Miss M. which Ellen and Sarah somewhat resented, but lately she'd gotten more careful. Mostly she just looked watchful now when they spoke of Mister or Missis. . . . The way she did this minute, her eyes half sleepy and half wary, shifting from Ellen to Sarah above her coffee cup. It rubbed Sarah the wrong way, and she looked at Nellie austerely as she got up and took her own coffee cup over to the sink.

"You'd better get up there and wake Miss M.," she remarked, "or we'll be diddling around here all day, before we can get the work done."

"O. K.," said Nellie, drawling it out. "O. K.!" But she lingered over the dregs of her coffee, and yawned again, to show she wasn't going to be bossed, or pushed around.

*　　*　　*

Sarah knew to the half minute just how much time she had to set the breakfast table. They could have set the clocks by Mister's bath water if they'd a mind to. And so, at twelve minutes past eight, as his decisive step came down the stairs, she had all the silver and china precisely laid and was on her way through the swing door with the rack of hot toast in one hand and the silver coffee pot in the other. She stood waiting as he pulled out his chair, pulled up the knees of his gray tweed trousers, and sat down. A tall, handsome man he was, in his early fifties. He had a strong-boned, slightly austere face, with a neat moustache half covering his mouth which was not austere at all, rather full in fact. He had gray eyes and light brown hair in which the white scarcely showed. He was the image of a successful and respected employer, and Sarah grudgingly considered him as satis-factory as any employer was likely to be. She waited until he had snapped out his napkin and laid it across his knees before she asked what kind of eggs he would have this morning, and when the answer came back, prompt and decisive, she nodded crisply and went off to the kitchen.

When the bell rang a few minutes later, she returned with the eggs and saw as she pushed open the swing door that Missis had come down meantime. She was not surprised, though she had not heard her on the stairs. Missis was a little thing, and quick moving, and you often didn't hear her going about the house. Sarah waited for her to remember to say good morning. Sometimes she did, and sometimes she didn't—though Sarah herself granted that it was more a matter of absent-mindedness than of varying temper. She put down Mister's eggs and took away the grapefruit, and had reached the swing door again before Missis suddenly looked up and smiled at her.

"Oh good morning, Sarah—I didn't notice—I'm sorry. I guess I was thinking of something else. . . ."

Sarah said, "Good morning, Ma'am," and went out thinking, poor thing, she looks washed out. Though, on second thought, her reason immediately rose to argue, I don't know why she should, I'm sure. She doesn't do so much in a week as I do in a morning, and that's a fact.

In the dining room, Mr. Fairlie, without raising his eyes from the paper, remarked reasonably, "If you do forget to speak to Sarah when she comes in, it doesn't do much good to go on apologizing and explaining about it afterward, you know."

"No, I suppose it doesn't," Mrs. Fairlie said uncertainly. "I suppose I do try to explain too much. I don't mean to, exactly, but I get started and then—"

"You're still doing it," he pointed out.

"Oh—yes, I am, aren't I?" She gave a sudden unexpected gurgle of laughter, and then stopped abruptly. After a long moment, starting on her toast, she said thoughtfully, "It's really better never to explain oneself, isn't it?"

He looked across at her then, but there was no guile in Madge's face; there never had been. Perhaps unfortunately. He knew it too well. Just a pointed little face which had been quite pretty at one time, though it hadn't lasted very well. She didn't have the bones that Margaret had, he thought, though he didn't quite follow out that thought to its logical conclusion, which was that Margaret had inherited his own good facial bony structure. Margaret had well-spaced gray eyes too, while Madge's were hazel. And hazel eyes were unsatisfactory to his notion, too changeable for beauty, too hard to pin down what was in them, if anything. They'd had a spark in them once, but too often now they had the look of burnt-out embers. Then there was her hair which had been curly and brown, but now it had a lot of gray running through it—no distinguished streaks or strands, just an indiscriminate sowing of whole threads. It sometimes occurred to Mr. Fairlie that Madge looked older for her forty-two years than he did for his fifty-three, since the white in his own hair didn't show if he kept it cut short at the temples. This pleased his vanity of course, but at the same time it irked him in an obscure way that his wife should lose her youth and her looks so early.

Not that he was thinking all this out at the breakfast table. He hadn't really sat and thought about her for years. He was merely conscious of her, and of a slightly irritated feeling which she stirred in him at times, through the layers of his various preoccupations. He turned back mentally to the latter, and to the newspaper, without quite being aware of having been diverted at all. But then, as Sarah came in with cereal for Madge, there was the dog edging in behind her from the pantry, the way he did every morning, and Mr. Fairlie's subterranean irritation transferred itself to the dog.

"That brute's going to get caught in the swing door one of these days," he said harshly. Brute (who had acquired his evil-sounding name just that way, quite innocently) paid no attention to Mr. Fairlie. He didn't hear very well any more, especially when he didn't care to. He went stiffly but directly to Mrs. Fairlie's chair, getting in Sarah's way of course, so that she had to reach over him to put the cereal dish in place, and there he stood pressed against her side, with his shaggy head lifted a trifle.

"Brute won't get caught in any door," Mrs. Fairlie said, gently but defensively. "He's much too smart." And she put her hand down on his ruff and twined her fingers in the long fur there until she could have taken a strong grip of it. Only of course she didn't. It was more than a pat on the head however; it was more like a clasp of hands, a reaching out for something that each needed, and Brute closed his eyes contentedly. It was their morning ritual, and it was all that he wanted. He didn't expect to be fed at the table, and after a moment he went, quite satisfied, to lie down in the patch of sunlight from the bay window. But Mr. Fairlie, observing the ritual as he had many times before, thought that there was something exaggerated in even that slight gesture of Madge's, something sentimentally overdone. It was all very well, Brute's having been Ronnie's dog, but it wasn't as though Madge had cared much for dogs ordinarily. She'd paid very little attention to Brute when Ronnie was alive.

Not that it mattered to him one way or another, as long as the dog didn't get under foot or start nipping the postman or delivery boys and bringing a lawsuit on him. He was very scrupulous about other peoples' rights and prerogatives, in business and civic relations. He began thinking about a complaint he'd had from one of his superintendents the day before, and so eased off again into one of those more congenial preoccupations. And presently he eased away from the dining room itself and the house, and the family, into that section of his life which absorbed him more than all the other pieces put together. He had driven off, on the back seat of the long black Lincoln, before Margaret had even put in an appearance downstairs, but Mrs. Fairlie was still waiting at the table, reading letters, half idly jotting down reminders about the meals, when the girl came down.

"Have a good time last night?" she asked, with quick interest, but gently, not as though she wanted to pry. And Margaret said, "Not bad. Not bad at all," in her light, offhand way. But presently she began telling her mother about the evening before, who was there, where they'd gone—not too much, just enough to make her feel that she was not being shut out. Or so Margaret believed, not examining the matter too closely.

They had a pleasant enough relationship, these two, although at times it might have seemed a little formal. And that might have been because Margaret, young and modern as she was, still was not exactly an informal person. It was typical that she had unconsciously appropriated the whole name of Margaret, and left her mother just the tag end of it. "Madge" fitted her mother so well anyway. It was only natural to think of her in diminutives, since she was such a small person. And that meant, in Margaret's mind, not only small in inches, but in some more intangible measure. Lots of little people loomed large in the world around them, but not Madge Fairlie.

Margaret's father and Margaret herself had been cast in a larger mold, mentally and physically. In fact it might have been because of that contrast with her father that, to the girl, her mother seemed such a little—even such an insignificant—person. Her father was, after all, rather a wonderful person, not only big and good-looking and generally to-be-looked-up-to as one of the prominent and successful men in town, but clever and astute, too, about so many things. To be sure, she didn't always agree with him; she even took an arbitrary pride in reserving some independence of her own, because she knew that really made her more like him. But she was deeply influenced by his judgment, whether she knew it or not. And possibly by his charm too, for she saw him as utterly charming whenever he wanted to be. He had a variable way of being charming, not so much in caprice as, it seemed, in appreciation of someone he approved. That was his way of rewarding someone who had pleased him—and his daughter was not insusceptible to that. She liked to please him, just as she wanted to live up to him. And though of course he had his typically fatherly and pompous moments, he always remained a compelling figure in her consciousness, and an interesting one too. So perhaps it was no wonder that while she loved and was profoundly proud of him, she was merely fond of—and often rather impatient with—her mother.

What she told her now was instinctively edited as she went along, trimmed to fit her listener's imagined capacities. And Mrs. Fairlie listened readily and without any outward evidence of missing what was not there. She had finished her own breakfast, but sat on at the table while Margaret ate hers. And when the small account was finished, it was Margaret, not Madge, who first inquired into the other's plans for the day.

"What's up?" she asked. "Have you got anything on for today?"

"Yes," her mother said promptly. "Several things. First, I've got to have a session with Ellen. And then some marketing and errands. And there's a Merritt Children's Home board meeting at lunchtime. And I want to stop and see Emmy Burns at the hospital either going or coming." She sounded rather pleased to offer Margaret such a busy-sounding schedule.

"Well!" said the girl, amused.

"Oh, and I'm going to stop in at Felice's and have the blue dress fitted too." But at that point Margaret grew firm.

"Darling," she said. "You're *not* going to try to have that altered when I'm not along!"

"Well, I thought you'd be busy."

"I will be. I'm playing golf. But you don't have to do it today. It's not warm enough to wear it anyway. And you'll never get it right without me."

Mrs. Fairlie looked a trifle unhappy, but not nettled. She sighed, looking down at her empty cereal dish with the little pool of cream left at the bottom. Margaret took the sigh for her answer, and pushed back her own chair briskly.

"That's a lamb," she said. "I don't know how you ever got dressed at all before I came along. Look, Mother, I'll take the coupe, that's all right, isn't it? You're taking Sims to drive the Lincoln, aren't you?"

Mrs. Fairlie lifted her chin.

"Oh, I don't know," she said perversely. "I just thought I might like to drive myself."

"Good Lord!" Margaret stopped in the doorway, and faced back toward her mother again. "*Why* should you want to do that? You know it makes Father and me nervous—and there's Sims just sitting there, eating his head off."

"But it seems so silly, keeping him waiting at all those places."

"That's what he's for, isn't he? And you know you hate parking. And you don't really want any more telegraph poles today, do you?" Margaret's voice was coaxing now, if ever so faintly satirical like her father's. They always brought up that telephone pole whenever she talked about driving herself. Madge sighed again resignedly, and got up from the table at last with a quick impulsive movement.

"All right, dear," she said. "You take the coupe and I'll take Sims."

Margaret nodded at her approvingly, and having gained her point, went swiftly on her way, without looking back again. If she had, she might have been puzzled by the small glint which came gradually into Madge's hazel eyes, as she stood there for an extra moment by her official place at the Fairlie table. Her head tilted just about an inch to one side—rather the way some men tilt their hard straw hats at the world—as she thought over what she had said. Well, I said I'd take Sims—yes, I did say that. But I *didn't* say I wouldn't have him drop me at Felice's, did I? No, she concluded, with a faint, arbitrary lift of spirit—I didn't. It wasn't enough of a lift to carry her very far of course, but at least it would get her started into one more day.

* * *

Her busy day was over by four o'clock. At least it was not much after that when Sims finally dropped her at home again. She rang the bell, because she never remembered to take a key, and after a long pause the door was opened by Nellie. (Sarah was off duty for her rest hour at this time.) The girl stood with a sullen, closed look on her face as she waited for the older woman to pass, and just for a second there was a curious hesitation in the latter; you might have thought there was a picket line which she was reluctant to cross. But then she stepped in, murmuring, "Good afternoon, Nellie," and when she saw Brute lying in the hall she added, "Hello, old Brute!" with almost a note of relief in her voice. He only raised his head and moved his tail faintly as she stooped to pat him, but his eyes were hopeful. Mrs. Fairlie sounded apologetic again.

"You want to go for a walk, old boy, don't you? Maybe after a while —can you wait awhile, Brute," she said ingratiatingly, "while I get cleaned up and rested a bit? You've been resting all day yourself, you know. . . ."

She kept on talking, with a self-conscious bright defensiveness, for as long as Nellie was in the hall. She knew that it sounded silly, but she couldn't help it. And Brute must have understood the gist of her remarks, even if they were silly, for he was standing waiting for her at the foot of the stairs when she came down a while later. She crossed quickly to the drawer in the hall table where his harness was kept, and put in on him while he stood patiently, but she didn't fasten the leash to it. He hated it so, and after all, he walked so sedately beside her nowadays that it surely wasn't necessary to put it on while they crossed the Square. Brute was resigned to having the undignified thing clipped on him whenever they went beyond that.

Outside, she crossed the street to the Square at once; they always went everywhere through the Square. The light was still pale and clear, though the sun was gone behind the houses, and people were beginning to come home from work, singly or in pairs, carrying packages in their arms. Delephant Square had been fashionable once, but it wasn't any more. It was too close to the railroad which ran half a dozen blocks west of it now, and to the run-down district which had grown up out that way. Some of the houses on the Square itself had even lost their early look of aggressive solidity. A tailor's shop had bored into the front of one, the drugstore had nicked the corner of another. Even The Haskell Arms, which had been one of the best apartment houses in town when it was built, had a seedy, indifferent look about it now. But the grass and the trees in the Square still made an oasis, as soon as they became faintly green. There was a refreshing, restful feeling about walking across it, though you had to watch your step for the warped and swollen places in the wide old-fashioned asphalt paths.

Mrs. Fairlie walked slowly, but with a lift in her step which she seldom lost. She paused now and then for Brute to investigate a tree or a trash basket, but mostly they walked along together so that the tips of her fingers just touched his ruff. Halfway across, they met Mr. Henry Delephant, who lifted his hat far off his head in his thorough, old school way, and gave them an almost courtly greeting as he passed. But Mr. Delephant was never one to pause and bandy the time of day about. You'd hardly suspect him of the whimsical turn of mind responsible for putting up the bronze baby elephant which spilled water into the edge of the children's wading pool. Yet he was the one who had done just that. It was his late father, old William Delephant, who had opened up the Square and built the narrow brick house on the west side, over fifty years before. But by the time Henry had come along to middle age the "D" had long since been chipped away from the street sign on the corner nearest town—the sign which had once said Delephant Square. And since everybody had taken to calling it Elephant Square instead (and no doubt thought that was its proper name) it had amused Mr. Henry to put up the fountain in an appropriate shape. The children loved its smooth bronze back, and the small curving trunk which playfully tossed a stream of water into the pool. In fact its back was kept smooth and shiny by the seats of all the children who had slid on and off it during the last thirty years.

There weren't many of them around now: a few on roller skates, often one skate to a child, since they didn't belong to the well-equipped and nurse-guarded breed which had once played there. They had thin faces and shrill raucous voices too. Madge Fairlie, reaching the edge of the Square and fumbling with the leash in her hand, preparatory to crossing the next street, was startled for a moment by one of the children's sudden shrieks. It was only a shriek of glee, but she had turned her head sharply to look back, and in that second, Brute, feeling no restraining leash upon him, had started impatiently into the street without her.

He had a certain scorn for traffic, shared by many other ancients, who either feel they are invulnerable, or that the world will wait for them. Furthermore, he had never quite taken in that the south side of his own private Square was its busiest boundary line, especially between the hours of five and six in the afternoon. And further still, Brute no longer heard nor saw very well. He didn't seem to hear Mrs. Fairlie at all when she suddenly called out to him. She had turned back to see him just stepping sedately off the curb, and seeing the truck coming from the left at the same instant, she made a quick desperate grab at the dog, her fingers just missing the long hair of his tail. She even took two steps out into the street as she called him sharply. But she had to stop, and her next call was a wail which mingled oddly with the honking of a horn.

The truck stopped not so many yards farther on, and a big man got out and came back, swearing, to look at the heap of fur lying in the street, while the traffic went around them both. He stooped over, and then looked up and saw the woman standing there a few feet away. Just standing, staring, with her face all crinkled up like an old woman's—or a child's, maybe.

"Say, I'm sorry, lady," he said, the bellow dying out of his voice. "This your dog?" She nodded her head up and down, and then began shaking it forlornly instead.

"He was my boy's," she said.

"Well, Jesus Christ—I beg your pardon ma'am . . . but that dog came right out without looking, and I couldn't miss him, that's all." He sounded aggrieved and defiant and ashamed all at once.

"I know," she said, and watched the man as he picked Brute up and brought him over and laid him on the grass beside the curb. He took his cap off then and turned to the woman awkwardly and helplessly.

"I'm sure sorry, Ma'am," he said again. "D'you think the kid's going to be so cut up about it? Can't you get him another?"

"He's dead," she said, looking up at him with wide blank eyes.

"Yeah—I know." The man spoke gently, but he was beginning to sweat, and he was puzzled too. The lady seemed to be only just realizing that the dog was dead. . . . And then, still looking at her, he saw those blank eyes had filled up with tears, and the tears were beginning to run down her middle-aged face. He didn't know what to do. He felt like a sure enough murderer, instead of a guy that had had an old dog just run out under his wheels. He guessed he couldn't leave her there alone on the street though, with her dead dog and a bunch of curious, calloused kids that had begun to come up and crowd around and stare at the dog, and at her too. She was getting to be more of a curiosity than the accident.

He took her home in his truck, finally, cruising slowly around the Square—like a hearse, with the dog in the back—to the house she pointed out. He hoped the kid the dog had belonged to wouldn't come tearing out now: he couldn't take it, on top of all the rest. But it was only an elderly maid that opened the door, and she never seemed to bat an eye at the whole performance. Just went off to get a lanky fellow she called Sims to attend to the dog, and then took the little gray-haired dame on into the house, sort of firm but kind, like she was a kid. She thanked him, that one, before she went in—"for all his trouble," she said, which didn't make him feel any better about it. Her voice sounded faint and kind of lost, and the tears were still running down her face as if the tap was on and nobody could turn it off, her least of all. He was glad to get out of there, and that was a fact.

But back in the Fairlie house, Madge's unaccountable grief did not seem to make as much of a ripple as it had in that one stranger's consciousness. There were a few clucking exclamations, and then the routine of the house flowed over the hole the slight disturbance had made. When Margaret came in she was told about it, and went up at once to see her mother, and when she came down presently she rang for Sarah and told her, in a tone of quiet constraint, that Mrs. Fairlie would not be down to dinner. She and her father sat down to the meal together. She was still wearing her small cloche hat, as she was going out again later, and that seemed to give a slight air of formality to the occasion. Especially since they talked carefully of superficial, non-private matters as was their way when Sarah was in the room. It wasn't until the main course had all been served and they were alone again that a pause came between them, almost an awkward pause, which was broken by Margaret.

"Doesn't it seem—queer to you, that Mother should have been quite so upset about this?"

Mr. Fairlie picked up his glass of water and took a long swallow.

"It was a shock, of course."

"Oh, of course it was, Father! And having it happen like that, the same way Ronnie . . . It all makes it that much worse, I know—" She broke off for a second, genuinely distressed in her own reserved way. "But what I mean is—" (she seemed to find difficulty in saying it)— "I never saw mother cry after Ronnie's death the way she has this time."

"Now that you speak of it, I don't think she did," her father agreed judiciously. Even dryly.

"I remember so well how Mother was that day, even if I was pretty young myself," Margaret went on in sober earnestness. "She was dazed and—sort of pitiful. But she didn't give way—not this way. Why, she was still crying when I left her just now, just sort of hopelessly, as if she couldn't stop. . . . It's almost as if—she cared more about Brute than she did about Ronnie," Margaret said in a hushed tone, and her eyes met her father's across the table, uncomprehendingly.

He glanced away, and then after a moment looked back and smiled at her slightly, as though to comfort her bewilderment, as though indeed their lack of comprehension of another person actually made a closer understanding between the two of them. He even shrugged his shoulders very slightly.

Chapter Two

IT WAS IN AUGUST OF THAT SAME YEAR, WHEN THE HOTTEST DAYS WERE past, and the Square lay in a sort of lull, not panting any more, just breathing softly and lazily, that Mr. Fairlie began again to speak of Entertaining. It was always a slight jolt to his wife, like coming down a small step that she didn't know was there. The Fairlies were all back in town again and ready to start the fall: Margaret after a month's visit out west, Madge after the same length of time up north at a mountain lake with her sister Lou. Hugo had suggested her taking Lou on a vacation, and though it was rather dull, and Lou took up bossing her around precisely where Hugo left off, she had seen little use in protesting. He himself had remained home, except for a vaguely sketched business trip to New York. It really wasn't surprising—rather characteristic instead—that he should look about for a ceremonial gesture to consolidate their separate returns; but Madge was taken unawares nevertheless.

The conversation had begun so innocuously. Margaret had said idly that "everyone" would be home again now before they knew it. And without any further bridge than that, Mr. Fairlie remarked, with a thoughtful look at Mrs. Fairlie, "You haven't had a party for quite a long time, do you know it?"

"Why yes," she said innocently. "We had the Bryants and the Joneses to dine just before we went away. And Mona and Ned—don't you remember?"

He smiled slightly, not at her, but across at Margaret.

"I meant a regular party," he said, in the indulgent grown-up tone which he might have used toward a child about a birthday treat, though the tone itself was not addressed to Margaret.

And it would be no treat to Madge. Her heart dropped a notch

16

as she stepped off that small jarring stair which she hadn't noticed in her way. Yet it was about time for him to think of something like this.

"People expect to be invited to a house like this every now and again, you know," he said. "To some kind of jamboree that they don't get everywhere else."

"I suppose so," Madge admitted reluctantly.

"Of course." He said it firmly and finally, agreeing with himself, since he knew that she did not. "We've got a certain position in the city, thanks to—a number of factors." (He passed over those, modestly.) "And since we're well able to do something a little extra for people, I feel it's up to us to do it."

"I know," she murmured. She'd heard all this before. But he was quite aware that she dreaded those big, tiresome expensive functions, and so he brought up his smooth array of arguments each time, though she never tried to oppose them any more. She just waited to see what kind of party he would feel properly represented him this year.

She sat passively and listened to the discussion going back and forth between Margaret and her father. The respective merits of a dance—a tea—cocktail party—reception; it didn't really matter to her. But it seemed that it should be something the older people would enjoy this time, after the dance for Margaret and her young friends last year. Gradually Hugo's idea evolved. A musicale, that was it; someone really good, from Chicago or even New York. A trio or a string quartette—something outstanding, to start off the season, give zest to peoples' return to town. About the first week in September, late in the afternoon, say, or quite early in the evening, with a really excellent supper afterward, and a good punch; none of this bathtub gin—and not just tea and cream puffs either . . . Hugo unfolded his thought with an air of creative largesse, until Margaret said indulgently, "You don't think people would *come* to a thing like that, do you?"

But even then he was not diverted.

"I certainly do," he said calmly.

"It sounds mid-Victorian," said Margaret.

Her father leaned back in his chair at the dinner table, and looked from one to the other as if regarding a directors' meeting.

"In the first place," he stated, "you have to remember that people will always come to this house, simply because they are flattered at being invited." Madge wondered if that were true; perhaps it was, though it seemed a repellent idea—she didn't like to think that people were like that. But Margaret looked thoughtful. "In the second place," he added dryly, "many people actually do like music." Of whom, thought Madge, in ever-recurrent wonder, Hugo Fairlie was one. It wasn't an assumed or manufactured part of him, that liking, as some of his other attitudes were; he really liked it. To Margaret, it was quite in character that her father should be a patron of the arts. She was proud that that was so, and it was her pride which gradually reassured her doubts about the party. At least it would be something Different, in this year of 1928. . . . For Margaret, to tell the truth, rather liked anything which set them apart and a step above the rest of the crowd. She was her father's daughter in that. So, quite suddenly, she dropped her critical detachment and smiled across at him.

"You know, it's quite an idea," she said appreciatively. "Once you get used to it. We'll surprise people, anyway! We'll practically knock their eyes and ears out at the same time, won't we?"

Her father looked back at her, mellowed by her approbation.

"I'm sure you'll attend to their eyes, my dear," he said. "I can count on you for that."

Madge listened to them, not quite dispassionately. Not that she minded their flattering each other, for she was used to Margaret and her father playing up to one another. She was even used to the slight disparagement of herself which was probably implied in Hugo's appreciation of Margaret. But she didn't feel dispassionate about this party; the mere thought of it depressed her too much. She went to bed that night with one more small weight tied around her neck. She knew it was small; she had long since learned to distinguish between large difficulties and small ones. (Everything was comparative of course; in the great cities even Hugo's fortune and Hugo's position would be— not small exactly, but certainly not so large.) But she had learned that she was small too, too small for all the things that Hugo and Margaret wanted to do or be. They had made her feel that so often, and for so long. You'd have thought that she might have grown up to them by this time; that she would have learned to cope gracefully with large dinners, large receptions; with Big Men and their big wives who came to town; with a large house and five servants and two cars, and a beautiful and capable daughter, and a large, handsome—too handsome— husband.

But it had always been like that, and she had never quite been able to fill up the space allotted to her. She had never wanted so much space in the first place. When Hugo had started to plan the house on Elephant Square, she had been startled by the size of his plans. She had quailed a little at the number of its rooms and wondered apprehensively if she could ever train and manage the servants needed for such an establishment. And when it came to decorating and furnishing it, her own knowledge and taste had apparently been quite inadequate, for Hugo himself had chosen or dictated most of what they bought. It was his taste which was represented in the fine heavy draperies and the massive furniture, in the deep coloring of the rugs and wall papers. Hugo had a discerning eye, there was no doubting that. . . .

It was the same way with clothes, as Margaret grew up. Madge couldn't have said just when she ceased to be the one who decided what they would both wear, but even as a child Margaret had been impatient of the things she chose for her. And for a long time now, Margaret had been the one to pick out not only her own clothes, but her mother's, while Madge in her candid way had to admit that Margaret's choice was better than hers, just as Hugo's was better in decorating the house. She had begun to paint some salad plates once, for china painting had been rather a fad when she was a girl. Madge had had a nice steady hand and she had loved tracing a fine gold band around a tea cup, or a flower in the center of a plate. She'd painted gold bands and twined initials on six after-dinner coffee cups for her sister Lou when she was engaged, and she'd done a whole dozen dessert plates, for Judy. But Hugo hadn't cared for the salad plates, so she put them away after doing only two. Hugo wanted only Dresden, or Coalport, or possibly Limoges, on his table.

All she could really do was to try to see that Hugo's china and glass wasn't broken, that the heavy silver was kept brightly polished, and the big house in passable order. She wasn't even a very good housekeeper, as he had implied more than once in the course of the years. She would have loved to let things go a little, even let them grow a little shabby and more comfortable. But she had learned, by trial and error, the routine of running the big house, and she always kept on trying. She knew *how* to give a large party now, though she didn't enjoy it. She would arrange with caterers, plan the food with them, see that extra cleaning and repairing were done, rent the chairs needed for the musicale, order the flowers, have her nails done and her hair waved—and appear in due course in her newest dress at the head of the receiving line. But she would lie awake at night worrying lest some detail had been forgotten, and in the end some detail *would* be forgotten, inevitably—some mistake made. It always was.

And when the party came she herself would be swallowed up in it, almost without a trace, even in her best dress which Margaret would have chosen for her. She never knew how far outsiders were deceived by her efforts to fill the place assigned to her; not very far, she suspected. She only knew that she would never deceive her family. Only Ronnie had thought her wonderful and lovely and entirely satisfactory. But she was not going to think about Ronnie any more, because that was useless. She had always known it was useless, but Brute's death had released her in some way from continuing to look back. At first the shock of it had seemed too much to bear; it had cut Ronnie off from her more completely than ever before, like the amputation of a long-aching part of her. Or had it only brought to life the nerves of what had been cut off so long before? Like the terrible pain people were said to feel in the stump of an amputated part?

Now at least she knew that the severance was final. No one understood quite what had happened to her that day when Brute was run over. She didn't, herself. But she was ashamed of having broken down like that. She had been trying ever since, in her quiet, matter-of-fact little way, to make them forget that she wasn't really a very well-organized or dependable person. She was a *nice* person, she thought hopefully, sometimes, in a fitful effort to be as fair to herself as she would be to someone else. But it had turned out that a Nice Person was not really what Hugo Fairlie had wanted. She didn't pretend about that any more. And there was no use in pretending, to herself, that she liked these big overgrown affairs either—with their fruity flavor of patronizing grandeur. . . .

* * *

The dress was gray; gray lace, with long tight-fitting sleeves and a long blouse tightly draped at the hips. That was one thing Madge never liked about the present styles: she was too short to have her waistline wrapped around her hips and her skirts chopped off at the knees; she had a hard enough time looking dignified anyway. But at least the new uneven hemline was a help, and with the gray lace cut into long flaring points, it almost gave the illusion of a gown which came to her ankles. On the whole, Madge decided that she looked quite nice.

She got up from her dressing-table bench, and turned, regarding herself obliquely in the long oval mirror. Yes—quite nice. But there was a quirk to her lips even as she thought—without saying—the words. Because she knew that it would begin to evaporate like a thin fog the moment Hugo looked her over. He was in his dressing room now, tying his tie before his own heavy chiffonier. The door stood open, and she could see the shoulder of his dazzling white shirt, turned away from her. He would be in presently. . . .

But even as she began to wonder hastily if she didn't need a bit more powder, someone else came to the hall door. There was a firm knock, and Madge called "Come in" lightly, almost gaily, thinking it was Margaret.

The door opened and Nellie stood there, in her neat gray uniform with its thin organdy collar and cuffs and frivolous small apron and cap to match. She looked very pretty, and it struck Madge for the first time, with a sense of ironic surprise, that the maid's uniform and her own new dress were much the same shade of gray. Only, it was much more becoming to Nellie, with her glowing red hair and lovely skin. These thoughts hurried after each other in Madge's mind as she turned toward the girl and heard her say, without any preliminary "Ma'am"—or in fact without any sign of deference at all—"Sarah says you want me staying up in Miss Margaret's room to help the ladies with their wraps."

"Yes, Nellie, I think that's where you'll be needed most."

"Well . . ." The girl seemed to accept this, grudgingly. But she had not finished. "Well, I suppose after they're all here, I can go downstairs and help in the dining room, can't I?"

"Why—no, I don't think I'd do that," Madge said slowly, but pleasantly. "Someone may come up again any time and want something—a few stitches taken in something perhaps, or a pin. You'd be of more help up here."

Nellie looked sullen, and not so pretty as she had a moment earlier.

"I don't see why I have to stay up here by myself," she said, rather like a spoiled child.

"Well, for one thing," Madge explained carefully, "the caterers are bringing plenty of their own people who are used to that kind of work, and you really aren't needed there today." She knew she was absurd, even to explain. But Nellie was still standing there in the doorway.

"Nobody's going to come back up here, Mrs. Fairlie," she said obstinately—and not quite so quietly. Perhaps she wanted Hugo to hear her . . . and Madge felt a stiffness run up her spine.

"I'm sorry, Nellie, but—" She was holding her ground until she felt the girl's eyes move beyond her, and she knew that Hugo had come to the other doorway. She felt a sudden constriction, as though she had stepped into a trap between them. A crawling, slimy trap, but one which clamped hard nevertheless. Nellie hadn't said another word, but her eyes had taken on a different, softer look, and as she looked across the room she had lifted her chin in a certain confident and provocative way. Madge turned her own head to look at Hugo, who stood there, impressive and impassive, beautifully groomed even without his coat. She said with difficulty—with great difficulty now in making her voice firm and audible—"Nellie was just asking where she was to help during the party, and I told her I preferred her to be in Margaret's room."

"I see," he said. Madge braced herself to hear him continue—in a large, indulgent way, no doubt—letting the girl off to do what she wanted. But he didn't continue. That was all he said: "I see," coolly, judicially, even indifferently. So Madge herself continued, with a careful detachment, "She would rather be downstairs with the others, I think."

"I don't see what that's got to do with it, if you want her up here."

It was not what either of them had expected him to say, and Madge looked at him again, quickly. At him, and then back to Nellie. Hugo's eyes had that bland, cold look which she had seen so many times before, but the girl had flushed slightly.

"That will be all then, Nellie," he said with finality. "You understand what Mrs. Fairlie wants you to do." And he turned away, back toward the other room. Nellie stared hotly after him for another second before she too turned quickly and left the room. And that was all there was to it. "That will be all, Nellie," he had said, and he hadn't meant just for this evening. It was like him, just like him: a clean cold knife—without anesthetic. But Madge was not capable, yet, of feeling sorry for the victim. It simply meant, she thought, that he was through with that one. It meant that she could dismiss Nellie now, that at least she need not have one of them right there in the house with her.

She began to take bigger, easier breaths again. But she felt a bit shaky now that the tenseness in her was loosening—and that was a nice thing, wasn't it?—to go down to preside over a party, feeling shaky to begin with. At least, she reminded herself thankfully, Hugo had not bothered to focus his critical attention on her and how she looked. She picked up her handkerchief and looked herself firmly in the eye in the mirror. Very well then, she still looked nice, didn't she? Very nice, she told herself again. But there was no conviction, no comfort, in that sort of reassurance. She would stop in Margaret's room, and see if she were ready. Margaret would be sure to be looking lovely, anyway, bless her heart . . . And Margaret might even think that Madge looked—all right; might even tell her so. She did sometimes, even if it was only in approval of her own handiwork.

*   *   *

Hugo had been right about people *coming,* she thought, a while later. Of course the acceptances had indicated that, but she hadn't realized how many there were until she saw them actually pouring in, like a flood coming in over the threshold. She had a slightly hysterical notion that the flood would keep rising—to the second floor and the third, and then to the roof—and she remembered pictures of people floating around their roofs on rafts, in boats. (Only this time, she thought inconsequently, the people would all be floating around in their best evening clothes—no, no, that wasn't right. The people were the flood this time, not the refugees. . . .) At any rate, she felt as she always did in a crowd, especially a socially bent crowd, that she must keep up at all cost, keep her head above the surface, treading water valiantly. Hugo was on one side of her and Margaret on the other, and that should have held her up, though it didn't, actually. The trouble was, Hugo would never believe that anyone could be so stupid about names, and didn't even try to help in passing them on to her. He thought she just didn't make the effort, whereas she did, such a tremendous effort that it left her memory blanker than before.

Even people she really ought to know had a way of eluding her at times like this, so that she could only smile helplessly and say, "You know my daughter Margaret, don't you?" hoping that the omission of their own names was not too obvious. Or she would think triumphantly that she really *had* the right name for some face and pronounce it firmly, only to realize as that face receded down the line that that couldn't have been Mrs. Richie after all, because she was in Europe this summer. . . . It was a blessed relief when she saw someone like Mona Cressley coming toward her (her dear friend Mona, in the too-tight pink satin)—or a couple like the Henry Delephants. . . . She thought how utterly unmistakable the Delephants would be in the largest crowd, he with his neat goatee and high collar, she with her air of complete serene dignity despite the long-waisted lace gown which hung so loosely on her narrow frame and went so oddly with the velvet band around her throat. "Quite like old times," she said with gracious approval to Madge, and though the latter didn't know just what old times she referred to, she smiled gratefully back at her.

But then after a while, when the bulk of the guests had arrived and begun settling themselves in the long semi-circular rows of chairs, Hugo and Margaret drifted off. And Madge was left alone at her post to greet the stragglers. Mostly younger people now, who could never bother to be on time—though Madge couldn't blame them, herself. A group came toward her just as she was considering moving away from her official corner: two young married couples whom she knew quite well, and then there was a young man behind them—but who didn't seem to be exactly with them. She was worriedly conscious of his moving up on her as she spoke to the others, because she didn't even know his face, and couldn't possibly remember his name. One of Margaret's friends, of course . . . though older than most of them, not quite so much of a mere boy . . . He was well built in a stocky way, with brown hair so curly that it looked springy, like the hair in a mattress. His eyes were such a light blue that they were surprising in that brown face; and he approached his hostess with a noncommittal speculative look, as if betting with himself as to whether she was going to know him or not, Mrs. Fairlie thought uneasily. To make up for her inner sense of inadequacy she greeted him rather more warmly than was necessary.

"How *nice* of you to come!" she exclaimed, smiling up at him as at one of her oldest friends. He shook hands and a slow grin came back to her in response.

"D'you think so?" he said.

"Why, of course I do. I think it's really rather charitable of you young people to come to a thing like this. Or are you very fond of music?" she added ingenuously, on an afterthought.

"Music?" He looked surprised. "Why yes, sure. I like music. Especially if it's got rhythm."

That seemed a strange rejoinder under the circumstances, but there was no use in pursuing it. She wished there had been someone else coming along behind him so that this still unclassified guest would have been moved along automatically and she could have dispensed with him. But there was a lull in late arrivals and the young man was looking over toward the filled ranks of chairs, now, as if he had just discovered and was puzzled by them.

"Have you seen Margaret?" Madge inquired, and his eyes swung back to her attentively. There was a suggestion of wariness in his manner, which went oddly with his air of calm, even arrogant, assurance.

"Why, no—not yet," he replied.

"I saw her out in the hall a few minutes ago," she offered helpfully. "Or—perhaps you'd rather find yourself a seat. I think they'll be beginning soon."

"You do?" he said. He sounded thoughtful now. "Well . . . I guess I'll go back to the hall then, see if she's around . . ."

"Yes, do that," she urged quickly, "she can find you a place with someone you know."

He half turned away, and then turned back toward her, and she saw that he was smiling again.

"Thanks," he said. He had a sudden smile, surprising in the same way that those light eyes were surprising in a dark face. It was a silly thing to think of, but it struck her that it was a rather disarming smile for a face which was otherwise—was it bold? Defiant? Over-assured—or over-guarded? She had no time to figure it out, or why he was thanking her. She only said, slightly bewildered, "Why, you're very welcome, I'm sure." And she thought, What an odd young man, and immediately forgot about him.

She wouldn't have thought of him again if she hadn't caught sight of him a few minutes later, talking to Margaret out near the stairway. So he'd found her, she noted absently, and then she noticed that the two of them had an intent, arrested look somehow, as they stood there. But it didn't occur to her to wonder what they might be saying. She only thought in passing that she must remember to ask Margaret who he was. And she noted too how really lovely the child was in that lime-green chiffon. Now Margaret, she thought, was tall enough, and slim enough, and graceful enough for any style. . . . And she was so confident and capable too; she could always cope with any occasion— anything that might come her way. Madge felt a surge of pride in Margaret, in her clear quiet beauty, her naturalness and self-possession —her lovely *rightness* wherever she was. And riding that wave momentarily, she felt another one following in its wake, a sudden confidence in the party itself. For once, she told herself, waiting almost serenely for the first sounds of the music to begin, she really believed it would go all right, without a single mistake on her part to mar the whole well-planned performance.

* * *

Mrs. Fairlie would have been astonished if she had heard as well as seen that conversation in the hall. Margaret had noticed the man standing near the foot of the stairs as she came out of the dining room.

Her attention was caught first, because she had never seen him before. She felt a moment's wonder about it, since the younger people on the list had all been among her own friends, but then of course—she told herself—one of them had brought him. That was it. Only, he was not with anyone at the moment; he was standing alone smoking a cigarette, and studying her father's portrait which hung over the lower landing of the stairs. That was the second thing which caught her attention. His interest in it gratified some obscure instinct in her.

He turned a little and seemed to see her coming and she looked at him casually as she went by, as she might at any umbrella stand or rubber plant along the way. And then when she was nearly past he spoke, in a level tone, without raising his voice at all to catch her attention.

"Hi," he said. "Don't you remember me?"

She turned quickly, genuinely startled for a second.

"Oh I'm sorry—I'm afraid I didn't just at first—how are you?" She said it almost automatically, but even as she did so, and looked straight at him, she felt a renewed assurance that she had no remembrance of that face.

"I'm fine," he said calmly, and added, "you're looking marvelous, yourself."

"Well—thank you . . ." She was annoyed to find that she sounded suddenly self-conscious. What was the matter with her, and who was this person anyway? She went on quickly, trying to pick up the hostess thread as smoothly as though she hadn't fumbled it. "Don't you want to find yourself a seat? I think they'll be beginning any minute now. Are you with anybody?"

"I am now," he said.

"Oh," Margaret said, and paused, just momentarily. "I'm afraid that's only a passing illusion," she told him coolly.

"Is that all you are?" he asked. He had a slow way of talking, taking his time—and hers, she thought impatiently. There was something just too calm and smart about him. Of course she had to be civil to a guest, but she didn't like him, and she didn't care who'd brought him. And then he smiled suddenly, and it was like a dog confidently waiting to be taken for a walk—confidently, but appealing to you not to disappoint him. It was ridiculous. But she had to make some answer.

"I'm afraid someone's keeping a place for me," she explained, trying to sound polite and patient and ironic at the same time. She wasn't sure that she accomplished it, but she started on. And in that same second the music started too, in the room beyond.

"Too bad," he murmured. "Too late."

She stopped again and glanced at him in annoyance, and found him grinning, and for no earthly reason she wanted to laugh too; she had to choke it down. He pointed to the stairs close beside them and she shrugged, and sat down there, and took on a remote listening expression. She seemed not to notice as he hitched up his neatly creased black trousers and sat down beside her. Her eyes never even wavered sidewise, but looked ahead, a clear, faraway look across the hall. Though she was not hearing a note of the music in the other room.

The large square hall was almost empty now, though there were two or three men standing around the library doorway, listening uneasily from there, as though they hadn't wanted to be trapped in chairs in the main room. One or two late arrivals came in the front door and made an elaborate business of tiptoeing across the hall and perching themselves gingerly on the high-backed chairs over there. And over inside the dining-room door, Margaret could see Sarah moving around quietly, not deigning to stop and listen.

She herself sat easily erect, with her hands laid together in her lap, her clear profile toward her unwanted companion. She was thoroughly irritated with him, for detaining her, for being there at all, for being himself—whoever he was. And yet, in some fantastic way she was enjoying herself. At the end of the first number she clapped conscientiously, and gave him a politely questioning look to suggest that he should be doing the same. And when he leaned forward a trifle, she thought he was going to comment on the music.

"Tell me something," he said in a low mutter. "Who is this guy just behind me?" She gave a quick startled look over her shoulder at the landing, which was empty. Except for her father's portrait, of course . . .

"You mean the painting?"

"That's right. Looks like an advertisement out of that new millionaire's rag called *Fortune*. That a real person?"

"Oh yes," said Margaret. "Quite real. Don't you know him?"

"Know him? Me?" The other chuckled. "Not in my club," he said.

"Really?" she murmured. "Of course he just happens to be your host tonight."

The young man turned to look at her with a half smile; one of his eyebrows seemed permanently higher than the other.

"No fooling?" he asked.

"Of course not," she replied, as if she were above such things, and frowned to remind him that the music was beginning again. When it stopped for the second time, he remarked, as though there had been no interruption, "So happens he wasn't the one who invited me tonight."

"Oh?" said Margaret pleasantly. "You know Mrs. Fairlie then. Or Margaret perhaps?" She added that as a happy afterthought.

"That's right. Had quite a little chat with Mrs. F. when I came in!"

"You did?"

He nodded thoughtfully. "Cute, isn't she?"

"Cute!" repeated Margaret. "Cute . . . Well—I—never happened to think of her that way. . . ." She seemed to swallow that down, and the young man looked at her more closely as he saw her reaction. "If you know Mrs. Fairlie so well," she began again, but this time it was he who silenced her, nodding toward the drawing room.

"There they go again," he said resignedly.

She wanted to laugh; she kept right on wanting to, first at one thing and then at another. The whole encounter was so perfectly absurd. But all she did was to move over slightly, ostensibly to rest her back against the stair rails. That way she faced a little toward him, and could look him over even while she seemed to be looking over him into the space the music made around them. He really wasn't bad looking at all. Well built—in that heavy, muscular way of course, and not as tall as the boys she liked, but he had good though rather blunt features. His hair was much too curly too, but he couldn't help that. At least he kept it as short as possible. His eyes gave her an odd feeling though, whenever she looked straight at them; as though she could look farther into them than she really meant to. Perhaps it was their lightness in his dark face . . . like a light window in a dark house.

He reached over to take the small printed program from between her fingers, and her attention moved to his hands. Margaret didn't like hairy hands, and his were not; neither were they overlarge. They were just clean, uneloquent hands; she couldn't tell whether they were capable or not. She wondered what he did with them. Nothing, probably, if wandering into a strange house without an invitation (something for nothing?) was part of his general policy in life. He was frowning at the program now, and when the music stopped with an abrupt clash this time, he looked up.

"Are they really going to play all those things?" he demanded, and she nodded serenely.

"Oh, I'm sure they are. That's what they came for."

"It'll take all night," he said gloomily.

"You didn't really know what you were getting into, did you?" she asked. She meant it to sound detached, perhaps a little amused, but for a moment she suspected that she had sounded merely curious. Or—worse yet—sympathetic.

"Gosh, no," he agreed. "I thought it was a dance. It looked pretty good from the outside. I was on my way to a place downtown, but this looked better and I just thought I'd stop in."

"Nice of you," said Margaret. She added coolly, "I always wondered just how one crashed a party. There seems to be such a lot of it these days."

"It's very simple, really."

"So I gather."

"And it's just as easy to walk out as to walk in," he said, almost curtly. She looked at him quickly, not sure whether he was offering to go—or did he actually think that was a threat? He was not smiling; he was looking at her with a sort of challenge, and again she had that feeling of going too far into that intent gaze. "We could leave, for instance," he said. "Right now."

"We?" It drew a gasp of laughter from her before she could smother it. "Why, I can't leave. Not possibly."

"Why not? We could just stroll across the park—sit out there a while and listen to it if you really want to—sound a lot better out there anyway."

"You don't understand," she said. "I couldn't leave, that's all."

"Somebody miss you?"

"Well—yes. Probably."

"We can always come back for the feed," he offered generously. "If there is a feed, that is."

She really was laughing now, helplessly, half indignantly too—but laughing.

"Oh there is," she said. "There is!"

He watched her laughing, indulgently at first, then suspiciously.

"Look," he said suddenly. "Is your name Margaret, by any chance?" She stopped laughing and just nodded. "My God," he said, not so much to her as to the empty hall in front of him.

The music began again. It was rather a long piece this time, but all through it he sat looking at her fixedly. She thought he might have turned away in some sort of embarrassment, but instead it was she who kept her gaze carefully averted. And when the periodic pause in the music came again, with its polite patter of applause, he acted again as if there had been no interruption. "Well, what of it?" he said.

"What of—what?" she replied.

"Well—your name's Margaret Fairlie—O. K.—mine's Clay Ferguson. Nobody's going to miss either of us till this show's over. Are you coming?"

"No," she said. He stood up.

"Too bad," he said, and held out his hand politely. Apparently he was leaving. She gave him her hand mechanically, though she smiled uncertainly; somewhere she had lost her code book, had almost an instinct to grope around for it somewhere.

"Nice meeting you," Clay Ferguson remarked, still looking thoughtfully down at her.

"It was so nice of you to come," she retorted lightly, but her eyes at that moment were as serious, almost as speculative as his. He gripped her hand harder all at once, so that her muscles stiffened to withdraw it, and with one motion he pulled her easily to her feet. They stared at each other, just a foot apart now, and Margaret's gaze was startled, her protest now more than a reflex.

"I thought you understood why I couldn't leave," she said a little petulantly, but he ignored both her words and her tone.

"We've got half the program still to go," he said. "Now's our chance."

Her eyes wandered over his shoulder to the dining room and then back to the drawing-room doorway, not so much looking for an escape as for a sign of her normal bearings. There was no one else in the hall now; the other stragglers had filtered on into the big room between the other numbers. And the violins were beginning another soft preliminary strain.

"Coming?" the man said again, rather gently, and Margaret smiled an absent, slightly bewildered smile. He put a hand on her arm, and she moved across the few feet to the front door, smoothly, as though she were on roller skates, with no more impulsion than that slight touch on her elbow. Through the vestibule, and the big outer door and down the curving steps, which looked like the inside of a serpent tonight, under the arched and striped awning which covered them. At the foot of the steps they turned to the right and walked along in the shadow of the house until they reached the corner. Clay Ferguson took her arm again there, and they crossed to the west side of the Square and turned again, in tacit agreement, and walked slowly along, arm in arm, past the old Delephant house, while the polite music from the open window of the Fairlie mansion fell farther and farther behind them.

Chapter Three

MR. FAIRLIE WAS THE ONLY ONE IN A REALLY GOOD HUMOR THE DAY after the party. He dropped a few gratified comments at breakfast, spoke of the music with a lingering zest, and of the number of people who had come, rather as a theater manager might speak of a good house—and then he dropped the whole subject from his mind. He had done his duty in instigation of and payment for the project, and his approval was the stamp of finality upon it. He had, also, the faculty for leaving anything that was finished completely behind him.

Madge was not so fortunate. She was relieved that it was over, but she was newly oppressed by the necessity for dealing with Nellie. She had often thought how strange it was that one could never climb one hill without finding another directly ahead; the country never seemed to flatten out. She began anxiously pondering how to approach this problem, since she knew that it was one of the things Hugo had left behind him—and left in her hands. It was as plain as though he had made a written request, signed with his initials, like an office memorandum. Just what line she ought to take with the girl, though . . . what pretext to use in getting rid of her as smoothly and painlessly as possible . . . that was what she didn't know. She shrank from the interview, and thought she'd put it off for a day or two, and think of the other things around her, while her mind presumably made itself up without her conscious connivance.

She was always aware of the different undercurrents which ran through the house. Sarah was tired out, but she went about with a grim, worn look, clearly determined to erase every last trace of the celebration; get the place cleaned up, as she put it, if it killed her. Ellen had a fit of indigestion after jealously sampling everything the caterers had produced, so that even her cheerful disposition was the

31

worse for wear. And Margaret was preoccupied, and at the same time
oddly jumpy.

But of them all, Madge was most aware of Nellie, even while she
tried to forget her. She had come downstairs the morning after with
a puffed, white look about the eyes and a downslant to her variable
mouth, and somehow Madge knew that the girl was hardly speaking to
anyone in the house, even the other servants. She herself avoided her
by the gentle tactic of not going up to her own room until well after
the hour when she knew Nellie would have finished the second floor,
and by staying out in the afternoon until she was sure Sarah would be
back on duty at the door.

But by the second day she realized suddenly, when the girl vanished down the hall as she came upstairs, that Nellie was trying to
avoid her also. It occurred to her, too, that Nellie was probably trying to see Hugo, and that she was not succeeding. It became a curious,
lopsided game, with six people living in one house, and one of them
trying to talk to one other and escape all the rest. Madge wasn't sure
whether Hugo was playing or not. He was quite capable of being
too preoccupied to notice what was going on in his house, though
never in his office. On the other hand, he was equally capable of
ignoring the girl, theoretically letting her beat against the wall which
was himself. Possibly even proud of the fact that the wall was so stout
it could feel nothing.

It was not an edifying game from where Madge looked on. And yet,
with each day it seemed harder to find the right move to end it. Perhaps she was hoping that Nellie would stalk her prey (if hunting *was*
a game?) until on some turn of the stairs or end of a hallway, he would
have to turn and deal with her himself. Would send her off, in other
words, and save Madge the unpleasant responsibility. After all these
years with Hugo, it sometimes seemed to his wife that the chief emotion left to her was that one of cloying humiliation at being so irre-
trievably involved in his life that she appeared to condone it. Well,
that was her own fault, of course, her own cowardice. And habit was
a paralyzing thing, too.

One morning when she was late in coming down, and met Hugo
on the stairs coming up again after his breakfast, she stopped a moment as if unsure whether she herself meant to go up or down. She
had seen the door in the small passage from the upper hall open a
little and show a glimpse of Nellie's blue uniform, before it hastily
closed again. So she was up there waiting, and this time she would
find Hugo alone. She felt a surge of relief—almost pleasure—but just

for a moment Madge had had the unreasonable, wholly unaccountable feeling that she should warn him, and her involuntary halt on the stairs did make him pause.

"What's the matter?" he asked, but she was moving past him now.

"Nothing," she replied, her glance avoiding his.

"Well, what made you stop in your tracks like that?" he said impatiently.

"I—thought I'd forgotten something, that's all," she said, and continued on down the stairs. Now perhaps he would go, she thought, and settle his own overdue account. But instead, she heard his step turn and follow her, and on the lower landing she stopped again.

"What is the matter with *you?*" she asked, in her turn, a little startled.

"You reminded me of what I'd forgotten myself," he said, smiling slightly as she stared at him. "I left my brief case in the den," he remarked, but not, she felt, entirely relevantly.

"Oh." Her rejoinder was flat, disappointed. "You're off right away then?"

"Right away," he replied very amiably. He put a finger under her chin and bent to kiss her lightly. In approbation, it seemed. So her swift glance upward had warned him, in spite of herself, and he thought she had done it intentionally. Mrs. Fairlie turned and went into the dining room, and she couldn't have said at that moment whether her feeling of numb disgust was more for her husband or herself. The very idea of letting that girl stay on one extra minute in the house . . . And here it had been four—no, five—days since the party.

Disgust rode her throughout breakfast, so that she didn't eat much, and the same disgust drove her upstairs at once after she had planned the meals with Ellen. She couldn't let this go on, and live in the same house with *herself.* She would have to tackle the girl—now. When she reached her room, she moved around it nervously for a few moments, nerving herself for that one when Nellie would appear. She could hear her in Margaret's room. And then suddenly the strident whine of the vacuum cleaner took the air like a rising plane, and Madge actually jumped. Cleaning morning upstairs—of course; she'd forgotten. Well, she couldn't go following the girl around trying to out-talk that awful noise. And if she told Nellie to go right now, or if Nellie should suddenly depart in the midst of the upstairs cleaning, there would be Sarah to cope with then, and a very dour Sarah it would be. Slowly, the determination which her disgust had hardened in her began to melt down again, in a soft mush of indecision. Well then, she thought, resignedly, it would have to be another day. And what did one day matter, more or less?

So she went on with her engagements, lunch at the Town Club, and a drive to the country afterward to take two of the guests home. And then she was to pick up Margaret out at the Highlands as she came back. She was a little late, and Margaret looked faintly disgruntled as she heaved her golf clubs into the car and got in after them. Margaret's normally calm temper had not been as even these last days—ever since the party, in fact—and her mother didn't know why. Probably indigestion, like Ellen's. But even so, Madge had a sense of warmth as they drove home together. She didn't recognize it as relief that she wouldn't have to meet Nellie alone at the front door; she hadn't yet returned mentally to her problems at home. But as when one wakes from a nap, there was that slight unwelcome intuition of a weight which had never moved.

When they reached the house, and as they stood waiting at the door for Nellie to answer the bell, it all began to bear down on her again. And she saw immediately the different look on Nellie's face as she held the door open for them. It had always been a little contemptuous before, under the top layer of sullen civility, but now it was definitely hostile, and it was directed at her. Madge felt the girl hating her as she passed her, and wondered for a second why she had been promoted—in a way—from a merely stupid inanimate obstacle, to someone dangerous enough to hate. And then of course she knew. It was because Nellie had heard them on the stairs that morning, and thought that she was trying to protect Hugo. For herself. She went past her as quickly as possible, and turned immediately toward the stairs at her left, as Margaret followed more deliberately. There was a small tray on the hall table which was always kept for cards or messages, and though Madge generally forgot to look at it, Margaret now went across the hall to see what was there. She picked up a card and at once put it down again.

"Mrs. Delephant was here," she said wearily. "Party call, no doubt. Imagine that!" She gave a half laugh, without amusement, and turned toward the stairs to follow her mother. But as if on an afterthought, she spoke over her shoulder to Nellie, who was just closing the hall door. "No telephone calls, I suppose, Nellie?"

"No, Miss." Nellie had a way of making her tone so polite as to sound almost satirical sometimes. (Or was she the only one who heard it that way? Madge wondered.) But then the door below had opened wider again. "Oh yes," Nellie conceded, "there was one gentleman that phoned."

Margaret stopped with her hand on the newel post. Without turning, she said, "For me? What was the name?"

"I don't know, Miss. He didn't say." Nellie sounded bored.

"Didn't you ask the name?"

"No, I didn't. He just asked was you in, and I said you wasn't."

Margaret turned around squarely on that.

"Nellie, you know that when there are telephone calls, you are supposed to ask if there's any name or message to be left." Nellie looked back at her across the hall, a cool long-range look, without any further answer. "You know that, don't you?" Margaret said impatiently.

"I suppose so." Even the tone was hardly courteous now. But on the other hand, Madge thought worriedly, Margaret was being unduly sharp. She moved more slowly up the stairs, wondering if she hadn't better step into this, but as always, she hesitated.

"Of course you know it," Margaret snapped. "And if you're to fill in for Sarah on her afternoon off you'll have to do better than that, you know."

"Margaret!" her mother interjected mildly from above, where she had paused. "I'm sure Nellie will remember next—" She had started to say "next time" and then broken off, rather shocked at her own reflex. But Margaret heard nothing of that.

"Please see that you do," she said to the girl, coldly now, as if closing the incident. But as she started up the stairs again from the lower landing, Nellie let go the handle of the door which she had been gripping, and took several steps toward the center of the hall. And she raised her voice as though to be sure to overreach those few steps upward which Margaret had taken.

"What makes you think you can order me around like that, Miss?" she demanded, and this time the "miss" was used not as a sop to civility, but rather as though an older person were addressing a child, and an impudent child at that. Margaret stopped, astonished, and looked down at her over the railing.

"I don't know what you're talking about," she said, "or what you're thinking of, to speak to me that way."

"Oh, you don't, don't you?" Nellie retorted in a lower tone again, but a more deadly one, as she took a few more steps out into the hall. "You think you can talk to me any way you like, don't you, and I can't even answer back? Well, maybe you'd better think again, Miss Margaret, because I've got quite a few things to get off my chest."

To Madge, those last words held a warning, which suddenly chilled her. . . . She had stopped dead still on the fourth step from the top, as Margaret had stopped halfway down. It was as if they were on a moving staircase whose cable had stuck beneath them, while Nellie on her level ground steadily closed in on them. But Madge had found her voice at last.

"Really," she said, "I think we've had enough of this, from both sides. I am amazed at both of you. Miss Margaret may have spoken too hastily, Nellie, or too sharply, but—"

"I think I can handle this myself, Mother," Margaret said below her.

"Go on and handle it, Miss Margaret," said Nellie. "Just take a good hold of it. But maybe you'll find it kind of hot."

Madge took a sharp little breath, but Margaret was going right on, picking up the challenge rather as though it were a soiled dust rag which someone had carelessly dropped in the front hall—no more than that. She was quite self-possessed now, cool, but reasonable.

"I don't know what's come over you, Nellie," she said. "I asked you a civil question and you answered—not too civilly, I might add. You had failed to do what you were supposed to about the telephone calls, and I corrected you. At which you became insolent—"

"Oh, yeah?" Nellie said, a little more loudly. "It's insolent, isn't it, when *I* so much as open my mouth, but it's just lovely when you talk to me like I was dirt! That's just acting like a lady, isn't it?"

She had come all the way across the hall now, and she had stopped at the foot of the stairs, but put one foot upon the lower one as if she might come farther. The more reasonable Margaret had become, the more it had enraged the other girl, but it was a deep sulphurous rage that wasn't all the way out in the open, even yet. Of course she'd been just ready to go off into an explosion like this, Madge knew, but she'd never dreamt that it might break out in Margaret's uncomprehending face. The latter looked rather white now but Nellie was going right ahead.

"Maybe I don't think so much of *ladies* after what I've seen around here! No, nor gentlemen neither. Society folks, huh? Rich society bums, that's all you are . . . putting on the dog and giving your dead pan parties . . . and walking over the likes of common people like me that never asked anything of any of you except to get a decent living . . . and be let alone—" With all its passion, the girl's outbreak was strangely impotent, and pitiful because of that. It had a furious, helpless—and young—ineptness about it because she couldn't *do* anything to assuage her own hurt. But she could still hurt others. . . .

"Nellie!" Madge said sharply, her one idea now to penetrate the red fog in which the other had become smothered, to bring her out of it, somehow. She came down the stairs slowly, passing Margaret who murmured, "I think she's crazy! She must have gone out of her head."

"Go on upstairs," her mother said quietly. "I'll talk to her. This has got to stop—" (But she hadn't meant to do it this way, never this way, with Margaret being swept into the horrid mess. She'd waited too long, of course—stupid and cowardly as usual—until the one child she had left was about to step into the crevasse which she had never even known ran right under and through her own house.)

"Oh, it's got to stop now, has it?" Nellie jeered, more softly now that she saw Madge coming down within her range. "Yeah, it's about time, isn't it? Funny thing to me is you never tried to stop it before. *I* thought you didn't know, but you did, didn't you—all the time, I'll bet. Sweet set-up you've got here, haven't you? So sweet it stinks!"

Madge was trembling slightly, and she stopped again a few steps above Nellie, to hold on to the bannister to steady herself. What *could* she do to stop the girl—with Margaret still looking on and listening from higher up? Stupidity, she supposed, was still her only recourse. Her refuge.

"I don't know what you think you're gaining by such behavior, Nellie. I don't know what you're talking about and I don't think I care to. Of course you know you can't stay on here now—"

"As if I wanted to!" the girl shot back, passionately. "As if I'd stay if you begged me to—you—and him—and her too. All I want's to tell every damned one of you what I think of you before I clear out!"

The door behind her, the front door, clicked as a key turned in the lock from outside. It opened, and Hugo came into the vestibule, closing it behind him, putting his hat on the high table there as he came. The three on the stairs, as if on one controlling shaft, turned and looked at him. The hall was silent as he stepped into it.

"Well!" he said, and then, "Well?" on a note of well-bred, not too interested interrogation.

"Nellie is leaving," Madge answered, in a small but distinct voice, not knowing what—or who—would answer that. But something had to be said, someone had to say it. "She is not happy here any more, I think," she added carefully.

"Is that so?" He looked at the girl with mild disinterest, just a passing glance as though to identify someone he had scarcely noticed before. "Well," he said again, with an equally brief glance at Madge, "it's up to you, my dear. You know I'm not interested in these domestic matters." He passed around Nellie, deviating only a step or two out of his way to the library door.

Madge didn't know from the look with which Nellie followed his retreating, imperturbable back, what sort of an outbreak would follow now. With Margaret still up there, listening . . . If only the child had gone on to her room. If only . . . But there was no time even to pray . . . even if she had known how. She spoke quickly, and quietly, too, because she hadn't much breath left in her.

"I think you'd better go now, Nellie." The girl's glance came slowly back from the library door and up to Madge. Her rebellious mouth was working slightly, but there was a glaze of tears in her eyes. They looked at each other silently for a long moment; the only sound was a slight uneasy cough at the head of the stairs, the abrupt rattle of a newspaper being unfolded in the den.

Madge said, "Do you want to stay on tonight, as it's so late?"

"No," Nellie answered. "No—thanks," she added bitterly—but that was all.

"Very well, then. I'll see that your check is ready when you come down."

She turned away, and looked up the long, long flight of stairs above her, and at the same time she saw Nellie turn the other way, and start quickly across the hall, but not toward the den. Above, Margaret stood waiting for her, and Madge plodded up toward her, her knees shaking, and the palm of her hand sticky on the balustrade.

At the top Margaret said, "Of all the extraordinary performances I ever saw! Do you think she really is a little off?"

"I—I don't know," Madge said. "I think—she must be one of these radicals one reads so much about—resenting people who have any money so much that everything becomes a sort of, well—personal affront. You heard how she went on about the common people and so on." (If only she could lead Margaret's attention down that road.)

"Oh, I hadn't the faintest idea what she was talking about," Margaret admitted impatiently. "I never in my life heard such a lot of muddled nonsense."

"She's—a very emotional girl, apparently," said Madge. She felt dreadfully tired, from being pulled in so many ways. She'd even felt sorry for Nellie, and she resented having to feel that way. But there was still something—what was it?—that she had to say. Oh, yes. "And then," she went on, "it really wasn't nice, the way you spoke to her at first, you know."

"Seems to me she had it coming," Margaret said stonily. "Maybe—I spoke too fast. But I was annoyed and I think I had reason to be."

"It was a small thing, after all."

"Not to me," said Margaret abruptly, and started to move off.

"Why, dear?" Madge tried to think back to how it had all begun. She couldn't quite remember now.

"Oh, it doesn't matter any more." Margaret was offhand.

"Was there—were you expecting to hear from somebody special?"

There was a second's pause, before Margaret said, "No," rather bleakly, and then more firmly, "No, of course not," and went along the hall to her room.

* * *

It was two or three weeks after the party that Mrs. Fairlie ran across that same young man with the tight curly hair and brought him home for cocktails. But it was entirely accidental and coincidental on her part. If, that is, behaving the way one's character prompts one to behave can be called coincidental. The trouble was, Madge herself could never tell what her character was going to get her into, or how it would act when she got there. The dentist had kept her a long time, and it was late in the afternoon when she came down in the elevator. She scarcely glanced at the two other people in the car with her, until one got off at the twelfth floor and her attention was somehow called to the other—quite possibly because he was looking at her. He looked away as she glanced up, and she had that familiar guilty jolt within her, wondering whether it was someone she should have recognized. He did look just a trifle . . . yes, just a little bit—oh, it was coming to her now . . . the party, that's where it was. The young man Margaret hadn't been able to recollect for her afterward. She'd even sounded a shade irritable about it. "Good heavens, Mother," she'd said. "I don't begin to remember all the hordes who were there. Probably just a friend-of-a-friend who dragged him along." So of course Madge still didn't know his name.

"How do you do?" she said so suddenly that he looked at her again in surprise, though not as if pretending he hadn't known she was there.

"How are you, Mrs. Fairlie?" he said.

Madge was relieved to find she hadn't made a mistake, and broke into a hasty smile, a somewhat dentisty smile, she felt, the sort that lingers with you until your mouth resumes its normal shape after undue stretching. "We haven't seen you for some time," she said brightly.

"That's right," he agreed. "Not since that musical party of yours." (Sounded like Musical Chairs, she thought, and wanted to giggle.) "I suppose you've all recovered from that by now?" he inquired, making it sound like a minor accident, though it seemed to her there was something faintly ironic in his tone.

"Oh yes," said Mrs. Fairlie cheerfully. "We're all back to normal again now." (Ellen's tummy has settled down, and so has Sarah's disposition, and the housemaid my husband was sleeping with has departed, I'm glad to say . . . she went on blithely in her own mind, and wondered with one of her unpredictable bursts of inner hilarity what the young man would have thought if she'd said that aloud.) She had to restrain herself from smiling, because he didn't look a bit responsive, even to her most innocuous remarks.

The fact was, his manner was quite different from what she remembered of it before. He was so unsmiling this time—a little stiff, she felt. Well, of course it was the second time she hadn't recognized him right away. People were funny about that; they did like to be recognized. She was thankful when the elevator door opened and she could step out briskly, smiling sidewise in passing. "Nice to have seen you," she acknowledged pleasantly, and he nodded—and followed right along after her, almost beside her. Well, naturally he had to get out of the building too. He couldn't be expected to remain in the lobby. So, feeling rather impatient about it, she picked up the silly little conversation again.

"Our September weather seems to have turned rather sour, doesn't it?" she suggested chattily. He opened the outer door for her.

"Still raining, is it?"

"It was when I came in. Oh dear, I'm afraid it's pouring now."

She saw with relief that Sims was there with the Lincoln, right at the curb. And then she saw that the young man was turning up his coat collar, that he had no overcoat, and that he didn't have a hat at all, not even in his hand. Men had no sense about rubbers and umbrellas and overcoats—just silly smarty little boys, all of them, thinking they were so tough until they got a cold in the head! But she still had that slight sense of contrition about this one, she didn't know quite why, just because she couldn't remember his name she supposed. She wished she weren't such a fool, or could at least be hard-boiled about it.

"Oh dear," she said again, "you're going to get soaked. Couldn't I give you a lift—that is—I don't suppose you're going out toward Elephant Square, are you?"

He turned and looked at her, hopeful and skeptical at the same time, and then glanced from her to the wet street and the umbrellas mushrooming by them on the sidewalk.

"Matter of fact," he said, "I do live up a piece beyond the Square. But I don't want to take you out of your way."

"Don't be silly," she said, half impatiently. "Come along." And she made a little run for the car, with him following her. But once inside the car, and with him beside her, she had a feeling of rather bewildered surprise at finding him still there. A sort of now-that-I've-got-him-here-what-do-I-do-with-him feeling. What a nuisance. If only she had some handle with which to get hold of him; if only Margaret had been more helpful, recollected where she'd met him, whom he knew, where he'd come from. *Something.* And then too, she couldn't get away from the impression that he was on his dignity, offended in some way. He was civil but offhand. He looked straight ahead most of the time, and the couple of times he glanced at her, his glance was a trifle—was it hostile—or curious—or was it just the sardonic, protective expression of youth? Oh, well, it was only a matter of a few minutes, and at least she'd saved him a walk in the rain, or a wait for the bus. But as they came around the Square she began to feel less impatient and more compassionate, and to wonder whether she ought not to ask him in. Hugo always had a cocktail ready about this time. It wouldn't hurt anybody just to be friendly. But the young man declined at first. He looked at her sidewise before answering.

"Thanks," he said, "but I guess I'd better not accept that one." And there was no doubt, this time, that his tone was ironic. Good heavens, the young fool didn't think she was asking him in because she'd taken a special fancy to him, did he? Now really!

"Just as you like," she said quickly, and then to disabuse him further of any such notion she added, with that fatal urge of hers toward irrelevant explanation, "It just occurred to me that Margaret would be in by now, that was all. . . ." (Oh dear, she thought, whatever had made her say *that?* As if Margaret needed young men dragged in off the street to call on her!) The things she said were always surprising her; some of them often stunned her. But the young man's reaction to this last surprised her even more.

"Oh she will, will she?" he asked slowly.

"Why—I think so." Mrs. Fairlie was nonplused by his tone.

"And you think she'd like to see me." It was more a statement than a question.

"Why, I expect she would," she said politely, but stiffly now. What else could she say at that point—that Margaret couldn't even remember his name when she'd asked her who he was? Madge was tempted almost unbearably to say just that. But then he smiled, quite a nice warm disarming smile. It was as if he'd turned a different colored light on himself. She really didn't know what to make of him.

"O. K.," he said suddenly. "Let's go!"

Mrs. Fairlie felt a little shaken by this time. He certainly was a strange young man. After all, she'd only been trying to be kind, in a casual way. But something seemed to have gotten away from her, as events so often did. And the car had stopped now, and there was nothing to do but get out and go up the steps with him following her again. But her family was going to think she had taken leave of her senses, bringing in this comparative stranger for no reason at all. She thought she must have, herself, but it was too late now. . . . When the front door opened, Madge braced her shoulders and marched in and across the hall toward the arched doorway which ran under the stairs to the library.

"Hello there?" she called, in question and warning as she came, and realized ruefully that self-consciousness made even her voice sound a little arch.

"Hello," Margaret's voice came back, clear and calm as always.

"I've brought a friend in for a cocktail," Madge said, trying again to sound gay and casual, as though she were always bringing young men in for drinks. But she knew it sounded just plain silly, and her heart sank a little further as she reached the door.

Even so, she was not prepared for Margaret's expression when she saw them. She was sitting at the far end of the library, and she laid aside the evening paper and for a long second simply sat and stared past her mother, as if dazed. Oh Lord, thought Mrs. Fairlie, she *doesn't* remember him . . . and then the young man spoke, himself, deliberately.

"Well," he said. "Fancy meeting you here."

But Margaret had already come to her feet and started down the length of the room toward him, and her own first words seemed to cross his without even touching them.

"I didn't think you were coming back," she said.

The tone was strange to her mother; not cool, not in any way a rebuff. Instead, it sounded a little like someone who'd been waiting to be met at a railroad station, and had about given up hope. It seemed to be said in the haste of relief, without thinking it over at all.

"I didn't intend to come back," the man said dryly. "I thought you'd be too damn busy."

Mrs. Fairlie stared at them for a minute and then turned to put down her gloves and bag, trying to make some normal motions, to act as if she belonged there. But she couldn't seem to find any cue to re-enter that conversation—if, in fact, she had ever been in it. She had entered with it, and that was all, she thought dizzily.

"You mean," Margaret said now, "because I was—busy—that night, at the end of the party?"

"Yeah," he agreed. "Something like that. It was pretty obvious, wasn't it?"

"But I *had* to do something about the party, after all . . . especially after I'd been off—"

She broke off short. And she had stopped a foot or two away from him too, and instead of putting out her hand to greet him, had clasped both hands in front of her, an odd nervous gesture—for Margaret, Madge thought. Like that of an unsure singer.

"O. K.," he said coolly. "Maybe you had to." Margaret dropped her hands to her sides then. She lifted her chin a little and looked at Madge.

"You and Mother always seem to be—meeting," she remarked, and the man's glance turned to include Madge also—as if she had just come in! He smiled at her reminiscently.

"Oh yes. Your mother and I came down in the elevator together at the Boge building, and she was good enough to offer me a lift out this way, and ask me in for a drink. She mentioned that you'd be in," he added deliberately.

"How nice," said Margaret, in a mock-polite tone, and her gaze continued to rest on her mother as if in mild but actual wonder as to who this little woman was, and how she had gotten there.

But Madge, who had felt for several moments as though she were running along beside a train, trying to find a place to hop on (after all, she'd *started* the thing, hadn't she?) felt suddenly when it came to a full stop that she didn't want to get on after all. She didn't know where it was going, or even where it had come from. And she still couldn't find any opening in the words which apparently included her. Their words said one thing, but their manner said another. And what either words or manner meant, she could only guess in a slightly dazed way. Apparently, and despite Margaret's previous inability to recollect him, she must know this man rather well. At least it seemed that they knew each other well enough to ignore the usual preliminaries in their greetings, well enough to talk to each other in a sort of code which both understood. There was even a sense of intimacy, to Madge, in the suggestion of antagonism between them.

But now there was this small pause, until suddenly he said rather harshly, "Maybe I shouldn't have accepted, after all," and Margaret answered gravely, "Why not? We're very hospitable people. Remember? And Father's out fixing a cocktail now. Oh no—" she half turned her head and added, "here he is now." She was looking at the doorway again, past the young man. "Just in time, Father," she said. "You remember Clay Ferguson—don't you?"

So that was his name, Madge thought.

* * *

Margaret was like Hugo in that she never explained. So, no doubt, later on, she would just listen quietly and let her mother run on in careful explanation of exactly how she had happened to run across Clay Ferguson and ask him back to the house, while she herself would simply omit to mention when or where she had met him. And meantime, she listened quietly and a little absently as he sat talking to her family. Madge put in a few nervous, irrelevant remarks now and again, but Margaret sat there, apparently relaxed, sipping her drink meditatively, and offering hardly a word. Anyone watching her might have thought that the girl was bored, except for a certain deep thoughtfulness in her eyes, and a certain sense of suspension in her body, despite her pose of graceful negligence. And when he got up to go, one might have thought from the alacrity with which she got up too, and went out into the hall with him, that she was almost speeding the parting guest. Unless, of course—she might be just neatly forestalling her father.

But after that day, she began seeing Clay, not regularly, but frequently, and the frequency grew too fast for it to find any measured sense of regularity. The first week it was only twice; the second week it was three times—but by the third, the days were running heel to toe with no spaces in between, and everybody had lost count, even Margaret. Sarah grew accustomed to letting him in and granting him a grim but recognizing smile. The new maid, Esther, came to know his voice on the phone without even asking for the name. Ellen became so piqued by their comments that the first night the young man was invited to dinner she had to peer at him through the small leaded window in the pantry door, to satisfy her sentimental curiosity.

Mrs. Fairlie was the one who was quiet that night. There was a distant look of worry in her eyes when they turned toward Margaret, of faint apprehension when they reached Clay. And of inscrutable, suspended patience while she listened to Hugo and Clay discuss the market and business generally. Listening to Hugo expressing the views which Hugo always did express, Clay had a way of responding to the touch of patronage in the older man's manner with something curiously like it in his own. As though he forbore from disagreeing with an older—but not a wiser—man. Sometimes it almost seemed that his patently indulgent civility was more irritating than a forthright impudence would have been. Madge could feel exasperation and intolerance building up in Hugo, and knew that she would hear more of it later.

To be sure, Margaret never let it go on for long; somehow, she would manage to turn their conversation aside, with a light touch for one man's sensibilities or the other's, until she could get Clay out of the house again. For Margaret was growing more adroit—with both her father and with Clay—and more luminous too, as the days went by. She was gayer, lighter, and deeper all at once. She seemed to be going somewhere very fast, with a light, sure step, and a gentle determination—whether or not she knew just where she was going. At least that was the way it seemed to her mother. Madge watched her anxiously, yet doubted that she could be diverted. She was *so* like Hugo when she set her head in some definite direction.

As for Hugo, his displeasure was like a force not yet released, but it was there, and Madge was fearful of the collision which would come when he let it go. Hugo's conclusions never went undirected; they were planned, well-aimed, sometimes devastatingly so for other people. And much as he felt for Margaret—a love, Madge thought, which was chiefly a reflection of his own ego—he might not spare even her, if she tried to oppose him or some prejudice of his. What he objected to in Clay she didn't quite know; Clay seemed an unexceptional young man to her, a trifle brash perhaps, but that was all; she found him rather likable on the whole. It was the fact that Hugo did object which mat-

tered, however. He might have objected to any young man at all—
indeed, Madge rather thought he had shown signs of restiveness,
whenever one boy or another had looked a little serious. But Margaret
had always remained so blithely remote herself that nothing had come
of it before. Now, if it was really coming to a showdown, she didn't
know who would win. What she forgot, for a while, was Hugo's
cleverness with women—which could be adapted even to his own
daughter if he put his mind on it. She forgot that until she learned
of an interview that took place one Sunday afternoon toward the end
of November, not in her presence, but which was later described to
her—in part—by Hugo.

The three Fairlies had finished a quiet Sunday dinner, and Madge
had gone upstairs about something, leaving Margaret and her father
settled before the small fire in the big living-room fireplace. It was
snowing outside, thickly and softly, blotting out the buildings only
a block away, so that the deserted Square looked almost like a winter
scene deep in the country. Margaret was going out with Clay later,
but for the moment she was content to sit relaxed in the blue wing
chair. Mr. Fairlie had his long, well-creased legs stretched out in
front of him, and his long cigar in hand, but he was not as somnolent
as he appeared. He was watching Margaret, and when he spoke, it was
gently, meditatively.

"You're very happy this winter, aren't you, Kitten?" He'd called
her that often when she was a child; only occasionally, in tender moments, since she'd been grown up. She stirred, a little surprised, and
then gave a small self-conscious laugh.

"Why, I hadn't thought of it—just that way." He waited, and she
added, rather shyly, "Does it show that plainly?"

"Yes," he said somberly, "I'm afraid it does." And after a moment
he added, "I'm glad you are, my dear," and gave a deep sigh. He said
no more for several minutes. Instead, he got up, puttered around
behind Margaret's chair—finding an ash tray presumably—then on his
way back toward the hearth he paused, still behind her, and with just
a finger he touched the waves of her hair. Margaret had soft hair,
and she wore it in a soft wavy bob, not one of these sleek boyish effects
which wound up with fish hooks on each cheek. "That's all I want for
you, dear," he said. "I hope—it will last." He went back to his chair
and let himself down into it. Margaret was watching him now, uneasily.

"Why do you say that?" she asked, after a moment. She sounded
strained, disturbed out of her content. As he no doubt meant her to be.

"What?—that I hope it'll last? Well—it's rather obvious that you're in love, or think you are—isn't it?" His smile seemed tolerant, but rueful, as he made his attack direct and frontal, and she retreated by looking back into the fire. "That doesn't always—last," he said.

"There's no reason why it shouldn't, is there?"

"Perhaps not," he agreed equably. "If there's the right sort of feeling between you. If, in other words, the man's really the right one for you. And if you're right for him."

"He seems to think so," she said quietly.

"He's asked you to marry him, then?"

"Not—exactly," she admitted, "but he's sort of—skirted around the subject. He certainly has it on his mind." And she gave another laugh, half embarrassed and half complacent now.

"Sounding you out," Hugo said dryly, "without committing himself. Kind of fellow that won't take a chance on getting turned down, is he? Won't ask a girl until he's sure of her."

Margaret gave him a startled look, and then lifting her head with a sort of pride, "I don't see why you say that," she objected. "It sounds horrid, and small, and Clay isn't like that."

"I'm glad to hear it," her father said, more dryly still. "Well, let that pass then, for the moment. At any rate, you expect him to ask you."

"I—think so," she said. She sounded a little helpless now, and confused, like an animal in a roadway with a strong headlight on it.

"You don't know much about him, do you?" Hugo remarked, after a smooth, momentary pause.

"Oh yes," she said quickly, even hastily. "That is—all the usual things. Where he came from, and how many in his family and what he does. He's very much like all the boys I've known," she said, with an attempt at carelessness which nevertheless seemed to stress the point, to reassure her father, or herself, that Clay was no different from the others. And she added, with a catch of her breath, "But I feel quite differently about him."

"Yes," said her father. "Ye—es, I see that." That was all, but there was a good deal more in his tone—doubt, concern for her, a touch of sadness, and even a touch of cynicism, all skillfully blended.

"You don't like him," Margaret said, slowly and unhappily, not wanting to say it at all. But somehow he had made her bring it out in the open; had not said so himself, but had made her do so. And that made a very subtle difference: he had not allowed her to become angry with anything he said. He had only made her acutely unhappy by what he had not said. And finally, after a considerable pause, he spoke again, judicially.

"Whether I like him or not isn't important, Margaret. But what sort of man he is—what he amounts to, or will amount to—is important, to me—and should be to you."

"I don't expect to marry anybody as successful as you, Father." Her tone was only faintly ironic, and had a slight tremor in it.

"But I think you do want someone you can look up to and respect. Or am I wrong?" he asked gently. She waited a minute, examining that, or perhaps unwilling to answer it immediately.

"Yes," she admitted finally. "I'd have to, I suppose. I've always looked up to you. . . ." There seemed to be a shade of regret in her voice, that she had had so far to look up to him, as though it were asking too much. Or asking too much of any other man to come up to that height. She added firmly, "But—I do respect Clay."

"You may be quite right, dear," he said, with a dry quiet reasonableness. He seemed to be conceding the point, almost to be willing to leave the whole thing there. But he was waiting. And after a couple of long moments Margaret asked, a trifle painfully, "What—is it—that you find lacking in Clay, Father?"

"Well, let's put it this way," he said slowly. "My likes and dislikes are personal, of course. But my experience is general. I've seen a lot of men, Margaret, of all ages. I've hired them and fired them. I've had to learn to size them up, you know, to spot the good ones and eliminate the bad eggs, the no-accounts."

Margaret knew that was true. But she sat huddled forward now, her elbows on her knees, waiting for him to continue. When he didn't go on, she said in a hardening tone, "Clay is not a bad egg, Father."

"No—o," he admitted. "Probably not that, exactly."

"You think he's just—no-account then?" She made herself say it, but with difficulty, as if she didn't even want to use the words. His answer was complete silence, but it was louder than if he had said emphatically, "I certainly do." She broke the silence hurriedly. "Oh, but that isn't fair, Father! You can't know that—I don't care how much experience you've had! He's young still—"

"Over thirty, isn't he?"

"Yes, but—"

"That's old enough for him to show a few of the marks of what he is, or isn't. Of course," Mr. Fairlie went on, in a tone of deliberate distaste, "I can find out more about him, any time you want me to."

"Well, I don't!" Margaret replied swiftly. She got up suddenly, and

she looked rather white. "I think it would be intolerable—inexcusable
—going around inquiring about him before we're even—"

Hugo sat quiet, looking up at her taut figure and tense white face,
but he said gently, "I'm sorry, darling. All I want is for you not to get
too involved before you know whether I'm right or not."

"But I'm not rushing into anything. We've just been having fun,
and I like him," she protested, and he smiled.

"You're going pretty fast, Kitten. Why, you're considering marrying the fellow, don't you realize that? You're seeing so much of him
in such a short time that you've become involved without even knowing it!"

"You don't want me to stop *seeing* him?" she exclaimed.

"I'd like you to slow down on it."

"What good would that do? How would I know him any better
then?"

"Maybe you'd know yourself better then, get your bearings again,
and know your own mind. It would give you time and space to acquire
a little perspective, on him and on yourself."

"I don't know that I want perspective," she flared, and turned away
and went over to the window, as though to get as far away from the
conversation as the room would allow. Her father's glance followed
her with a sort of sorrowful humor.

"Oh Margaret," he said. "My level-headed girl!"

"And I do want to see him," she persisted, with a certain stubborn
passion, her back still turned to him.

"Naturally you do now. But if you'd wait a while, you might not
feel the same way about it."

"How long?" she asked. He waited a second, watching her slim,
rigid silhouette.

"Oh, a month," he said finally. "Or two. Even six weeks would
help, I think, to give you—detachment."

There was a stubborn silence. It began casually enough, falling
into place behind Hugo's words, as any momentary pause follows along
in the relentless march of minutes. But the longer it went on, the more
obstinate it became, backed on the one hand by the older man's
deliberate, ruthless patience, on the other by the girl's strong but
untried resistance. It was one of those silences which are designed to
wear down one participant, or the other. And suddenly Margaret
turned back. She came quickly toward him and stopped a few feet
away, in the center of the room.

"Well, I won't do it," she said passionately. "I won't, that's all!"

Hugo met her straight look, but he remained silent. After a moment he slowly removed his glance from hers and swung it over to regard the fire, as he recrossed his long legs. But that slight shift gave no impression of retreat, of losing ground on his side.

"You're trying to break up something that—that means a lot to me—much more than you think—and could mean even more than that," Margaret said. "I don't think you really care about that, about how I feel. You only think how you feel, from an older person's point of view. Not liking him yourself, and not even trying to see why I like him. It isn't the same thing at all—and it isn't *fair!*"

He let her go on, her words coming fast, and stormily, but uncertainly too, more in gusts than with unbroken force. She had turned away again, and started walking restlessly back and forth, stopping to look out the window, at the white Square, returning to the fireplace, to stand looking down into the flames with her back to him again. Finally he said, "I wonder just what all this feeling for him really is." He spoke slowly and thoughtfully, but anyone who had seen the speculative, considering look with which he seemed to measure her back, might have thought he spoke experimentally too. "There are different kinds of love, you know," he remarked. The back he was watching seemed to grow—not stiff, but still, and the look in his eyes grew more shrewd as they watched. "Naturally," he went on again, "many emotions are stirred up in any love affair. One expects the biological forces to play a certain part, since that is inevitable. . . ." He sounded rather dry about it, as if such things didn't greatly interest him, as though he knew of them more by hearsay or by necessity. "But sometimes," said Hugo, "they play a rather larger part than they should, Margaret. Than you would want in your life, I think."

She had turned slowly around now, though she was still not facing him, but standing very straight, looking off across the room. A wave of color had come up under her fair skin, and stayed there. Hugo still watched her for a moment, and then in careful timing, gathered up his long length and moved over to her and put one arm around her.

"If there's too much of that kind of thing between you, it's not likely to last—with you, my dear," he said rather soothingly and kindly now. "It would sicken a girl like you, rather quickly I'm afraid—and spoil your whole relationship."

She didn't meet his eyes, and it was plain that she couldn't.

"How can one tell?" she said, so low that he couldn't have heard her if he hadn't been close beside her.

"Give it time, as I suggested. Time—and space—between the two of you. You'd be surprised how they can change a situation like that."

"But if I did—suppose those weeks of not seeing me right now—would be enough to make him decide that *he* didn't care?"

"As a matter of fact," Mr. Fairlie said with flat authority, "if he's anywhere near the point you seem to assume, that period of being held off will bring him to the point, dear. If that's what you decide you want yourself."

Her eyes came back to his at last, as though finally trying to face the insistent headlight which had been turned on her this last half-hour.

"You make me—feel so ashamed, Father," she whispered.

"Oh, I don't mean to do that—quite. But you must be honest with yourself about these things, Margaret. Not make a bad mistake, and then perhaps have a certain sense of shame for the rest of your life."

She nodded carefully, as though it hurt to do so.

"What—would I tell him?" she asked.

"Why not the truth? If you think he can take it. That *I* believe you're seeing rather too much of each other, and want you to—take it easy, that's all. Take a short vacation from each other, see more of your other friends, for a time."

"Two months seems an awfully long time," Margaret said rather pitifully. "Even six weeks . . . That wouldn't be until the first of the year. Don't you think a month would do—till Chirstmas time?" Hugo squeezed her shoulder a little, braced her against his side for a second. But he said nothing. "I was going out with him this afternoon," she said plaintively.

"Go ahead," he agreed. "But then—make your break, and stick to it. I'd like to believe that my girl is strong enough to do that."

"Oh Father!" She gave a little wail and turned and buried her face against his shoulder. "I don't know if I *can*."

He held her close, tightening his arm as he looked down at her. Madge came into the room just then, returning from upstairs. She stopped short for an instant, looking at the tableau, startled by the lost sound of the child's voice, not like a child at all really, but like a spirit being led into a dark place—unwillingly. But led by someone trusted above all others. Then she saw the expression in Hugo's eyes, which looked up at her and over Margaret's head, and held an unmistakable flicker of accomplishment and satisfaction. Almost as if he had just closed a smart business deal.

For Hugo had said to her the night before, "That fellow's not for my girl, let me tell you that!" *His* girl, he had said, and though Madge's heart had felt constricted when he said it, she'd known he was right about that. She was almost glad that the responsibility wasn't hers, but his, for there was this twisting fear in herself, for Margaret. Margaret must marry sometime, she knew that; just because her own marriage had been a bad one was no reason to pull the girl back. She would not—she *would* not let her feel any of her own anxiety. So all she could do, really, was to watch, as from a house next door, and see this nice-looking girl going back and forth, so healthy and sensible-looking—so calm and radiant at the same time. To watch her going in and out more and more frequently with this strange young man, and wonder curiously, but never avidly (like a well-bred neighbor) just who he was and what he was like. And then to watch and *not* see him coming any more, and wonder again how it would all come out. As though it were a story that she had nothing to do with herself.

Chapter Four

THE NEXT COUPLE OF WEEKS WENT BY SMOOTHLY. HUGO WAS WELL satisfied, though Madge's own doubts continued to waver and twist within her. Poor Margaret looked so sweetly noble as she went around the house. Or else she had an almost grimly dedicated expression, even when she began going out with some of her other friends again. Her mother had always thought that keeping people apart was supposed to magnify the attraction between them. But Hugo saw the matter otherwise.

"Not at all, not at all," he said largely and impatiently. "He isn't her kind at all—and when it's only a matter of physical attraction, and you put space between them, it loses its potency. Like a magnet, my dear: beyond a certain distance it has no force—no pull."

An odd thing for Hugo to say, Madge thought. But he ought to know. At any rate, he and Margaret seemed to have a sort of unspoken pact of silent understanding between them; they didn't discuss their agreement, or the subject of it, at all. And to Madge he talked significantly of the Christmas present they would get for the child. Something very special this year, a ring perhaps, or a lovely bracelet; like a reward for a good girl. Madge started dutifully to look for it. She rather enjoyed Christmas shopping anyway, not the way she used to of course, when the children were both—children, and there was a hubbub of furtive excitement about it, but it did give her something else to think about now, at a moment when she welcomed it.

And then about the second week in December, there was a change in the atmosphere, both outside and inside the house. Outside, it began to rain, and freeze into sleet, and rain again. Inside, there was beginning to be a suggestion of strain in Margaret's manner. Madge suspected that she wasn't sleeping well. And when Hugo got his feet wet and acquired one of his bad colds, he became much less complacent.

There was an evening, for instance, when Margaret was late in coming in to dinner. In the first place, Hugo was a stickler for punctuality at meals; in the strange mixture of laxities and rigidities which made up the man, that was one of the small iron struts which —quite possibly—held him together. In the second place, his nose was badly stuffed up and he had used his sprayer just before coming downstairs, in order to eat his dinner more comfortably. So when Margaret, who was generally prompt and conformative about the household routine, failed to show up, he began to bristle with aggrieved irritation. Even his drink failed to soothe him because it didn't taste very good. They waited twenty minutes, and then went in to the table, and five minutes later Margaret arrived. It would have been better if she had been earlier of course—or much later still, for her father had not had time enough for his annoyance to subside, or for his food to take soothing effect.

He didn't call her to task at first; in fact he hardly spoke to her, but continued eating his soup in Olympian dignity. Margaret had pulled off her small hat in the hall and come straight to the dining room, so her hair was slightly rumpled, and that too was an offense to Hugo. Madge spoke cheerily, trying to avoid the actual subject of lateness, and yet seem natural about the girl's comings and goings.

"Have a good time?" she asked.

"Oh—all right," Margaret said indifferently. "Nothing much."

There was a short ceremonial silence while Sarah brought in her soup plate and set it down before her. Then as she left the room Hugo inquired with acidly polite detachment, "Might I ask where you've been?"

Margaret glanced at him, not in the least unaware of his tone, but still indifferent to it.

"At the Cochrans'," she said. "For cocktails."

"And are cocktails supposed to go on all evening?"

"Sometimes. A few of the people stayed on tonight. Some of them had left."

"If you don't intend to come back for dinner, and leave word about it, that's one thing. But since you didn't—I suppose you'd forgotten what time we dine," Hugo observed, finishing his soup and wiping fastidiously around the edges of his neat moustache with the corner of his large napkin.

"No, Father," Margaret said rather stiffly in her turn. "I know the dinner hour here, I think. I just didn't notice the time particularly."

"Really?" he said. "I suppose it didn't occur to you that we would wait for you?"

"I hadn't really thought about it. It didn't seem so very important, after all."

"We waited twenty minutes for you," her father said portentously.

"That's too bad," Margaret rejoined calmly. "You shouldn't have." She was looking at him coolly, her tone quite courteous, but her manner as unbending as his own. She was in one of her moody spells, Madge had seen that from the moment she entered, but it was unfortunate that it had to be tonight, with Hugo feeling the way he did.

"Oh well, it doesn't matter now, does it?" Madge put in gently. "Hurry up and eat your soup, dear, so you can catch up with us."

"I prefer not to wait," Hugo stated. "Ring the bell, Madge, and have Sarah go ahead."

Madge sighed and pressed the button under the table, and Margaret, if anything, began to dawdle over her soup, nibbling her cracker with a deliberative air.

"I should think," Hugo remarked, still worrying away at the subject, like something he couldn't keep away from no matter how much it irritated him, "that if you weren't even having a particularly good time, you might have had some consideration for someone else."

"Well," Margaret said lightly—too lightly, and not even looking at him now, "a drink's a drink, after all."

Hugo flipped the chop Sarah was offering him onto his plate, and glared across at the apple of his eye.

"That," he said, "is the sort of remark I don't care to hear my daughter make."

"Oh—h?" said Margaret.

"The gin-drinking flapper is not your type, Margaret. I shouldn't have thought I'd have to remind you of it. Furthermore, I think there's getting to be definitely too much of that kind of thing among the people you see, and I don't like it."

He seemed, for once, to have forgotten Sarah, still impassively circling the table with the vegetables. Or perhaps he had made himself think that he had risen to the plane of righteous indignation on a matter of national, or at least civic, importance. But Margaret did not take it as a large issue; she took it as a small and intensely personal one. She had forgotten Sarah too.

"I thought you wanted me to go back to seeing my old friends," she retorted. "After all, a person has to do something—"

"I wanted you to show some discrimination about the company you kept," he said sharply, and at that Margaret was suddenly on her feet, her gray eyes blazing.

"Well really—I think I can do without this particular company tonight!" She dropped her napkin by her place and started to turn. But her father's glance had crossed hers and his mouth was grim.

"Sit down!" he said shortly.

"I'd rather not. I don't care for anything more."

"*Sit—down,*" he repeated. "You've disturbed our dinner enough already."

"*I've* disturbed it!" Margaret flashed. But she didn't leave. She stood her ground for another second, with her father's cold gaze seeming to pin her there, and then she sank back on her chair and pulled the napkin slowly back onto her lap. Her mouth was a tight line and her face was white.

Madge sat there, a little limp. She realized that she had picked up her fork but was not doing anything with it, so she began carefully to eat a bit of mashed potato. Sarah had faded out of the room at some point, Madge didn't even remember when, and there was silence in the room except for the sudden sound of Hugo blowing his nose. Madge tried to think of something to say to ease them both back into an ordinary conversation, but she knew if she said something stupid it would only irritate them both. So she kept quiet, but Margaret didn't. She was still seething.

"Just because I come in a little late once out of a hundred times," she said in a voice that was low, but still tense, "why you should go on this way—about my friends—and as if I didn't know how to behave . . ." She broke off for a minute, looking steadily at her plate. Then suddenly she looked up and across at Hugo again. "You're a little hard to please," she said, not appealingly but resentfully. "After all my effort to do as *you* want, when I've been trying to follow your advice."

"I wonder," Hugo said nastily, "how much you actually care about my advice. How much you want to please me—"

"Well if you don't even believe me! If you don't trust me—" Margaret interrupted hotly.

"Your whole manner tonight," Hugo went on—but his nose was so stopped that he was having trouble with his n's and m's and he stopped, and tried again. But it came out the same way. "Your whole badder," he repeated, and suddenly it was Mr. Fairlie who had put his napkin aside and risen to his feet. "I've had about enough of this for one didder," he said.

"Oh Hugo, do sit down and finish. This is all so unnecessary!"

"I don't want any more. I've had enough, I tell you. Had to wait so long in the first place the damn spray's worn off and I can't taste a thing!"

Madge sat there and watched him go stalking out the door, and for a moment the impulse to break into peals of laughter was almost uncontrollable. A dinner of jack-in-the-boxes, that's what it was— first one popping up and now the other, as if working on alternate springs . . . Madge sneaked a sidewise glance at her daughter, and if there had been the least softening of her mouth, the least hint of amusement in her eyes, Madge would have broken down. Instead, she picked up her glass of water and took a hasty swallow.

So on the whole, she thought it was rather fortunate when Hugo announced the next day that he had to go to Chicago on a business trip. If it really was business, she reflected . . . but she didn't give it much thought, really. It was just that these things crossed her mind from old habit, without her inviting them to. On second thought, she was inclined to believe it was business, because otherwise he probably would have stayed home and taken care of that cold. As it was, he went off with an extra supply of handkerchiefs in his suitcase, coughing in short grumbling barks and complaining heartily. He was to be gone a week.

But there was no real relaxation left behind him. Madge went along in a preoccupied way with her Christmas shopping, but she was increasingly aware of the constraint in Margaret's manner. She remembered that more than half of the probationary month was gone, and wondered once more what good it had done, or would do. She asked Margaret brightly about the things she was doing and the people she was seeing—and then felt perhaps she hadn't been very tactful to do so, after all. She knew that the girl's time wasn't as full as it had been before Clay Ferguson's advent; she'd let him monop- olize her evenings, too many of them, for nearly two months, and now she was not in as much demand. There were three evenings in a row that Madge and Margaret spent together after Hugo went off.

They spent them in the library, which they preferred, but which was generally left for his use when he was at home. The fire was going quietly in the fireplace and the lamps made small islands of light for their reading in the dark-walled room. But they were not

comfortable evenings. Madge was too conscious of the girl's concealed but consuming restlessness. She smoked far more than she was
used to doing, she changed from one book or magazine to another.
Her usual calm habits of concentration seemed to have failed her and
she went upstairs earlier and earlier—to bed, or to brood, Madge
didn't know which. For once, Hugo's plans were not working, she
thought. This one was only deepening Margaret's interest in that
boy. . . . And her restlessness began to work upon her mother, who
was a trifle uneasy and unsettled anyway whenever Hugo was away.
You'd think, she told herself irritably, that I'd be glad enough by this
time to have him away, really out of town. . . . But it was always the
same: she never missed him in the daytime, and at night she was
thankful to have the bed to herself; but in the evening, at dinner,
and even later on, she was uncomfortable in his absence, as though
one wall were gone from the room, leaving it open to the elements.

On their fourth evening alone, the telephone rang at nine o'clock.
Both women looked up at each other, though neither moved at once.
Then Margaret muttered, "I expect the girls have gone up," and she
got up hastily and went out to the hall and across to the den. Madge
didn't hear the door close, but she didn't hear any conversation either.
Margaret didn't come back for several minutes and when she did, she
didn't come into the room, but stopped in the doorway.

"I'm going out, darling."

"This late?"

"Is it late?" Margaret said lightly, but Madge felt there was a
slight defensiveness in the mere lightness.

"Well—I suppose not. It just surprised me, making a date at
nine o'clock."

"Not very flattering, is it?" The girl laughed, a very brief sound.
"Well, I don't have so many dates these days. My stock has gone
down, you see." She sounded brittle, and Madge said instantly, "Oh
darling, you know that's temporary! You mustn't—"

"Oh yes—" Margaret seemed to brush that aside, impatient that
she'd mentioned it. "I'm bored, that's all. Terribly bored. And that
might not be so temporary." Her whole manner seemed to her mother
to be a queer mixture of intensity and self-consciousness. It was as if
she were trying to cover up a vehement sincerity with an artificial
bravado. "You don't mind my going, do you?" she said, perfunctorily
now.

"Why no, of course not, dear. Will you be late?"

"Probably."

"Going to dance somewhere?"

"I—expect so."

"Well—have a good time . . ." Madge said slowly. Then wondered suddenly if she'd sounded wistful. She hadn't meant to. She was quite used to being left alone for the evening, anyway. No—it wasn't that; it was, she realized almost shamefacedly, just the idea of dancing. . . . It came over her that way, once in a while, without any warning. She had so loved to dance, herself, but Hugo hadn't cared for it. It was one of the few things he didn't do very well. On the other hand, he played a very fine game of bridge, and was completely impatient with Madge's inability to master the game. Oh well—what did it matter? She was forty-two years old, and she hadn't danced in ten years (well, six or eight anyway) and why she should suddenly envy Margaret—not her romance or her unknown beau of the evening, or even her youth—but just her dancing for the next few hours, Madge couldn't imagine.

She heard Margaret running upstairs, moving around up there. Then before long she heard the doorbell, and immediately Margaret's step on the stairs again. She heard her call, "Good night, Mother" with a cheerful, even an excited breathlessness, and the front door opened and shut again—and that was all. It occurred to her that she didn't even know who the girl's date was this evening. But that didn't matter either, really. Margaret was as particular about the people she chose to go out with as she could have been for her, Madge was sure.

She went back to her book and read on. It improved slightly for a while, and the fire went down and she grew chilly without knowing it, and suddenly she yawned. She might just as well go up. Silly, reading on here in the cold, when she wasn't very interested in the story. It was 'way past eleven. She turned out all the lights except the one in the hall, and went upstairs. One reading lamp had been left on in her room, and the bed turned neatly down, with her gown laid across one side. And no pajamas on the other side she noted, with a renewed feeling of pleasure. She moved about mechanically and sleepily, and after a leisurely half-hour was just ready to get into bed when the long-drawn-out ringing of a bell downstairs brought her up short, her chin lifting and her eyes staring at the opposite wall.

Telephone—? No, that was the doorbell. What on earth, at this hour? Margaret had forgotten her key, perhaps, but no—Margaret wouldn't be in yet. She'd said she'd be late, and in Margaret's code midnight certainly wasn't late. As Madge stared and wondered in consternation, the bell rang again, persistently, and she realized belatedly that it was up to her to go down, since no one else was likely to. She went out into the hall and started reluctantly down the shadowy stairway, when all at once the idea of an accident occurred to her and she fairly ran down the rest of the way. Margaret in an accident—oh *no*—but after all she *didn't* know who she was with—and so many of them did drink and drive wildly nowadays.

It was only that image ahead of her which got her across the lower hall without hesitation and made her open the door without even peering out through its curtain-covered window first. And when she saw Hugo standing there, with one hand on the door jamb, she was so taken aback that she couldn't speak.

"God, I thought you'd never come!" he said irritably, and came past her into the vestibule.

"Hugo!" she said finally, "What on earth—? I thought you weren't coming till the end of the week—and this hour, without warning—I thought it must be an—"

"Took the noon train," he muttered. "Had to get back somehow. And I couldn't find my damn key . . ."

Somewhere, a remote part of her mind recorded that it was a remarkable thing for the orderly Hugo not to be able to find his key. But something caught her conscious attention nearer by.

"Where's your bag?" she asked.

"Couldn't bother with it," he mumbled. "Didn't go back to the hotel there . . . For God's sake, don't stand there asking questions!"

She saw that he seemed to be groping for the knob of the inner door to steady himself. He had simply left the outer door open for her to close—and a surprisingly detached question came to her mind. She had never in her life seen Hugo drunk, but she had never seen him waver and lurch either, as he seemed to be doing now, and he didn't generally swear that way, at her or even before her. Hugo wasn't the swearing kind of man, generally. . . .

"Are you drunk, Hugo?" she asked now, in a tone of naively polite interest.

"My God, no—I'm sick!" he said irascibly. "Can't you give me a hand there—don't you see I need some help, you little fool?" And as she looked at him now, with a rush of compunction, readjusting her mind still again, she saw that he did look very queer.

*   *   *

Somehow, she got him upstairs, though he was breathing hard, and complaining that his legs were like rubber. She helped him to get his clothes off, and when she felt his skin she began to believe him when he said that he was burning up. His face was flushed, certainly, and his eyes had a suffused glazed look, as if he hardly knew her. It was that cold, of course; he'd caught more, traveling about, or else it had gone into some kind of influenza. But Hugo often got these heavy colds and Madge still wasn't so much alarmed, exactly, as bewildered by these midnight events. She was inclined to soothe and discount his own alarm, and when he told her thickly that she'd have to call the doctor, she even demurred a trifle.

"Do you think we should, at this hour? It's just a very bad cold, my dear. It's sure to be better in the morning if you'll just take some aspirin and get right into bed, and I'll fix a hot drink for you—"

"Oh, all right, if you want to let me run into pneumonia," he said with a sort of pettish anger. She took him up quickly, chiding and soothing him at the same time.

"Don't be silly, Hugo. Of course I'll call him if you want me to."

She helped him into the wide bed which had been opened up so invitingly for her alone. She propped her own pillows as well as his under his shoulders, as that seemed to ease his breathing. And then she apologetically telephoned Hugo's doctor and went downstairs to fix the hot drink for him. She was still in the kitchen fifteen minutes later, trying in an unaccustomed way to find what she wanted, when the doorbell rang again, raucous in the still house, and she trotted out through the hall to let the doctor in.

"I'm so sorry to call you out, Doctor," she apologized once more. "But he does seem awfully miserable, and I'm afraid he has some fever, though I couldn't find the thermometer. . . . It's just a bad cold, of course," she went on explaining, padding up the stairs beside him, tripping a little on her long dressing gown.

She was still trying to explain the whole thing away, partly because she was a little frightened now, but partly because it all seemed so unreal to her. But when the doctor came out of the room after examining Hugo, there was something in his manner which cut through her private fog, and made the dimly lighted upper hall quite clear and actual at half past one in the morning. The sound of Hugo's breathing, even out there, seemed all at once not only extremely audible, but believable as well.

"I don't like the look of it," the doctor said abruptly. "We've got some râles there now, and the temperature's nearly 104. You ought to have a nurse, Mrs. Fairlie."

"Why, of course," she agreed in a small voice. "Though I'll do whatever you tell me to—that I can . . ." she added, her words trailing off apprehensively. It was so long since she'd even nursed the children through anything.

"I'll get one over to you within an hour, if possible. Meantime, there's nothing for you to do except to get a kettle or something steaming in the room. And keep him where he is. . . ." That seemed a silly thing to say, she thought, but the doctor paused and then went on more slowly, as if to impress it on her. "He *must* be kept quiet, and he may not be—entirely clear-headed, you know, with that temperature. That hypo I gave him will make him less restless after a little, of course."

"Yes," Madge said. "I see." But she continued to look at the doctor wide-eyed, as though to see more, presently, than he had already told her. "Is it—pneumonia you're afraid of?" she asked.

He returned her look, searchingly. He didn't know this little woman very well; she didn't look like the kind who could stand up to much. But still, the little ones had to take it along with the big ones. . . . He shrugged, mentally, impatiently.

"I'm not afraid of it, Mrs. Fairlie—I'm sure of it," he said. "By tomorrow we'll have a consolidation of the lungs. We'll have to accept pneumonia as a fact, right now, and just do all we can with it from here on out."

That was all he had to tell her, really, though she asked him a couple of questions over again—to delay his going, perhaps. And then she watched him go down the stairs and let himself out, and thought in utter, overwhelming consternation, that she was alone with a very sick man. She'd been alone earlier, but it hadn't meant anything then. Now she thought desperately of Margaret. Margaret ought to know, she ought to be here, but Madge hadn't the remotest notion where she was or whom she was with. She turned and went back into hers and Hugo's room.

"What'd he say?" Hugo asked gruffly, his eyes moving restlessly to find her.

"He said you were to stay right there, and drop off to sleep if you can. I'm going to get a kettle steaming in here for you, and the doctor's going to send over a nurse who can make you more comfortable."

"Says I'm pretty sick, doesn't he?"

"Why no, of course he doesn't," Madge denied quickly. "He says you have a bad bronchial cold of course, and all this traveling around hasn't helped it. But all you have to do is to be quiet and take care of yourself." She felt rather proud of the way she was ad libbing for the doctor, but Hugo only grunted again, shifting his body uneasily.

"You never were much of a liar, Madge," he said.

She stood uncertainly beside him, and he turned his head away and then restlessly turned it back to fix that glazed bright look on her again.

"I'm damned sick, and you know it," he said.

"That's nonsense," she retorted stubbornly. "You feel awful of course, with the fever and congestion in your chest, but you mustn't exaggerate it, Hugo, and you mustn't keep on talking."

He paid no attention to that, though each time he spoke it seemed an effort.

"I never exaggerate," he said morosely. "And I know when I'm sick, too. I've got a feeling—" He broke off, only to add abruptly after a moment, "I don't think I'm ready to die, Madge."

"That's an absurd thing to say. Nobody thinks you're going to die—I don't think even you do," she chided him, but he ignored her.

"I don't suppose we're ever ready." There was a pause: "Or do you think sometimes people are?" He was looking at her anxiously, as if forgetting how little he ever cared for her opinion.

"I think you're being very silly even to think of it," she said gently. There was a sort of gloomy excitement in him, a childish insistence on how sick he was—that's what it was of course. Yet at the same time she saw that the apprehension, the deep foreboding, was quite real, and she didn't know what to do about it. He looked strange and helpless, braced on his pillows that way, with that animal-like expression of fright in his clouded eyes. Poor Hugo. She could only feel sorry for him now, though it was hard for her to comfort him, for they were not close enough. She felt such a long, long distance from him. She had no idea how to reach him. She didn't know whether he even wanted her to hover over him. She put her hand on his wrist in a tentative way, and his own hand turned over and gripped hers, unexpectedly.

"I've given you a pretty bad time, haven't I, Madge?" he said, staring up at her, and for a second, though she wanted to speak, she was dumb. What *did* one do at times like this? Say "Oh no, not at all—" or "Of course not, dear—think nothing of it—" One read that at times of crisis one did forget all the rest and pour one's self into the pure channels of love and compassion. But she hadn't loved Hugo for a long time; he had killed all that in her slowly, painfully and effectually. And there was something too deeply honest in Madge for her to perjure herself now. In fact it seemed as though, if one were ever to be honest, it should be when (or if) a person was going to die. Madge had a simple conviction that the person concerned would be able to see through any deceit too soon to make it worth anything.

But compassion she still had, and that was what she felt for Hugo now. She was sorry for him, as she had never dreamed she could be. He seemed, all at once, to have so little to go on. The big successful man, not quite so successful as he had thought, or so big . . . Aware that he had failed in some important way, after all. It shocked her to look at him, because she knew it wasn't decent for any person to be exposed to another in that way. In all the years, she had never seen him naked, in that way. And she had to drag her eyes from the sight to be able to think of something—anything—superficial to say.

"It's no use thinking of things like that now," she said quietly, and his grip on her hand loosened sluggishly.

"No, I suppose not," he said heavily. "No use apologizing now— to you or God, either. Besides, you wouldn't be much good at getting me into Heaven, would you? You never even wanted to go to church —for me, did you?" She didn't try to answer that; she could only gaze at him helplessly, not sure whether he even knew what he was saying now. He moved his eyes with apparent difficulty from her to the footboard of the bed. And then, as she was about to move softly away, he spoke again. "Well, anyway," he said grimly, "I've left you pretty well provided for. In fact you'll be damned well off."

That stopped her at the foot of the bed, as sharply as if something had struck her in the back, between the shoulder blades. What an awful thing for him to say to her now, she thought. . . . But perhaps it was no worse, no more shallow, than the silly words she had had to offer him in his extremity. She turned around, but still there was nothing more that she could offer.

"I wish you wouldn't talk that way, Hugo. You're not leaving us at all, you know, and you're only exciting yourself. And that's—not a pleasant thing to say."

"I'm . . . not . . . excited," he said slowly. "And why should I be pleasant this late in the game? It's the truth. The only reason you ever stuck it out, Madge. Be provided for . . ."

"The doctor said you mustn't talk," she insisted, rather desperately, and her face was white. "You *must* be quiet." She put her hand on his scorching forehead—as if she could quiet the thoughts there, though it was an effort to touch him at all—and he turned his head now to shake it off. She reached up to turn off the light over the bed, and then moved definitely away. Keep him quiet; that was the least—and the most—that she could do for him.

She busied herself carefully around the room for a few minutes, bringing in from the bathroom the little steaming kettle that she used to use for the children's coughs, putting things away which she'd had no time for earlier. Hugo was still now, and his breathing seemed quieter and less difficult. Perhaps the hypodermic was beginning to take effect. She took a small blanket from the couch and wrapped it around her knees, and sat down in the armchair across the room from the bed. To wait. And wonder where they were going now, she and Hugo. They seemed to have started somewhere rather fast, not so much on the earth as away from it. She had a sense of hanging, loose, like some dangling unattached part, in a large dark universe. But of course it was only a large dark bedroom, late at night.

* * *

For a while, her mind kept darting from one corner of the room to the other, one end of the house to another, as if unwilling to come to rest. And then as the minutes went on, it settled down in one spot, the spot where she found herself physically and mentally—sitting in her own path, at it were—waiting to learn whether her husband would die, or not.

She began to think about it, quite sensibly and conscientiously and consecutively—one thought after another. Of course she was an alarmist even to consider such an extreme. Men always made a fuss about being sick. To think of it at all was only a reflection of Hugo's childish fear, and the doctor's pompous solemnity, and the palpable fact of the dark night around her and her virtual aloneness in it. But still she knew, pooh-pooh it how she would, that pneumonia was not just a name to frighten children with. It was a dreadful thing, and people did die of it. And that was an overwhelming realization to come upon so suddenly, even as a possibility. Madge hardly knew how she would feel presently if the possibility became a fact. Perhaps she would feel grief, later on, find that something she had thought paralyzed had the capacity for pain after all. She hadn't thought that he could still hurt her—much—until he'd said that, a few minutes ago. But perhaps the most painful part of it would be the irony of learning that one could miss a person even when he had hurt and humbled and humiliated one past loving him. For without Hugo she would be very much alone.

It was strange, now, to sit there alone with this man, and stranger still to try to find her way back, wondering how she had ever come there. She had been so very much in love with him at first, carried away by it, almost drowned in it. And she had been such a green little fool, the wonder was that he had ever looked at her. It was her sister Julia whom he'd looked at first; Judy, with the dark eyes and chestnut hair and the flair for the dramatic. Madge was the youngest sister, very much the youngest. She was the only one who didn't remember their mother very clearly, or miss her very much either. Lou, the oldest, had been sixteen when their mother died, four years older than Judy, eleven years older than Madge. Lou was the one who had taken over her mother's responsibilities, who had run the house and counted the pennies and tried to manage Dad.

Madge had been too young to bother long about anything. She wasn't too fond of Lou's dominating ways, but she had grown used to them before she really recognized anything else. And her Dad was always a great source of comfort, and fun too. He'd ridden her on his knee, which was well-padded and comfortable, and taken her to the zoo and to the circus. And he hadn't cared whether she went to Sunday school or not. He'd said everybody got religion somehow, one way or another, sooner or later, though they mostly called it different things. It was God to some of them, clear and concrete; and it was a kind of courage to others—not the blustering, bloody-nosed kind of courage, he'd explained carefully, but just the courage to live. (She never knew what he meant by that until years later.) And some of them called it love—and there were different kinds of love too, her father had said, breaking off absentmindedly. Not that he'd gone into those abstract things with her when she was six, or ever, very thoroughly. Just once in a while, through the years, he'd drop something into their conversation, half absently, as if he were still figuring it out himself.

And when she was old enough for school he hadn't cared how bad she was at arithmetic, either. He said it didn't matter for girls—while Lou in the background, counting her pennies, gave an unpleasant little laugh. Madge realized now that Dad hadn't been too fond of Lou's firm hand himself. He was too easy-going, and besides, he liked a drink now and then, and Lou disapproved of that. Madge knew now that he'd liked many more than one drink at any one time, and Lou had had something on her side; but then again she didn't think he'd done much drinking before Lou took over. Maybe he just missed Mother; felt empty without her and tried to fill himself up with something else. It was all rather vague in Madge's mind; clear in its small pictures, but hazy in the larger background. Yet it had seemed quite a satisfactory family to her, on the whole. Her father was bald and untidy and soft-spoken; Lou had straight auburn hair and a good profile, and she was a good cook. Julia was the temperamental one, but charming—and she brought young men to the house later on, which was pleasant, and at times exciting. She had brought Hugo to the house.

At that time he was a department head in the machine tool company which he was eventually to buy into and make over and rename in his own image, so to speak. He had no mustache then, and his features were even more clear-cut and striking than they were now. Everything was so clear and clean about him: his gray eyes and smooth light brown hair, and fair skin. His nails were immaculate, and his shoes well shined, and if his suits weren't as well cut in those days, they were least well pressed. But of course it was more than that which had first attracted Judy, and then her nineteen-year-old sister; it was that way he'd always had, of looking at a girl closely and intimately, without apparently giving an inkling to anyone else. The first times he looked at Madge, Judy hadn't even been aware of it. And she'd had him to Sunday dinner especially to show him off, and Lou and she had taken great pains with it. She'd been quite keen about him, and was putting on all her best effects. Maybe she'd been a little too sure of their effectiveness, or a little too sure of Hugo. One or the other. And his eye had wandered and found Madge's across the table.

She didn't know, to this day, just how she'd caught that eye and held it, even temporarily, though he'd told her often enough that it was her utter artlessness which did it. She'd been pretty in a way, she supposed, and certainly very natural compared to Julia with her more studied wiles. She'd had a sad little feeling of contrition about Judy for a while afterward, though the older girl pretended scornfully that it didn't matter. Later on it really didn't, for Judy had married a very different sort of man, who had made her far happier, for the time she had to live, than Madge had ever been. In the end, Madge could even feel that since Judy hadn't been permitted a very long life, she had at least saved her spoiling what little there was of it.

But in the beginning it had all been confusing, and it had happened very fast. It probably couldn't have happened at all, otherwise. And Hugo had brought her here as a bride, not to this house of course, but to the smaller one down on Sixth Street. And she had gone through a period of engulfing, unbelievable enchantment with him, for a little while. (No wonder it was unbelievable, since there was nothing real about it.) The adjustments people spoke solemnly about didn't seem to matter. Even then, Hugo had been a deft and experienced lover, though she didn't fully realize that fact, and beyond all that, she was more than ready to do all the adjusting there was to do, to fit herself to him in any way demanded. Even after the days began to seem less touched with absolute magic, she was still quite happy, for she was still in love with a man whom many women before and after her found curiously compelling.

Perhaps if she hadn't been so much in love, or in such an immature way, she wouldn't have been so frightened by the first faint recognition that he was still capable of an interest in other women. For it was her own fright, in the long run, which had weakened her and made her so vulnerable. That first intimation was so slight, and in retrospect seemed so childish, that it was a wonder she still remembered it. But she did, with surprising clearness. They had been at a dinner party, during the first year of their marriage, in a group they were only just beginning to know. Madge still had a little way among strangers of looking to Hugo, not for support exactly, or anything so crude as approbation; perhaps it was just for recognition, in a warm, intimate, reassuring sense. She would look up and find his glance moving toward her with something like amused indulgence, almost unaware of its own direction. Their eyes would meet just for a flash, like the touching of hands, and move on instantly, not even acknowledging each other.

But that night she didn't once catch his eye. Not from down and across the table where he sat by an attractive blonde girl with a large pompadour, and not later in the drawing room when the party broke up into fours and settled at the bridge tables. (Always an ordeal for Madge, though they called it auction then.) He was still seated with the blonde, a young married woman, a visitor in town without her husband. He seemed to find her very entertaining, and said afterwards that she played a surprisingly good game, for a woman. That was all; there was nothing more to it than that. Madge was never even sure of her name. But Hugo had forgotten Madge herself for an entire evening, and it was not so much jealousy she felt, then, as a faint faraway breath of desolation. As though she had dreamed something which had depressed her, but could hardly remember when she woke up what it was that she had dreamt.

The next day, of course—or the next week, perhaps—she had told herself not to be so silly. But it seemed now that her naive instinct had been more deeply right than her carefully sensible second thought. And perhaps even from then on, she had begun to lose the complete serenity of confidence, had begun trying a little too hard, and so inevitably had given herself away. Once her artlessness was gone, she had no art to replace it with, or not enough for Hugo, who knew what art was. She was so mortally afraid to lose him. He was attractive and—absorbing somehow, beyond anyone she had ever known. But much more than that, he happened to be the first person in her life with whom she had that feeling, deceptive as it was, of mutual and exclusive Belonging. It was a little tragic as well as ironic that such a strange garment should ever have been tried on a man like Hugo, for it certainly never fitted him. But it was only natural that the bare notion that she might not be able to hold him, against time and other women, had scared and shaken her.

She thought now that whatever she had been, Hugo would still have been the man he was cut out to be. But in a way, she supposed that she had invited some of his impatience, brought down his ever-decreasing opinion of her capacities, both physical and mental, because she was so afraid, and so increasingly unsure of herself. She had made him more arrogant and careless of her, no doubt. And he had made her into a pretty poor thing, in the long run.

The children hadn't seemed to make the difference that people often said they did. Unless in fact her pregnancy before Margaret came had been the immediate cause of his first actual defection. Madge had a small frame and she looked enormous and distorted when she was carrying a child. Hugo would look at her inadvertently, and look away deliberately. It had hurt her sharply, but she had thought perhaps that was the natural and inevitable reaction for any man, and that it would be all right when the baby came. Actually, she had never known just who had been the first, or when it had happened, and she was glad now that she hadn't. And when the recurrent wonder, and then doubt of him had come to stay in her, she had refused to acknowledge it to herself, even while she felt it lying like a weight at the bottom of her heart. As though a fear could not really exist as long as it remained unrecognized.

Hugo had been disappointed in the baby's being a girl, of course, but Margaret had won him over in spite of himself, and that had given Madge such hope for a time that she was even glad when she found Ronnie was on the way. That was the time when they built and moved into this house, and it had seemed then that surely they were building something new and permanent into their lives. Finally, when the same old doubts began to weigh her down again, she told herself, listening to other women talk, that all men were like that and one just had to expect and accept it. It was a long time before she realized that all men were not quite like Hugo Fairlie.

She was ashamed of that period, and her own part in it. Of the way she had accepted his increasingly frequent absences (his Evenings Working at the Office, his Business Trips) without inquiry or even apparent interest; of the way she accepted his returns, almost as though she were glad to have him back—without ever admitting that he'd been away. How had she done it, she wondered? *Had* she been glad to have him back on any terms? Had she still been proud to go out with him when he condescended to take her? Possibly she had; it was hard to say now.

She was ashamed to remember the night when that period came to an end (at least insofar as being unacknowledged between them), when she had failed utterly to meet the challenge that it brought. By that time Hugo's attitude was so careless of the usual amenities or marital conventions, that it must have been obvious to even the stupidest woman. It must have exasperated him to think she could be that stupid. In fact he had said just that. She still remembered that evening, when he had gone upstairs shortly after dinner, and after a while—perhaps a half an hour—she had gone up also, not to follow him but to look at Margaret who had had a cold, and then at Ronnie, just for the pleasure of looking at him. She really thought Hugo had come down again and gone out without bothering to speak to her.

She hung over Ronnie for a few minutes, and fussed around the room, doing nothing, and then went back across the hall to the big front bedroom, whose English chintz and curtains hadn't yet lost their freshness. Hugo was there in his white dress shirt sleeves and black silk waistcoat, tying a black bow tie.

"Oh—" Madge said involuntarily. "I thought you'd gone . . ."

He looked into the high mirror of the chiffonier, where her small image was reflected from across the room, and gave a slight smile.

"You just take it for granted that I'm going out, don't you? Why, I wonder?" he said, almost idly.

"Why, I suppose because you often do," she said helplessly. It seemed an absurdly futile question, but he seemed to expect an answer.

"Do you feel I go out at night very often, Madge?" he inquired, with a sort of scientific interest.

"I never counted up, particularly," she said, trying to sound as casual as ever. "You have a great many business things which come up, I know," she murmured, trying to pull that old fiction up around her shoulders; but it wouldn't quite cover her face.

"Hm—yes. I suppose I have," he agreed judicially. He gave a complacent glance down at his shirt front, down the length of his long black legs. "I'm a very well-dressed business man, wouldn't you say, Madge?"

"You're a very well-dressed man, Hugo," she acknowledged in a small tone, as though reciting a lesson she had learned, without knowing why. And she didn't know what was coming next, what he was trying to do, why he was goading her this way.

"You think I'm quite suitably turned out for a business conference tonight then?" he pursued, as if anxious for her opinion.

"I don't . . . know what you mean," she faltered.

"Oh don't you? Come now, Madge, you can't be quite as stupid as that."

She could feel the color coming up in her face, until she was scarlet. She was horribly aware of it; yet why should she be the one who was ashamed? She turned away finally, as if wrenching herself out from under his cynical gaze.

"You won't answer that one, will you?" he said, following her amusedly with his eyes. She turned again, trying to make some stand—a little farther away from him.

"I don't know what you're trying to do, Hugo. I don't know what you want—with such a conversation. Surely it's no use—"

"I just wanted to know how much of a fool you really were, my dear. I've often wondered," he said.

"Was that why you married me in the first place?" she asked softly. "Just to find that out?"

He laughed; actually laughed out loud. Oh yes, Hugo had enjoyed that interview.

"No. . . no," he acknowledged, "there were a couple of other points."

"Which you explored—and exhausted very soon, didn't you?" She stared at him, without tears, but with all the hurt in her eyes which tears could neither have hidden nor expressed. And then she broke out suddenly, the only time she ever had. "What do you *want* of me, Hugo?" she cried out at him despairingly. "Why are you trying to humiliate me this way, on top of everything else? Do you want a divorce—is this your strange way of telling me?"

"Good Lord, no," he said abruptly. "Certainly not. Where would I ever find another wife so—complacent, shall we say?"

She moved back a step, and put her hands out behind her to catch or brace herself against the chair she had backed into.

"If that's what you think I've been," she began, very low, but his own smooth tone overrode hers.

"And unless I miss my guess by a wide mark," he said calmly, "you don't want a divorce any more than I do."

He came toward her, and she stood her ground now, though she wanted to turn and run from him. He put his hand under her chin and raised it; he bent and kissed her, not carelessly as he generally did, but lingeringly and with relish.

"*Good* night, my dear," he said.

Yet even after that, she had stayed. No wonder Hugo could say— what he *had* said to her tonight. She had gone back into the nursery again that evening, and sat there, quiet and blank and empty. She had sat there for an hour, two hours perhaps, watching Ronnie, who slept so beautifully. And she had stayed. . . .

*   *   *

She should have left Hugo, of course. Any other self-respecting woman would have. But then, she wasn't a self-respecting woman, and never had been, and that was her trouble. Hugo seemed to have left her very little to respect herself with, even while he had built a high and handsome wall of money and position to shelter her from the world outside. She simply hadn't the courage to climb that wall, or throw herself off the top of it either, and meet whatever she would have to face outside. Somehow, by the time their situation was finally acknowledged between them, it was already an old and settled shame which she had accepted and, in a sense, made her own. You can leave in the first flush of anger or humiliation. You're not so apt to leave, she found, when the first has worn off and you've become accustomed to the last. It's astonishing what you can grow used to, Madge thought.

She was not yet twenty-four at that time. She didn't know whether she ought to have had more courage at that age than she would have later, or whether one had to build up a fortitude to meet what lay ahead, and she had had too little time to build or grow before she ever met Hugo. In the meantime, her father was gone, and both Judy and Lou had married, and there had seemed nowhere to go, no one to turn to, even to ask what she should do. They hadn't liked her marrying Hugo anyway, and she'd had a sort of poor, pathetic pride about that too. She told herself that if it hadn't been for the children, she might have found enough courage just for herself. . . . She didn't know. Sometimes she wondered with horrible candor whether she hadn't made the children only another excuse for her cowardice, not a reason for her endurance. But there it was; and they had all gone on together, for nearly ten years, until Ronnie was killed. And then it was too late, too late for anything. She would probably never feel older than she had at thirty-three; no one ever did, of course. Anyway, she had gone on again, more numb than ever in the center of her, but with all the little outer nerve ends quite alive, surprisingly, to feel the funny and ridiculous and irritating things as they went by. And now, perhaps, it was nearly over. . . .

Only she couldn't believe that. She had come full course around the circle, and she could believe it no more now than at the beginning of all this remembering. Hugo would be better in a couple of days, and they would go on as they always had. If only that nurse would come. The doctor had said something about cold baths or ice packs, and surely it had been over an hour since he had left. She was getting stiff and chilly herself, but still she didn't want to move as long as Hugo was quiet. He was stirring now and then, but she thought he was asleep.

And then he spoke again, muttered something she couldn't understand. She got up and went over to him, but still she couldn't make it out. Something about the present . . .?

"Yes, Hugo, I'm here," she said, but he was not satisfied.

"Present," he said, in an uneasy feverish way. "Got to get that present."

"Present?" She was puzzled.

"Christmas present," he said, much more loudly this time, glaring at her as if she were either very deaf or very dull, or both. Oh yes, of course—of course; the present he had wanted her to get for Margaret. That was it. Odd that he should think of that now.

"The bracelet?" she asked, and he nodded, rather uncertainly, for Hugo. "Yes dear, I got it," she assured him. "It's quite all right." But he was looking at her so doubtfully still, with the same dull glare. Perhaps if she brought it and just showed it to him he'd stop worrying and settle down again. She went over to her desk and rummaged for a moment in the deep lower drawer, and brought over the small square box, and opened it. It really was a beautiful little bracelet, gold, with sapphires set in and spaced around it. Madge turned on the light above him, and Hugo took it in his hand and looked at it for a long moment. Almost automatically, Madge began to wonder if it was right after all, if he would approve of it; he was staring at it so. And then he looked up slowly, from it to her.

"Is that for Lucy?" he asked suspiciously.

Lucy, Madge's thought repeated. Not Margaret then; not even now. She didn't know who Lucy was, and didn't in the least care to. She took the bracelet out of his hand gently, but he had closed his eyes again and hardly seemed to notice. She was glad, as she took the box back to the desk, that Margaret hadn't been there to hear him.

Chapter Five

MARGARET ARRIVED A FEW MINUTES AFTER THE NURSE DID. MADGE had barely finished showing the latter where things were, and just begun to wonder whether she could lie down for a little while herself in Ronnie's old room, when Margaret appeared in the doorway, her eyes as wide and dazed as a night animal's by the lights she had found on everywhere. Madge had not heard her carefully quiet entrance, but even so, there would have been no way of leading her gently up to the night's events. She told her simply, coming quickly out into the hall and closing the door behind her first. She was prepared for a shocked reaction, but not quite for the stricken look on Margaret's face and the way she faltered, "Oh *Father* . . . if I'd only known . . ." as if speaking to him, and not to her mother at all.

"Darling, you couldn't know," Madge said. "None of us could. His cold must have gotten much worse suddenly, and he just wanted to get home and didn't even think of telegraphing us to meet him. I couldn't have got hold of you, anyway, because I didn't know where you'd gone or even whom you were with—"

"I know," Margaret said, almost in a whisper. "That's the awful part of it."

"But there wasn't anything you could have done," Madge said gently, trying to reassure her. "There was nothing to do except to keep him quiet, till the nurse came. That's what the doctor said. He's dropped off now—but you'll be able to see him in the morning, even talk to him a little then, probably. He'll be better then, dear."

But Margaret was never to hear her father speak coherently again. Though, on the other hand, in the few vague words he did say, there were no more revealing names or implications for her to overhear. Something spared them both that. His sentences simply

75

made no sense at all, and then lapsed entirely in his fight for breath itself, as his lungs filled and his fever mounted, always a little higher. It was painful to hear and watch, even if you felt you hardly knew the suffering creature lying there in the oxygen tent, which in itself gave him a fearful strangeness. He knew no one, not her, nor Margaret, nor the minister who came and said a prayer beside him while Madge listened with a sense of acute embarrassment—not for herself, but for Hugo. Or was it for Hugo's soul, lurking there trying to find some place to go? Madge's religious concepts still had a vague but primitive simplicity. If it hadn't been for Hugo, she might have learned to go to church quite happily, for she sometimes thought she was the sort of person who really belonged there.

But Hugo, strangely enough, had always set great store by appearing in church at regular intervals, by the contributions he made to it, by being known as a member in good standing. He had liked her to appear with him, or even for him sometimes, and that had raised an impassable barrier in her mind, between herself and any honest belief which she might have found there. She knew very well that many other men liked their wives to do the churchgoing for them, even expected them to act as go-betweens for themselves and God. She even saw now, from what Hugo had said the other night, that he resented the fact that she had never held up that end of her job. But as things were with them, she had been able only to sit in the pew, passively and with great detachment, and wonder how many others in the congregation were as self-deceiving—as inconsistent—or as hypocritical—as her own husband. And yet now she was wondering if there had been some obscure base for him there, after all—which a man like that could seldom touch, but which he kept reaching out to, nevertheless. She remembered again her father's saying that everybody looked for the same thing, but had to arrive by a different route that he'd hacked out for himself. So maybe there was a base—a permanent goal—for everyone, to go out to or come back to (whichever way you saw it). Even for Hugo. Maybe he was returning even now, finding his way right there before her, behind that unconscious face which she could no longer penetrate. . . .

It was three days before Hugo Fairlie died, two days before Christmas, but those days and hours all seemed to run together in one queer misshapen blur for Madge, spent as they mostly were just sitting waiting, in the dressing room off the big bedroom. A room which was darkened in the daytime, faintly lighted at night. Bits of meals eaten hastily at queer irregular hours . . . Later, as she looked back, she could remember very little of it distinctly. It was only that first night, when she'd been alone with him, which stood out in every clear detail and remained a dreary but indelible picture. And then, when Hugo was actually gone, her mind, which had been in a sort of suspension, following her body around rather than leading it, gave a painful jerk and began to function again.

Everyone said, with a certain respect (surprised respect, no doubt) how calm she was. Because for once in her life Madge Fairlie seemed to be more efficient, to have more wits about her, than anyone else in the house. Margaret was a lost shadow with a washed-out, haunted look in her eyes, wandering from room to room, as if looking, despairingly, for something that wasn't there. Ellen dissolved in an emotional flood of sympathy and watered all their meals. Even Sarah was flustered in her grim way, while Esther and Sims looked scared and apprehensive, respectively, as if unsure of their roles and wishing themselves anywhere but where they were.

But Madge went ahead steadily and quietly, despite the fact that she was coming down with a cold now, and felt achy and queer. In those next three days she saw all the necessary people: the undertaker, the florist, the clergyman, certain of the friends who came to the house. It occurred to her once, fantastically, that she must have learned her job of managing the—"social"—affairs of that house better than she had ever realized. Christmas coming just then made it awkward of course. . . . Hugo, with his sense of the proprieties, would never have chosen to die two days before Christmas, so that the funeral would have to wait until the day after the holiday. He would have considered that unsuitable and badly timed. But that was not Madge's fault. All she could do about that was to concentrate intently on holding up the burden of that extra day, to keep things running, carefully in balance, suspended through the period which was inevitably bridged by a sort of emotional tension anyway. And since there was no emotion in her, she must ease the tension for others as best she could. For those three days at least. Beyond that, she refused to look.

Christmas, she knew, had better be ignored between Margaret and her, left unacknowledged—except for one thing. Just one, which she must attend to somehow. But how to do that, she didn't yet know. There was such a remoteness about Margaret these last few days. She had moved off to a greater distance than ever before, just when they should have come closer together. Perhaps the wall between them was sheer numbness now, the merciful deadening which follows great shock and shuts off any feeling for a time, from within or without. But Madge had a miserable suspicion that it was there because her own feeling couldn't match Margaret's, and the girl knew it in her heart. That made it harder than ever to approach her, yet something must be done about that bracelet which still lay in her desk drawer. No matter what Hugo had said in a wandering moment, that had been his idea for Margaret. It was his present far more than Madge's, and she had no right—had she?—to keep it back for fear of upsetting the child still more. And so she waited, all through that day, waited for the moment to come which might make it a little easier.

Through breakfast, which they ate stolidly, without the faintest acknowledgment of the date, despite the large streamer in red ink which ran across the top of the newspaper, lying on the table between them. Through the morning, and the trip to the undertaker's, and the return to the house, where Madge's friends Mona and Emmy were waiting together to answer telephone calls, and see any people who came to the house. Through the early afternoon when Mona took Margaret and Madge back to her own house for a quiet lunch. And then on through the late afternoon, at home, when the servants were in again, but people had stopped coming, and Margaret and Madge consulted in carefully matter-of-fact detachment about details: black clothes for Margaret, whether they should use the den for the minister the next day, or have him go upstairs.

Through supper, where they sat almost in silence, finding less and less that could be said. It was the first evening meal they had eaten alone together. Emmy had stayed with them the night before, and the nurse had been there the first night, just after. . . . Madge had made the nurse take home to her own family the turkey which had been ordered for the Fairlies two weeks before. So now they had cold ham and a souffle, and artichokes from Florida. And afterward they went in tacit agreement into the drawing room rather than the library, and Margaret picked up a book and sat looking at some one page, without turning it, for a long, long time. Madge settled herself at the small desk and tried to write a couple of notes. People had been so kind already, leaving messages, and flowers, and there would be so many more flowers tomorrow that she must keep ahead as well as she could.

But it wasn't long before Margaret got up abruptly.

"I think I'll go up," she said. "You don't mind, do you, darling?" She touched her mother's shoulder half apologetically.

"Of course not, dear. I'll be along in a very little while anyway. I'll stop in your room—to say goodnight."

She let her go, and sat on at the desk for a few minutes more, finishing the note. But this was the time, she thought. It was the only time left, for Christmas was almost over—and it might help just a little, give the child some sort of comfort. It might even help Madge Fairlie to reach her own child at last. . . . She closed the desk, and crossed the floor to turn off the lights, and as the room dropped into darkness which was like a hole, she stared back into it for a moment, and gave a little shiver. The whole place was so strange now; how were they ever going to live in it? Everything was strange, and everyone was a stranger to the other.

She went upstairs, quietly and quickly as usual, making no sound, though she was unaware of that. She heard no sound from Margaret's room either, though the door was open. She turned into the room which had been hers and Hugo's, where she had not slept for almost a week—though she supposed she would have to move back here soon. She refused to let herself shiver again and went quickly across to the desk, to stoop and open a drawer, and feel there for a moment. And then without lingering she went out with it in her hands and started along the hall, and suddenly halted at the door of the small sitting room. For Margaret was there, not in her own room. She was sitting in the low chair by the telephone table, and one hand was resting on the telephone itself, though she was not talking. Madge hesitated and then came into the room.

"Darling," she said, and hesitated again. Margaret looked up at her slowly, and for a second she looked almost at bay, defiant. "Darling," Madge said again, urgently now. "I haven't known what to do about—this. I've been worrying about it all day. I hated not to say anything, but I just wanted to do what would hurt you least. Or comfort you most—" She stopped short, her eyes searching Margaret's, but there was nothing she could find there, nothing she could take hold of. "It's something your father . . ." Madge faltered and looked down at her hands and at the thing in them. "It was his idea," she went on carefully. "He suggested it—Oh, weeks ago. I—we—got it then. He saw it before he died," she said, and stopped again. But somehow she had to go on through this, clear to the end of it. "I wouldn't have brought it now," she said jerkily, "but after all it was—I mean it *is*, his Christmas present for you, and it's nearly the end of the day, and I thought maybe—now—was when you needed it."

Margaret's gaze was still fixed on Madge's hands and what was in them: a small box, not wrapped or anything, just a box. Her mother held it out to her suddenly, rather like a child poking it at her in embarrassment. Margaret lifted her own hand from the telephone, at last, and took the box in it, and laid it on her lap, her eyes following it as though it were alive, moving of its own accord and not because one hand had passed it to another. And then she opened it, and picked up the bracelet, and looked steadily at it as it hung over her fingers.

"It's beautiful," she said in a whisper. Her arm sagged slowly till the fingers reached the box again, and laid the bracelet back in it. And then she raised both hands to cover her face, and sat that way, utterly still for a moment. Madge reached out anxiously, half fearfully, to touch her shoulder, and when she did, she could feel the sobs coming before they were even audible, and when they came, they were like a storm which had been a long time gathering its force. Madge had never seen Margaret give way like that, not even when she was a child. She had never seen anyone cry like that.

"Oh my darling," she said, "I didn't know—I didn't know . . . I thought it might comfort you a little. I didn't know what to do—" She repeated pitifully, and a little forlornly too, "I never know . . ."

*   *   *

By the next day, Madge's cold had come on in full force. She had become thoroughly chilled that first night of Hugo's illness, pattering up and down with bare ankles, sitting that way by the hour in her nightgown and wrapper. And then of course she was tired; she must have been tired, just from lack of sleep, though she hadn't really thought about it. She'd tried to fight the cold off and ignore it, but now the morning of the funeral, she needed a handkerchief constantly at her nose, and even her eyes would start to stream and weep every now and then. The flowers, too, the masses of flowers banked all around the two big rooms and out in the hall—they didn't help any.

There was a moment that morning when she had dropped down in sheer weariness on a chair in the drawing room, clutching a moist rag of a handkerchief in one hand. For that second, she was alone. Margaret was upstairs, two or three women who supposed themselves to be helping with the flowers were in the den talking in low voices, and the undertaker's assistant who had stayed behind the others had gone out to his car to bring in more chairs. That was when Mrs. Henry Delephant came in from the hall, saw Madge sitting there abjectly, staring across at the flowers banked around the coffin, and she stopped and put one hand on Madge's shoulder.

"My dear," she said quietly. Madge looked up, and the light from the window beyond the other woman's head made her eyes start watering again. Mrs. Delephant shook her head from side to side, and her own eyes reddened slightly. "I haven't had a word with you alone," she said, "but I can't say anything—there isn't anything to say. Only that I know what you're feeling, because I know how it would be with me—if it were Henry."

"You're awfully kind," Madge murmured, shamefacedly, dropping her eyes to her lap and the damp handkerchief in her hand. "Everybody's so kind—"

"And everybody says how brave you've been." Brave, Madge thought; she, the completest coward there ever was, giving a show of bravery now, when none was needed. Mrs. Delephant dropped her long slender hand from Madge's shoulder to squeeze Madge's hand, and Madge pressed it in return—and then hastily put up her wet handkerchief to her nose, while the other woman slipped quietly and tactfully away. She meant it all so sincerely and so deeply, poor dear old soul, who had lived with and loved her own husband for nearly forty years. Poor soul? Madge didn't know why she called her that, even in her own mind. She supposed she'd heard other people say "The poor Delephants—did you know . . ." just because the Delephant fortunes were commonly supposed to be on the wane in these booming days of 1928. But that had so little to do with it, or with anything important. She had something that Madge had never had—and she had it still.

Madge herself felt such an arrant, nasty little hypocrite. All this sympathy, all these people coming in and out, stepping softly, speaking warmly of how brave she was. Speaking respectfully and admiringly of Hugo. While all she felt at the moment was a throbbing head and a streaming nose, and a naked sense of mortification, as though she could hardly cover herself with the few shreds of shock and grief which really belonged to her. Maybe it was just as well, she thought, that her eyes wept and her nose was red, in spite of her. She ought to be thankful for the cold in her head which was the only thing that would get her through all this with some decency.

The service was at one-thirty, in deference to Hugo's large business acquaintance. There was music—there had to be music for

Hugo, though it was something to suffer through; there was the simple service and a less simple prayer, and then the minister talked about Hugo for ten minutes by the watch on Madge's wrist. She had been afraid to tell him not to, but she sat there shivering at the top of the stairs—with Margaret sitting stiffly just beyond her reach, as though if they touched each other, it would give both of them away. She wondered what all those people thought down there as they listened to that man praising Hugo; did they believe him? And did the man believe himself? Perhaps. None of them knew much about Hugo after all. Perhaps—But she was thankful when there was no more to come, thankful that there was no trip to the cemetery. And by quarter past two it was over, and everyone had gone.

It was over, she told herself insistently, as if trying to make herself hear and understand. It was over, she repeated, all of it. Even the undertakers and the chairs and the flowers were gone at last. She had had them take all the flowers away. Even the few closer friends like Mona and Ned, and Emmy Burns, had gone away, finally. Madge had come downstairs again, rather dazedly, and begun directing Sims about some of the furniture that the undertaker's men hadn't put in the right places, because Sims himself behaved as though he'd never seen the house before. And then suddenly, and finally, she didn't know what to do next.

It seemed as if there must be something that had to be done. There were all those hundreds of notes, of course—but she and Margaret were going to go over the list together and divide it up between them. There were Hugo's things to go over—but surely she could wait a little before trying to move that mountain with her bare hands. She didn't know where Margaret had gone. She must find her, she thought. Poor lonely child—the only one in the world who really loved Hugo . . . She went upstairs again and saw at once that the girl's door was closed. She stood outside for a moment, tentatively. She knocked very softly and said, "Margaret, darling—" but there was no answer. No sound in the room at all. She put her hand on the door knob and turned it, hesitantly. The door was locked. She was like a small terrier, she thought, sniffing anxiously at a door which was always locked—to her.

She turned away, to Ronnie's room, where she had been sleeping these last nights. She thought perhaps she'd lie down for a little while. That would probably be the most sensible thing to do for her cold. And she might even drop off for a nap. She was still tired, and it would pass the time—the time of this particular afternoon which somehow stretched away in front of her, as long as a lifetime. Or was it a lifetime that she really meant, in her mind, and was trying not to think about?

It occurred to her all at once and with relief that she could go outdoors instead of lying down. A walk and fresh air would do her far more good. It was quite mild out again after the cold raw wave they'd had the week before. It might not be considered quite the thing for a newly widowed woman to go walking—but no one would see her anyway, no one would think of it. She turned to the closet where her few black things had been hastily collected together, and got out an old coat and hat. No one would see her, she repeated to herself. And she saw no one as she went downstairs and across the hall. She didn't even hear any sounds from the back of the house. The whole place seemed rather strange to her, like a public building without a soul in it. She let herself out the door, remembering to put it on the latch, as if she were almost afraid there would be no one there to let her in again. She would have to learn to remember things for herself now.

She crossed the street to the Square and started out the way she always went, along the diagonal patch which ran from one corner to the other. The air really wasn't cold at all, and she felt freer outdoors, even though the clouds were low overhead, and the square had its gloomy winter look. As she walked farther into it, she noticed someone sitting on a bench near the dry wading pool, and thought how odd it was for anyone to sit down out there on a late December day. And then as she came nearer she saw that it was a woman and she was crying. Just sitting there quietly, with her hands in her lap and the tears running slowly down her face, almost as if she were unaware of them. Madge looked at her again, and then she looked away hastily. . . . The only decent thing was to pass by as if one didn't notice anything—and yet that didn't seem quite human. She slowed a little, and glanced again, and thought perhaps the woman couldn't even see anyone passing through her own private blur. So she went on again, relieved by that reflection, but with a peculiar feeling still as though she were trying to pass unseen, evading someone who had called to her. She stopped finally after a few yards, simply because she couldn't quite go by.

She turned and left the walk to cross over the hard turf, so that the woman's shoulder was toward her now as she approached, and that made it more difficult, somehow. She really didn't seem to see her, and Madge stood there hesitating, wishing she hadn't stopped after all. But now she had, she couldn't suddenly dash off again; she'd have to find something to say.

"I'm *so* sorry," she said timidly after a long moment. "Is there anything anyone can do?"

The woman turned her head a little way toward her, and then turned it away again. She was a good-looking girl, or would have been if her face hadn't been all streaked. Tall and dark and dressed all in black, and not much over thirty, Madge guessed. But she didn't speak, and Madge felt herself shrinking up inside.

"I'm very sorry," she said again, but in a still smaller voice than before, "I didn't mean to intrude. But you seemed to be in such trouble . . ."

"I am," the other said, in a flat tone, as though nothing mattered enough now to make it worth dissembling.

"Isn't there—haven't you anybody to help you?"

"No."

Oh dear, Madge thought, I've probably said the very worst thing. And then aloud—"I don't suppose there's anything I can do, but— I was just coming across the Square when I saw you sitting there—"

"It doesn't matter," the girl said dully, "where you were going or where you were coming from. What the hell do I care—unless . . ." She broke off for a second, staring across the Square. "Unless you came from that house," she added slowly, nodding straight ahead of her. It seemed to be Madge's own house that she meant; it must be, because there was no other in such direct line or which stood out more clearly from here.

"Why—yes," Madge said, as slowly now as the other had spoken. "I did come from there, as a matter of fact."

"Were you at the funeral?" the young woman asked abruptly.

"Yes, I was," Madge acknowledged. And then she added simply, "I live there, you see." That seemed the most tactful way of dropping a hint, to steer away from the unexpected direction this conversation was taking. But it had a different effect than she anticipated. The girl was staring at her now, with an intense scrutiny which had a sudden, hopeful urgency about it.

"I think I know who you are, now," she said quietly after a minute.

"Do you?" Madge said uncomfortably. "Well—it doesn't mat—"

"Yes, I do. You're Sarah," the other said, with a rush of confidence, and something almost like tender recognition. Madge opened her mouth, and no sound came out. Sarah indeed! Sarah, who was twenty years older than she, not to mention any other differences . . . Of course she did look a wreck today, and her hair *was* gray in spots, and she supposed this ancient coat . . . But altogether, the encounter had rendered her more helpless than usual, and she couldn't even think what to say, before the other was going on again, quietly, but with a sort of deep reminiscent sadness. "I've heard so much about you, you see," she said. "I know the whole house and everybody in it, even where all your rooms are . . . And yet," she added, with a reflectiveness which was resigned, and bitter, at the same time, "I couldn't go there today. No. I couldn't see it for myself. I knew which room it would be in, but not just where they'd put him—nor what the flowers were like. Were there a great many flowers?" she asked, almost wistfully.

Oh dear Lord, Madge thought. She had almost recoiled. She had very nearly turned and run, straight through the Square as though pursued. Anywhere—to get away from here. But instead, somehow, she had managed to stand still, if not very firmly, on the same spot. And after a minute she said quietly, "Yes, there were a great many. They were very beautiful."

"Would you mind telling me about it?" The woman moved over slightly and put a hand out on her cold bench, as if in invitation, or mute entreaty. Madge moved forward carefully and sat down beside her (the support was a relief, in a way) and began slowly and dazedly to describe Hugo's funeral. The way the flowers were hung or banked together around all four sides of the drawing room, and on into the library and some in the hall too. The colors: more red roses, and yellow and white chrysanthemums than anything else . . . Just exactly where the coffin stood . . . Where the family had sat upstairs . . . It all came out, all of it, a little more slowly with each sentence. And all the time, the other woman's eyes gazed at her, and one hand was raised so that the back of her thumb was pressed against her half-open mouth, like a child trying to keep from crying. It was incongruous, and difficult to watch. But Madge kept on, quietly and mechanically and monotonously until she couldn't think of anything else. When she stopped the other was silent. Finally she said, rousing herself, "Thank you. You *are* kind. I knew you would be, when I realized who you were. I think you liked and admired him very much yourself, didn't you?"

"Why I—" Madge felt herself growing dizzier, her feet going out from under her on a slippery surface. What was she supposed to say to that, she wondered? Who was she supposed to be answering for, herself—or Sarah? But of course it was Sarah. She, Madge Fairlie, hadn't come into this encounter at all; she wasn't *here*. "Why—yes," she said, after a moment. "He—uh—he was a very good employer, I think." She realized how prim she sounded, but perhaps that was in character too, for Sarah. The girl smiled a little bleakly, but she nodded.

"I know he was. I was a receptionist in his office, once," she said simply.

"Oh—" Madge acknowledged, unable to think of another word to add to that one.

Slowly the other got up, and stiffly, as though much tireder and older than her thirty-odd years. She stood looking down at Madge.

"Thank you," she said again. "I know I can depend on your— loyalty—as well as your kindness."

Madge took a breath, lifted her eyebrows a little, though she was looking at the ground near her own feet. "Yes," she said, constrain- edly, but wearily too. "Yes, of course."

"This has been strange, hasn't it? I didn't know why I came out here . . . just to see the cars come, and go away again . . . at a distance. But now I know. And it has helped."

"I'm very glad—if it did," Madge said.

"Thank you, Sarah." The other woman stood there for a second longer, as if uncertain how to leave, then she turned and started walking away toward the downtown side of the Square. Madge con- tinued to sit there for a few moments, wondering if her legs would work when she got up, if she could still walk, or rather, go for a walk. She wondered if that girl's name was Lucy . . . Not that it mattered. She wondered if she really felt sorry for her, and thought she did, though perhaps she shouldn't. The other *had* something still, apparently: some feeling left, some honest grief. Maybe she was lucky, after all. Madge sneezed suddenly and violently, and reached for her handkerchief which she had forgotten for a while—and got up and began walking hurriedly, not paying much attention now which way she went.

* * *

She felt worn and battered when she reached home again, but not from walking. She hadn't gone far, just a dozen blocks over toward the Boulevard, and then back again. Her head felt clearer, but it seemed a long, long time since the day had started, and it was not over yet. Margaret and she still had the evening to go through. She couldn't help the child, she knew that now; but there was an obligation laid upon her, not to let her down further by exposing her own lack of grief. It was as much the thought of keeping up the right front before Margaret, which hung darkly over her, as it was the eerie realization of their aloneness together. She was emotionally tired, which she had a right to be, from anyone's point of view, but the trouble was that she had been struggling with all the wrong emotions, which was perhaps even more wearing.

She was glad she'd remembered to leave the front door on the latch for herself, so that she wouldn't have to face anyone else just yet, even to get into the house. But that respite was brief. She'd hardly come through the outer door when she realized that two people were standing talking just inside the hall. Esther making excuses to someone—oh dear, who now? she thought. A man with his back to her; overcoat on, no hat—those wide flapping trousers . . . She had actually forgotten Clay Ferguson for—was it a matter of hours, or days? She had to stop short and readjust her mind to the thought of him.

"Oh . . . Clay," she said slowly, and a little vaguely, with a shade of wonder in her tone. He turned quickly and she saw Esther quickly fading across the hall, as if glad to be relieved.

"Mrs. Fairlie! Gosh, I'm glad to see you—that is—I didn't want to butt in, but . . . You know, I'm awfully sorry about everything," he said abruptly. She was surprised by that somehow, because he sounded as if he meant it. She wouldn't suppose that he would be sorry about Hugo, everything considered. But he had come straight across to her, and taken both her hands, and was holding them hard now, looking down into her face with a close and anxious distress. She felt suddenly warmed, overwhelmed by a kindness where she would least expect it.

"Thank you, Clay. It was nice of you to come." He shook his head almost impatiently, as if that wasn't worth mentioning.

"I've been here several times," he told her.

"I didn't know."

"No, I know. I didn't want to bother you. But I did want to do something if I could. And I wanted to see Peg—Margaret," he corrected himself a trifle grimly. "She knows I've been here. But she won't see me. She won't even answer the telephone," he said, and he sounded angry and anxious too.

For a second Madge had to think about it. Yes, of course: her father had asked her not to see him for a month or two, and Margaret would feel she had to carry that out. But this was carrying the thing to an extreme, wasn't it, under the circumstances? It wasn't quite kind, when the boy was obviously trying to be kind, himself.

"I'm sorry about that," she said, rather carefully. "Margaret must appreciate it, I know. But you see—I don't know if you fully understand, Clay, but her father suggested her not seeing quite so much of you as she was doing for a time, so now I suppose she feels—" She paused. This was very awkward. And he was looking at her as though he wasn't sure they understood each other.

"I know that," he conceded finally. "But things have changed, Mrs. Fairlie." For a moment Madge had one of her mad impulses to laugh out loud in the wrong place. That, she thought, was one of the completest understatements she had ever heard. But all she said was, "Yes, Clay, they have."

"And I've got to see her," he broke in. "You don't realize what— my God, I've been going nearly crazy thinking about her and wondering—I guess you'll think that sounds pretty childish, with all you've been through," he interrupted himself, as though forcing himself to a stop. He had let her hands go and thrust his own deep into his overcoat pockets. He was looking moodily at the floor, but Madge was watching him, and she had never liked Clay Ferguson quite so much as she did at that moment. Perhaps because his feeling about Margaret seemed so strong and so genuine. And so, though she didn't really want to, though she was moving against the undertow in her own mind, she said, "I'll try to get Margaret to see you." He raised his eyes and Madge had a sudden feeling of looking into an open room from which she drew back startled, because it was so large and light and—somehow—rather beautiful.

"You will?" he said simply. "Thanks." And he gave a great sigh of relief.

"I'll see if she's upstairs now."

"I think she is. In fact I know she is, even if the maid was trying to tell me differently."

"Go into the library, Clay, and I'll go up—"

"No thanks," he said with abrupt stubbornness. "I'll wait right here." And then he added purposefully, "And you tell her if she doesn't come down this time, I'm coming up."

Madge turned, astonished.

"I hardly think that's—necessary—or suitable, Clay," she said, rather coolly now. "And give me a little time to talk to her, please, before you—leave." What a queer combination of gentleness and brashness he was. No wonder Hugo . . . and now if he and Margaret really . . . but she refused that thought hastily as she went up the stairs. All she had agreed to, after all, was to get Margaret to see him, this once. That was only fair, but that was as far as she went.

She saw when she reached the second floor that Margaret's door was open now, but she didn't go to it immediately. She went into Ronnie's room and hung away the old coat and hat. She wanted a moment or two to think what to say. But before she emerged from the closet Margaret had come into the room. Madge still lingered among the hangers, trying to prop something under her spirit, but of course she had to come out of there, sooner or later. And when she did, Margaret said swiftly, "Darling, I'm so sorry."

"Why?" her mother asked, off balance, hardly able to remember all that had gone before.

"For not answering when you came to my door earlier. I'm such a pig. I was just thinking of myself, and it seemed as if I just couldn't bear to talk then. I've been—sort of out of my mind, I guess, this last week."

"I know, dear."

"But you're the one I ought to have been thinking about. You're the one it's hardest for." She put her arms around Madge. "Will you forgive me?" she said, softly and warmly. "I'll try to be more comfort to you. I truly will."

Madge stood in the circle of her embrace, surrounded by it, and touched by the sudden wonder of it. After all her inept reaching and striving for the child's love and understanding, to have it come like this, so naturally . . . Margaret was tall enough so that Madge could lean her cheek against the girl's firm shoulder, and it was a comfort to stand that way and feel encircled again. But even as they held each other, Madge had to brace herself anew. Because she was taking comfort for something she had no right to. This wasn't understanding, but the very opposite, and how could two people come closer on that basis? She let out a little sigh and then they stood a little apart and looked at each other. Margaret looked badly, Madge thought, and she felt a renewed ache of sympathy for what her child was going through—and without her, in a way, even though she didn't know that. She wondered how to bring up Clay's name.

"Did you know that Esther was looking for you, dear?" she asked.

"Yes," Margaret admitted. Madge waited a minute.

"Did you know that Clay was here?"

"I supposed that was it when she came up, though I didn't answer her. He's been phoning and calling . . . every day." Her tone had no expression in it at all. She sat down on the edge of the bed, and looked at her legs stretched out in front of her.

"I hadn't realized that."

"Yes," Margaret said again.

"It was kind of him. Don't you think you might see him or talk to him, this once?"

"I can't, Mother!" Her voice was very low, but there was feeling enough in it that time. Feeling that sounded rather like despair, Madge thought, but she couldn't be sure; Margaret looked so rigid as she sat there, with her arms braced straight at her sides. Madge moved to sit down beside her.

"Why not, darling?" she asked gently. "Don't you want to see him again?"

"*No,*" Margaret said, almost between her teeth. Madge was silent. And then precipitately, the girl broke out, "Yes, of course I want to see him—more than anything on earth! But I can't—I can't."

"Can't you?" Madge said.

"Oh Mother—Mother, you don't know! It was *Clay* I was with that night." She turned, groping for something to cling to herself, and put her arms blindly around Madge again, but this time it was Margaret's head on her mother's shoulder, and Madge's arm which tried to shelter her.

"No dear," she said. "I didn't know. You mean the night—"

"The night Father came home, so sick . . . The night you and I were alone again, and he was away, and I was going slowly crazy, I guess. And then Clay called, and he was getting so sore and hurt over the way I was treating him. . . . He sounded as if—if I didn't see him, he wouldn't even give me a chance again. Oh, it doesn't excuse me. I promised Father that I'd give it a try, and I had no business to go. But it just seemed as if it wasn't working out, and I *had* to see Clay."

"Yes, dear," Madge said softly, just to say something.

"I thought if we could just talk things out, I could make him understand. And we did—for hours and hours. Till it was pretty late . . . But then—"

Margaret began to sob now, in a queer dry way, and Madge held her shoulders tighter, as though trying to keep her torn feelings from tearing her apart.

"He didn't notice, dear," she murmured.

"I didn't mean to be underhanded about it, truly, Mother."

"No, of course not," Madge said quickly.

"But Father and I both got sort of on edge—you know, that night before he went away. And I thought he'd never understand. And now he never will," the girl cried brokenly. "And I can never even explain to him. And the last thing I did to him was to let him down."

"Oh darling, darling, you mustn't," Madge said urgently. "You can't help all that now. It doesn't matter to him now, I'm sure of that."

"It would matter to him that I'd deceived him," Margaret said, very low, her words half muffled. "He was always so straight himself. Always."

Madge couldn't speak for the ache (or was it something else?) that stuck in her throat. Slowly the girl sat up again.

"It would matter to him, too—the way I did it. I feel as if I could never face the memory of him again," she said. "And his memory means so *much* to me. You know, Mother—it's all we have left." She looked at her mother with a sort of anguish in her eyes, and her mother looked back, with pity—with the utmost pity. But what could she say? Strange, that it was she who was called upon to give sympathy, now to one and now to another, for her own husband's death. And she wasn't up to it, she knew. She tried to send out her own small despairing protest—where it echoed back at her, down some private corridor—tried to let someone know that she wasn't up to that. She was small and petty and lacking in any real life-sized emotion herself, wasn't she? So what could she offer to anyone else?

"You'll have the memory of his love for you," she said. "And that's more—than you can even realize just yet, darling. As for the rest, it was a sort of tangle of purposes that you got into, your father's and yours and Clay's, all wound around you. The whole thing looms up very large for you now—"

"Yes," Margaret said suddenly, throwing her head back, with her eyes closed. "Yes, it does. You see, Clay and I got married that night."

"Oh—h—h," said Madge, on a long, faint breath.

"So . . ." Margaret went on, with a sort of inexorable irony, opening her eyes again, "it does make it a little difficult, doesn't it? I can't just *see* him, and say, it's nice of you to call, and stop in again sometime, next month or next year."

"No," Madge admitted, almost stupidly. "Not that." Her face was stricken, and her eyes were suddenly full of fright—and pain. But Margaret hadn't looked straight at her yet.

"Well, now you know." She got up slowly. She brushed her hair back from her forehead with both hands, straightening her mouth, her whole face, as she straightened her body. Then she looked down at her mother and put out her hand to touch her cheek. "And I've hurt you too," she said sadly.

"My baby," Madge said, and tried to smile at her. "Why—did you do it that way?"

"I've told you. I was half crazy, I *missed* Clay so. And everybody else I saw bored me into a frenzy. I couldn't even listen to what they said, because nobody mentioned him, ever. If I could have talked about him, even—" she gave a faltering, shaky sort of laugh— "maybe I could have stuck it. Or if I'd been sure when the time was up that he'd be there and we'd both go on from there. But I wasn't, don't you see? He was so hurt, his pride was hurt, he couldn't see any sense in the whole agreement anyway. And I guess he thought— I cared more for what Father wanted, than for what he wanted."

"I see," said Madge.

"And then when I went out that night and we talked—and talked, we just didn't seem to get anywhere. It seemed so useless. I knew Father wasn't going to change his mind about him in a month —or a year. And there we were, and—how *does* one get into these things?" Margaret asked all at once, quite simply.

"I don't know," Madge said, scarcely above a whisper.

"Well, we did, that's all," Margaret said, turning away. "We went over the state line, to Dorsey. Very convenient little place, Dorsey. And then we drove back to town, and came out to the house to get a few of my things. I was going to leave a note for you, so you wouldn't be worried in the morning (all the proper melodramatic touches, you see) and then we were going to drive up to the Lodge at Deer Lake. It was too late—that's what I thought—to wake you up and tell you then. I came in so quietly. . ." Margaret went on, in a spell of remembering that was almost hypnotic. "I hadn't noticed all the lights from outside, I don't know why except that I was in too much of a trance, I suppose. It wasn't until I got halfway upstairs, still creeping, that I suddenly came to, and realized—that things were all different. And then you came out and told me. And I went down and told Clay and he went home." She stopped speaking and stood motionless in the middle of the floor, looking ahead of her at a spot on the wall, just below a framed water color.

"But you've seen him—since then?"

"No," Margaret said stonily.

"Or talked to him on the phone?"

For a second the girl didn't answer. "No," she said again, finally, though it seemed to come with difficulty. "I couldn't—at first. I just couldn't. And then each day I got a little more desperate, because I didn't know what to do, and I didn't even know how I *felt*. I was just torn up—every which way. And then—you remember Christmas night?" She looked at Madge, as though in sincere question as to whether she might remember a night like that, so long ago, and then she saw her expression and said, "Oh—yes. That was only yesterday, wasn't it? Well, I stood it all day—that horrible day. . . . And then after dinner, you remember I said I thought I'd go up early?"

Madge nodded, once for agreement, but her head kept on nodding, slowly, as though she couldn't stop it.

"I went upstairs, to the sitting room—where you found me. And I decided to call him. I was just going to," Margaret said, her voice curiously still as she spoke, "when you came in—with my present from Father." She turned again to look at her mother, it seemed, but her eyes were so full of tears that she couldn't have seen her clearly. And Madge thought, I tried to pick the best time, the moment when it might help her. . . .

"I'm so very sorry, darling," she said humbly. Margaret turned away toward the bureau, and after a second she picked up a handkerchief of her mother's which was lying there, and carefully blotted her eyes with it. "So you still haven't seen him, or talked to him," Madge said finally.

"No."

"But you'll have to, sometime."

Margaret merely shrugged her shoulders.

"You—don't care for him after all, then?" Madge persisted steadily. She didn't know where she was going. She only knew she had to find her way out of this jungle somehow, and lead her child out if she could.

"I love Clay," Margaret said in a level tone. "But perhaps he was right."

"I don't know what you—"

"That I loved Father more."

"The two aren't comparable," Madge said quickly.

"Of course not. I didn't mean they were. But this awful sense of desolation—I feel as if I couldn't bear it, Mother, because it's swallowed up everything else, nothing else seems to exist, or to be alive any more."

"But we have to bear it," Madge said in a small voice.

"Then what I mean is that I can't bear Father's loss—knowing how I failed him—and Clay's love, at the same time. The way things have happened has made it—impossible, Mother."

"But you have no choice, darling," Madge said, with difficulty.

They looked at each other for a long minute, the tall forceful girl and the small ineffectual, middle-aged woman.

"You mean you think I have to see him? That it would do any good at all?"

"I mean—you married Clay," her mother said.

"I could get an annulment."

Madge was silent. Finally she said, "I—wish I could help you, my darling. I wish it—so much." She had always wanted to help her, protect her; that was natural, it was what a mother was for. But now, the first time—the first time since Margaret had been a child, she'd turned to her, and she could do nothing. This was something only Margaret could do, herself. And so her mother sat there, not even getting up to go to her, to touch or put her arms around her again, and after a moment Margaret turned away from her, for the last time. She turned and stopped, facing the door which still stood open, and then she went slowly through it, into the hall and turned again toward the stairway, out of the line of Madge's vision.

Madge sat on the side of the bed where she had been ever since Margaret had sat beside her and thrown her arms around her and cried on her shoulder. Sometime she would move again, no doubt. But there didn't seem to be any point in it at present. In moving, or anything else. It was the house which seemed to be moving, not she. It seemed to be moving up around her, closer, shutting her in, and yet the walls were higher and the rooms larger . . . and there were more of them. How many were there, actually, Madge thought, and began counting to give her mind something to do, to offer it any little straw to nibble at. Drawing room, den, library—kitchen, two pantries, maids' dining room—laundry, furnace room, fruit room—six bedrooms on the second floor, no, seven, counting the little back one, and four bathrooms. And then the three on the third floor, and the storeroom too—was that twenty-five or twenty-six? Oh dear, she was getting confused, and she was so tired. . . . She thought it was twenty-six, but it didn't matter did it, one or two, more or less? Either way, there seemed to be rather more than enough for one woman.

Interlude

The World Outside

Chapter Six

A MONTH LATER, IN FEBRUARY OF 1929, MADGE SAILED FOR EUROPE with her sister Lou. She didn't want to go; she had quailed at the mere suggestion when Margaret first made it. She didn't like traveling anyway. It always made the world seem larger, and herself smaller, the farther she went. There were so many strange things to cope with: strange people, strange customs, the strange *places* themselves, in which she never felt that her feet were on solid earth. She couldn't even sleep decently on trains or boats.

But then there had been the alternative; there had to be some alternative because she had to go, or stay, somewhere. She had to exist. There was no point to it, of course, but she had to go on. And there had been a sort of windy desolation blowing all about her, even in the well-built house which had been put there—presumably —to shelter her. It had come right into the house and kept on blowing silently through it, from the moment when Madge had waked up the morning after Hugo's funeral, and remembered as one does— suddenly again, after sleep—that he was gone, and that Margaret was married.

It wasn't sorrow that she'd felt for Hugo. And yet, on the other hand, she hadn't felt the relief she'd expected to, the release from an insufferable pressure. From the weight, both physical and mental, of his demands. That weight of belittling indifference and scarcely tolerant contempt which had pushed her down for so long. So long. No—it was queer—it was rather horrible, but she had found that she missed the weight a little, as if it had been a heavy blanket, which when it was taken away had left her colder than before. It was dreadful to miss a person whom one didn't really want back again; she had hated the feeling, and the deep sense of indignity which it

97

brought her. It would have been so much *decenter* if she could just have felt the sorrow she was assumed to feel.

Even so, she would probably have stayed right on in the house, following the line of least resistance, if it hadn't been for Margaret. Margaret's conscience wanted her taken care of, and she'd suggested the trip—any trip—for a few months at least, until Madge could begin to find herself and make the adjustments to a different life. (People talked such a lot about Adjustments, as if there were a lot of little screws and valves to turn and then you'd have just the right combination.) Aunt Lou would love to go, Margaret had said. She'd jump at the chance—that was what she'd said. But Madge had shrunk back from Margaret's anxious pressing, and kept making her own little transparent excuses. Till all at once Margaret had dropped her persuading arms from around her, and with a sort of quick uncontrollable impatience, had said, "Oh Mother, why *are* you such an absolute rabbit?"

So, in the last analysis, Madge Fairlie went to Europe because her daughter had called her a Rabbit. There were all the other reasons, of course, the ones which seemed reasonable and wise to other people, but that was the real one. She had gone abroad to show Margaret . . . something, she hardly knew what. And Lou *had* jumped at the chance as Margaret had said she would. They planned to go for three or four, possibly even six months. A cruise in the Mediterranean, a leisurely trip up through Italy and France in the late spring, part of the summer in England . . . And so on . . .

Actually, they were gone for more than two and a half years. It wasn't that Madge came to like travel so much better than she had expected, though there were parts of it that were pleasant enough . . . especially after they came around into the Mediterranean. The bright glassy sea which emptied one's mind of thought, as effectively as any crystal ball . . . That had been a help. And a few pleasant people emerging into clear focus from the blur of being merely faces which looked all alike . . . The nostalgic, yet rather quiet detachment with which one could watch the young people playing deck tennis in the mornings, or dancing on the lower deck in the evenings . . . The trips ashore, with the drives, by car or by carriage, up the steep hills or down the narrow streets . . . And then the slow progress up the peninsula after they'd left the ship at Naples: the stops and starts and movings on, the pleased remeetings with people they had run across earlier . . . Some of that wasn't bad, either.

But that was not why Madge had kept on doing it for two years and eight months. She had stayed on because of Lou.

Lou had taken over the management of their tour from the first day—even the first hour. In fact, Madge had only come down to the stateroom a little while before, finding she couldn't bear to stand at the rail looking down at the black space of water widening between the ship and the dock where Margaret and Clay were standing—just a couple of pale blobs in the indistinct pattern of faces below. When she saw the water widening from a mere crack—to a river—to an ocean—she had turned quickly and edged back between Lou and someone else at the rail, and found her way finally (after a couple of blunders) down to their room. But Lou had caught up with her there, not long after, had come down to ask her whether she had attended to their seats in the dining saloon.

"Oh," Madge had said, looking startled. "Do we have to? I'd forgotten."

"And having our deck chairs put in a good place," Lou pursued.

"No, I never thought—"

Lou regarded her with a mixture of pity, impatience and superiority.

"If that isn't typical!" she said. "You, the accustomed traveler, as vague as ever—while I, who never got any place—"

"You always were more practical," Madge said, soothing and smiling.

"I had to be," Lou retorted dryly. "Well—do you want me to go up and arrange about it?"

"Do you mind?"

"No, I don't mind," Lou drawled, with an effect of indifference which Madge had known was not quite genuine. She'd glanced around the stateroom with a critically approving air, as though already taking credit for the appointments, and then added, still offhand, "I could attend to all that sort of thing for you if you like. Arranging about shore trips and reservations and tickets and so on, after we leave the ship. And the tipping—I could even do that for you—that is, if you want me to manage the money end of it."

"I hate tipping," Madge admitted at once. "I never know what to give."

"That's what I thought."

"You mean I haven't been doing it right?"

"Well—" Lou shrugged her wide soft shoulders. "Ten per cent's all right enough for the average person. For the likes of me," she added satirically. "But for people like you, dear . . . You have more to live up to, if you see what I mean. If you travel in a certain way —look rich, in other words—you have to pay for it, that's all."

It had always puzzled Madge a little to find how ready people were to spend your money for you: not for themselves, but for *you*. But she had accepted Lou's dictum, nevertheless. And it *was* a great help to have her take all the bother and responsibility of details. At home Mr. Hawley, Hugo's old stock-and-bond friend, who was coexecutor with the bank of Hugo's estate, had taken over all her business affairs. While out here Lou had taken over the personal details of her life. As someone always had: first Lou, then Hugo, then Margaret and now Lou again, around the full circle of her life. Madge saw the whole thing, in certain isolated moments of rueful clarity; she even knew that she was wrong to let them manage and direct her life—her own, and only life—for her. But she was used to its being that way; it was easier.

And yet it had made for a curious situation. Lou enjoyed managing the show, but it went to her head just a little, and Madge was faintly embarrassed at times to realize that people often took Lou for the rich sister, and Madge for the poor relation who had just come along for the ride. It would have been funny if they could have laughed about it together, but she had discovered long since how abnormally sensitive Lou was on the subject of money. And now she learned that if she made the smallest suggestion about doing things differently, Lou would be offended.

"Oh well, after all," she would say with a shrug, "it's your money, my dear. Don't think I ever forget it . . . I try to do my best—but naturally, if there's anything you prefer otherwise . . . you have only to say the word."

Madge had wondered often, in a worried way, during the first months of their journeying, how it would be if she and Lou were to go on living together for the rest of their lives. It would be less lonely, of course, but they weren't really close, the two sisters; they never had been. Like many families, they took each other for granted most of the time, and the things they talked about were rather general, with only a few personal ones thrown in. They talked about the people they used to know, and the people they met now, casually —about whom they seldom agreed. They talked about Dad and Judy, and Judy's swift dreadful illness. Lou talked about her husband George, and in return, Madge talked about Margaret. Never about Hugo.

Lou had tried to get her to do that years ago, when they had been together on some occasional visit or vacation trip, and sometimes Madge had longed to unburden herself. But it was strange, perhaps, how little a non-self-reliant person like herself had ever really relied on sympathy, or even asked for it. Her own queer negative pride had taken its place, and in this case, the more she felt the pressure of Lou's often devious, insistent curiosity, the more she had resisted it. It was the same way now, until one day Lou said, "You know, sometimes I think you try to bottle everything up inside you too much. It might do you good to break down and talk about Hugo."

Madge shrugged. "Maybe, but it never was very easy for me to talk about personal things."

"I know!" Lou retorted with a perceptible touch of resentment. "You never were one for giving yourself away, for all you seem so sort of ingenuous. I never could make out," she said, with a sudden stroke of boldness or impatience—Madge didn't know which— "whether you loved Hugo so much that you couldn't express it—or didn't care for him at all!"

There had been a moment's thick quiet in the stateroom that time, while Lou had waited, and Madge had remained turned away from her. And then, still without turning, "Can you really ask that?" she said, in a small, remote voice. And Lou had said rather abruptly that she was sorry, and they let it go at that.

Madge wondered if they deceived each other at all. People went to such elaborate lengths to be casual, to be subtle, to be disarmingly frank, but how often did they congratulate themselves on their concealed hearts, when they might as well have had cellophane windows over them? And then again, when you thought you knew someone completely, there would be some unexpected, inexplicable turn in the complex of personality, and you would wonder in bewilderment if you really knew him—or her—at all. At least that was the way it was with Lou and herself.

There was the matter of men, for instance—not George and Hugo, but the men they met now, just passing acquaintances for the most part. Women of their age shouldn't be looking for anything else, Madge felt; she even had a dim, unanalyzed conviction that they had used up any capacity they might have had for any interest in men—as men. She'd had enough herself, and could do quite nicely without them from here on, except of course as porters to carry bags, and drivers of cars, and persons behind cages who understood about such things as letters of credit. But she had realized with a slight shock of surprise, not long after they had sailed, that Lou didn't feel that way. Not at all. She said quite frankly, when they were alone, that she preferred the company of men to that of women.

Madge had conceded to herself that most women did. Most women didn't have the blind recoil that she had. The only thing was . . . that Lou didn't stop there. There was something purposeful in her attitude toward each man she met, though her manner varied from one to another, as if she were trying on one hat after another, not sure which style became her best. There was a Mr. Hough on the boat going over, a dark-jowled business man from the south, without visible attachments. Lou had taken the hearty, good-pal tone with him, played bridge with him, walked on deck, sat over long drinks with him in the bar. Then there was that thin nervous man, a widower he was, with ulcer trouble, who was staying at the same small hotel with them at Naples. He went on automobile trips with them and gloomily showed them all the beautiful views which he had first seen with his wife some thirty years before. Lou was motherly with that one—and sympathetic about his diet. And then there had been that awful man in Rome . . . Jarvis.

Madge had watched these episodes uneasily from the sidelines with an increasing sense of—squeamishness?—or was it anxiety or apology for Lou?—in her own mind. But that last one was the worst. She'd become involved in that herself, in the end, or rather, to be honest, she'd been in a way responsible for it from the first.

*   *   *

It had all begun by her getting quite fed up with Lou one day, directly after they had arrived in Rome. Lou had gone off to look up a couple of shipboard acquaintances she'd heard were staying at the de Russie, promising to be back by lunch time, or very shortly after. But she hadn't turned up, and Madge, who had been content to spend the morning washing gloves and writing letters in her room, had grown increasingly bored as the afternoon wore on. Though quite possibly what irked her as much as anything was her own lack of enterprise about striking out for herself in this big foreign city. She was still being a Rabbit, and she knew it.

So it was much the same spirit which sent her off to Europe—to *show* Margaret—that started her off now, in Rome, in an open carriage which the concierge got for her. She'd told him that she wanted to go to some nice place for tea, and presently she had found herself driving in lonely luxury along a pleasant winding road, up a long cypress-fringed hill, until eventually she arrived at a restaurant with a lovely view back over the city. She'd been quite pleased with herself, and with her table by the window, and the music, and even with the people dancing. They'd been the usual assortment one saw at these places; two or three American girls with their own parties, one or two more exotic creatures of both sexes, several women of Madge's own age—or more—and certainly more than her girth. She'd noticed them dancing with men considerably younger than themselves, and wondered about that for a moment, and then realized that the men were gigolos—of course. She'd never seen any before, to her knowledge. She sat there thinking about it, tapping her foot on the floor without knowing she was doing so, tilting her head a trifle in that way she had, and then insidiously, the thought had crept up on her. Well—why not? She didn't know a soul in the entire place, she would never see any of these strangers again. No one would ever know. . . .

Madge had suddenly lifted her fork and tinkled it against a glass, the way she'd seen Hugo do, though the sound of it startled her and she hastily put her finger on the edge to still the echo. But it had been as simple as that: someone had come up immediately—some kind of sub-headwaiter—and Madge had lifted her chin and stated firmly that she wished to dance. And after a few minutes another man had materialized, coming toward her across the end of the room. Somewhat older than the others she had seen; late thirties—early forties, perhaps—slight and dark of face, with narrow dark eyes and black hair with a restrained wave in it. A touch of white in it too, not at the temples but just above and behind the ears. It gave him a slightly incongruous look, had made Madge think inconsequently of an aging faun, with the white tufts for horns. He bowed and asked if Madame would care to dance, and Madge had accepted primly and gotten up a little stiffly.

For a minute or two it had been rather awful. The music had sounded odd, now that she tried to keep time to it, and Madge realized suddenly what she'd so unaccountably forgotten or ignored a few minutes before—that she hadn't actually danced for years. She tried to concentrate on following him, reminding herself anxiously that she used to be a very good dancer.

And then she'd stepped on him. She looked up in confusion, her eyes dark and apprehensive, her lips parted.

"Oh, I'm so sorry," she faltered, and he smiled slightly, rather as a formal concession it seemed, as he murmured, "Not at all. My fault, of course."

He had very white teeth, Madge thought irrelevantly, and spoke English without any accent at all, which somehow reassured her. For a few minutes then it had gone better, and their steps fitted nicely and she had begun to lose herself in the swing and the motion which she had always loved. She'd even closed her eyes for a minute to try to forget everything else, and then realizing that dancing with her eyes closed must look simply maudlin in a woman of her age, she'd hastily reopened them. But just for a few turns she had captured some sort of illusion again, and it was fun even if it wasn't quite real, and she'd at least known that she was still light and alive. . . .

It was only when the music stopped and she'd gone back to her table and the man had left her, murmuring that he would return, that she had seemed to recover not so much her breath as her balance. Good heavens, she didn't want him to come back! She couldn't go through that again. It made her feel old and silly, now that she'd stopped. After all, she'd only wanted to see how it felt to dance again, just once. But to—*hire* somebody to dance with you, all at once it seemed quite abject to her. Almost shameful. Why, she'd have died at sixteen, rather than do such a thing. (Only, of course, she wouldn't have needed to—at sixteen.)

She hadn't even known what to do about paying him: whether it was included in the check or not. She couldn't decipher the latter anyway, with its queer foreign writing and queerer figures; she asked the waiter and he beamed and nodded, "Si, si, Signora" vigorously, and Madge prayed that he'd understood what she was asking. She paid the check and started across the room toward the entrance, and then on the way to the door she'd run into That Man, and his eyebrows had risen, and he'd asked most pointedly if Madame was not going to dance again. And it seemed then that his fee was not included in the check she had paid, and she had to stop and paw through her bag again, till she found a wad of those bewildering liras, while she felt her face turning crimson and the man stood there studying the tip of his cigarette or looking off distantly at the dance floor.

It had all been a horrid, humiliating performance. More than that, Madge had felt as if something—some undeveloped, shut-off section of her youth had betrayed her into doing something incredibly cheap and silly. The only thought she had found to comfort herself with all the long way back to her hotel, was that she would never go near that place again, and would *never* have to see that man. And nobody else, least of all Lou, would ever know what a little fool she had been.

But of course—she had seen him, and not a week later. At a sidewalk cafe on the Corso, when she and Lou and the Hunzikers (the shipboard couple Lou had run to earth) were stopping for an *apéritif*. The place was crowded, and they had paused in their search for a table, and there was this Creature, sitting alone—right under her nose—before she knew it or had time to look away and pretend she hadn't seen him—had never seen him before, in fact. She gave a small but startled gasp, and Lou turned her head interestedly, while the man looked straight at Madge with a slightly satirical, politely appraising smile. If only she'd had the poise not to see him, she thought afterwards. But that instant of surprise had done it. He had stood up, directly in her path, and with a sort of mocking deference had asked, since it was so crowded, whether she and her friends would not sit at his table. She could have killed him, she thought. He also murmured, softly but distinctly, his own name, and though he had spoken it too quickly for the others to hear, they had heard the offer. They were looking at her with a surprised but expectant approbation, and Madge was trapped.

Anthony Jarvis. That was his name. She'd hardly spoken to him during the half-hour which followed, while they all sat there sipping their various drinks. But the others, amazingly, fantastically, had liked him. They'd found him interesting. It seemed he knew Rome very well. He'd been extremely helpful about suggesting several places where they might enjoy going. Damn decent of him, Mr. Hunziker said later. And so distinguished looking, his wife had added artlessly. While Madge found herself wondering, rather creepily, at the combination of extreme softness and hardness which the profession of gigolo must call for . . . And then, some days later they had run across the man again at one of the very places he had suggested to them, and Lou and the Hunzikers had welcomed him almost like an old friend. Madge had kept stubbornly silent, while the others had asked him to join them for dinner—if by any chance he wasn't engaged? Of course, she thought dispiritedly, he wouldn't be —and he wasn't. But it was worse than that. For that very evening he had told them about more places to go and he seemed to know about museums and churches and out-of-town trips, as well as shops and restaurants. In fact, it wasn't long before he'd agreed to join them on one of their regular sight-seeing tours.

To Madge, it was like one of those continuing dreams from which you can't quite waken yourself, even though you know dimly that these things can't actually be happening. She couldn't understand why it wasn't obvious to the others what sort of person he was; she suspected now that he had been a regular tourist's guide at some time or other (until he'd found an easier trade?) and she was sure he got a rake-off whenever he steered them toward restaurants or shops of his own choosing. But of course there was only one actual fact that she could have told them about the man: that he accepted money for dancing with stray women. And that was the one thing she had no intention of mentioning to anyone, ever; least of all to Lou. When Lou asked where she had met Mr. Jarvis, she had told some vague tale of having run across him at the American Express Company office, where he'd been civil about directing her where to go. (A nice young boy *had* done that one day, which had given her the idea, and after all, the American Express Company did seem like a sort of chaperone for Americans abroad.)

It was strange, Madge thought, that she had first taken the man for someone in his late thirties or early forties, for in the daylight she had decided that he must be in his fifties. His skin looked weathered, not by the outdoors, but by some synthetic process—like a rather unpleasant leather. And though he was quick and wiry in build, his eyes were old. *Old.* Catching their glance one day, Madge thought with a sense of shock—why the man might be—I believe he could be—sixty or more. She didn't know just why it was shocking; one didn't feel that way about the average man of sixty. It was just an age, like any other, to be taken for granted in the natural progression of years. But with Mr. Jarvis, who appeared to be something else, the realization had something eerie about it. And when Madge, who was generally unobservant about such things, suddenly realized that those very white, too-even teeth were probably not even his own, (European dentistry was always inferior, one heard) the sense of shrinking from something unnatural deepened in her. Maybe the wavy, faintly frosty hair wasn't his own either . . . not that that mattered.

But what she wondered, more and more uneasily, was what he wanted with them. And then, gradually, she had begun to worry more explicitly about Lou. Lou's manner this time had become one of almost playful archness, and Madge watched it with a certain horror. What was the *matter* with Lou, anyway? Surely she couldn't think—she couldn't believe that she was making a conquest . . . or could she? Madge even wondered if it had anything to do with Lou's age. Women did get weird infatuations at that time, she'd heard. Of course if Lou had had money, that would have explained at least what *he* was up to. Money or sex, it had to be one or the other, didn't it? Madge reflected drearily. Madge's thoughts had paused there, rather blankly, in midair, as if waiting for something to catch up with them, something which should have been there ahead of them. And then it had come to her. He *thought* Lou had money, that was all.

Oh good Lord, Madge thought, now she would *have* to say something to her, wouldn't she? It wasn't fair to let it go on. So she tried first just to persuade Lou to move along to some other place and forget about these people. They'd been in Rome long enough now anyway, she suggested, hoping desperately that this oblique approach would work. It didn't, and Lou's little coppery eyebrows had gone up in mild affront.

"Well, for goodness' sake—you were the one who said you didn't want to go rushing around from place to place on this trip," she'd countered at once. "Always packing and unpacking, you said."

"I know. I suppose I did. But—we just seemed to be doing the same thing—seeing the same people all the time," Madge said weakly.

"Do you think it would be pleasanter for you and me to go paddling around Europe all by ourselves, never speaking to another soul? I thought you liked the Hunzikers!"

"Oh, I do!" Madge said.

"Well then . . ." There was a slight but ominous pause. "Have you some objection to Mr. Jarvis, perhaps?" Lou's eyebrows were still up, and Madge was silent, because she knew, when she came right to it, that Lou was going to be very angry. She probably wasn't even going to believe her, either. "So that's it," Lou said slowly, and the eyebrows settled back into place again and the blue eyes narrowed slightly as they regarded Madge. "Do you know what I think?" she asked then, and Madge looked back at her in a troubled way, still without answer. "I think you're jealous," Lou said flatly. Madge gasped as though she'd been slapped.

"Oh *Lou*, how can you!"

"Well, aren't you? You saw him first, of course."

"I can't bear the man," Madge said stiffly.

"Really! Maybe you just can't bear to see me getting more attention—from anybody at all. You used to get plenty when we were young of course," Lou said grimly, digging down toward some old buried bitterness. "You were such a pretty, dumb little thing—and I never had the *time* to be either. But that's no reason to think things are the same now—"

"Lou, I don't see how you can think or say such things," Madge broke in desperately. "At our age! Why you're making absolute fools of us both, talking this way. I wish you'd stop it!"

"You started this conversation," Lou said deliberately. "Now you want to stop it because it isn't going your way. What did you think you were getting at, anyway?"

Madge took a large unsteady gulp of air.

"I was only trying to head you off from—getting too involved with that kind of a man. That's all."

"What—kind of man?"

There was a moment's stark silence, and then Madge said carefully, "Hadn't you ever thought—that he was—the sort of man who just drifted around looking for rich women to—to get something out of?"

That struck Lou as very funny, and she gave one sudden, hearty laugh. "*I* don't have to think of things like that," she said, with a mixture of complacency and contempt. "Nobody's interested in me for my money, my dear!"

"You don't seem to realize that people could take you for the one who is—well, financing this trip." Madge looked steadily at Lou, and the other stared back at her unflinchingly. "After all, you *do* attend to all the most obvious things, like arranging for cars and settling with Mr. Hunziker for the meals we all have together. . . ." She paused, wavering, and didn't try to go on again. She saw that she'd said enough, from the color rising in Lou's face.

"That—is a perfectly *stinking* thing to say!" her sister spat at her. "Now I know you're jealous, and I see why. It's because your rotten money isn't getting the results you've learned to expect from it, and you can't bear that, can you? So you have the nerve to imply that *I* couldn't even attract the attention of Anthony Jarvis on my own but just because he thinks I have *your* money. Really, Madge Fairlie! I knew money did pretty nasty things to people, but I never thought my own sister—My God, I'm glad I haven't any! I really am, for once in my life. I'd hate to think the crawly sort of thing you think, about myself or anybody else. . . ."

There was more of the same. Lou had gone on and on. She'd always had a temper, of course. It hadn't been a very pretty scene, all in all, and Madge had felt herself shriveling inside it, like too small a potato in too hot an oven. But when it was over, or nearly over, she had said in a small stubborn voice, "All right, maybe I'm all wrong, about the whole thing. If I am, I'm terribly sorry, Lou. But I should think you'd want to know, yourself—be sure whether it would make any difference in his attitude. We could—well, we could just pick him up on the way to the bank you know, as if it were just one of our usual errands. Let him see that I'm the one who draws the money and turns it over to you. That's all it would take to let him know. We wouldn't have to say anything, or act as if we thought anything about it, or dreamed that *he* would. . . ."

* * *

In the end, of course, Lou had agreed, though still contemptuously, to that naively simple suggestion of Madge's, because after all she had to, for the sake of her pride. It was several days before she cooled down enough to agree, but when she did, the errand at the bank was smoothly accomplished, and quite casually, with Mr. Jarvis in seemingly detached if not indifferent attendance. It seemed almost too easy. Yet there was no slightest change in the man's attitude toward either of them, as far as Madge could see, and by evening Lou's own manner had acquired a new assurance, like a new coat of make-up, though she had scarcely spoken to Madge for these last few days, anyway.

On the day following that, when they went up to their rooms after lunch to get their wraps for a drive in the country, Lou had gone down again almost immediately, ahead of her sister, as if she didn't even want to stay in the same suite with her unnecessarily, and certainly couldn't be bothered waiting for her. Well, Madge thought in a baffled way, she'd made a silly mess of things as usual, and she couldn't blame Lou now for being hurt and angry. But she stopped to change her dress, rather perversely, taking her own good time about it. At this rate, she reflected, their traveling together wasn't likely to last much longer, and she might as well start learning to be independent too. When she went down into the small foyer of the hotel, there was no sign of her sister. So she'd just gone off and left her this time, had she, Madge thought resentfully. And then she saw Mr. Jarvis coming toward her, alone. It seemed, according to his suave explanation, that Mrs. Naughton had grown a trifle—should he say, impatient?

"You were—perhaps—just a *few* minutes late in coming down?" he suggested, smiling, and it struck Madge in a vague way that he was proffering an amused indulgence for her own tardiness rather than siding with Lou's impatience.

"I expect I was," she agreed calmly.

"Yes, of course," he said cosily, as if that were quite understandable. "Well, your sister thought we should not keep the others waiting too long, so she went on in the car. . . ." He made it sound somewhat like a subtle personal triumph on his part, but Madge said, "Oh," rather flatly, and added in a practical way, "Are they coming back for us here? Or are we to go after them?"

He gave a rapid, considering glance toward the door.

"I tell you what I think," he said confidentially, "I think we might take the carriage here—the one which always stands by the fountain outside, you know?—and then we will go around to them. It would save time, no doubt, since it was only a moment since Mrs. Naughton left. Then we can all start out together, without their troubling to come back."

Madge turned to regard him thoughtfully. She felt quite sure that it was more than a moment since Lou had gone on, for she herself had been upstairs—how long? Ten minutes? Fifteen? And if they started off in the slow-going carriage now, they certainly could not catch up with the others. But after a moment Madge felt herself relaxing into a sort of bored resignation. Maybe this was the best way.

"Very well," she said gravely, "Whatever you think."

It was to be one of the strangest afternoons she had ever spent, however, and not entirely boring. For of course by the time they reached the Hunzikers' hotel the others had left. Jarvis was very calm about it all. They might as well, he said, go their own way, using the slower carriage to take in just a part of the expedition planned. Madge hadn't even any clear idea of where they had been going— she never had—except that there was some church "without the walls" which they were to see, and then drive on into the Campagna. (How Lou loved that word!) Then she thought there was a place they were to stop for tea on their way back; in fact Mr. Jarvis had said carelessly that they might even get that far eventually, and find the others there.

As for the man himself, his manner toward her was a shade different now—perhaps; it was hard to be sure. But if so, he was clever enough not to make that difference too clear. The mockery behind his deference was gone, or faded out, and there was a kind of flattery in the speculative look which he turned on her now and then, in place of the faint sardonic amusement which she had felt there before. That was all. He continued to be the urbane sight-seeing companion and guide. He kept talking carelessly of the places they passed, giving her bits of information like little bites of pastry. And so they continued on their leisurely way into the open country, in their slightly decrepit open carriage with its top laid back, like a shabby neckpiece sliding off an old lady's shoulders; it didn't seem to matter in the least just when they reached one objective or another, since they didn't really expect to meet anyone now.

At times, Madge almost enjoyed it. She even laughed at some of Mr. Jarvis's dryly satiric remarks. She didn't like him, of course, but her dislike had nothing personal about it; he'd been only a symbol from the beginning, first of her own foolishness and then of Lou's. And Madge had a sense of relaxation this afternoon, which came partly from her feeling that this would *show* Lou, at last. The game was nearly over now, and she would be released from the nagging sense of responsibility which she had had. Already the situation seemed to have nothing more to do with her personally; even her being there in the carriage with Mr. Jarvis was quite incidental and irrelevant now, like a bus ride from place to place. All she had to do was to sit there and look slightly amused, to let him know how clearly she saw through him.

For once in her life she had a comfortable sense of superiority to the situation in which she found herself, and it was really rather pleasant because it was so unusual. She had no idea that the amusement or intoxication of it would show in her eyes, or that the relaxation of relief would sound in her laugh. And when she saw Mr. Jarvis turn that half-speculative glance toward her once or twice, she only thought he was trying to figure out his own behavior—not hers.

Once, as the afternoon wore on, and they worked a lazy course back into the outskirts of the city again, he said, "You *are* enjoying the afternoon, Mrs. Fairlie?"

"Oh yes," she said calmly. "It's been very pleasant. And educational," she added, with a touch of primness.

"And educational," he repeated, smiling at the driver's back rather than at her. After a moment he added, "One cannot always tell just what you enjoy. You are a very reserved little person, aren't you?"

"Oh, I don't think so," Madge said, rather resenting the diminutive adjective from him, though of course she couldn't argue about it. "I'm a very simple person, that's all."

"I wonder if that's true."

"Of course it's true," she assured him in a nettled tone. "I'm a very simple person, and I've lived a very humdrum life. Not even worth inquiring into."

"That is at least the front you present to the public, isn't it?"

She looked at him in surprise.

"What on earth makes you say that?"

"Because I think there is a sort of protective grille-work—a fine, strong, wrought-iron screen—which you put up before you. Even your sister is a part of it."

"My sister?" she repeated, in still sharper surprise, and he nodded thoughtfully.

"Whether you build her into it out of consideration for her own —shall we say vanity?" he suggested delicately, "to let her feel more important, perhaps . . . or to put up a stronger buffer between yourself and the world, I'm not quite sure."

"I really don't know what you're talking about," Madge said stiffly.

"Don't you, Mrs. Fairlie?" He sat there looking at her, not moving an inch from his corner of the carriage; enclosing her in a look which was long and penetrating, contemplative and appreciative. It gave Madge a sudden and subtle sense of discomfort. She was not just embarrassed, but a little breathless, as though they were in a close room rather than out-of-doors. She didn't like being enclosed, and she didn't like this man—who seemed to her more like a mannikin come to life, thinking for itself.—Thinking about her, what's more. Though of course it was true, in a way, what he had said. And he proceeded now to underline it. "I think you must know that you retire behind someone else for protection, or convenience possibly. Don't you realize," he added, "that this, today, is the first time that you and I have been able to talk—together?"

Oh come, come, Madge thought. That was just too much.

"It seems to me that we've seen each other quite frequently, Mr. Jarvis. Quite often enough to say—whatever we might have had to say to each other."

"You see?" he said. "You retreat at once. Why do you do it? Is it the habit of shelter that you're used to, or is it people themselves that you're afraid of?"

"I'm sure I don't know!" Madge said impatiently, but defensively too, she was afraid. She didn't seem to know how to deal with this man and his approach after all. It was at once so pointed and so elusive, like some very sharp but almost invisible weapon which he used, now like a foil and now like a delicate probe. She knew it in a dim instinctive way for a form of flattery: the interest, the pretense of understanding which feeds the hungry ego. But, dear heaven—she didn't *want* him to understand her! "I suppose," she admitted almost unwillingly, "that I am used to someone standing between me and the rest of the world, as you say. My husband was—a very able man," she ended, with an abrupt irrelevance which was unexpected even to herself. Now, why on earth had she brought that up, she asked herself in annoyance.

"Do you know, I find it quite difficult to realize that you've ever been married? It's left you—curiously untouched, in some way, hasn't it?"

"I shouldn't have thought so," Madge said, with a sort of stiff dryness which she seemed actually to feel in her throat. "I have a married daughter," she announced then, firmly.

"I know." He seemed amused by the idea. And then she saw that he was gazing past her, meditatively. And she began looking along the way they were coming, conscious of it for the first time in some minutes, wondering why it should seem familiar. For they had been gradually winding up a hill, and Madge realized that they were not coming into the part of town she was used to. Partly to change the subject, she said abruptly, "It's getting late, and we don't seem to be getting down toward where the hotel is."

"But I thought we were going to have tea," he objected reproachfully. He hadn't mentioned it for some time, and of course she couldn't understand the directions which he gave the driver in Italian. But it seemed to her that this part of this whole fictional ritual was superfluous.

"This isn't where my sister and the others were going, is it?"

"Oh no," he admitted easily. "That would have been too far out, without a car."

"But it *is* getting late," she persisted. "If the others are back they really will begin to worry."

"Does that matter?" he asked calmly, looking at her with no expression at all except that his eyebrows had lifted slightly. He was only stating after all, that conspiratorial indifference which had been accepted between them—tacitly of course—all through the afternoon, and Madge felt trapped by it now.

"I suppose not," she said unwillingly, "except that I—really don't want to be much later in getting home, myself."

"We won't stay long," he said, smiling and reassuring.

The tired horse in front of them plodded around a last curve at the top of the slope, and stopped in front of a low building with lights already showing in the windows. It must be a beautiful view from up here, Madge thought, if the sunset hasn't faded too quickly . . . and then she realized all at once why the road had seemed familiar. It was that place: the one she'd come to weeks ago, alone, the first time she had seen this man. For a moment she was speechless, and then she turned on Jarvis, rigid with something like indignation.

"What on earth made you bring me up here?" she demanded.

"Why not?" he said, his glance conveying that he was not sensitive about it, and asking if she were; challenging her perhaps, or was it only mocking her? She didn't know, and that made her more indignant. "You love to dance," he reminded her softly, "and it's a charming spot."

Why not, indeed! she thought. He had an astounding nerve to bring her here, but she couldn't let him think the incident had intimidated her, after all. She shrugged her shoulders almost impatiently and stepped down from the carriage.

The place was just the same: the same view, the same sort of people, the same discreetly decadent air. (Well, she didn't expect it to change in a few weeks, did she?) At least they weren't shown to the same table, which seemed for no good reason to help a little, but she had a prickling consciousness of the way the sub-headwaiter greeted Mr. Jarvis—knowingly, yet not even by name, and without any of that unctuous deference which one could usually feel. They gave their order, and sat looking out over the room, and Madge hardly knew whether the silence between the two of them now could be taken for the stiffness of strangers, or the ease of old friends. She wished suddenly—of all things!—that Lou were there.

The music started up, and he looked at her and rose, saying nothing. Almost gritting her teeth, Madge got up too, and they moved out onto the floor together again. After a few steps she seemed to recognize a certain pattern, a design which was familiar to her feet, and she didn't have to grope any more. Yes, he was an excellent dancer, no question about that. And so was she, she thought grimly—so was she. She would have enjoyed it so—years and years ago. But she didn't enjoy it this time.

They returned to the table and had their tea: Madge's tea and his vermouth. Looking across at her thoughtfully, he said, "You're really very young, you know." And Madge found that she could laugh, quite naturally, not at all hysterically.

"Oh no, I'm not," she said flatly.

"You don't know quite what I mean," he persisted. "Or possibly you refuse to admit that too. You seem to me to have stopped living some time ago—quite young—and in some ways you have never used up your youth, as most of us do. As most of us have," he added in a curious dead tone, yet one which sounded almost real, made one wonder if there were a person there after all. A human being. But she didn't pursue that thought; she didn't want to regard him as anything but the dancing automaton which he was supposed to be.

Between times she asked for the check and paid it, as calmly as though she were used to this sort of thing, even hardened to it. And when the music started up a third time, she said quite definitely that she must go now.

"Once more," he said.

"I'm sorry, but I must get back."

"Just a couple of times around then, as we go out?" he said, smiling persuasively with his too-handsome store teeth, and she shrugged again. What earthly difference did it make? Lou would be furious by now, anyway. But Lou would herself be cured, quite cured, Madge reflected, and that was what did matter.

They stepped out on the floor and he put his arm around her again, in the same efficient way which was a part of the whole routine. But this time, as they slid smoothly from one corner to another, it was different though she was hardly aware of what was happening at first. The music was good, and it was a piece she had heard often, heard Margaret singing it at home, in fact. But gradually, distastefully, she had to realize the difference. He had held her stiffly the first time, weeks ago, in the more formal manner that Europeans used in dancing. Now suddenly that was gone, and his arm was farther around her and holding her unpleasantly close. She tried to ignore it for another moment, but it was too insistent. And she didn't like it. He had her so close now that it was impossible to ignore. His whole body seemed suddenly inescapable. His cheek was against her hair too, so that she could feel his breath . . . the young people danced that way all the time, of course, but she wasn't used to it, and she found herself wishing wildly that she had worn a bigger hat. Though what good that would have done . . . She made a slight, imperceptible effort to put a little space between them; made it as imperceptible as she could because for some reason she didn't want to admit even to him that she was aware of his closeness. But it did no good.

She tried to work herself loose, on a turn where their steps made a wider pattern. But that didn't work either; only for a second, and then he seemed to have swung her closer still, and his hand seemed to have crawled farther around her so that it was almost touching her breast. She realized that he was not only not taking her hint, he was deliberately holding her against her will, forcing her to accept something she didn't want—unable to believe, perhaps, that she didn't want it. She wondered frantically what the man was thinking of, and what in the world one did to get away from someone on a public dance floor, without actually making a scene. After all, you couldn't scream, or slap him, right there—and he knew it.

He was counting on that, or on her inexperience, perhaps, or even upon some unfed hunger or vulnerability which he could prey upon. What he didn't know was that the one approach to Madge Fairlie that he couldn't take was the physically amorous one. What he couldn't know was how strong that guard in her was, conditioned by how many years of plain endurance. She had hardly known, herself. But this was intolerable, not merely repellent. She had stood it as long as she could, and now suddenly, she reacted to the implication of deliberate force like a small animal, as desperately and uncontrollably as though she were in real danger. She put her free left hand between her own shoulder and his and pushed, as hard as she was able; she wrenched her body back from his and tugged with her other hand to get it out of his grasp. And in that small convulsive struggle, she let out one vehement gasp.

"Let *go* of me, will you!"

He let go, of course. He had to then. "You disgusting fool!" she said, almost under her breath, and gave him one furious glance as she stepped back, staggering a little to catch her balance, and then went past him toward the edge of the floor without another word or look.

It had taken only a few seconds. Possibly no one else realized it, though the two couples nearest them gave them a look of amused surprise, or curiosity. Madge turned toward the corridor blindly as she left the dance floor. Thank heaven she had already paid the bill.

But she found she was going the wrong way, and had to turn again through another short hallway to reach the outer door. She looked feverishly for the carriage as she stepped out on the gravel, and when she saw it—horse, vehicle and driver all suspended in one inclusive coma—she almost ran toward it, knowing already that there were rapid steps behind her. She stepped hastily into the carriage and sat down with a sudden giving way of the knees. And before she could rally what words to say to the driver, Jarvis was there. He got in and sat down beside her and spoke to the driver, curtly this time, and she noted that he was breathing hard. The Aging Faun himself, she thought derisively, trying once more to grab at some saving, stabilizing sense of the ridiculous.

But for several solid minutes the two sat there in a sort of smoky silence, while the horse started down the long winding slope into town. Madge didn't glance at the man, but she could feel that he was very nearly as angry as she was. Until, recovering a certain degree of equanimity first, he said dryly, "For God's sake, what is the matter with you? Are you really as much of a puritan as all that, Mrs. Fairlie?"

For still another second she stayed silent.

"I don't like being—*squashed*—and by someone I don't even like!" Madge burst out, almost childishly. "If that's what you call being a puritan."

"So you don't even like me?" he observed. "And yet, I think you did not give that impression earlier this afternoon. I think you knew that you attracted me—surely you have known that all the time."

"Oh nonsense!" Madge said sharply. "I knew very well what attracted you, Mr. Jarvis."

"Oh yes?" he said. There was a sibilant stillness in the last word which hung on the air for a second, waiting, as the man himself seemed to be now braced, wary, waiting to see which way to spring.

"Yes indeed," Madge said. She took it up almost briskly. The brake had been released by that terrific recoil which she had suffered. She was tired of being made a fool of, that was all, whether she herself or someone else had made her one. "I think that's fairly obvious," she said. "It has been to me right along—but my sister didn't realize . . . you see she hasn't had the unfortunate experience of having people nice to her—solely on account of money!"

"But surely," he said suavely, making one more hasty side step to recover his former footing, "surely you can't think that mere wealth is what draws people to you? A woman like you, if you wouldn't shut yourself in . . ." His breathing was audible, as though pumped by real emotion. It must be an exhausting game, after all, this sort of thing. But Madge's pity was dried up.

"Oh do stop it!" she said impatiently. "We're really not all such fools as you think. You pursued my sister right up until yesterday, when you saw me draw that check. Today you pretend it is I who interest you . . . if only I weren't so reserved, so unapproachable," she echoed him scornfully. "There isn't one thing you could say, Mr. Jarvis, that would change my opinion, so you might as well save us the discussion."

For a moment he said nothing. Then, "That being the case," he inquired in a flat, hard tone, "why did you go along with me all this afternoon?"

"I suppose I had some silly idea of letting my sister see you and your motives for herself, since she wouldn't believe what I might tell her. Certainly I had no thought of acquiring your—attentions—for myself." Her own voice was very dry, with a scorching touch. "I had some idea before, of course, of the sort of man you might be, but it's always hard to realize how contemptible people *can* be. You must like the very proximity of money—anybody's money—very much, Mr. Jarvis. Even to dance with!" she said scathingly, and broke off suddenly. "Oh yes, I forgot," she added. "I *beg* your pardon." She opened her bag, took out the wad of notes remaining, riffled them with her fingers half carelessly (yes, there was plenty there, for *three* dances) and handed them to him. For a second he looked at them in his hands, then took out his wallet, placed them carefully in it, and returned it to his inside pocket. By now they had reached the level, lighted streets at last, and she could see that his brown face had flushed a dark unhealthy red. He had been grim before, sardonic, but the glance he gave her now was malignant.

"Most of us do like it," he said. "Even the feel of it. Even the feel of someone who has it. You're quite right there, Madame. Most of us haven't lived as close to it as we would like."

"Even so," Madge said stiffly (or was it only primly?), "most people are willing to work for it. There's a limit to what decent people will do to—overtake it."

"That comes very well from you, I'm sure. You know so much about it, don't you?" he said, in a queer silky voice, almost a whisper. "You never did without a single goddamned thing you wanted in all your blessed little pampered life, did you? Never worked a day in your life, for money, did you? Or a night either," he added venomously.

He stopped short on that. "Or—*did* you, I wonder?" he asked suddenly, and ran that penetrating look of his through her.

It felt to Madge as if it went straight through, from the exquisite sharpness she felt piercing her somewhere, in some spot she couldn't touch to ease it. How *could* this man see the things that no one else guessed at, or even looked for? Her gaze wavered from the horse's bony back to the driver's fat stolid one. Oh dear heaven, would they never get there, she thought imploringly. She hadn't looked at the man at all; only that one swift glance as she had handed him the money; but still he had seen something, or picked it out of the air between them, as though he wore antennae, instead of a faun's pointed ears. For he went on now, with a sort of ruminatory relish. "Yes—yes, of course . . . That might explain it. That must be the thing I felt about you and your marriage all along, though I couldn't—quite—place it. So it was real work after all, was it, Madame? Night work at that . . ." He waited for an answer, but none came. Madge couldn't trust herself to let her tongue go now—not one step.

"You—little—bitch," he added softly, savoring the taste, almost the smell of the words, it seemed, leaning toward her a little way the better to enjoy the closed look on Madge's white face.

* * *

She had never told Lou the whole story of that afternoon; surely, surely, she had reassured herself, that wasn't necessary. She had received the thrust of Lou's resentful questions against a hard little core of calm which seemed to have petrified inside her. She'd carefully recounted the various stages of the expedition with Jarvis, omitting only that last quarter of an hour as they had come down the hill, and Lou had listened, with her small mouth compressed and her small eyebrows pushed upward like a pair of amber spectacles worn on the forehead.

When Madge finally paused, Lou had said grimly and defensively, "Well, I suppose you're dying to say I told you so!" To her surprise, tears came into Madge's eyes and her mouth trembled slightly.

"No," she said, very low. "No—I don't—want to say anything more about it, Lou. It's just been one of those hateful, unexpected things that you get into, traveling alone, I guess."

"Well, of course," Lou said, with an effect of picking up her dignity and putting it on again, "I must say I don't think you used much judgment in the first place." Madge gazed at her wordlessly. "Well—" Lou repeated impatiently, "you were the first to make his acquaintance, weren't you? And introduce him to the rest of us? Why—he probably would have been trying to borrow money from us before we knew it!"

"Yes—I suppose he would," Madge said faintly. She had been going to confess finally, just to soothe Lou's humiliation, how she had met Jarvis at that tea dance. It had seemed like a sort of expiation, to make Lou feel better, because it would make Madge look rather the sillier of the two sisters. But it didn't seem quite necessary now. Instead Madge had turned quickly and gone into her own room, unable to keep down another moment the wild laughter which was trying to get out. She shut her own door and began to giggle quietly, in little gulps, and then louder, as she put her handkerchief up to her mouth. And then for about five minutes she had begun to cry and hiccough quite uncontrollably, until—as though someone else were steering her—she had turned and gone into the bathroom and firmly swallowed half a glass of water.

They had left Rome very shortly after that, and the Jarvis episode was not mentioned between them again. If Lou's vanity had been really hurt, she didn't let Madge know it, but at least she was more circumspect for quite a while. For almost exactly a year, in fact. She was more careful now, also, not to let any confusion arise as to which of the sisters was paying the way for both of them. She continued to manage them both, but she had adopted the line that she really did it for her keep: that she was only a paid poor relation after all. Somehow, through this new method she succeeded in making herself seem appealingly comic and faintly pathetic at the same time. Madge didn't like it; indeed, she hated it, but there was nothing she could do. She decided that she really didn't understand Lou at all. It took all of that year before she suddenly realized the very simple thing that Lou wanted, and had wanted right along.

But in the meantime, their trip together proceeded comfortably, if a trifle guardedly on both sides. And the time passed. Up through Italy that spring, into Switzerland and on to Holland presently, while Margaret's letters came after them like a happy following breeze. In the fall they had come down to France, and of course there were wild tales of a market crash at home, which Lou for one didn't take at all seriously. Just at first she had shown a little concern—when the concierge at their hotel, even the waiters in the restaurants, hovered over them with a certain solicitude, rather like that shown to the newly bereaved. They hoped, delicately, that this bad news—this tragic circumstance—would not affect Madame. . . . Lou had looked at Madge searchingly, then, and asked, "What about your affairs, dear—do you think they are safe?" and Madge had said confidently, "Why of course! Hugo's old friend Mr. Hawley looks after everything—and he was very reassuring in his last letter—says people have been unduly alarmed."

"Oh well, you know how our papers go in for anything that sounds sensational—and make it more so," Lou had said then, shrugging off the news. "It really would be silly to let that affect our plans."

So they'd stayed on in Paris through the autumn and into the winter, and then gone down to the Riviera for several months. Madge's funds were always forthcoming with soothing regularity, though Mr. Hawley's letters did sound an occasional gloomy note. Margaret wrote brightly and casually however, and though Madge had a furtive wish now and then to see Margaret and Clay together for herself, it seemed to grow less pressing as time went on. The picture of Margaret as a busy young married woman seemed so unreal; it was almost as if that world of hers was as much beyond Madge's reach as the one Hugo was now in . . . if he was anywhere. They had both moved on into some inaccessible place, while she herself was left in a sort of half-world in between. No doubt it was her own life which was the unreal one, without any roots, sliding easily over the surface of the earth, never quite resting on solid ground. But it was easier to follow along and do what Lou wished, since she at least seemed to be enjoying all this. And of course it *was* lovely in the south of France . . . and later on that next spring, in England.

They'd meant to stay longer in London, but after a few weeks there they had drifted down to Devonshire for a weekend, and—somehow—had lingered on; for a month, and then still another month. They had found a place on the side of a hill overlooking a deep green inlet of the sea: a little hotel, not nearly so grand as the ones Lou generally chose for them. Not grand at all in fact. There were never more than a dozen people staying there at one time, and there wasn't a great deal to do—but it was all so lovely to look at, and there were walks for Madge and bridge games for Lou, and crumpets, and scones, and jam and Devonshire cream—for both. And finally there was a certain Mr. Budleigh, who not only liked bridge and afternoon tea, but Lou as well, and he had a two-seater Morris-Cowley car to drive farther afield when it seemed desirable.

Madge smiled a little, inside, over Mr. Budleigh; he was so ruddy and amiable, and at the same time so staid and cautious. He was a bachelor of sixty-two, a solicitor who lived in London and came down here for a month's holiday in June, as he had been doing for many years. He belonged to a pattern, like that of the green and brown fields, quilted by hedges, or like the dark plaid of his own wool socks, an unchanging pattern with which he was completely satisfied. He seemed rather dull to Madge, even mildly absurd like some of the cartoons in *Punch*, and the sight of Lou and him going off for an afternoon's spin in the small car made Madge smile, in an inward and elderly way. Lou was showing Symptoms again, after all these months; she was being wholesome and womanly this time. But if she was flattered by this portly interest, these cautious little dabs of attention —what on earth did it matter, after all?

Madge and Lou sat late over their breakfast one morning—the first of July, it was. It was warm and lazy, and Madge wondered if she had the ambition to go off for her regular walk this morning—and whether Lou and Mr. Budleigh would go for one of their "spins" in the Morris-Cowley. That's what he always called them: "spins." But she didn't care in the least. She had reached the point, some time ago—months ago perhaps, she couldn't have said just when—beyond which nothing seemed to matter. Pleasant or unpleasant, it was all more or less the same. There was not much point in any of it, but there was no point in having any strong feeling about it either. In fact, it was safer not to.

She spread jam on another piece of toast, and waited for Lou to read her bits of the *London Times*, which was much easier than to read it for herself.

"Well," Lou said, "the French troops finally pulled out of the Rhineland yesterday. Interallied commission and all. And about time, too."

"Think so?" Madge said docilely.

"Of course. What do we want to stay in there any more for? We've all got to get on about our own business, haven't we? Why, the war's been over for nearly twelve years!" After a minute she said, "I see where they're talking about digging a tunnel between France and England, under The Channel."

"For goodness' sake. Who's talking about it?"

"Parliament. Quite a lot of debate about it yesterday. I don't

know why it wouldn't be a good idea. But some of the military seem
to object."

"Why?" asked Madge idly, without any real curiosity.

"I don't know. Something about the danger of it if there should
be another war."

"Oh *dear*," Madge said. "How can they even talk of such a thing?"

"Silly," Lou agreed. "Imagine any country ever getting dragged
into one again." She went on reading, and turned a page. "The
tennis at Wimbledon ought to be exciting," she said presently. "So
many of our players, and all." And then she added, a shade self-
consciously, "As a matter of fact, if we were in Town, I think Mr.
Budleigh would take us to see some of the matches."

"Is he going up this week?"

"M—m—I think so. He's already stayed on longer than he meant
to." Lou sounded faintly smug about that.

"But it's so lovely here," Madge murmured, drawing back as she
always did from making any new move. Almost as if to fend off the
idea, she got up from the table. "I guess I'll take a little stroll down
to South Sands before it gets any warmer," she said.

She went out to the desk, where the mail had just been sorted.
There was a letter from Margaret, but she didn't go back to the dining
room to read it to Lou. Instead, like a dog with a bone to hide, she
went out the front door and down the two flights of steps through the
pergola which followed the descent of the hill. She turned into
the lane from the gate at the foot of the steps, and went along to the
wooden seat a little farther down, under a tree, where she often took
her mail to read, before starting out for her walk. She sat down
there now, and ran through the other envelopes, saving Margaret's
for the end; but finally she started on that, taking it slowly so as to
make it last a long while.

Even so, she couldn't have been reading it as carefully as she'd
thought, because she came to a sudden stop and went back the way
she'd come as if she'd missed a turn. She couldn't have understood her.
. . . She was so *casual* about it, as though it were just another piece
of news along with the Larrimores having to sell their house. And
more than that, it sounded as if Margaret meant July—*this* July,
which was right here upon them, now. Couldn't be next July, Madge
thought confusedly, because that would be twelve months instead of
nine. But if so, why in the world hadn't she told her before? For a
moment, there was a kind of blank which seemed to surround Madge.
She couldn't see through it or feel through it either. She just couldn't

understand. It was as if something heavy had hit her on the head and knocked her out temporarily, even while she sat bolt upright on that bench. And then as the numbness faded, the pain began. It hurt terribly, so much that for another small period of time it seemed to possess her entirely, and she could only think, Why did she do this to me? Let me go right up to the very end before saying a word . . .

She must have failed Margaret dreadfully, she thought, that Margaret could in turn have failed her this way, denying her mother access to the most important thing in her own life, and to what she must have known would be the most important thing in Madge's life too. It just didn't seem believable. . . . And she thought she'd forgotten how to feel anything. . . . But after a few long seconds she got hold of the pain in her, almost with a sense of physically taking it in her hands and pushing it out of her way. Because after all that wasn't what mattered. What mattered was Margaret. For Margaret was going to have a baby—"probably the second week in July"— within two weeks! And here was she, her mother, way over in England.

"I knew you'd fuss and worry and spoil your whole trip if I told you at the beginning," Margaret had written. "And you do seem to be having such a nice time . . ." Well, but good heavens, Madge didn't want to stay on here—*now*. Why couldn't Margaret have understood that? Have known that her mother couldn't possibly feel any other way? If she'd only given her more time . . . Madge wondered feverishly how soon they could get a passage, and she skimmed back hastily over Margaret's first two pages, to make sure she'd really got it all this time, and then her eye settled, rather heavily, like a weight dropping slowly through water, on what she had said toward the end. "Please darling," she'd written, "don't get excited now and try to come racing back. I'm getting on beautifully. Clay and I have everything all arranged, and it will be all over before you know it, and then I'll have my hands full, learning how to take care of an infant. I know you and Aunt Lou were planning to stay on till the end of the summer anyway, and that's just what I want you to do."

Didn't she even want her mother there, Madge thought? It was a slow, unwilling thought. But of course that was just silly sensitiveness on her part—or it was just Margaret being conscientious in her own funny, unperceptive way. She, Madge, was just being petty and personal and possessive, and she was ashamed of her own first reaction. The only thing to do, the *only* thing now, was to get up there to Lou just as fast as she could and send wires or telephone, or whatever one did, to get the first possible passage back to New York. They could just do it, she thought, if they had any luck.

She gathered up her letters in both hands, not even putting them back in their envelopes, and went back up the lane, hurriedly, still clutching the oddly assorted sheets of paper in front of her. She climbed the two stages of steps through the pergola without pausing, and kept right on up the flight inside the house, to the second floor where Lou was now sitting by the window in her room, rocking and placidly reading her own mail. Madge had barely breath enough left to gasp out the news, but Lou appeared extraordinarily unmoved by it.

"Well, that's fine. They usually do have babies after a while. I don't see that that's anything to get so upset about."

"I'm not upset exactly—at least I wouldn't be if I were *there*."

"She's all right, isn't she?"

"Oh yes, at least, she says she is. . . ."

"Now look here, Madge," Lou broke in firmly. "Of course you're excited over the news. But there's no sense in your getting yourself worked up and being in a lather about it for the next seven or eight months—"

"But that's just it!" wailed Madge. "It isn't eight months—it's *two weeks!*"

Lou just looked at her.

"What do you mean?" she said finally. "Has she waited until it's almost time, before telling you?"

Madge nodded, and her cheeks flushed a little as she dropped down into a chair opposite Lou.

"She had some silly idea that I'd fuss and worry and want to go right back—"

"She seems to have made a pretty shrewd guess," Lou remarked dryly.

"Oh, don't be tiresome, Lou!" Madge snapped at her. "I want to be there when my only daughter is having her first baby, can't you understand that? Tell me how soon we can make it."

For a moment Lou looked away from her and didn't answer.

"Don't you think you're being rather—hasty?" she said.

"But there are only two weeks before it's due, I tell you! Of course, it may be late, being the first . . . but I can't count on that."

"Do you think Margaret wants you to get there?" Lou asked coolly. Madge's color had died down, but she didn't meet her sister's eyes immediately.

"That's not a very kind thing for you to say to me, Lou," she said quietly. Lou shrugged and got up, and as she passed Madge on her way to the bureau, she patted her shoulder.

"I'm sorry, dear. I see how you feel, of course, but it seems to me it doesn't make too much difference—your being there, I mean. . . . Unless Margaret is anxious for you to be."

Madge was silent, looking down at the mess of papers still in her lap, bits of blue and white and gray, sticking out at all angles.

"She had this absurd idea of not breaking into our trip," she said finally, in a low tone. "She's so terribly conscientious. And she doesn't know how she'll feel when the time actually comes. Oh, I don't care— I've got to! I'm going back, if I can possibly get there. And it's up to you to figure it out."

"My job, h'm?" Lou's voice had a slightly bitter tinge to it.

"Oh dear! I didn't mean it that way, and you know it. Why do you have to get a chip on your shoulder now, of all times? All I meant was that you have been looking after tickets and so on for us, all this time, and naturally I depend on you now."

"Very touching, I'm sure. We poor relations do have our uses."

"Oh Lou, don't be exasperating. What *is* the matter with you? Why do you have to be so difficult all of a sudden, when I have so little time?"

"I don't have much time, myself, apparently," Lou remarked. Madge looked at her uncomprehendingly.

"I don't understand you," she said.

"No—it hasn't occurred to you to ask whether *I'd* like to go back right now, has it? You don't consider me at all."

Madge, sitting taut and upright, seemed to crumble a little in her low chair.

"Lou dear, I didn't mean to be selfish and inconsiderate, but this thing has broken on me so suddenly. There's just that one idea in my mind—I must get back, can't you see?"

"Yes, I see," Lou said flatly.

"But my dear, won't you try to understand? This is so important to me, and we've already stayed over longer than we first meant to, and I didn't think it would make so much difference to you, after all. . . ."

"Well, it does," Lou said.

The flat statement stopped Madge in her tracks.

"Why?" she asked after a moment. Her sister turned around and looked at her—a cool, level look.

"Because of Mr. Thomas Espe Budleigh," she said.

"Oh *Lou!*" Madge said. It was a protest, an incredulous, gently deprecating protest. Lou shrugged again. "You can't mean it," Madge said, still gently, still unbelieving. "I mean—I know you like him and all that. But you don't—love him, do you?" She felt oddly embarrassed even to use the word in that connection.

"No—o, I suppose not," Lou conceded slowly.

"Well then—" Madge was only the more bewildered. "How can you even bring that up now, in comparison to something that's so terribly important to me?"

"Because this is important to me," Lou said, "whether you're able to take that in or not."

"But *why?*—if it's just a pleasant interlude with a nice elderly bachelor whom you don't even care about."

"I didn't say I didn't care about him. I like him, in fact I'm rather fond of him. What's more important is that he likes me, and if given time—plenty of time, mind you—I think I can work him around to asking me to marry him."

"And is that—what you want?"

"Of course it's what I want," Lou said impatiently. "Why wouldn't I?"

"Well, I don't know," Madge said helplessly. "I don't know why you *would.*"

Lou was walking up and down the room, rather heavily, but purposefully. There was a sullen sort of anger in her now, dull-burning but hot, like coals growing redder as they are blown upon. And when she paused in her pacing for a moment, she eyed Madge almost truculently.

"No, I suppose you wouldn't know. It wouldn't enter your little head that what Mr. Budleigh could give me would be a simple matter of security for the rest of my life. You've been lucky, Madge Fairlie. You never had to worry about money the way I did when we were kids. *You* were too young. I was the one who had to make Dad's pay cover about twice the ground it was big enough for. And I didn't marry just out of school, the way you did—and I didn't marry a man who made a million—or several million—or whatever Hugo did make, before he was fifty . . ." (Even then, at a time like that, Lou waited a moment, to see if Madge would fill in that amount—which Lou had always wanted to know.) "I didn't have any fortune left me when George died, either," she ended flatly.

"Lou dear, I *know!* I know you haven't had an easy time, and I've tried to help you when you'd let me—"

"Yes, you've helped me," Lou admitted. "I'm not denying that. You and Hugo have been darned decent, and don't say I don't appreciate it, because I do. But there's something else you don't know about, because you haven't had to learn any part of it, and that's taking money from somebody else—yes, even a sister. Maybe you think it's easy. Just take it and say thank you and be grateful . . . . Well, it isn't, and I don't care how nice the giver is about it, either. It isn't *yours,* and you can't do just as you'd like with it—and the hell with it if it isn't a sensible thing to do! You have the feeling all the time that the other fellow wants to know just where it goes, and whether maybe you couldn't get along with just a little less if you were a little better manager—"

"Lou! I never felt that way about it!" Madge exclaimed, shocked out of her silence.

"All right, maybe you didn't—but *I did,* I tell you. And that's what gets a person down. What's more, you never know what you can depend on. How did I know if you'd keep on helping me when Hugo died? How did I know if he'd do anything for me if anything happened to you? How can I tell what you'll be able to do for me five years from now—or ten—or if Margaret and Clay get in trouble, and their children need educating . . . or if you even want to go on living with me when we get home again. We don't get along so well together, Madge—we never have, and we both know it. But all the time I'm taking, taking, taking from somebody, and it doesn't belong to me, it's always a *favor*—it's almost as if somebody did me a favor to let me go on living! It makes me feel like a low-down boot licker the whole time."

"You don't act like it," Madge said suddenly.

"No, of course I don't act like it," Lou retorted, "and because I hate the feeling I go to the opposite extreme, just to convince myself that I'm not always playing for somebody else's favor."

"I'm sorry you feel this way, Lou. I must have been awfully stupid and clumsy, but I had no idea . . ."

"Oh, I know you hadn't. How could you, living the way you have? And it isn't the kind of thing one's generally frank about, some way. Even in the family. I don't know why. It gets too raw, I guess. But now you do know how I feel. Now maybe you'll see why Thomas Budleigh is important to me. He's decent and solid and kind, and he likes me even if I am nearly fifty-five and fat in the bargain. I don't have to tell you now, I guess, what it means to be left all alone. . . . And I'm getting older every day and every month, and I don't have enough to live on without help from somebody, and I hate the thought of going back to that damned little hat shop, and people just won't hire women in their fifties for decent jobs. Or for any jobs at all now, from what we hear . . . And I hate skimping along in that one-room apartment down in that one-horse town for the rest of my life—and I hate taking more from you to get myself a better place—"

"Oh Lou, stop!" Madge said, though she didn't know whether she wanted to save her sister from further exposure—or herself from hearing any more. At any rate, Lou stopped, and while there was still that red glow of anger around her, it had dulled again, having worked off some of its heat.

"All right, I'll stop. I'll spare your sensibilities. But now you know. Now maybe you can see why I don't want to be yanked off to America, away from the last chance I'll ever get."

"All right," Madge said, in a sensible tone. "You'll stay on, that's all. There's no reason why you can't stay for as many more weeks, or months, as you care to, even if I do go back now."

"Oh no," Lou said. "Me stay on in England after you leave? That's a mite too obvious, isn't it? I haven't made any bones about the fact that I'm not traveling around on my own money. I made that mistake just once, thank you. . . . So if Thomas E. Budleigh thinks I'm lingering around on his account—as he would, being a man—that would just about tear up the whole account in a week. That man's a bachelor—not a widower—remember? If I ever do pry him out of that state of mind, it'll be only by dint of much time and more diplomacy. No," she said again, abruptly. "If you go now, I go too; there's nothing else for it. You'll just have to make up your mind whether seeing your grandchild into the world is more important than giving me a chance at winding up my later years in comfort and companionship—and security. Especially security."

"That's nicely put," Madge said.

"Well, those are my cards on the table, that's all. It's only a gamble, I guess. I'm not kidding myself, or you either. It's your money and your choice. And you can decide what you're going to do about it while I drive into the village with Mr. B. I expect he's waiting for me now. If you want me to try for the nearest sailing, I'll send a wire when I come back."

Lou left her sitting there. Poor old Lou, Madge thought dully.

Queer how one knew so much about the people one was with every
day, and so little. And the queer obsessions they had . . . There wasn't
any reason for Lou to feel the way she did, whether she and Madge
were to go on living together or not. Madge had never quite faced
that, herself. She looked blankly out of the window, off at the horizon
where the brilliant green V of the inlet widened into the sea. Then
she looked down at the vari-colored letters in her lap, and began sort-
ing out Margaret's, and slowly reading it through again. When she
had finished, she continued to stare at the last words, not even seeing
them. Margaret didn't want her to come back now, and didn't need
her—that was about the size of it. Lou was right about that. So there
really wasn't any decision for her to make, was there? She could lean
back on that, at least, with a sense of relief. She did so hate making
decisions.

Part Two

Chapter Seven

SHE KEPT TELLING HERSELF, FROM THE TIME THE TRAIN LEFT CHICAGO, that this was the last lap. First, she had been planning to go home; then she was on her way; now she was almost there . . . after two years and eight months away. That was a long time. It had taken much longer than she had realized it would on that day in July, in Devonshire; over a year ago that was now. Lou's project had taken all that time, and there were times when they had nearly given it all up.

That fall of 1930, when they had discreetly retired to Brittany for a while, Madge didn't see why they couldn't just as well have gone on home, and come back the next year, perhaps. But Lou was too wise to let her go then, too unsure that they would ever come back. There was all that talk of the depression, which it seemed had not ended after all but was going on and on. Lou had even used that as an argument. After all, Madge didn't want to go back into that gloomy atmosphere, did she? And suppose she *was* having a few dividends cut, everyone knew that they could live more cheaply in Europe than at home. So they had stuck it out. And now the job was done. Thomas was really a good soul when you knew him; Lou would have stability for the rest of her life anyway, and that was what she had wanted. Well, it was what most people wanted, wasn't it?

Madge thought about her a good deal as she crossed the ocean, but when she had reached New York and started west on the train, her mind pulled itself upright from its backward leaning, and leaped forward instead, toward Margaret and the baby—and Clay too, of course. It was like a mental trapeze act, and there was nothing solid beneath her during the long trip; she was still swinging through thin air, it seemed, till she could reach Margaret, and home. Perhaps all aerialists had that feeling of breathless insecurity until they made contact again, that same feeling Madge always had when she had to travel alone. Especially during this last, long drawn-out hour or two before arrival. Margaret would have the house open for her at any rate, she thought, but it would be so very different now that Margaret herself was away, in a home of her own—with a husband—and a baby! She wondered if they'd bring the baby to the train. But no— of course not, it was too late.

It was dark outside the windowpane, and had been for some time. She'd had coat and hat and gloves all on for an hour now, because she couldn't tell where they were, just from the lights and an occasional crossing flashing by in the darkness, and she wanted to be ready, to get off calmly. Like the world-seasoned traveler she was supposed to be. But she'd forgotten that the porter would come to take her bags out . . . as he was doing now . . . forgotten that she didn't have to push her bags out of the windows over here. So this . . . was it! They were slowing down. Her stomach suddenly seemed to have left its moorings and fetched up with a jolt somewhere under her breastbone, because she was home again.

Out on the platform she looked anxiously up and down; no sign of them, she thought, in ready alarm. And then she realized that that was Margaret, that girl standing only a dozen yards away—why it must be, because she was coming toward her, smiling. And she hadn't even known her for a minute, Madge thought in horror. She hadn't remembered that the girl was so tall. And thin! Of course these longer skirts, halfway down the calves, made tall girls look taller, and she'd let her hair grow in and had it drawn back into a neat little bun on the back of her neck, and that made her face look thin, Madge supposed. And then she forgot everything else, as they put their arms around each other, and kissed each other, and stood off again to look at each other, Margaret with her hands on her mother's shoulders, smiling at her fondly, indulgently, a little patronizingly, as she always had. Madge had almost forgotten that look, and it suddenly made her want to stamp her foot, in rebellion, like a badly behaved child. But she laughed instead.

"Margaret honey—you look so grown up!" she said.

"Great Scott! I am. I'm an old married woman—remember?"

And then Clay loomed up, and he looked different too, but she didn't have time to figure out why, because he had stepped closer and leaned down to kiss her, in a brief effort at gallantry. After which he immediately grew very business-like and began asking her about her trunk, and getting her bags together, and Margaret put her arm through her mother's and steered her out through the noisy station, which seemed just as strange to her at that moment as any other station in the world. And when they were on the sidewalk and getting into a taxi Madge laughed suddenly and said, "You know, just for a minute I fully expected to see the Lincoln standing there—and Sims beside it, as dour as ever! I'd completely forgotten that we let him go a couple of years ago."

"Two and a half years," Margaret assented thoughtfully, and seemed to forget to say more for a minute, as if she were living them over as thoughtfully as she had said the words. But after a minute she added abruptly, "We'll have to get another driver for you. I just hadn't attended to it. And then too, I didn't know just what arrangement you wanted to make now."

"Well—I don't know about the Lincoln," Madge said. "It seems enormous for me alone. I suppose I'll have to get another car, do you think so?"

Margaret smiled a little oddly.

"That's up to you, I guess, darling."

"What about the coupe?" Madge asked. "Is it still in good condition or have you got another one yourself now?"

"Oh I sold that," Margaret said carelessly. "Some time ago. But we haven't gotten another one—just yet."

"Don't you need it?" Madge said, in some surprise, but Margaret said lightly, "Oh well, I'm not playing golf these days, with an infant to look after—and Clay didn't seem to need a car, so it was foolish to think of one." Perhaps the mention of the infant was deliberate for it caught Madge's whole attention at once. She put her hand on Margaret's.

"I can hardly wait another day," she said. "If you knew how I've felt all these months, not being able to see her grow week by week —and smile—show her first tooth—"

Margaret squeezed her hand. "You won't have to wait another day, darling. She's in bed at home—at your house. You see," she added, "we've moved in with you for a few days. I thought it might be easier for you than to go back alone just at first." It was Madge's turn to squeeze the other's hand, which she did almost convulsively, and then she turned impulsively to Clay too, sitting on her other side, but he was stolidly looking straight ahead of him. For a moment she couldn't say anything. Why, oh why had she sometimes thought that Margaret was unperceptive? For this would make all the difference—to have them there with her, if only to start her off.

And it did. It seemed as though Margaret still lived there, to have her open the door with her own key, and then ring for the maid to come and take the bags—even to have her introduce the new girl to her mother. For when Madge stood in the square hall and looked around, with every detail so familiar as to strike her like an old pain starting up again, she didn't think she could have borne it alone. She hadn't known how a place, a mere house, could stand up before you, to have its features counted and recognized, one by one. She hadn't dreamed how many things one forgot to notice while living there, and certainly never thought of while away, which leapt to the attention like flashing signals when one returned. The way the rug in the living-room doorway always ruffled up a little—those silly old Jacobean chairs sitting like empty thrones with their arms stuck stiffly in front of them—the way the light caught the portrait on the landing and made Hugo's eyes gleam as if he were watching her. She wished at least that Margaret hadn't thought to have that light turned on.

"I tried to have everything just as it should be," Margaret was saying as she looked around. And Madge was quick in apology for the wish which she hadn't even uttered.

"You've done a beautiful job, dear," she said warmly. "I'm afraid it was a lot of work." And then they went upstairs together, as they had so many times before, and down the hall to the corner opposite Margaret's old room.

"We're in there," she said carelessly, "but I put Joan across the hall, over here."

Madge had a queer, tentative feeling as she went into the room, and she leaned over the crib almost anxiously. It was Ronnie's old crib, which Margaret had had brought down from the attic. And the baby was deeply, beatifically asleep in it. Pink-faced, fat. The hair in moist curls at the back of her neck. And suddenly it didn't matter that it had all happened while she had been away. The sense of belonging, of absurd, unreasonable pride, was just as strong as though she had been here all the time, had even had some part in the process, instead of being a useless member whose active part in it had been played years and years before. Madge gazed at the baby steadily for a long time without even looking up, without saying a word, but when she did glance up to find Margaret's eyes, her own were shining.

"She's perfect," she said simply. "Just perfect."

"Well, don't forget, she yells and drools and a lot of other imperfect things in the daytime," Margaret said, smiling. "She's teething, you know." But she was pleased, just the same. And Clay, who had come in after them, having carried the heaviest of Madge's bags upstairs, stood behind her, grinning too.

"Good job, eh?" he said, and Madge thought he seemed more natural in that moment, with more of his old arrogant cockiness, than he had at all up to now.

They went back along the hall again presently, and Clay went on downstairs while Margaret stepped into Madge's room with her, and looked around once more, to see if there was anything she had overlooked. Madge stood in the center of the room beside her, looking around too, but more slowly, her glance making that same involuntary inventory which it had downstairs. The rug here was blue, as it always had been, and the chintz was the same English one which Hugo had chosen, eight—or was it nine?—years ago. Those good materials and dyes seemed to last forever. . . . And the chaise longue was the one where she'd spent a lot of fruitless hours, reading, sewing, waiting. . . . And the dressing table, and the chiffonier, and the desk—all the heavy old walnut furniture that she knew by heart, even to the places that had been chipped or scratched, and repaired and polished again. . . . So here she was, back in the same spot. Funny how one went off on long, long journeys, in time as well as space, and it was all one big circle after all. Surely one must make some headway finally—come out somewhere a little farther along . . . But at the moment it didn't seem that way to Madge. And Margaret was watching her.

"All right?" she asked softly, and Madge smiled at her.

"Of course," she said. "How about you, darling? Has it been all right with you? Are you happy?"

Margaret stood smiling back at her in the old way, as if making up her mind whether to answer or not. But then she did, after a fashion.

"I love Clay very much," she said. "If that's what you mean."

If she hadn't known her Margaret, it might have seemed an ambiguous answer; not evasive exactly, but not quite complete, perhaps. But it relieved Madge.

"I'm glad," she said simply, and let out a long slow breath of thankfulness, as if she had been holding it for two years and a half.

* * *

At first, there was just the pleasure of being with Margaret and Clay, and having them with her, and Madge didn't try to look further. She hardly looked beyond Elephant Square, which seemed in some way to shut out the disquietingly strange and yet familiar city. And she hardly dared look beyond the first weekend, when she was afraid the young people would be moving back to their own place. But after a few days, Margaret casually let drop that they were going to find a new apartment anyway; that they had just left the old one, which had made it easy for them to fit in the little visit with her. So Madge's heart bounded up again, and she said eagerly, "Don't look too hard just yet, darling! Make it more of a visit, if there isn't any real hurry." And Margaret smiled indulgently, and a little absent-mindedly.

But when her own feeling of hurry had dropped away—that feeling of having to savor every moment of their company before they left her again—Madge began to look at them more carefully, and wonder more closely about them. She had had a little hope that Margaret and she might come closer to each other now, since married women were always supposed to have a certain fellowship of understanding. It was the same old obstinate, unyielding hope that some day her child wouldn't just turn her away when she approached her; a perennial hope, which died down as it sprang up. And gradually, once again, she saw that that day was as remote as ever, and Margaret herself a little more remote, if anything. She was as lovely as ever, of course, and her mother's eyes followed her fondly, even respectfully, as she watched her filling the role of Young Wife and Young Mother, so calmly and capably. Margaret was so much more *adequate* than she had ever been, she thought. But at the same time, she seemed almost to live with care, as though to fit that certain pattern which she had always seen as designed for herself. Care—discipline—caution—reserve—Madge didn't know what it was. It remained strange and baffling to her. She wondered once or twice whether Clay understood Margaret better than she did. He must, of course.

But his attitude toward her was a strange thing too, to Madge's mind. She wouldn't have said that he adored Margaret so much as that he admired her, and that seemed a peculiar way for a husband to feel. It was almost as if he acknowledged the excellence of everything she did or stood for, because he couldn't deny it. But sometimes he seemed to accept it with an odd hostility, and sometimes with an equally odd touch of humility. On the other hand, as if to neutralize any intangible loss of stature beside her, there was a lack of what

Madge could only call physical respect toward his wife, which startled
and almost shocked Margaret's mother at times. Little familiarities
that he took with her before Madge which were not in themselves
important or even unusual in this day, she supposed, but they made
her subtly uncomfortable and sometimes inwardly indignant. A slap
here—a way of fondling her there—well, it was only a matter of good
taste, perhaps, in which he was lacking, or a matter of asserting his
masculinity—of which he seemed to have plenty anyway. If it had
been done affectionately, with a fondness so self-evident as to make
any roughness seem tender, that would have been very different. But it
did seem to Madge sometimes as though Clay meant—not to humiliate
his wife—no, surely not that—but to take her down, in some subtle
way, and she was surprised that Margaret, with all her air of quiet
superiority, didn't appear to mind it. Or if she minded, she gave no
sign that she did.

Well, most marriages had their surface oddities, to the outsider's
eye, and what went on inside them was only a matter of guesswork.
But though Madge thought they were happy together on the whole,
there was something . . . something unsettled about them still, despite
Margaret's pose of confident serenity. Of course that might come
from the fact that they were not in their own home at the moment,
that their routine and rhythm of life was all mixed up with somebody
else's. Though it did seem that Clay's routine was rather variable
anyway. Generally, he left the house soon after breakfast, as any
business man would, and was not seen again till late in the afternoon. But on some days he appeared at the house again much earlier
than on others, before four o'clock once or twice, Madge noticed in
some surprise. Once she was still more surpised to hear his voice
coming from Margaret's room well on in the morning, as late as
eleven o'clock.

And then there was another morning when they all sat late over
breakfast, and the clock in the hall struck solemnly—once, and
Madge (thinking aloud, and with no malice intended) said innocently,
"Is that only half-past eight? Oh no, it can't be—"

"No," Margaret said, glancing at her own small wrist watch.
"It's half-past nine." There was something rather measured in the
way she said it, and she picked up her coffee cup with the same effect
of deliberation. "We're all late this morning," she added calmly.
Madge had the feeling that the simple words meant more than they
seemed to, but the expanse of newspaper behind which Clay had
retreated gave no indication that he had even heard. Madge changed

the subject, talked about something she was going to do that day herself, and Margaret sat there, not quite listening, she felt, her long fingers playing a silent scale on the table top. She had finished her coffee now; she seemed to be waiting for something. Madge herself was in no hurry. She found it very pleasant to sit with her family again after a leisurely breakfast. But presently Margaret pushed her chair back, not abruptly, but with a sort of decision.

"Well," she said lightly, "you two may have nothing to do all day—but I've got an infant upstairs, and a few other little chores. And it must be nearly quarter of ten . . ."

There was nothing in the least disagreeable in her voice that Madge could note; it was the lightest sort of inconsequent remark, even if it had an implication of teasing in it. But the newspaper suddenly came down.

"All right, all right!" Clay said, loudly. He folded the paper over roughly, almost savagely, flapped it down on the table, and shoved his own chair back. "I'm going, damn it—that's what you want, isn't it?" His glance at Margaret was a brief glare as he got to his feet with an effect of violence in the quick motion. And then he had left the table and the room without further look or word to either of them. Madge was so surprised that she stared at his back through the doorway, but when she moved her glance again toward Margaret, she saw that there was only—was it pity, in her eyes, or sort of regretful resignation?

"Sorry," she said to her mother, in the same light tone that she'd used earlier. "I've got to go up to the baby."

"Yes, of course," Madge agreed quickly. "I'll be up presently, after I've talked to Mildred."

There seemed nothing more to say, but she didn't understand the little scene at all.

So after that she did begin to wonder rather more about Clay himself, whether he was a little lazy, perhaps. . . . She had no idea what his work really was, what a bond salesman did from day to day and hour to hour. She discovered only accidentally that he was no longer with his old firm. She had asked some casual question about it, trying to show a polite interest in what presumably interested him, and Clay had ignored it. Just rudely left her question hanging in the air, though Madge was sure that he had heard her. He hadn't picked up the newspaper until after she had asked it. But when in her surprise, she glanced at Margaret, the latter answered for him, in a smooth offhand way.

"Clay hasn't been with McGinnis and Company for a long time, you know," she said, as if it were really rather a foolish question on Madge's part.

"Oh, hasn't he?" Madge said, uncertainly. "No—I didn't realize . . ." She supposed she should have known, and that Clay was slightly insulted by her not remembering, but she simply didn't recall their having told her.

"Oh no," Margaret replied carelessly. "He changed a year or two ago."

"I just didn't realize," Madge repeated awkwardly. She was on the point of asking where he was now, but Margaret was looking so dreamily into the fire, as though she'd forgotten the subject, and Clay was so immersed in the paper, that she thought better of it. She would ask Margaret more about him sometime when they were alone. But when she did, the girl was still offhand, and not very illuminating either.

"Oh, I couldn't possibly describe his work. It—varies so," she said vaguely. "He's been doing some rather intensive research work on markets and market cycles lately. Clay has a good mind, you know," she added with sudden firmness, as though she needed to convince someone. Though Madge agreed at once.

"I'm sure he has, dear. He always seemed very intelligent and well informed to me. I just—don't feel I know him very well yet."

But in spite of their gradually extended stay in her house, she made little headway. Clay treated her with an odd combination of patronizing gallantry and a detached indifference which seemed to conceal some faint, indefinable hostility. She didn't know what to make of it. She had always rather liked him, and still felt she would be fond of him if he ever gave her a chance. He still occasionally had that little cocky way with him which had always had a certain irritating charm about it. But there were other times when he had little to say to anyone, when he was morose and almost surly. Madge felt uncomfortably that she must have brought a discordant note into their home atmosphere, just by her presence, and she tried harder than ever to be as pleasant, as unobtrusive and unobjectionable as she knew how.

But there were such ridiculous, unexpected things which came up. Like the episode of the apples. They had been sitting idly together one day—it was a Sunday afternoon that time, a couple of weeks after her return, and a fire had been started in the library fireplace against the first fall chill outside. Margaret had the baby on her lap, tired and dozing after a rampant play hour, and Clay seemed to be in one of his more cheerful moods, had even asked Madge some questions about her wanderings. She found herself reminiscing—foolishly, she thought afterward, because nobody was ever really interested in anybody else's trip abroad. But her remarks had seemed so innocuous. She'd been talking about the colorful outdoor flower stalls that you saw in the cities over there—the lovely ones on the Spanish steps in Rome, and all the flower sellers around Covent Garden in London, and on street corners here and there . . .

"I used to love to stop and get a handful for our rooms," Madge said idly, and then she laughed as she thought of something else. "You know that was one thing that struck me in New York this time. They've got a way of selling apples on the street there now—did you know that? I liked it because it did seem rather picturesque for us— more like Europe than over here." There was something flat and unresponsive in the silence of the other two, but she went on quite innocently, "Except that it did seem so very American, somehow, that we should sell something to eat rather than just to smell or look at."

"And did you buy an apple, Mrs. Fairlie?" Clay said, deliberately. His tone was queer, almost—ominous, Madge would have said, and she looked at him in a puzzled way. But she answered him smilingly.

"As a matter of fact I did," she confessed. "I couldn't resist it. I bought a beautiful big red shiny one when I was walking around the afternoon I was there—and then I felt so silly because I didn't know what to do with it, and it was too big to put in my handbag. Imagine walking into the lobby of the Ritz with a large apple in one hand! But I did," she wound up, with a little reminiscent chuckle at herself, and her unusual temerity.

"Oh for God's sake!" Clay said, and got up suddenly and went over to look out the window, though it was getting dark outside. Madge looked at Margaret, whose face looked very still and set.

"What on earth is the matter?" she asked. "Have I said anything so very odd?"

"Didn't you know, Mother," Margaret said quietly, "that people are selling apples on the street corners this year, because they haven't any jobs—because they can't find any other work?"

"Why no . . . no, I had no idea that was why they did it. I shouldn't think they'd make very much at that sort of thing," Madge said mildly.

"No—they don't!" Clay almost shouted, turning back from the window for a moment, to glare at her across the dusky room. "They're lucky if they make a few cents to get a cup of coffee or a hamburger. That's how picturesque it is!"

Joan had waked up and begun to make fretful noises and wriggle on Margaret's lap. The latter spoke firmly, though not to her. "Clay," she said quietly. "Mother didn't understand about it. There's no reason to shout—and wake the baby," she added, bending her head to press her mouth against the child's hair.

"No." Madge spoke meekly, rather appalled by the flare of feeling which had lighted up in the quiet room. "I didn't understand at all. It was very stupid of me, I suppose. But I just hadn't happened to hear of that—custom."

"Sorry," Clay said abruptly. "I forgot how little you seem to have heard of our American customs, Mrs. Fairlie."

It was hardly an apology, the way he had put it, and Madge sat there quietly, but with a tenseness inside her, like that of an animal drawing itself together against further attack. She felt almost tearful for a moment. She had been awfully stupid she supposed; she'd admitted that at once. But how was she expected to *know?* It was so unfair of Clay to act as though she were being deliberately callous. Why should he burst out at her that way, as if he held some personal animus against her, as if she were in some way responsible for what went on in the country while she'd been away from it?

And then, again—a week or two later, there was the matter of the hat: that silly, silly little hat which Madge had fallen for. It was what they called a Eugenie hat; there were hundreds and thousands of them that fall, but Madge hadn't seen them before. They hadn't been in evidence where she'd bought her French clothes earlier in the year. She saw it in a window one day after she came home, and felt its impulsive pull on her, almost like the appeal of a puppy in a pet shop window. She went in and tried it on. It was made of dull green velvet, and had a luxuriant soft ostrich feather which swept over it and wound up in a lovely curling sweep just below the ear. Madge was entranced; she'd had a hat once—a large one—with plumes, soon after she was married, and it seemed now as though she'd been waiting half a lifetime for another hat with another plume. So she bought it. And she bought a blue one for Margaret, too—not like it of course, but a little on the same order. That was utterly reckless of her of course; because Margaret had never approved Madge's taste. But she had the saleswoman put it in the bottom of the box, and thought she'd see how Margaret liked the one she'd got for herself.

When she reached home, she went in the front door past the new maid, eagerly and buoyantly. The girl said Mr. and Mrs. Ferguson were upstairs with the baby, so Madge went up briskly and along the upper hall to the big corner room and found all three of them sitting on the floor and laughing. She came in and put her box on a chair, and stooped over to ruffle the baby's hair and hold out a finger for her to grab at. She put off displaying her purchases for a moment, feeling suddenly a little shy—or maybe only a little demure—about them. But Margaret could hardly miss the round yellow box sitting there so smugly, and she asked curiously, "What have you got there, Mother?"

"I'll show you," Madge said smiling. "Something I fell for, that's all. But I think you'll like it."

She took off the hat she'd been wearing, opened the box with an air of proud discovery and took the new green treasure over to Margaret's dressing table. She put it on with a sort of smiling tender care, and as any woman would, she said, "My hair is mussy. It will look better when it's done properly, but—there!" She turned back to them expectantly.

They all stared at her, without a word, even the baby caught up, uncomprehendingly, in the momentary mesmerism.

"Don't you like it?" Madge asked, turning her head to show them the side view with the sweep of feather from brow to nape of neck.

"It's very nice, darling," Margaret said constrainedly.

"I thought you'd really think it was becoming to me," Madge said, a trifle urgently now.

"It's a nice soft line," Margaret acknowledged. "It's a little different from anything I've seen on you, of course. . . ."

Madge looked at Clay, who had turned back to playing with the baby. Her glance was still a shade demure, but more doubtful now. "What do you think, Clay?" He glanced up at her briefly.

"I don't know much about women's hats, Mrs. Fairlie. I guess it's all right. Looks expensive anyway. That's what you wanted, wasn't it?"

"Why no, I never thought of that." Madge laughed somewhat ruefully. "I suppose it was a bit expensive really, though that certainly wasn't why I got it. It just bewitched me, I guess. I thought you'd all like it," she added in a crestfallen tone, turning back toward the mirror as if to look for what they saw. "*I* like it anyway," she said, suddenly a little defiant.

"Well, that's what matters, dear," Margaret said gently now. "If you like it, you'll enjoy wearing it."

"And I'm sure you needed it," Clay remarked, in a tone that was too heavily facetious to be quite pleasant. He'd gotten up from the floor in an abrupt scrambling motion, and he stamped one foot— to shake down his trouser leg of course, but somehow the effect of the move was that of a gesture of impatience, of exasperation even. Madge took off the hat and turned with it in her hands to see him regarding her dourly.

"Why no, Clay," she answered him coolly and literally. "I don't know that I needed it particularly. I still have a number of hats that I brought back with me."

"Yeah, that's what I thought," said Clay dryly. "Well—" He turned toward the door. "I'm going down."

Margaret got up also and leaned down to take hold of the baby's hands and let her pull herself to her feet and stand there, proud in her achievement.

"Got to get undressed, punkin," she said to Joan. But Madge, who had crossed over to the yellow box and put back the hat, on top of the one which had never emerged from the tissue paper, spoke in a small even voice.

"Really, Margaret," she said, "I don't quite understand why Clay should use such a tone to me. It's rather—disagreeable, you know, aside from anything else. And after all, if I choose to buy a hat with my own money, whether any of you care for it or not—it *is* my money."

"Yes, of course it is, Mother." Margaret was standing there with the child in her arms now, looking over her head at her mother. Her look was strangely somber. "I'm sorry we didn't sound more enthusiastic."

"I'm sorry you didn't too," Madge said a bit frostily. "Well, you never did like what I chose. You always did try to take the pleasure out of anything I bought myself. I should be used to it by now."

"It wasn't that—" Margaret began, and stopped.

"What was it, then?" Madge had picked up the box, and she looked across at her daughter; not hopefully, but still willing to listen.

"Well, it's just . . ." Margaret spoke again with a certain constraint; "just that people here don't go around any more, buying things they don't need. It isn't done, that's all. So I suppose—it does seem strange to us."

"I see," Madge said slowly, though she hardly knew just what it was that she saw. There was something illogical here; it didn't make sense in some way. If one had the money to buy something, if people had things to sell—if business was to go on at all . . . And yet, if people criticized each other, resented it in some way when one bought something one didn't actually need . . . Madge shook her head slightly, as if to shake off a touch of dizziness. Perhaps the resentment was not really against the purchases one made, or even the extravagances one might fall into. It was against the fact that anybody had the money to make them, wasn't that it, really? But for Margaret to feel that way—Margaret and Clay, her own children!

The girl was continuing to explain, going on in a quiet, forbearing way. "You see, so much has happened during these last two years, Mother. The depression has been much worse, for lots of people, than you can realize all at once."

As though she were not quite bright . . . her mother filled in in her own mind. There was a sort of apology implied in what Margaret had said, and yet Madge realized that the apology was not offered for Margaret's husband, who had been rude, but—for her mother, who was stupid.

* * *

Of *course* she knew that there had been a depression, and that it was still going on. They had talked about it in England too, and people had written about the depression in their letters from home for the past two years. Even the papers abroad had mentioned it, in their dignified way. But Madge hadn't quite realized that people over here, the people one knew, were so utterly preoccupied by it, so—so *absorbed,* in the sense of being blotted up—in it. They didn't always talk about it, to be sure. Sometimes—like Margaret—they rather avoided mentioning it, as if it were not quite in good taste. But others wanted to talk about it all the time. They even seemed anxious to have you know how badly off they were, that they had a part in it personally, almost as if there might be a certain dishonor in not being affected by it, when everyone else was . . . or pretended to be. She discovered, to her bewilderment, that one woman whom she knew, who had just bought a new pair of brown oxfords, had actually had them well rubbed down with a dark polish so that the newness would not be easily marked.

There was a great deal that Madge didn't understand. And when at length she went in to see Mr. Hawley, her puzzled but still detached confusion became quite suddenly a close and personal bewilderment. He had telephoned two or three times, first to welcome her home, next to suggest that there were some questions which they ought to go over together, but she had kept putting it off. Finally, one day when she was downtown, she turned into the building where his office was, as if she had suddenly decided to have a tooth pulled. Even as she rode up in the elevator, she told herself that this was foolish, going in without a definite appointment, because of course he would be out or busy. He was in, however, and strangely, he was not busy. She was shown into his big corner room, with its wide-windowed view of the city which lay beyond, but she forgot to admire the view this time, as her attention was at once caught by the impression that Mr. Hawley looked older, much older. Her next thought was that he must be ill; he seemed to rise with such an effort, and his skin looked such a bad color too. His hair had been white before, and she knew that he had been considerably older than Hugo, but she fell to figuring again, hastily, just how much older he must have been. She greeted him with an unexpected feeling of warmth, and they sat talking for several minutes in a friendly, unfocused way. Suddenly Madge asked him whether he had been well.

"Oh—yes," he said, pushing some papers from one side of the desk to another with his large white hand. "I'm well enough, I guess. It's been a bad time though, the last couple of years. Most of us feel ten years older instead of two, that's all. I don't—sleep much any more, without this dope they give you."

He was tired, poor soul, she decided compassionately. The downward-running lines in his face, the droop of his eyelids, the sag of his shoulders, even the way his hair lay down on his head instead of standing up from the parting in a comb, as it used to, all said the same thing. He was just plain tired, that was all. She smiled at him sympathetically and for a second they looked at each other without speaking.

"Well—" he said at last, and then paused again before he went on. "I'm not sure whether you know quite how bad things have been, Mrs. Fairlie."

"I know they say it's a bad depression," she agreed in a docile, conciliatory way.

"It's the worst depression in this country since the 1870's," he told her rather sternly.

"I . . . see."

"I've tried to write you about conditions in a general way, of course, in a way which I thought might give you some idea, without unduly alarming you." Madge felt guilty, listening to him, knowing how sketchily she had read his letters. Sometimes she was afraid she hadn't really read them at all. "However, it is taking a much longer time for the situation to improve, than any of us anticipated. It has become a sort of endurance test—of men—and of their resources too. Of how long each can hold out." Mr. Hawley kept pausing every now and then, as though he lost his own thread and had to fumble for it. "You were fortunate of course, in having a large enough income at the start so that it could stand some shrinkage and still give you plenty to live on. But you realize that there have been reductions, don't you?"

"Why yes, I guess so," she replied meekly. "But I seemed to have the same amount to live on." And Madge smiled at him confidently, paying due tribute to his cleverness in managing that.

"Yes. Well, as I say, there was still enough coming in to allow you the same rate of living income which we had agreed upon before you went abroad. But as time went on, there has been less of a margin above your living rate, less surplus to reinvest, say, in order to make up the capital losses. In fact," he said heavily, "the principal has shrunk in value—very markedly. You—understand that, of course?"

"I'm afraid I don't really understand much about it," Madge admitted honestly. "Or even what some of the words mean."

Mr. Hawley seemed to brace himself, both against her ignorance and his own immense weariness. "The principal—that is, your capital —has shrunk about in half," he said after a moment. Madge stared at him, her eyes wide and uncomprehending. "Do you remember my telling you," he went on, "soon after Hugo's death, that he had a firm belief in common stocks, and that the bulk of his estate was invested in them?"

"Ye—es," Madge said hesitantly. She did seem to remember some such talk; the trouble was, she had never been quite sure what a "common" stock was. It had a rather snobbish sound to her.

"Well, that being the case, I didn't wish to advise you to change the whole plan of his investments—too drastically. But, that being the case, also, when the bottom dropped out of the market, naturally the market value of your securities dropped with the rest."

"Yes, of course," Madge said, doubtfully but dutifully.

"We made some changes in 1930, as you know," Mr. Hawley said, "moving into some preferred stocks, and some—uh—railroad bonds, as they were considered a reasonably conservative refuge. A reasonable retreat, say, without sacrificing your whole position."

Madge blinked at him and nodded. He cleared his throat.

"Unfortunately, even the senior stocks, even the bonds, have not held their ground during this sweeping period of deflation. The rails have had a very bad time. Some—have had to go into receivership. So the shrinkage of the property as a whole has continued," he said firmly. "I feel you must understand that: must recognize how much less the size of your holdings is at present than it was. Much less. The shrinkage has in fact amounted to sixty-three per cent of the appraised value of Hugo's estate," he added, with an effect of laboriously, meticulously crossing his t's. "I have all the figures if you care to go over them, right here."

"Oh no!" Madge protested, instinctively recoiling. "I can understand a little of what you tell me, this way—but not figures!"

"Of course it should recover, some day, when production and business generally recover," he said.

"Oh, I'm sure it will," Madge told him comfortingly.

"But there's one aspect of your affairs which has worried me considerably for a long time," Mr. Hawley pursued, refusing to be comforted. "That is the matter of your holdings in the Fairlie Company itself."

"Oh?" said Madge.

"You realize that that is your largest holding, don't you, Mrs. Fairlie?"

"Why, I suppose . . ."

"Very much the largest. Quite naturally," Mr. Hawley said. "That was Hugo's own greatest interest, his own personal achievement, I might say. He built it up from a small outfit, believed in it—would believe in it today, I'm sure. It's a good company. But machine tools are part of heavy industry, Mrs. Fairlie."

"Are they?"

"And durable goods, as we call them, are the hardest hit in a depression like this. They are heavily capitalized, they have to operate at a high rate of capacity to break even, and when production is cut down to a mere trickle as at present, when the buyers of the machines are having to retrench in every way themselves . . . Why, Mrs. Fairlie, earnings on industry generally are off fifty per cent from last year. They're down over seventy per cent from 1929."

He saw that Madge was just staring at him again, with a slight pucker between her brows, and he stopped. "They just can't earn any money," he said abruptly, after a minute. "That's the long and the short of it. They cut down on wages and dividends, and let out all the employees they haven't got work for, and reduce maintenance—but when they've used up the surplus left over from the profitable years, they *have* to keep on paying operating expenses—and that means they go deeper into the red. As you know, the Fairlie dividend rate has already been cut, a couple of times."

Madge was still looking at him with her eyes wide, but perhaps she understood more than he thought she did. Or perhaps she had merely absorbed the idea, rather than understanding it. He stopped leading up to it. "They're probably going to pass the next dividend entirely," he said flatly.

"Not—pay anything, you mean?"

"That's right. And they may not pay anything again for some time. Some years, maybe. How long I don't know. Nobody does. It's still a good company, you understand," he said again, carefully, "but it's what we call a business man's investment. I never should have left you in it," he added suddenly, almost fretfully.

"You think we ought to sell it," Madge said, not even asking it as a question, because she knew that was what he meant and didn't want to say.

"I hate to see you do it at these prices," he sighed, at length. "It really depends on you and whether you would rather get some income on the money, rather than waiting for the stock to come back. Several years, maybe."

"Well, I'd rather have the income," Madge said promptly.

"That's what most people say," Mr. Hawley muttered. "It isn't smart, but I can't say I blame them, with the way things have been going." He sat and looked at her for a long few seconds. He seemed to be studying her, not so much in a professional way as a personal one. As if wondering what made her tick, Madge thought. Then he nodded, and gave a slight, a very slight shrug, as one who has done his utmost. After a minute he went on to explain that it would take a little time to dispose of the stock, even in small blocks, in this thin market, and then he had her sign some blank forms, and when she lifted her head in the middle of signing one and asked, trying to be intelligent, "What are you going to put it in?" he sat back again in his chair, and cleared his throat.

"That's something else," he said, and Marge couldn't help wishing that she hadn't started him off again. "You remember, soon after Hugo's death we talked about the advantages and disadvantages of trust accounts? [*We* talked! Madge thought. He went on and on and I never did know what it was all about. . . . And here he was, going on again now.] Well, I have retreated somewhat from my position at that time, Mrs. Fairlie. I'm going to suggest now that when you have the funds from this stock, you use them to establish a trust fund for yourself. In that way, you will have a backlog of the most conservative investments, limited by the trust laws of the state, and of course, taken care of in all the routine details by the regular trust company machinery of some good bank."

Madge was bewildered again, and looked it. "The rate of income on such bonds as are stipulated will not be large," he said inexorably, "but in that way, even the management of your property will be divided, in responsibility and judgment. It seems a reasonable compromise to me," he said, more slowly still, as though the long record he had been playing for her for the past hour, was finally running down. "A reasonable hedge—against the uncertainties of the future. None of us is infallible, Mrs. Fairlie. We all make mistakes."

Something new, and at the same time something curiously final, seemed to have come into the interview, and Madge wasn't sure that it was just because it was reaching its natural conclusion. She was suddenly conscious of a breath of real fear, now, breaking through her uneasy ignorance, and she didn't know what to make of it. She had already accepted, in a blind sort of way, all the dire and depressing things he had said earlier, but this was something quite different.

"You aren't disowning me yourself, are you?" she asked with a wistful, slightly forlorn smile. "You'll still keep on advising me about all the other—stocks and things, won't you?"

For a second he didn't answer. Instead, he reached into a pocket and brought out a handkerchief, touched his mouth with it, and his forehead, and then his nose, which he blew briefly and sharply. It was a puzzling pantomime. But then he seemed to pull himself up, in his chair and in his speech.

"Oh no," he said in his large, kind way. "We'll keep on checking the other things for you. The rest of the stocks are the kind which can stay put, I think—and the real estate of course, which is completely stagnant—for the present. For the present," he repeated. "And you ought to meet my younger partner, too," he went on. "I don't think you knew Dick Purcell before, did you?"

And that was the way he eased her out. He called in Dick Purcell and introduced him to her, a large young man with large brown eyes in a solid, responsible-looking face. Together they moved into the outer office. And as they reached the door and Madge put out her hand, Mr. Hawley took it and held it firmly.

"You'll have to be more careful, you know, Mrs. Fairlie—watch the scale of your expenses and so on. We have a lot to learn you know, even if we aren't young any more. Especially if we aren't—" he broke off suddenly. "But you're still very well off, relatively speaking. You'll get along all right."

It seemed a strange way to end the interview, with that last admonition intended to be reassuring, no doubt, but trailing off into thin air, as though there were no substance to it, no real breath behind it. Madge walked dazedly down the hall to the elevator, wondering what he really meant. It was as if she'd followed trustingly along the way he'd said to go, and now suddenly she was left with the feeling that he was just pointing the way, not leading any more. But of course, she told herself quickly, that was just her imagination, and sheer nonsense. The man was tired out, that was it, worn out by worry; he didn't have the energy of reassurance left in him at the moment. Even Madge's imagination did not go so far as to tell her that that was actually the last time she would ever see Mr. Hawley

Chapter Eight

THE DAYS WENT ON, AND THE DISTURBED CONCERN WHICH MADGE HAD felt that afternoon subsided easily as though there had been no center of reality to it. Mr. Hawley telephoned her several times to report on the sales of the Fairlie Company stock. It was moving slowly, he told her; the price was soft, and he didn't want to press on it. But presently he reported that all but 400 shares had been taken, then all but 200. And then when it was all sold, he reminded her again that she had better see Mr. Briggs, her lawyer, as well as the trust officer at the bank, and arrange about having a trust deed drawn up to take care of these funds. Madge's heart sank promptly at the thought of trying to arrange anything, and her mind automatically postponed the actual making of any appointment. Mr. Hawley's voice on the telephone was measured and steady and business-like, and she couldn't imagine now why she'd ever had that unreasonable sense of apprehension and uncertainty, of shock and distress, like a sudden stiffening of inner muscles, as though her feet had felt shifting sand under them.

She kept on running the house in the same way she always had. The new maids Margaret had found were fairly good and would do for the present, Madge thought; a man had been engaged to drive the car and do the chores around the house which Sims had always done, and she had also insisted on engaging a nurse for Joan, when she found Margaret had none, though Margaret herself had been quite unresponsive about it. As for herself, she dropped back quietly into the ways she had followed three years before. At Mona's urging, she went back to several of the committees on which she felt so futile and out of place, knowing that all they wanted from her was financial support. She went back to her old sewing club which had knitted socks and sweaters during the World War, and suits and dresses for themselves

153

during the twenties. Now they were sewing on children's clothes for unemployed families. Down through the years they had talked about their children and their diets; and Wilson and Harding and Prohibition. Now they talked about their grandchildren and their diets, and Hoover and the Depression. They always came back to the Depression these days, and more especially to what one or another woman's husband said about it. Madge, having no one to quote, sat quiet as usual.

But there was a conversation one afternoon which she remembered longer than some of the other ones, if only because—for her—it pointed up so sharply what followed right after it, like a heavy black exclamation mark in her own mind. One of the Girls had said, with a wistful sort of nostalgia, "I wonder if things will *ever* get back to normal again?" and another, whose husband—Fred Ownsley—was head of Associated Industries in that region, had spoken up briskly.

"Well, why not, for goodness' sake?" she said. "We've had these depressions over and over again. This just happens to be a worse one than some of the others, and so people have gotten scared to death, and defeatist about the whole future."

"I don't blame anybody for being scared," Emmy Burns said in a quiet tone, "when one's income just melts away like a butterball in the sun. . . ." She smiled slightly as she said it, but then she added a little dryly, "You know what someone said the other day—that you can always adjust your living to a smaller income, but you can't adjust it to no income at all."

Madge looked over at her, wondering what on earth there was that she could do for Emmy that her friend wouldn't resent. Next to Mona, she was fondest of Emmy; sometimes she almost thought Emmy came first, because Mona was so capable about life, but Emmy had had a great deal of illness and seemed to need her friends more. Emmy had never married; she'd been a teacher when she was younger but hadn't been strong enough to keep it up, and for a number of years she had been living on a small income left her by an aunt. With all her doctors' and hospital bills she must have found it terribly difficult to make out. But it was so hard to help people sometimes. They were so sensitive . . . And just then, after the slight pause which had followed Emmy's remark, another woman spoke in a rather hushed and puzzled way. "Do you know," she said, "*I* read somewhere the other day that eighty per cent of the people who had money when they were forty have lost it by the time they're sixty-five?"

It seemed an almost indelicate thing to say just then—and not quite relevant. Or was it? Mrs. Ownsley, for one, seemed to consider it irrelevant.

"Oh that's another thing altogether," she said decisively. "That's just bad management—carelessness and ignorance about what to do with money when one has it . . . But what we're talking about is the business cycle, really. Fred says we're at the bottom of that now, and we're just like someone who's been awfully sick and can't even imagine ever being well again, when he's actually starting to get better already and really can't help getting well—if he doesn't throw himself out of a window or off a precipice, like jumping off into socialism or something." She looked around the group with her bright, roving glance, as if to gather them in, to fuse and infuse them with Fred's robust common sense. And then she stood up with decision, as if there were no more to say. Later on, Madge remembered her standing there, smoothing her skirt down over her stomach and waiting for a moment for the others to get up too. As she stood there she reached out a hand idly, to pick up the evening paper which had been brought in and left lying on a table near her. She glanced at a couple of headlines and was about to lay it down on the table again, when she gave an exclamation.

"Good heavens!" she said sharply, to no one in particular, but since Madge happened to be nearest her, she was the one who said, automatically, "What's the matter, Mary?"

"Why, this says—I can't believe it—it says John Hawley died last night."

Madge just looked at her.

"Died?" she repeated, stupidly.

"Last night. At his home. Why, I saw him only the other day—leaving the Town Club I think—yes he was just coming out after lunch—and he seemed perfectly all right." After a second Mary Ownsley added in a puzzled way, "I didn't even know he'd been ill."

"So did I," Madge said dazedly. "See him, I mean . . . Not long ago, that is. He looked very tired. . . ." She heard herself saying the words, but they didn't seem to mean anything. From the others there was a slight flurry of interest in Mrs. Ownsley's news—for she seemed to have appropriated the news from the paper. Some of them didn't know who Mr. Hawley was, so she told them.

"One of the oldest investment houses in town," she said. "Oh really, one of the finest firms—I've often heard Fred say so. He was the senior partner I think, since Mr. Funk's death. Fred thinks a great deal of him. Oh, I am sorry about this."

But it was Emmy who turned to Madge as they went out to the hall. "Isn't that the man who looks after your business affairs?" she asked, with a suggestion of concern, and Madge nodded.

"Yes," she said. "He does. I mean he—did." She couldn't seem to say any more. And driving home, she couldn't seem to think about it, or him, at all clearly. She was shocked, yes, and a little numb from the shock, as though Mr. Hawley had been much closer to her personally than he really was. But there was something else besides the shock: a feeling of trying to see around that small item in the paper, as if there were something to be grasped behind the bald announcement of his death.

She came into the house feeling small and forlorn—and tired as though John Hawley's fatigue had settled down on her. She was glad to hear Clay's and Margaret's voices in the library. It must be later than she'd realized, nearly dinner time. But she went back to the library to speak to them, just to feel them closer, before she went upstairs. Clay was standing with his feet apart, and his back to the fire; Margaret was lounging with her feet tucked up, in a big chair near the table. The paper was lying there near her, but she wasn't reading it. Madge said hello to them, in a subdued way, and then as if she couldn't keep it to herself, she asked, "Did you see the notice about Mr. Hawley in the paper?"

Margaret looked faintly surprised.

"Why, no. I haven't read the paper."

"What about him?" Clay asked.

"He—died last night," Madge said in a small voice.

"Why Mother! How dreadful—had he been sick?"

"I don't—think so. It's right there—lower down—on the front page," Madge said, making a small gesture toward the table.

"And how many stories up might the offices of Funk, Hawley and Purcell be?" Clay asked suddenly. Margaret, who had picked up the paper, gave him a rather sharp glance, as if to stop him.

"He didn't die in his office," she said quickly. "Or—"

"Or even jumping out of it?" Clay said imperturbably. "You don't say." And then he seemed to feel some sort of compunction, and turned toward Madge, though she didn't know what they were talking about. "I'm sorry. I guess you'll miss the old boy at that."

"Yes . . . yes, I will." There was a moment's silence, while Madge hesitated inside the doorway. "I must go up and get ready for dinner," she murmured, and half turned, and stopped again. "What did you mean then, Clay?"

"Me? When?"

"A minute ago—when I first spoke of Mr. Hawley. You said something about how many stories his office building had."

"Oh, that. I didn't mean anything." Clay sounded awkward.

"You must have meant something."

"Oh, just some of my misplaced humor, I guess. Better skip it."

Madge looked from one to the other of them. Margaret had laid down the paper and was sitting looking at her long hands lying on her lap.

"I don't understand," Madge said, and Margaret spoke quietly.

"You said it, Clay. You might as well explain it."

"Oh hell, all right," he said irritably. "I was talking about another of our little American customs, Mrs. Fairlie. Maybe you hadn't heard of that one either." He was suddenly on the defensive again, speaking harshly as if impatient of her. "These guys have a way of jumping out of their forty-story office windows when the going gets too tough for 'em. The Big Boys, I mean—pillars of industry and all that. The ones the country's built up into a great golden legend. Their finances get a little too fancy, see—they get themselves into very fancy jams, and they can't take it—the yellow-bellied—" He stopped himself short, as if with some effort and then went on heavily. "There've been dozens of 'em, Mrs. Fairlie, believe it or not—hopping out of New York office buildings, and Chicago office buildings and points west and south . . . well, that's that." Clay said again, abruptly. "You asked what I meant —and that was it."

"You shouldn't joke about such things, Clay," Madge said in a tone so low that it was nearly a whisper.

"I wasn't exactly joking," he said grimly. "They make me sick to my stomach, if you want to know." But he turned around, away from Madge and toward the fire, as if through with the subject, and when Madge spoke again, it was more as though she spoke to herself.

"Oh no," she said softly. "No . . . He died at home, in his sleep. A heart attack, that's what the paper said. One never knows about a heart . . . Poor man . . ." Then after a moment, as though reminding herself, "I must go up," she murmured again, "and change my dress for dinner."

*   *   *

She didn't sleep much that night, though she went early up to her room. All through dinner, and while the three of them sat together in the library, there was no further mention of the subject which was surging back and forth through her mind. It was as if someone had made a rather coarse remark (as perhaps, in one way, Clay had), and they had all decided tacitly to ignore it. Madge was really afraid to bring it up again. She'd spoken to Margaret once recently, about the changes which Mr. Hawley had advised her to make, but there was always something like a deliberate withdrawal in her manner whenever her mother touched on such things. As if to say, almost pointedly, that they were no concern of hers. As for Clay, she didn't want to give substance to his monstrous suggestion, even by referring to it again. Because it *was* monstrous. It must be.

And yet she took it to bed with her, and there it hung in the upper shadows, all night, though every now and then she would try to turn the light on it, both actually and metaphorically. After all, what was this idea that he'd put into her head? That Mr. Hawley might have committed suicide, that was it; and so, by implication, that Mr. Hawley might have been in some awful financial mess, and quite possibly taken advantage of his clients . . . No, no—she couldn't believe that. That was just her silly imagination again. He might have lost money, yes; everybody had, apparently. But there was no sense in looking for anything worse. There was no *sense* in fancying that his death was anything but that of an overworked, overtired man in his late sixties.

And yet—and yet . . . The trouble was that Madge herself had felt something puzzling and out of place, even before Clay had put the notion in her mind. Or maybe it was the other way around, that certain things fell into an unexpected pattern, too neatly. Mr. Hawley's anxiety to see her, his immediate pressure to make such big changes in Hugo's holdings so soon after she came home; his careful, measured explanations to her, which he knew perfectly well she didn't half understand. His sudden concern to introduce Mr. Purcell to her. And finally, as soon as he had finished up all those sales, his—disappearance, you might say, just as if he had planned to go away. Even those remarks of his which had had such an air of final admonition about them . . . and if he'd planned to go, there must have been some reason. Perhaps he *had* gotten terribly involved, used peoples' securities to try to extricate himself; perhaps he'd already used all the money from the Fairlie stock. Maybe it was all gone, that very minute . . . Madge didn't know how these things were accomplished, she only knew they happened. You read about them in the papers, though you never expected them to happen to you.

She wasn't even sure now where that money from the Fairlie stock was supposed to be. Generally, she thought worriedly, funds from sales like that were held there at Mr. Hawley's until they were reinvested. But he'd suggested having the Trust Company invest this for her (why had he ever suggested that?), and she had no idea whether he had transferred the money to her account in the bank or not. She was so hazy about that kind of thing, never was quite sure what those deposit slips stood for. What her balance was, even. Oh, she was such a *fool* about it all. She didn't even know how much of Hugo's estate had been in the Company. Mr. Hawley had said a large part of it, but she didn't know how large. *She just didn't know.*

She turned on the light again. It was quarter to three. She had tried reading a magazine two hours ago, but couldn't keep her mind on it. She had been up and down three or four times already, sipping little drinks of water, adjusting the blankets, lowering the window part way. Now she put on her slippers and quilted dressing gown, and shut the window all the way. The nights were getting cool now. She started walking up and down, from corner to corner of the big square room, in the hope that if she walked long enough maybe she'd be too tired to think or wonder or worry any more.

The fact was that it was the first time in her life that Madge Fairlie had ever worried about money, and she didn't even know how to go about it. There was nothing she could take hold of, to make comparisons, or see how well or badly off she really was. Mr. Hawley had said she would still have "Plenty"—but maybe he just meant she would have plenty to live as Emmy Burns did, in a two-room apartment; or the way Lou had, with handouts from others to help her along. Only Madge was the one who had always given the handouts . . . she'd never even stopped giving Margaret her ample clothes allowance.

Hugo never should have left her so much money, unprotected, Madge thought suddenly. For it wasn't she, it seemed now, who was unprotected; it was The Money, like a member of the family itself, at once the most powerful and the most vulnerable member. A sudden puzzling question came to her, whether, after all, the Money was supposed to take care of her, or she was supposed to take care of it. It was a sort of entity in her life, but she had never tried to figure out her relation to it as such. What was it that that woman had said only that afternoon? That eighty per cent of the people who had money at forty had lost it before they were sixty? (Or was it the other way around?) Madge wished now that she hadn't heard that remark. It was not a very nice idea to come back and haunt you in the middle of the night.

She moved restlessly, enlarging her circuit, on into the small sitting room next her own room, where the shades were up and the light from the street lamps was spread about as clearly and more evenly than from the reading lamp in the other room. She went over to the window and stood looking out on the Square below. Elephant Square, which had seemed such a stronghold when she'd first come there twenty-five years ago. The leaves on the trees were going now, and it looked drab and cold with its clothes partly off. You could see through the ones that were left, see all the paths and the benches, even the empty wading pool, as though you were looking through a threadbare piece of cloth. It was a discouraging view at this time of the year, and yet Madge was so used to it that it held a certain comfort for her. Until she thought with a kind of shock, maybe she'd even have to sell this house . . .

Strange, that the thought of that should spread such a chill all through her, when the house itself had so often appalled her. She hadn't even known that she was very fond of it, after all she had lived through there. But there was a fright and loneliness in her tonight, lying coldly at the heart of all her confusion. It was different from her accustomed sense of inadequacy, though it fed and grew on that. She knew how little use she'd be if she ever had to get out and earn her living. And she knew that other people lost all their money—so why, after all, shouldn't she?

She turned finally and padded slowly back to her own room, crawled back into bed and lay there very quietly now, with such a feeling of waiting helplessness as to be almost drained of worry. Whatever was coming was lying ahead of her there in the unborn but already conceived daytime. She must have dropped off to sleep at last somewhere between half-past three and four. She slept uneasily at first, and dreamt a little now and then, as though continuing to think even in her sleep. She turned and twisted a good deal, and then grew quiet and slept heavily for a couple of hours.

When she woke, her first realization was of how utterly battered she felt, as though she'd rolled down a steep hill, or been run over by a heavy truck. Or as though she were sixty-five, instead of forty-five, perhaps . . . And then she remembered the reason, but it didn't seem quite real now. One always magnified things so at night. Perhaps all that mental night-sweat had been nothing after all: just a passing thing like a sudden infection. Yet she knew the cause of it was still there.

Mr. Hawley was still—dead. Perhaps she would know soon what had really been the cause of his death. At least she would call as soon as the bank opened and find out whether any large deposits had been made for her lately. Or not . . . Meantime she had to get up and get dressed and go down to breakfast. One always had to get up. If you didn't even bother to get up, that meant you were really through, didn't it?

They were all rather quiet and abstracted at breakfast, and Madge was thankful for it. Afterwards, she went about her usual routine, consulting with the cook, planning the meals for the day, telephoning the orders to the shops. It seemed a footless routine today, but she knew she had still an hour or more before the bank opened, and she could call. It never occurred to her that she might have called Sidney Corey, one of the vice-presidents whom she knew quite well. She took for granted that she had to wait for time and tide and regular banking hours.

And so she went about arranging the flowers as usual. She generally enjoyed that, but this morning she began wondering in a somewhat masochistic way whether there were any shops that employed flower arrangers. There must be lots of women who could do that, and little else. She could even imagine what a rush there would be if anyone were mad enough to advertise for Middle-Aged Ladies to Arrange Flowers Artistically. . . . She thought of the day not long ago when she had advertised for a nursemaid for Joan. She'd gone out very early for some reason, and returning before the morning was half over, had found, to her surprise, that two women were waiting in her own vestibule. They started to speak to her, but the new maid who had opened the door had spoken up first, quickly and firmly.

"There's other ones ahead of these, Mrs. Fairlie."

Madge didn't know what the girl meant until she followed the gesture of her head and moved on into the hall, where she stopped short in consternation. There were women all over the hall, sitting on all the chairs, on the carved chest, on the lower stairs, leaning against the long table, standing along the wall. It was unbelievable—but there they were. Young women, and girls in their teens, and middle-aged women, some decently dressed and some shabby, several even rather unkempt. There must have been forty or fifty of them crowding Madge's front hall, for most women, it seemed, knew something about children, or thought they did. It didn't take training to be a nursemaid. That appeared to be the general assumption, or the common hope.

Well, arranging flowers was even simpler and easier, wasn't it? Madge had finished the last bowl now, and going into the hall again she saw that it was suddenly time to call the bank. She didn't hurry, but went up the stairs steadily, to the little sitting room, where the upstairs telephone was. She sat down on the straight chair beside it, because it was better to be sitting on something solid when bracing oneself against the unknown. She had to look up the number of the bank because she never could remember it. Then she had to wait while she got the right department. And then she had to explain, and as always, Madge's explanation grew a little involved, and made for some confusion and delay.

She waited with the receiver at her ear, for several long, eternal minutes. Margaret came to the open door and paused there, holding the baby on one hip, and Madge looked up at her blankly.

"Good morning, dear," she said, as if she hadn't seen her since the day before. "Are you going to take her out to the Square yourself today?"

"Yes, I thought I would. Want to come with us?"

"Why—I don't know . . . I—" she broke off vaguely. "I just had to put in this call at the bank," she started explaining. "I wasn't sure about my balance, whether Mr. Hawley had transferred the money from these last sales . . ." She hadn't meant to go into that at all, and as it got away from her she tried hard to make her voice sound casual. But she ran the palm of her free hand down the knee of her skirt, because it seemed to be a little damp. And then as Margaret still stood there, frowning in a puzzled way, shifting the heavy baby from one hip to the other, Madge spoke suddenly, rather hurriedly, into the receiver again.

"Yes? Yes, if you'd just give me the deposits on this month. I wasn't sure if I'd entered them all. Yes, and the dates too, please. What was that last date? I see. Thank you. That's the final balance, then? Yes I think—that's all. . . . Thank you very much."

She put the receiver back on the cradle, and looked up again at Margaret. "It's all *right*," she said, and her tone went up a little, in slight, puzzled surprise. "Perfectly all right, apparently. I guess they made the deposits at the bank as each sale went through."

Margaret looked uncomprehending. "That's good," she said politely. "Well—do you want to come with us?" Madge's eyes were looking straight at her, but absently, as if she were still listening to the voice on the telephone. "Mother!" Margaret said, in a half-irritated query, and her mother's glance came back to focus on the two in the doorway.

"Why yes, dear," she said, rather groggily. "Of course I'll come. I'll be with you—in just a minute. By the time you've got the baby's things on . . ."

But she still sat there after Margaret had left the doorway. At first, the relief was so great that she felt a trifle lightheaded. It was a relief now, just to laugh at herself again for being such an idiot. And then after a couple of minutes, a feeling of guilt began to rise in her, of deep compunction and apology to poor Mr. Hawley. She was suddenly and deeply ashamed of herself for having had the least doubt of him, when he'd been so good to her. She hoped he didn't know. It was strange, the feeling one had that when a person left his body, his mind might still be hovering around, could even see into other minds. But if he could, he would know she was sorry too, wouldn't he? Would know how she appreciated all his careful planning for her?

Madge got slowly to her feet, but her mind seemed to pause again to consider. Her thoughts had found another block in their way. Because he *had* planned all that purposely, she was perfectly sure of it; more sure now than she had been in the night. She remembered, suddenly and clearly, his remark about not sleeping, about taking something to make him sleep. So that was it: sleeping pills. It would be quite easy, wouldn't it, to dispose of a little box, say, before the contents took effect? The doctor would know, of course, but that part just hadn't been published in the papers. That was done, surely, sometimes?

Madge walked slowly into her own room, and blindly toward the closet to get—what was it? Oh yes, her hat and coat. There was complete conviction in her now. She *knew,* just as if he had told her. John Hawley had been decent and honest, and conscientious, but he was a tired man, too tired to begin all over again. "A lot to learn," he had said, "for those of us who aren't young any more." That was the thing, Madge thought. He was getting older—and he had no family, of course. When the world changed, young people could change with it. But when you had learned to live and think along certain lines, you didn't know how to begin all over again. And sometimes you couldn't sleep. . . .

It wasn't night now, and the fantasies had faded. But the fear which had come to her—a flash of purely personal fright, which is the only thing that teaches people what fear is—that was still there, something she would have to live with now, as other people did. Not wondering where her next meal was coming from. No, that was still just a figure of speech. Not wondering—yet—whether she would have to sell the house, or let the servants go, or cut down Margaret's allowance. But something akin to that, nevertheless: a third or maybe a fourth or fifth cousin of that primary fear which she had just begun to realize lay all around her. And she would have to learn to be careful, very careful, so that she wouldn't be one of that fated, submerged eighty per cent . . . by the time she was sixty. Or was it sixty-five?

Chapter Nine

IT WAS NOVEMBER NOW, AND THE LIGHT WAS BAD, EVEN AT THREE IN THE afternoon. Clay began feeling his side pockets for cigarettes, remembered that he couldn't smoke here anyway, and reminded himself, with that extra twist of the knife which he kept turning on himself these days, that it was just as well. Spending your days where you couldn't smoke cut down on the outlay for cigarettes. But then he began to be aware of the rotten light; it was just at that point where the electric lights didn't make much impression indoors and the daylight was a poor dim effort outside. His eyes were tired and his brain was tired, and all at once the ever-simmering resentment in him boiled up, and under his breath he said the hell with it, and snapped shut the book on Technocracy.

He got up and went out of the reading room with the book under his arm, nodding from habit rather than friendliness to the scrawny woman behind the desk. He didn't have to return it to the desk; he didn't come to the library just to read books which couldn't be taken out. He came there to get out from under Mrs. Fairlie's eye. But he was damned if he was going to stay there till the respectable businessman's hour of five o'clock, that day. Some days it got him right down to the raw, this set-up, and he wasn't sure how much longer he could stick it. This pussy-footing around his mother-in-law's house, this put-up job that Margaret had euphoniously dubbed his "research work" . . .

Not that he could blame it all on Peg. She *had* suggested that they go back to the Fairlie house for a while; that much had been her idea, all right. She'd pointed out that she'd have to open up the place and get it running for her mother and it would be easier being on the spot. Otherwise, he'd have to stay with the baby every time she went across to Elephant Square. What was more to the point, though, was that they were behind with the rent, and if they went over to her mother's they could use the rest of her allowance that month to get paid up. It would give them a breathing spell then to catch up for a while; no rent—no food—no lights—no gas for cooking. It would be a godsend, and they both knew it. And she had tactfully dwelt upon the fact that it would be a real comfort to Mrs. Fairlie to have them there for a while; it wouldn't be so lonely for her. And it needn't be long, just till they got in the clear again.

"And what," Clay had argued bitterly, knowing himself already licked, "is your mother going to think when she comes back and finds me cluttering up the house all day and every day?" Margaret had been silent for a minute then. "You know how much your family thought of me in the first place," he reminded her, "and I'm damned if I'm going to have that thrown up in my face from the start—that her good for nothing son-in-law can't even find work to support her little girl."

"She wouldn't say that," Margaret said gently.

"Well, she'd damn well think it."

"You wouldn't have to stay around all day, dear. You could—well, you could go to the library. You often do."

"Or out to sit on a park bench," Clay said. "Thanks."

Margaret forbore to mention that he had spent a good deal of time that very way during the past summer. She just said patiently, "But you have been interested in reading up on all that economic stuff. You could just make a little routine of it for a while, go over at regular enough times to give a suggestion of working hours. Mother isn't very observing, after all. And then you wouldn't have to feel sensitive about what she thought. Goodness knows, I don't want to make it any tougher for you, Clay. I just thought . . ."

It was the only thing to do of course, because they needed the breather that the visit with Mrs. Fairlie would give them. So he'd stuck it out, carried off the bluff like a goddamn grease paint actor strutting his stuff. But twenty-four hours a day was a lot stiffer than any job under Equity rules. Sometimes he sulked in his tent, and sometimes he just about blew his top over the whole business. He could feel the pressure rising in him this afternoon, and he walked fast against the wind, partly to work it off, partly to keep warm. He had no heavy overcoat, and he was toughening up, keeping the old medium-weight one against the really cold weather. It made him feel better with himself, gave support to his own opinion of himself to know that he was tough physically. Some day maybe he'd get a job digging ditches. God knew he'd tried everything else.

The bond house had let him out early in the game, as he'd been one of the late comers. Cut off his salary first, then let him ride along on commission. Only there weren't any commissions. He tried to sell insurance for a while after that . . . "on commission" again. Unquote! Then he'd taken on some electric appliances and gadgets, house to house. But people didn't want gadgets. What's more, housewives got so sick of opening the door to real panhandlers they got so they wouldn't open them to anybody half the time. Clay persuaded the appliance company to take him on at the downtown office during the Christmas season, but then the whole branch closed that February. He hadn't had any job at all for over five months now. He still kept making the rounds, like a dog on a watchman's beat after his master was dead, or like a horse on a milk route—without any driver—without any clients—without any milk. That was all the good it did. Meantime they'd been living on that putrid clothes allowance and the baby wasn't paid for yet.

And here he was now, living directly on his mother-in-law and hating her for it. Not the usual mother-in-law stuff; she didn't bother him much personally; in fact he'd never stopped to think whether he liked her as a person or not. He regarded her more as a child than as an older woman, partly because she never seemed to belong in any special age classification, and partly because he had absorbed Margaret's patronizing attitude toward her and thought her a good deal of a little fluffy fool. What Clay really hated was what she represented in his mind: the people who had too much money—especially the people who didn't work for it.

He'd never liked Mr. Fairlie; he'd thought he was a chromium-plated, gold-zippered bastard. It was one of the unsolved but touching mysteries about Margaret that she could believe her father to be the finest and cleanest man who ever lived. But that belief was untouched, as far as Clay was concerned. He supposed what people said about a man's family being the last to hear anything about him was true, anyway, and he'd let it go at that. But for all his unvarnished view of his father-in-law in some respects, he had had a certain grudging admiration for his business talents. As far as he'd ever been able to learn, the Old Man had been straight in that line, and Clay would have been glad enough to emulate him. In fact he had every intention still of making a pile of his own whenever this stinking hell hole of a "depression" began to fill up again. He'd been studying business cycles—everything he could find that the wise guys said about them; he'd been plotting graphs and compiling endless averages until he felt he could have given odds to Hugo Fairlie himself and shown him a thing or two. Jeepers, what he could do now—right now!—if he could have laid his hands on some real cash. And there was that little bright-eyed, dim-witted dame with no more sense than a chipmunk, sitting on a pile of it as smugly as though it were . . . nuts. Yeah, nuts! It might as well be, Clay thought.

He went across the Square, not even seeing it. He knew it by heart and by fanny anyway. He'd tried every bench in it, last summer. He'd fished the kids out of the wading pool, and picked 'em up when they fell off that fool bronze elephant. He'd talked to all the bums who used to come there and spend the day, and sometimes the night if they could get away with it. All the *other* bums, Clay corrected himself mentally. The only thing he hadn't done was feed the fat dusty pigeons with dry bread—because that was a rotten waste of good food, and it made him mad every time he saw somebody doing it. Like old Mrs. Delephant, who cooed like a pigeon anyway . . . Oh, he knew the place all right, striding through it with his light blue gaze straight ahead of him, not even looking to one side or the other. It was like a climate he passed through; not November, and not August, but a definite and well-remembered atmosphere just the same. And he was in no better temper by the time he'd gone across it and reached the house.

The Fairlie Mansion . . . He let himself in, and swung the big door to with a hearty slam. He hoped the old girl had heard it. He was in the mood for some kind of gesture; a gesture of defiance, independence. Riot and Rebellion, maybe. And if she came out and asked, ever so mildly, in her naive surprised little way, how come he got home in the middle of the afternoon, he was just about ready to let her have it, in words of one syllable—and four letters too. It would be a pleasure.

But no one came out. The hall was completely quiet. He would have whistled to Peg, except that he didn't feel like whistling at all. He took a look into the empty library and drawing room, not really expecting to see anyone there, and then went upstairs. The door at the head of them, the one to Mrs. Fairlie's room, stood wide open with no stir of sight or sound beyond it. Clay felt a distinct, unreasonable sense of disappointment that she wasn't there to question him. He went along the hall to their own room, and there was no one there either. With a feeling of absent-minded frustration, he went to the bathroom, came out again and looked around, stood there and rubbed up his hair with both hands. (He couldn't even keep it as short as he liked any more.) Then realizing that his feet were wet, or anyway cold, he pried off his shoes without bending over: first the toe-sole of one against the heel of the other, and then vice versa. He looked down at the big darns in the toes of his socks, had an unformulated thought that he didn't care if Ma Fairlie did come in and see them and, leaving the shoes lying in the middle of the floor, he went silently out the door again and across the hall to the kid's room. He had another passing, unformulated thought that it might scare the new nurse into a cat fit, his coming in on her like that, without a sound, but nobody was in there either. No baby, no nothing. All out, damn them. Why couldn't somebody be around when he came home?

His exasperation was formless and foolish and he knew it, but that didn't make him feel any better. He needed a drink, that was what. That was the only thing that could make him feel any better. He thought of it standing in the baby's room, in his stocking feet, turned and padded down the hall again and down the stairs, but he wasn't at all sure there was anything fit to drink left in the house. Mrs. Fairlie didn't seem to mind having the stuff around, but on the other hand, she was oblivious of it, and since he and Margaret had laid off buying supplies of any kind, it just didn't get attended to. Clay had mentioned his favorite bootlegger to his mother-in-law, offered to put in an order for her, and she'd thanked him but never thought any more about it. Well, he'd look and see anyway.

Nothing in the sideboard cabinet but some old pre-prohibition, pre-war cordial: filthy sweet stuff to Clay's way of thinking. Nothing in the pantry cupboard except some de-likkered Virginia Dare—and yes, by golly—a bottle of gin, stuck way at the back. He thought it was full till he lifted it, but it was empty instead. He swore, took it out to the kitchen passage where there was a big zinc barrel for cans and bottles, and threw it in there. It would have been a certain microscopic satisfaction to him if it had broken, but it didn't.

He went out to the front hall again and stood figuring whether it was worth going across to the drugstore to see if old Hogan would loosen up on anything. But Hogan was as fussy about his clients as he was about where he got his stuff, and he'd said once, in flat terms, that he would make no charges of that kind on Mrs. Fairlie's bill, unless she gave the order herself. Clay felt in his pockets, and pawed over with one finger the handful of change he found there. He'd had a dollar that morning, but he'd split it for a sandwich and cup of coffee at lunch, and that was all there was. That meager handful of change seemed the last straw to Clay, in his aggrieved state of mind. Couldn't even have the satisfaction of turning alcoholic—without any dough, he thought morosely.

Even the afternoon newspaper hadn't come yet. He went to the front door and opened it to look around for the paper, then slammed it harder than ever, even if there wasn't anybody to hear it. He stomped up the stairs again, in a dull rage with everything—the house —the world—everybody in it, including himself. And on the top step, somehow, not noticing there was another tread there, or just blind with his own irritation, he stubbed his big toe horribly. He limped on into the bedroom again and let himself down into the large chintz chair by the window, picked up the injured foot and laid it tenderly on the other knee, and sat there nursing it, rocking back and forth in pain and muttering words to himself.

It seemed at that moment as though the whole place had conspired against him in small insidious ways until here he was left in the ultimate, silly humiliation of howling in his mind over a stubbed toe. This fat, plushy house, serving him up every luxury that a guy could want, but couldn't buy; his little nondescript nincompoop of a mother-in-law who probably saw through his bluff all the time; even his wife, the exquisite, composed, slightly superior girl who had married him, who looked cool but wasn't, who tried to barricade and defend him in her own inherited fortress but who had actually reduced him to just a helpless, fuming, non-paying guest. No—that wasn't fair to Peg, because the depression had him flat on his back before they'd moved in here; him and how many other millions like him? Only—well, it seemed as if Margaret's quiet, forbearing, anxious protection made him feel his impotence, not as a man but as a Person, more than ever.

He put his foot flat on the floor again after a while, and leaned his elbows on his knees and ran his fingers through the thick mat of his hair once more. And then dropping his hands and letting them dangle between his knees, he sat there staring across the room, his eyes a little lighter in their dark setting, as they always appeared when they looked both blank and intent. Clay Ferguson was a young man still, not yet thirty-five, but there were certain things about his face and posture, the look in his eyes, which belied it these days. Lines from nose to mouth, the drawn look and the flat color of the flesh across his wide cheek bones, the forward-growing set of his head on his stocky shoulders. As for the look in his eyes, it was one which flickered past, under guard, never quite pausing to reveal itself when anyone was there to observe. But that afternoon the look was plain; it was full of the war going on inside him, the confused and shifting battle between bitterness and bewilderment. If he only knew what to *do* to get out of this bog; it was the inaction, the deadly, day after day, unproductive waiting that got him down, that even seemed to paralyze his brains and guts as well. If he had any of either . . .

* * *

He sat there for fifteen or twenty minutes. Just sat. And then he finally picked up the book on Technocracy and jerked on the chain of the reading lamp beside him. He heard the nurse come in with the baby presently; he could tell who it was by the running, cooing murmur of the woman's voice as she came slowly along the hall talking to the kid. And about time, too, he thought, but made no move to go in to inspect Joan. He heard the telephone ring downstairs and someone go to answer it; so the maids were down now, and the velvet routine of the house was being smoothed out around him again.

It was nearly five when he heard the front door open and close and Margaret's and her mother's voices, at a distance first, and then coming nearer on the stairs. About time, he thought again, grumpily, and realized he was repeating himself to himself—which is much worse than repeating yourself to somebody else. But he made no move and didn't even look up when Margaret came in.

"Oh, hello there," she said. "I didn't know you were in yet."

He didn't answer and she went across to the bureau and began taking off her outer things. "Did you come in early?" she asked idly— just conversationally—but it was the wrong thing for her to say.

"Yes, dammit, I came in early!" he shot back, in a what're-you-going-to-make-of-it tone. But Margaret made nothing of it.

"Sorry I wasn't around," she said, knowing he'd missed her and was sore with idleness and loneliness, rather than with her.

"Nobody was around," Clay grumbled. "That woman had the kid out somewhere till it was practically dark."

Margaret had hung her things in the closet and was sliding into a kimona now, and sitting down on a low chair to change her shoes for slippers. She didn't answer until she had picked up the oxfords in one hand and was sitting regarding them.

"Well, I guess it doesn't matter too much what she does. We're going to let her go."

Clay leaned back and moved his gaze at last from the book to Margaret's face.

"What do you mean by that?"

"Just that," Margaret said. "Mother said this afternoon that she thought she'd been mistaken to insist on getting a nurse when I didn't really want one."

"Well, I'll have to admit," Clay said in a tone of badly strained patience, "that I just don't understand the way your mother's mind works. Not that it matters."

Margaret shrugged and got up, and then stooped again to pick up Clay's shoes which were still lying on the floor.

"No, it doesn't matter. I didn't really want the girl, you know—I certainly don't need her while we're staying here and I have all the time in the world, and if . . . when we move away and I have everything to do again—well, we wouldn't be able to pay her. So there it is. It was silly anyway, but Mother had this idea that I was too tied down, that we ought to get out more with our young friends—" Margaret gave a little laugh as she disappeared into the closet again.

"And what would be her idea now? She seems to change 'em like her hats."

"I think," Margaret said lightly as she reappeared in the doorway, "that she has some idea now of—economizing."

"You don't say," said Clay politely. "D'you know what brought on this burst of thrift?"

"I don't know. Maybe it was what I said about that silly hat a while ago, and people buying unnecessary things. Seems to me she's been a little—sensitive or something, about expenses since then."

"*She* should be sensitive about expenses!" Clay remarked, still in that carefully balanced, deliberately weighed voice.

"Well, I suppose even Mother has to think of expenses sometimes," Margaret observed. "Maybe she's had a dividend cut or something," she added carelessly.

"Maybe she's getting down to her last yacht," Clay said. "Like some of the other people we hear yowling about the depression." The pressure was building up in him again; Margaret could tell by the unnatural evenness of his speech, that he was just holding the lid on with his bare hands, and that it would presently be too hot and too strong for him.

"Darling, you mustn't mind her so. She just doesn't know what it's all about, because she's never had anything to worry about. I wouldn't have understood myself probably if—" She stopped abruptly.

"If you hadn't married me," he said.

"No I *didn't* mean that. I meant one has to work at least a little to know what values mean. People who don't do anything are shut off, some way. . . ."

Clay had held on about as long as he could.

"And they're the ones we're at the mercy of—all of us," he said, not so quietly now. "Absentee owners—lousy fat employers who are just living on their fat and don't give a goddamn if the wage earners starve when they're laid off—women stockholders who own more'n half the securities in the country, and have just as much intelligent interest in it as your mother!"

"Oh Clay, we can't help that—there's no use getting worked up again."

"That's what I said," he retorted, more loudly. "We can't help it —we're at their mercy. We can't get jobs—but that's when *they* begin to economize—corporations and individuals both. That's when Mrs. Fairlie turns off this poor devil of a what's-her-name—"

"Mildred," said Margaret.

"Mildred—Myrtle—Maisie—what the hell does it matter? Your mother knows the swarm of 'em that came trying to get that job. The house was crawling with 'em—fifty women for one lousy little job— and she takes her on for two weeks—"

"Three," said Margaret.

"I don't care if it's three or six!" Clay shouted, slamming the book down on the small table so that it rocked. He thrust himself to his feet. "It's all the same—there aren't any more jobs now than there were a month ago. Probably there are less. And here's this poor damn drab, thought she was settled down and doing all right, and now she's going out on her ear again with no more reason than—"

"Clay!" Margaret said urgently. "Honey, she'll hear you. She's probably right across the hall."

"She might as well hear," Clay said, striding around the room in his stocking feet. But his footsteps were the only quiet thing about him. "She might as well have some warning of what's going to fall on her. Isn't that fair? To give a yell when you see a ton of bricks coming down on somebody? I don't mind her knowing how I feel about it, believe me! She needn't think it's any of my doing. I'm not having any part of it, see?"

Margaret had been sitting on the side of the bed, watching him helplessly; her eyes following him, distressed and pitying, yet somehow clear and undeceived, seeing him as he was instead of as she'd hoped he might be. They'd been all through this before, not this incident, but others like it. Some small impetus that set off the train of all Clay's explosive frustration. She couldn't stop him and she couldn't help him, and yet she couldn't let him be overheard, all over the house, maybe. The door was closed, but even so . . . Perhaps if she just went out, herself, across the hall—he'd stop, and she would see whether the girl really was there or not. She got up and went past him to the door, and Clay turned in the center of the room, to follow her now, with his eyes and his words too.

"How'll you feel if she decides she'd better economize on us too?" he asked. "I eat a lot, you know, when I get the chance."

Margaret opened the door and closed it behind her and went quickly across the hall, and as she did so, some image registered in the corner of her eye, though not for the moment in her brain. She saw at once as she went in that the room was empty. Mildred was giving the baby her supper downstairs then; thank heaven she hadn't been there to hear Clay. He was getting beside himself these days; not that she blamed him after all these discouraging months—not really. She had tried and tried to reassure him that it was no fault of his own, that everybody was in exactly the same fix. Well, almost everybody. Her father wouldn't have been, of course . . . No, not ever, no matter what conditions might have been around him, or on whatever rung on the ladder he might have been. But there was no possible point in thinking of that now.

And then, as she stood there, she realized suddenly what that image in the hall had been, which she had caught out of the tail of her eye. It had been her mother, standing hesitantly in the doorway of her own room, down the hall, brought there no doubt by the sound of Clay's loud voice. Margaret knew quite well, even in the midst of her own sense of guilty shock, that her mother wasn't trying to listen, only that she'd been startled by the noise, probably wondering what it meant, or if she should do something about it. At that distance, Margaret was almost sure she couldn't have heard his actual words, which was lucky. She must have thought they were having a terrific fight, but that was better than for her to hear what he'd really said; she'd just have to think what she wanted to. Margaret recrossed the hall, glancing that way, but Mrs. Fairlie was gone now. Her daughter went back into her own room again, and her face was expressionless. Clay was still standing in the same spot, with a baleful eye on the doorway.

"Well?" he began immediately.

"She wasn't there, thank goodness," Margaret said, even more quickly. "But Mother was—down the hall—standing in her door."

He grinned, not altogether pleasantly.

"Maybe she heard something that'll do her good," he said.

"She must have thought you were raising the roof, even if she couldn't hear what you said. Clay dear, you must be more careful. There's no use going off the deep end this way. You're only harrowing yourself up, and it does no earthly good."

"And I might get us thrown out—with Mildred—if she knew how I really felt, mightn't I? You wouldn't like that, would you?"

Margaret stopped close in front of him, and looked straight into his eyes.

"Would you?" she asked.

The color rose in his face, dark and painful, from his neck up over his jaw and cheek bones. Margaret came closer quickly, put her arms around him and her cheek against his. It was hot, as though he had a fever, but not as painful to feel as to watch.

"I'm sorry," she said quietly. "Oh Clay darling, I wish you didn't have to take it. I wish we could go, too. You know I do. But not right now—not till things begin to break—just a little . . ."

* * *

Dinner that night was like every other evening meal at the Fairlie house: there was a carefully set table, silver and glasses in geometrically accurate position, four courses carefully prepared and ceremoniously served. A delicious soup, a roast, two vegetables, celery and olives on the side, and jelly on the table; salad served separately with cheese and little crackers, a light dessert, and afterwards, coffee in the library. Margaret and her mother had both changed into afternoon gowns, soft dressy ones which had once been "best," but were now a little lower on the list. Clay had put on his coat and shoes again, had washed his hands and combed his hair down into its usual tight mat.

But there was some difference among them all, nevertheless. Coming to the table in his present mood only sharpened his awareness of it. The very way the table was set, the food, Myra's silk uniform— the whole gilded cage set-up—while here *he* was, just another unemployed bum. As for Margaret, she was putting on one of her best acts, taking pains with the desultory conversation, keeping it light. She was talking as if she were at a party, Clay thought. And Mrs. Fairlie rallied to meet her at times, and then seemed to wander off and leave her chatting by herself. Mrs. Fairlie had a slightly pinched, preoccupied look herself.

When they had nearly finished their coffee in the library, she seemed to want to say something. She looked from Margaret to Clay and back again with a lingering little smile. Suddenly she said, "You'll never know how lovely it's been for me, having you all here. I think if I'd had to come back to this house alone, especially at first . . ." She broke off.

"Why darling, we wouldn't have let you," Margaret took her up quickly. "And it's lovely for us too, don't forget that. I'm getting too spoiled for words again—and I love it!" She gave a small laugh, not quite spontaneous, and then she gave Clay a quick look across the corner of the room, as if to remind him of something.

"Yeah," he said, rising to the prod with a certain deliberation, "just think of the style you're getting us accustomed to. Why wouldn't we like it?" It was labored of course, even a bit lumbering, but you couldn't say he hadn't tried. Sit up, Fido, he told himself savagely. Now lie down—roll over, damn you. . . .

But Mrs. Fairlie didn't want to pursue the matter, it seemed, possibly because Myra came in for the coffee things just then. They were always so god-awfully well-bred and impersonal before the help, Clay thought scornfully. At any rate, she let the subject turn and slip off into something else, and drop to earth, like a paper plane which has not been properly cast upon the air. Clay picked up the newspaper, and Mrs. Fairlie turned to the incipient pink jacket which she was knitting for Joan. Margaret went upstairs to have a good-night look at the latter, and when she came back she glanced around the room restlessly, and then suggested a game of rummy to her mother.

They played for an hour or so, rather absently, without much conversation. Both looked up, a trifle startled on their respective side-tracks, when Clay knocked out his pipe and got up with one of his sudden movements.

"Guess I'll go up," he said. "I've got a book upstairs."

"Coming down again?" Margaret asked carelessly.

"Nope, I guess not."

Mrs. Fairlie put her hand on the table, face down, rather carefully, but she looked up with the air of catching at a decision before it slipped past her.

"There's something I must say to you both—if you don't mind waiting just a minute, Clay. It won't take long." Her glance had a faint appeal in it, and her voice was a little shaky. He stood with his hands in his pockets, looking down on her, one eyebrow higher than the other. "I've been putting it off," she said, as though making a confession, "but I know that's wrong, and it might as well be now." She stopped again, and the other two waited, in wonder chiefly, though there was a sort of stiffness in the air: it bristled with antennae. "I tried to say something earlier," Madge began again. "To let you both know how—how deeply I've appreciated your coming here and helping me over this first couple of months. It was one of the sweetest things anyone has ever done for me—" She spoke faster for a moment, with a touch of breathlessness. Clay and Margaret did not look at each other; they kept their glances apart, like skillful drivers avoiding each other at a crowded intersection.

"Well—" Madge took another breath—"I can't seem to say it properly. I just hope you know what I mean. But I know I've been selfish in letting you stay on. I know you both want your own place again. It's only natural and right, and I know you've just been waiting to see me established."

"We've been quite happy, Mother—very—comfortable," Margaret said, in a still, constrained voice.

"Oh, I know. You've been sweet and adaptable—even when it must have been a strain at times, being in someone else's house. I know it's different, dear, once you're married," Madge smiled across at Margaret. "But you see I realize that it has been a—strain, for you both, and that's why I can't let it go on. I've been selfish—but I'm not quite blind."

She stopped, and there was complete silence in the room. Margaret's fingers were resting on the edge of the table and she was looking steadily down at them. Clay had walked over to the fireplace and was standing there looking into it, though there was no fire going that night.

"You've both been so considerate that it's—awfully hard for me to say all this—but—"

"But you think it's time for us to move on," said Clay.

Madge lifted her head.

"It doesn't sound the way I mean it when you put it that way, Clay. I'm—trying to be unselfish about it."

"Sure," Clay said. "Oh, sure."

Margaret spoke quickly then, as if to cover up his tone, to muffle its echo in the room.

"Do you think you can get along all right alone now, Mother?"

"After all, she won't be alone, will she, with only five people in the house?" Clay said hardily. Madge moistened her lips and pressed them together, and then opened them again.

"No," she agreed. "I won't be alone."

"And that's really what you want us to do now?" Margaret pursued with a sort of relentless quietness.

"Yes," Madge said, after just a second's pause. And then there was silence again. They weren't helping her out very much. "Of course it will take you a little while to find a place you like," Madge suggested hopefully. "Though—I suppose there really are plenty of apartments available now. . . ."

"Matter of fact," Clay said abruptly, "this will free me to do what I've been threatening to for quite a while. Get out of this burg and—"

"Oh!" Madge broke in, involuntarily. "Go to some other town, you mean?"

"Yeah," Clay said, eying her with that cold, offhand look which he sometimes wore. "Why not? This place is dead on its feet anyway. I've been considering an—opening down in—well, down in Dorsey. So now that we're . . . free to move—" (he said those three words with a sort of relish) "I guess that's the thing for us to do. Don't you agree, Peg?" She looked up at him at last.

"I don't know," she said. She sounded as if she really didn't know what she was saying, or thinking either. "If you think that's the thing to do—now—at a time like this . . ." And then she seemed to break out of her trance, which was a sort of sleep-talking. "Mother," she said, "I think it's time for us to be frank with you. I'm sorry we haven't been before, but there's so much about the way things have been around here, all through the country I mean, that we felt you wouldn't know how to take it at first—wouldn't even understand—"

Madge looked away from her daughter's gaze as though a trifle bored, as if she'd heard about all she wanted to along that line. But it was Clay who broke into Margaret's desperate opening.

"Oh, I don't know," he said. "I think your mother is being particularly realistic. I don't think she needs any diagrams or explanations at all. Fact is, I think it's a darned good thing she brought this all up and put her cards on the table. Me—I'm ready to play 'em as they lie. Ready *and* eager!" he said, with rising emphasis. Margaret's lips were open, her eyes wider yet, staring at him, but he was cutting off any escape for her, any last minute capitulation, any throwing of herself and him on Mrs. Fairlie's small-minded mercy.

"So that's that," he said. "All very simple and clean-cut. We understand each other all right. No need to go into anything further. So now I'll go up and read my book—okay?"

There was a rough sort of bravado in his voice. Some of the old cockiness which repelled some people and appealed to others, which even now had one effect on Madge and another on Margaret. There was a suggestion of primitive, rather brutal elation in it, and Madge looked up and met the hard, half-insulting, half-engaging mockery in his eyes, with an apparent attempt at gallantry in her own.

"I knew you'd be glad, Clay," she said simply. "You've been—a very good sport all these weeks."

She picked up her cards again and looked at them as if wondering where they had come from, who had dealt them to her, as he went down the room.

"Do you want to finish the game?" Margaret said.

"All right."

"We're going to finish this game, Clay," Margaret said, without turning her head. "I'll be up in a few minutes."

He went out of the room and up to the second floor without even seeing the stairs in front of him. He *was* feeling savage, of course. He was possessed with rage, reasoning or unreasoning, and it was directed entirely at his mother-in-law. The stinking little hypocrite, he thought, pulling all that palaver about being unselfish, about setting them free, when all she was thinking about were her own precious, shrinking dividends. That was her revenge for the remarks she'd heard him bellowing this afternoon. Very neat too; no reference to that at all—complete ignoring of his crudity, his raw ingratitude. But if he didn't appreciate her hospitality, he could damn well get out and sell apples himself, and take Margaret and the kid with him. And *that* was about as raw as anything he'd ever run across, personally.

But thank God they'd held out. He'd thought for a minute Peg was going to cave: to come crawling in at long last with the tale of his joblessness through all these months. That would have put the cap on it for Clay. Sometimes he'd even thought it was foolish, himself, keeping up the pretense; sometimes his own puny pride didn't seem worth it. But Peg had bolstered him up in those moments. And then sometimes, when she'd weakened and said, "Oh Clay, let's quit struggling to save face and just tell her how things really are—" then *he'd* had the guts to hold out. So if they'd broken down after all that, just at the moment when Mrs. Fairlie had decided to call the turn on them . . . he didn't think he could have taken it, that was all.

He'd have just walked out on the whole bunch. And he didn't want to do that. He didn't want to walk out on Peg, because he still loved her, even if she did make him feel pretty small sometimes. He guessed she didn't mean to. And then he had to show her somehow, some way, that she hadn't made a mistake. He couldn't have done that, ever, if she'd broken down this time and shown him up before her mother. So he was thankful he'd been able to shut her off.

But what they were to do next . . . This idea of Dorsey—it might work. He knew he was right about the cities being the worst places to get jobs now. But of course he hadn't anything waiting for him down there, or he'd have gone long before this. It was just a jump in the dark, with a girl and a baby in his arms, not knowing if he'd land on his feet or his fanny, if he'd be able to feed them or not. Probably not. Well, then they could come back to Mother, couldn't they? They'd have taken the chance, and if he didn't win, he'd be the only one who had lost anything. Everything. Because he'd be through then, sure enough, and that was God's truth. Probably that was what Mrs. Fairlie was hoping for right now. Counting on, maybe. Booting him out subtly and temporarily, just to give him the chance to boot himself out for good. For keeps.

His anger against her was the stronger, of course, because it was tinged with terror. There'd been a fine bravado about it downstairs, and a sort of desperate determination which kept it up as he came upstairs, but now that he found himself in the bedroom again, it was the relentlessness of fear which kept him at it, damning her, when he ought to be making plans, being practical. He realized that, dimly, and tried to work it out, sitting on the side of the bed where Margaret had sat before dinner. Whether he'd better go down to Dorsey first, leave Margaret and Joan here . . . But if he did that, maybe he'd never get them again. They could manage for a while again on that allowance, if he didn't get something right away—that is, of course, if . . . *it*— the allowance was going to be kept up. Maybe she meant to cut that off too; maybe she was *really* economizing this time. Right down the line.

He sat there looking at this core of his immediate fear, which he'd felt like a lump at the center of his thoughts. He kept turning it over and over, in abject fascination. What in the hell *would* they do, if Mrs. Fairlie cut that off before he could get set? He'd had a contempt for it, and for himself all the time they'd been depending on it before, but he knew damn well that they couldn't have made out without it. The door opened, and his head jerked up as he seemed to put away hastily this thing which he'd been looking at. Margaret came in, closed the door, leaning slowly back against it until it latched, and staying there as she and Clay looked across the room at each other, steadily.

"Well?" he said, harshly.

"It's all right, dear," she replied, her tone as steady as her look.

"I really fixed it this time, didn't I?"

"I'm glad you—held out. I almost gave in, myself."

"I know," he said.

"And I'm glad you stopped me."

"Are you?" She came slowly across the room and sat down beside him. "Maybe we can swing it," he said grimly, "if . . ." He waited for her to say it, but she didn't. Finally he brought it out, miserably, shamefacedly, not looking at her. "I mean—well, what's she going to do—about the allowance? She going to cut that off too?"

There. There it was, the hard little core, taken out in the open again, and offered to her as if held in his hand between them, for both to look at.

"That's what she was talking about after you came up," Margaret said quietly.

"Yeah?"

"Yes. She—thought she ought to cut down a little, on everything, she said, especially as I felt the way I did about buying unnecessary clothes and so on."

"I see," Clay said. He gave out something which was meant to be a laugh.

"But she's going to do it differently from now on. I mean," Margaret said carefully, "she thinks it would be better if I had something in my own name, rather than just calling it an allowance."

"What the devil do you mean by that?" Clay demanded, staring at her.

"I mean," Margaret said again, "that she's sold a lot of Father's company stock; Mr. Hawley told her to before he died, apparently. So she's got that money in the bank now, and she's going to get them to figure out how much it would take to make about the same income as my allowance—maybe a little less, but then she's going to put that in my name. I mean the principal, is that what you call it?"

"The hell she is," Clay said, almost stupidly, and then he added suddenly, "In trust? Or as a gift?"

"No, she said *give* it to me. She said she thought maybe that was fairer, that we'd feel better about it, to manage it ourselves, and so would she, because she doesn't like the responsibility of it all anyway."

"My God!" Clay exploded. "Do you realize what you're saying?"

"I think so," Margaret said simply.

He had shot to his feet and was standing over her, still with that look of incredulity and amazement, but it was gradually being topped by hope, relief, elation, one climbing rapidly over the back of the other.

"Why, it changes the whole almighty picture—that's all it does! This way—well now we've got something to go on, don't you see? Something to work with."

Margaret looked up at him, not so much doubtfully as searchingly.

"But it's going to bring in less, if anything, than we had before."

"The hell it is! That depends on what's done with it. My God, this is *it*, don't you see? This is what I've been crazy for—it's what I've been working for, all the past five months—without even knowing I could use what I was learning. Markets—cycles—long-term trends—and this is the point, the very point in a life-time, where a fellow could break in at the bottom. Capital—that's all you need right now, if you know what to do with it. Capital to go into business on your own, capital to build up in the market as it starts to revive. Capital's what I've been crying in my sleep for, baby! Oh Peg, Peg, don't you even get it?"

He had caught her under the arms and lifted her to her feet. He was gripping her shoulders so hard that his fingers hurt, but she was beginning to smile now, with the contagion of his own exuberance, and with something more, which seemed to grow in her eyes as she watched him.

"That is—" He broke off suddenly; it was a short break but a sharp one, as if a pain had caught him in the side and shut off his breath. "God—I don't know what I'm saying. I'm off my head these days, I guess. It's your money after all—I haven't got any right to touch it, even for you and the kid. . . ."

"Don't be a fool," Margaret said, holding him still with the tenderness in her eyes. But his own look was strained and shocked.

"I couldn't have said that a couple of years ago," he muttered. "I don't believe I could have thought it. Your money—your family's money—was in the way then. You know that, Peg. I wouldn't have wanted to use it. Even that damned allowance always made me gag. But that's what a couple of years can do to you—make you grab at anything. like a pig in a trough."

"You're not—grabbing, at anything," Margaret said steadily. "I'm asking you to use it."

He ran his tongue over his lips once, as if they were dry.

"You mean you really—want me to try? Lord, Peg, if I could just use what I've learned these months, and build up something *for* you, make it into something that's ours together. My God, then I could hold my head up again, feel there's some excuse for my living. The thing is though—" and his voice cracked again almost as if he were sixteen— "whether you've got the faith left in me, to let me try. . . ."

"Why, of course I have," Margaret said quietly and sensibly. "You've just never had a break before, that's all. And if this is it, I want you to use it." Her own voice was as steady as her gaze. She kept it so. And if that gaze was still searching, as well as yearning, no other person could have assayed it, to find how much of each element it contained. Margaret herself couldn't have been sure just then. She loved Clay so that he seemed a part of her. And in that other part of her (even the part which was still Fairlie perhaps, and never Ferguson), she wanted very much to believe in him, to be convinced at last beyond all doubt or question that she or anyone else might raise against him.

Interlude

The Imaginary War

Chapter Ten

THE 1930's SEEMED INTERMINABLE TO MADGE, AS THEY DID TO SO MANY other people; but her reasons for thinking so were often quite different from those of the next person. She visited Margaret and Clay several times during those years, in Dorsey where they went first, and then out in Salt Lake City, where they moved next. Clay appeared to be doing well during the middle thirties, judging by the house they lived in, the car they now had, and so on. Actually, Madge knew nothing of his situation beyond those surface signs. She never asked anything about it any more, just as she forbore from ever referring to the property which she had turned over to Margaret, and which Clay was presumably managing for her. That, Madge felt, had nothing to do with her any more, or she with it. She had, simply, a sense of relief and satisfaction that she had taken that step when she had; Margaret's rush of almost emotional surprise had made her realize that there must have been resentment in her heart before, because none of her father's estate had come directly to her. It even seemed for a while that that might have been the main barrier which had stood between them, and with it gone that Clay and Margaret would be closer to her.

But that was one more false hope, because the barrier, whatever it was, remained there just the same. So she never stayed very long at a time with the Fergusons. She couldn't have said why, but she was uneasy in her daughter's house, and more so rather than less as the years went on. Margaret had become so terribly efficient, and the old habit of running her mother's life seemed to grow on her a little more each time Madge stayed with them. She was so calm and competent about everything: her house, her husband, her two children (young Fairlie had appeared on the scene in 1935) who were being brought

187

up in the modern manner yet who, strangely enough, were quite
well-behaved and agreeable children. Madge thought that Margaret
must have inherited Hugo's genius for organization, along with his
gray eyes and good bones; her efficiency was always reaching out for
more things to manage. She was active in the Junior League and
served on several boards and committees besides, and when Madge
came to visit, Margaret took her on too, like another committee
which had been poorly run and needed directing along the proper
channels.

Madge gave her child full credit for all that she did so well, but
she found herself wishing that Margaret would make a mistake just
occasionally. For Margaret, in her early thirties, was no longer quite
fluid, as a person; she was like something which had begun to
harden, slightly but unmistakably. Her patience with all of them—
her mother—the children—Clay—was quietly forbearing, almost too
rigidly forbearing at times, as though it too were set in a carefully
shaped mold. Madge wondered once whether Clay must not get tired
of that quiet patience, that bright determined steadiness, and then
she dismissed the thought hastily as a disloyal and frivolous one.
Margaret was just trying to live up to the pattern she had made for
herself, and it was a good pattern, and she came closer to it than
most people did, and that made them realize their own inferiority,
that was all.

As for Clay, he was nicer to Madge, in a patronizing sort of way,
than he used to be, but somehow she had a feeling that there was
still some guard in him which he kept up against her. Distrust—dislike—she supposed she would never know what made it. Just merely
being a mother-in-law perhaps. He was a moody man anyway, and
she wasn't at all sure that her visits didn't make him more so. She
became more sure of that when she visited them in the spring of
1938, for there was a stiffness and tension about him then, an irritability which seemed to be growing in him. Forlornly, sometimes, in
the Fergusons' pleasant guest room, Madge pondered why she should
irritate him so much, when she herself really rather liked Clay.

But after that spring, she didn't go back to Salt Lake for some
little time. And then, later on, Margaret suggested bringing the children to stay with her instead, which was much nicer, and seemed to
give her a more logical reason for keeping the house on Elephant
Square, too. For herself alone, the house seemed almost more than
she could bear. She often thought that she ought to sell it, and be
done with it. Except that you couldn't sell houses like that in those

days. You couldn't sell any house, Mr. Purcell told her; real estate was a drug on an already sodden market. Well then, she ought to give it away, she thought impatiently. But there were two things which held her back, aside from the simple fact that she didn't have so much to give away these days. One was that Margaret did seem to love to come back there for those visits, as though she found something both refreshing and sustaining in the shelter of the old walls. The other thing, the uneasy, illogical thing, was that Madge herself remembered, at disconcerting moments, the lost and rootless feeling she had had that one night in 1931, the night after Mr. Hawley's death, when she had thought she might *have* to move.

So she kept the house, to come back to. She would stand it as long as she could, for six months, or three—or a year, and then she pulled herself up bodily and went almost anywhere, to get out of it. She had gone to England a couple of times, once in 1933 and again in 1936, to visit Lou and Thomas who were living in a village in Sussex now. She would have gone once more in 1939, but then of course the war was imminent, and Madge was thankful later on that her perennial timidity had kept her home that year. And in between times she had gone south, to Florida perhaps, or out to California, not because she liked to travel any better than she used to, for she didn't; she still had to drive herself to attend to the smallest details, like getting her tickets and engaging reservations. She still couldn't sleep the first night on a train. But she went anyway, to get away from the House, which swallowed her up, and echoed back at her, and which she could never quite let go of—and she knew that she was inconsistent.

She knew also that traveling was frowned upon during the depression, not by the railroads or the hotels who desperately needed the business, but by people who could not go themselves. Just as, when she had bought a small new car to replace the old Lincoln, they had had a way of looking at it and saying in a subtly significant tone, "What a *beautiful* car . . ." which made her feel she had unwittingly, but nonetheless extravagantly, bought one with jeweled door handles or something. Madge listened to her hard-up friends talking about the depression, and realized now that they really were having a bad, and often a frightening time. She was shocked when she caught herself envying them from the bottom of her heart, just the same, because no matter how poor they were, they all seemed to have something that she didn't have: somebody close, somebody who cared whether they came—or went—or stayed . . . But she always managed to keep up the pretense that everything was quite all right with her, because she would much rather they went on feeling sorry for themselves, than for her, if it came to that.

She listened to them talking about the New Deal too, and President Roosevelt, and then the Recession, all in turn. Depression—New Deal—Recession—New Deal—it was a circle which they kept going around, at lunch, at dinner, year after year it seemed, like a record which had stuck in one groove. She would hear Ned Cressley, or Mr. Purcell down at Mr. Hawley's old office, declare roundly that the President was playing on the country's dormant class consciousness, that he was really out to ruin anybody who had any money left—and that meant innocent bystanders just like her, they would tell her. That Man, they called him . . . And then she would hear Clay Ferguson denounce other men—like good, honest old Ned for instance, who had worked hard and conscientiously all his life—and call them Reactionaries and Crooks and Economic Royalists, who didn't care what happened to the country as long as they saved their own tough skins. And it all seemed completely confusing and irrational to Madge, and she wondered if anybody really knew what he was talking about.

Even when the war in Europe began, she felt the same sort of confusion as to who was right about whether we should or should not—would or would not—get into it ourselves. The larger reasons for things always seemed to be hard for her to grasp, but in a small, personal way, she felt a new sort of lonely bewilderment as she worried about Lou. She urged Lou and Thomas, in 1940, to come over to stay with her for as long as they would, but they wouldn't come. They went right on, stubbornly sticking it out as things got worse, through one year—and then two, and strangely enough, the longer it went on, the less real they seemed to Madge. They had become a little larger than life size, like all the English people, in the unbelievable things they were facing and the jobs they were doing daily. They were super people now, it seemed, not just her own sister and brother-in-law. Madge kept sending them parcels of food and clothes, as much as she was allowed to send them, but that seemed to be all she could do. No more than for any stranger.

So there she was, still sitting on the outer edge of things, working down at the Red Cross, and knitting for Bundles for Britain, oh yes . . . but there was never the feeling of being inside, anywhere near the center of reality. She remembered the last war, and her thankfulness because Ronnie was far too young, and that queer unholy feeling mixed of guilt and gratitude, because Hugo was too old. And now, this time, they were neither young nor old: they were simply not there. Even in Margaret's family, it was Clay who was too old this time, and little Fairlie was too young. She visited Margaret and Clay again in the spring of 1941, and found to her surprise that he was doing defense work, something in an aircraft factory. Of course he couldn't say just what his particular job was but she suspected that he rather relished his code of secrecy this time, like a small boy in a mysterious game. As for Margaret, she was deep in the A.W.V.S. and several other things; Madge trotted after her, but never quite caught up—and she stayed only two weeks that time.

It was that same fall that she decided to go out to California and take Emmy Burns with her, for Emmy had had pneumonia the year before, and the doctors said this winter in the north might go badly with her. Madge had a hard time persuading her, for though Emmy's heart was bad and she was increasingly crippled with arthritis, she was still proud. She still needed some self-respect; just enough to live on, she told Madge, with that slight wry smile of hers, which was never really bitter. But it was finally agreed between them that she would take the trip down and back as Madge's guest, if they could stay in some small hotel or boardinghouse where Emmy could afford to pay for herself.

They went to a place Madge had heard of several years before, a big, old house overlooking the sea, in a small town two-thirds of the way down the California coast. The house was run by a stocky little woman named Mrs. Oakley, and called—not surprisingly, perhaps—Oak Lea. As comfortable as a hotel, Madge had been told, but more personal, and with just a few nice people staying there. It had a large living room with large sea windows where they all met and chatted in the evenings, and beyond that an uncovered deck stood out over the side of the hill, where Emmy could sit in the sun all day. Her bedroom was on the ground floor, so there were no stairs for her to climb. And for Madge there were walks to take, around the clover-shaped beach, or up the hill behind the village, and the weather was perfect all through November. She still went conscientiously to the Red Cross branch twice a week, but the war seemed even more remote to her here, perhaps because none of the other guests at Oak Lea seemed to have any close connection with it either. They talked about it of course, but it was academic—part of the news rather than a part of their personal lives. On the 7th of December Madge went out late in the morning—not to church, for she seldom went to church any more, now that she didn't have to represent Hugo there—but to walk around the curving cliff above the beach. It was a beautiful day, and she sat for a while on a bench, looking out over the sea, half hypnotized by its brilliance. She thought, not for the first time, how impossible it was to believe that a war was still going on over on the other side of that peaceful, sparkling stretch of water . . . in China or any other part of the world, for that matter.

*   *   *

The first impact was already over. That first day . . . when people took the news from the radio, like a bolt of lightning running through them: when they rushed to their telephones to pass it on, as though the current was more than they could bear, or contain, in their own bodies and minds . . . And then returned to the radio again, as if frozen to it by the shock . . . or went outside and spoke with stark frankness to complete strangers passing by. Or just walked by themselves, dazed, in the streets.

That first day was past, and with it some of the unself-conscious-ness which had rushed to the surface for a moment. Now people were beginning to think of themselves again, and of how this would affect them individually. Some had expected it to come, and some had not, but none of them had expected it to come in quite that way. Most of them were confused, between a bewildered impulse to do something, and an uncertainty as to what was the right thing to do. There were the young men who poured into the recruiting offices of course, driven by basic instinct more than any reasoning, perhaps. But among those who remained civilians, there was a certain lack of direction, a certain uncoordinated enthusiasm—or apprehension. People rushed out to buy blackout materials. They volunteered hastily as air-raid wardens, plane spotters, nurses' aides.

And on the coast, some of them wondered nervously whether they ought to stay there or move inland, and it was hard to tell whether they were the realistic ones, or the ones who were letting their imaginations run away with them. At Oak Lea, the Smiths had gone right out, the first thing on Monday morning, before Congress had even met to declare war, and got their train reservations to go east. And Ella Holcomb was wavering audibly—should she go home or not?—and whimpering a little again about how she missed her Harry —who had been dead two years, but who had always known what to do, always taken such care of her. Madge and Emmy wondered quietly, just between themselves, whether they should stay on or not. But neither one knew what to do, and each one said she would do whatever the other preferred.

"If you think it's wiser not to—" Madge said uncertainly, and stopped.

"My dear, I don't know what's wise or what isn't," Emmy countered. "But if you'd rather go—"

"Oh no, *I* wouldn't," Madge said hastily. Yet she herself was the worst coward in the world, and Emmy would find it out soon enough, if she didn't know it already.

So when Margaret called her mother on the telephone late that same day, on Monday afternoon, Madge was surprised to discover that she was feeling rather annoyed with the concern in Margaret's voice.

"This is the very first time I've been able to get through to you," Margaret said rapidly. "I've been trying for two days. Are you all *right,* darling?"

"Why yes. Of course I am," Madge said rather airily.

"Well, you must get out of there, you know."

"Why?" asked Madge.

"Good heavens, Mother, you're right there on the coast, with airplane plants above you and military camps below you, and goodness knows what else, though I suppose I shouldn't even be saying this on the telephone . . . And nobody knows *what's* going to happen next."

"Well, I don't think the Japs are going to land on the California beaches just yet," Madge replied mildly, unconsciously quoting somebody who had made some such remark at lunch that day. But Margaret didn't know that, and anyway, she had fully expected her mother to be irresponsible in this crisis.

"Now look, dearest, you don't know anything about it. Nobody does, actually, but there's no use in taking chances. There *may* be bombing any time. I want you to get on the train and come back here to us."

"Oh no!" Madge said at once, quite involuntarily.

"Why not?"

"Because—well, I think it's rather silly."

"Oh *Mother!*" Margaret exclaimed. "If you weren't always so impractical—so . . . Well, I can't keep this wire indefinitely you know, they ask you to limit your conversations. . . . What *are* you going to do, then?"

Well, what was she going to do, anyway? Madge hesitated. "I suppose—just wait a while until we see how things are going. . . ."

"And then it'll be too late," Margaret said ominously. "Look, Mother, if you don't want to come to us—though I don't see *why* you won't—but anyway, if you won't do that, will you go *home?*"

"No," Madge said perversely, "I don't want to go home. I've closed up the house for the winter."

"Honestly, Mother! As if that had anything to do with it!" Margaret's voice had a note of helpless exasperation in it, and then she softened it quickly. "Mother dear, don't you understand, I'm *worried* about you?"

"That's sweet of you, darling," Madge said, with a sort of gay insouciance now. "But there's no need for you to worry, I'm sure. We won't stay on if people really think we ought to move inland. But I think we'll just wait a little bit and see. . . ."

There *had* been talk all day, about one family or another who were moving or going to move back into the hills, though she hadn't admitted that to Margaret. Rather scornful talk, to be sure, but with an undercurrent of uneasiness in it, as though the speakers themselves weren't quite sure whether the movers—or the stayers—were the wise ones after all. It was a war still being fought in their imaginations, as far as civilians in America were concerned. A sort of imaginary war. And somehow the idea of picking up her suitcases and running for the next train or the nearest mountain did not appeal to Madge Fairlie at the moment. It seemed foolish and a little undignified, that was it—and here she'd been trying all her life not to be any more undignified than she could help. The fact was, she felt a trifle stubborn about the whole thing since Margaret's call.

It was while they were at dinner that night that the first alarm came. For a moment, listening to the siren from the fire house two blocks away, they all looked at one another wide-eyed, almost stupidly. It was only just after sunset, so it was not yet dark, but there was a hasty rallying around to cover the windows if the so-called blackout should continue through the evening. Mrs. Oakley came into the dining room with a harried expression and some heavy gray blankets over her arm and Mr. Wells started tacking them up over the big windows on the sea side, while Mr. Smith stood by and awkwardly tried to help him. It was a fumbling but earnest sort of business. There had been a rush on black materials to line curtains with, that day, and Mrs. Oakley hadn't been able to get enough for her large windows. The others looked on, wanting to help, not knowing quite what to do; trying to behave properly, not knowing exactly how to go about that either.

They all settled down in the living room presently, and made talk, bit by laborious bit. Nobody knew what the alarm was for, but the radio was off, and that gave them the sense of being quite cut off from the world. The women started to play an uneasy game of bridge, and the two men sat smoking and talking in low tones in the corner. Then after a bit, Mr. Wells got up with such an elaborate air of casualness that Madge couldn't help noticing it, and he went off— out the front door, to look at the blackout from outside apparently —while Mr. Smith sat stolidly on. They must have agreed that one of them should stand by, with the women, just in case anything should happen. Men were rather sweet sometimes, Madge thought. Some men. But funny too . . . because what could either fat, slow-moving Mr. Smith or long brittle Mr. Wells have *done,* actually?

Emmy revoked once, apologized with her wry little smile and said something about not being used to wondering whether a bomb was going to drop on the table any minute. The others laughed a little self-consciously, except Mrs. Spencer who remarked detachedly that one got used to it; they all turned to look at her then, until she explained, still matter of factly, that she had been out in China when the Japs came in there in 1939. Madge eyed her with new respect, but Ella Holcomb kept on sighing every few minutes, and tremulously wishing that *she* were used to going around the world alone and taking care of herself, but she just wasn't.

And then Mr. Wells came back and reported unemotionally what he had learned in the village. It seemed that the radio had been on for just a few minutes after all, and he had heard that there had been two enemy squadrons sighted off the coast near San Jose, about fifteen planes in each group. One had flown north past San Francisco and turned out to sea again; the other had flown south, and disappeared. No one seemed to know where it had gone. There was a complete silence in the room after Mr. Wells had given his report, in a rather apologetic not-to-make-too-much-of-it voice, and then Mrs. Spencer turned to Ella Holcomb.

"I said two spades," she reminded her.

But it really was a very queer feeling, to realize that those planes —the ones which had disappeared—might still be up there now, quite near, and heading their way. Queer to realize that the thing they'd heard about and read about, happening so far away, could happen quite near by too. It might not be just an imaginary war here, after all. There had to be a first time everywhere in the world, maybe, the way the world was now. Madge wondered what the others were thinking; she herself felt rather resigned and fatalistic all at once—but not calm. Oh, no. She might have pretended to herself that she was calm if it hadn't been for her stomach, but that gave her away to herself. It wasn't a matter of butterflies, the kind she usually had when she was nervous. No, this time her stomach had shrunk up into a tight little knot in the middle of her, that was all. She recognized the feeling with surprise, because it was just what she had read about.

* * *

Some people doubted the reality of those unidentified planes, and some swore they had been seen by too many eyes to be doubted. But nobody ever seemed to know what had become of them. There had been another alert toward dawn, and Madge was wakened by the howl of the siren in the fire station near by, and lay shivering in bed, wondering whether to get up or not, until surprisingly she went off to sleep again. It struck her later on that day as rather funny that the people who invariably complained of being light sleepers, all those who "wakened at the slightest sound," were the very ones who hadn't heard that siren at all. Emmy had one deaf ear, of course, so that was different; when she slept with the good one down she didn't hear anything at all.

Madge was beginning to worry about Emmy, beginning to feel responsible for her. She was pretty helpless in lots of ways: the arthritis made her so lame she couldn't move very quickly, and with her bad heart, any shock—if anything really should happen, that is . . . Madge thought maybe they were being foolish after all, to linger on. The Smiths had already left; Ella was still wavering about where to go, and when. And the war news was all bad. Madge wished she knew how Emmy really felt about going or staying.

And then one day she came in late in the afternoon from the Red Cross, where she was spending more days and longer hours now, and she heard voices in Emmy's room as she came into the front hall: one voice even more familiar than Emmy's, though she couldn't quite believe that she was hearing it, at first. She stopped at the open doorway and stared into the room.

"Margaret!" Madge said, in a stunned little voice. Margaret looked up and smiled (like an angel, Madge thought—she was so glad to see her!) and then she got up and came over and put her arms around her mother, almost protectively it seemed, and Madge found her eyes beginning to smart with unexpected tears. "Oh darling," she said, "it's so *good* to see you! I can't quite believe it. How did you get here?"

"By train," Margaret said easily. "Mere civilians can't get on a plane these days. Bad enough to get on a train—though it's easier at the moment because people aren't exactly crowding to get to the coast."

"Oh . . ." Madge said, a little startled by the implication, and then— "How are the children?" she asked suddenly, not knowing quite why she asked it, because of course Margaret wouldn't have left them if they hadn't been all right.

"They're fine. I left them in charge of Miss Moore—you know, the little retired schoolteacher I told you about."

"Oh yes," said Madge. "And Clay?"

"Clay's very well," Margaret replied. It sounded rather formal.

"He hasn't—well, of course he *wouldn't* go off and enlist, at his age, and with a family," Madge said hastily. "I don't know what even made me think of it."

"No, he's still working at the defense plant."

"And you—? How did you ever get away?" Madge smiled her question in tribute to all the projects which she knew Margaret must have left behind.

"I told them I was going to take four days off, come hell or high water," Margaret said, and she added gently, "I came to take you back with me."

"Oh," said Madge. She sounded more startled that time. So that was why. There was something like the beginning of a chill just touching the extremity of her senses. Something, which she couldn't possibly have identified just then, had touched the farthest edge of her pleasure in seeing Margaret. "But darling," she said, "I told you that we wouldn't stay if it didn't seem wise. We just haven't decided yet, that's all." She looked beyond Margaret to Emmy, who was sitting there knitting, watching them both interestedly, fondly, and noncommittally.

"Well, we'll talk it over after a while, shall we?" Margaret said casually. She had that pleasant, casual—and forbearing—tone, her mother thought, which she had heard her use so often with the children.

But that night, when they went upstairs together (fortunately, she'd been able to get the Smiths' still unoccupied room for her), and Margaret came into Madge's room and sat down on the bed to talk, Madge felt definitely oppressed, as if she were going into a committee meeting, or even as she had felt when *she* was a child, and was told to stay after school. Margaret would want, now, to go into the whole thing—and she didn't even want to talk about it. She had no real argument to offer when Margaret began, so reasonably and persuasively. Margaret said that people seemed pretty uncertain about what was going to happen out there on the coast, and she agreed. Margaret said that of course it *might* be all right and there would never be any bombing over here, but on the other hand you couldn't tell—and Madge might be taking a dreadful risk to stay in such an exposed place, so near to camps and factories too. The Japs could so easily miss a factory and hit Oak Lea, for instance. Madge didn't answer that, because she was ashamed to admit that she had dreamt the night before that that very thing had happened. Margaret said that, after all, nonessential people on the coast might be an actual handicap to the war effort. She said that Aunt Emmy was really pretty frail, and might prove quite a heavy responsibility if anything did happen. And Madge had to agree.

But then she added suddenly, "Did Emmy tell you whether she'd really rather leave?"

"No," Margaret admitted truthfully. "She didn't. She wouldn't say, I guess. She said whatever you preferred would be all right with her. But I can't understand why you would *want* to stay, under the circumstances."

"I don't know," Madge said. "I don't know that I do . . . We only came a month ago, though. And it seemed to be doing Emmy so much good. And I like it here, I guess."

"Oh, but Mother, that's so—"

"I know," Madge said quickly. "That doesn't matter. There's a war on."

Margaret watched her mother thoughtfully as she stood over there by the dresser and began to unscrew her small pearl earrings.

"There's no sense in it you know," Margaret said in a reasonable tone. "I mean, I don't see why there should *be* any question in your mind at all, under the circumstances."

"Maybe not in my *mind*," Madge said hesitantly, groping to express something, but behind her Margaret gave a little laugh.

"No, perhaps I shouldn't have used that word," she said. She probably had no idea of being offensive; that remark, indulgently

made, was just a reflection, if not a reflex, of the way she had been
used to regarding her mother all her life. But Madge turned slowly
around to face her again.

"Why can't you just let me decide the whole question for myself?" she said quietly. "Let Emmy and me decide it between us,
that is, not try to force me—"

"I'm not trying to force you," Margaret said. "Only to persuade
you of what seems so obviously sensible to me."

"But why should I do what seems sensible to *you*? Surely what
I do or where I stay is personal to me, isn't it?"

"Why, yes—except perhaps for the larger aspects of the war,"
Margaret began, a trifle sententiously.

"You just don't think I'm capable of making a sensible decision,
do you?" Madge spoke with a gathering intensity.

"Why, of course I do, darling," Margaret said indulgently. "But
you need just a little shove, you know, to get you going. You always
have."

"I always have," repeated Madge. "Well, maybe I have. But maybe
I hate running away from things too, even if I've always run before.
And maybe I hate being *pushed* around, even if I always have been
pushed!" There was an odd combination of petulance and passion in
her voice now, and Margaret seemed to be studying her, like an interesting problem, with a puzzled but still patient air of giving it her
careful consideration.

"Well, I'm not pushing you, dear," she said at last. "You sleep
on it tonight, and then we'll talk about it again in the morning.
You know I only want you to be where it's *safe*, don't you, Mother?
And I'd love to have you back there with me again—with us, I
mean. You know that, don't you darling?"

She stooped to kiss her.

"Yes. Oh yes," Madge murmured, that strange, stiff resistance in
her beginning to dissolve again into a wobbly contrition. "Of course
I know it. And I'm so lucky to have you, even to have you worry
about me. And I'm *not* just trying to be difficult. Truly I'm not."

She stood in the middle of the floor after Margaret had said
goodnight and gone along to her room, and put both hands up to
either side of her head, and thought, Why did I have to act that
way? Why do I feel like this, when she's come all the way out here
to get me? She came just because she was worried about me and
wanted me to be safe. (Safe . . . she thought in parentheses, I've always been safe, haven't I?) And I've always wanted her to love me,

and want me—and now she tries to show that she does, and I behave like a difficult child. I'll have to go, of course, even if I don't want to. . . . And I *don't* want to. I don't want to go home again so soon, and I don't want to go back to stay with them, with Clay being irritable and tense, and Margaret too rushed and busy already, but still trying to manage me—

Her thoughts broke off short at that point, like a string snapping, but she picked it up again, and followed it along. Was *that* why she didn't want to leave here? Was she really being as small as all that, in the face of all the danger, and grief, and turmoil all over the world? She dropped her hands to her sides resignedly. What earthly difference did it make? She was always trying to make some decision like this, where to go or stay—go or stay—and each time it *seemed* momentous to her. And of course it didn't matter in the slightest degree what a couple of detached and useless women did with themselves. They were just like a couple of stray cats anyway . . . nursing their own comfort where they could find it. She'd tell Margaret in the morning that she'd do what she wanted her to. And Emmy would probably be relieved, after all. They would all start east together; only Emmy, once ensconced, could just stay on the train and her brother would meet her in Chicago. . . .

But she and Margaret didn't discuss any of that at breakfast. Margaret was being very sweet and light and casual, and Madge was feeling meek and submissive again. However, she thought it was only decent to speak to Emmy before capitulating officially, so to speak. So when they finished, Madge went into Emmy's room alone. Emmy always had her tray in there and didn't appear outside until late in the morning. She was sitting in her big chintz-covered chair, and Madge noticed that she was fully dressed—same dress she had on last night, at a matter of fact—and wondered absently why she bothered to get up that way, why she didn't stay comfortably in bed, or at least in her dressing gown, the way she used to. Probably some little fetish in her own mind, she supposed, like an Englishman dressing for dinner in the jungle. Emmy was very conscientious. But Madge didn't ask any question about that; she spoke only of the subject uppermost in her own mind. She asked her if she wouldn't tell her how she really felt about staying on.

"I have told you," Emmy said simply. "Honestly. I would rather do what you prefer. I'm not trying to be self-effacing, my dear; it really doesn't matter."

Madge looked at her with a slight worried frown between her eyes.

"You were nervous the other night. We all were," she said quietly.

"Yes," Emmy acknowledged. "I guess we all were. It was such a new thing for any of us to face the thought of that kind of physical danger . . . But on the other hand—" She smiled and shrugged her shoulders. "In the day time, the sun—and the view—are very lovely."

"You do like it, don't you? And going back to that cold weather may be very bad for you."

"On the other hand," Emmy said again, "a bomb might be equally bad for me! So you see? It doesn't make much difference, when your life is close to the margin, either way."

"You won't help me," Madge said sadly.

"I can't, Madge. You must let Margaret help you, if you need someone's advice, or do what you want yourself, my dear."

"Well, you know what Margaret wants." Madge smiled rather wistfully, lifted her hands in a gesture of surrender. But that was all she had actually *said,* before Margaret came to the door.

"Oh, here you are," she said cheerfully. "May I come in?"

"Come in, dear," Emmy spoke up. "We were just talking about you, and what we ought to do." And there she left it for Madge to pick up and carry on. Margaret came into the room and put her arm around her mother's shoulders.

"Well, we're not going to argue any more about it, are we?" she said lightly. Madge looked up at her in surprise, and Margaret squeezed her arm gently. No, Madge hadn't been going to argue any more . . . but now, for some reason, because of something so sure in Margaret's manner, she couldn't seem to answer; not right away. She waited to see what Margaret was going to say. Maybe she'd even changed her mind. But Margaret went on easily, "I've just been on the telephone, talking about reservations."

"Reservations!" Madge repeated.

"Yes—for tomorrow night. And we're in luck, believe it or not. That's because I spoke to somebody on the way out, a man who just happened to be in the office here. He was very nice and said he'd see what he could do for me, if I called him direct."

"You mean you've already got something—for tomorrow night? For all of us? Or just for you?"

"You can make it by then, can't you dear? With me to help you both pack?" Margaret's arm was still around her; protective, or persuasive—which?

"I suppose—I could," Madge said very slowly, dragging her feet. "But Mrs. Oakley may not—"

"I've already spoken to her, too. She was very decent about it. She can see how people feel, after all—the ones who don't really live here—and she won't have the least trouble filling her rooms, with all the army and aircraft people who *have* to stay."

Madge moved slowly away, out from under Margaret's arm; just a few feet away.

"But I hadn't even told you whether I'd decided what to do," she said, in a constrained tone.

"Oh darling, don't let's go all over it again," Margaret said firmly. "You agreed with everything I said last night. I know how you feel about not wanting to seem to run away, but you can see it isn't being cowardly in this case; it's just being sensible and practical, from every angle. You know I'm right."

"Perhaps," Madge said. "But aren't you being a little high-handed also?"

Margaret threw a half-humorous glance at Emmy, as if to enlist her more urbane support, but Emmy, who never needed to look at her knitting, had her eyes firmly fixed upon it.

"Don't you think *you're* being a little—difficult, Mother?" Margaret countered. "You said last night that you wouldn't be."

"I said last night—" Madge began, and stopped. She was looking straight at Margaret, whose eyebrows were lifted slightly in annoyance. Yes, Margaret was annoyed, because she liked to have her plans work out. She was executive, like Hugo. She liked to manage things, and people, because she did it better than others did. And when she met opposition, she went right through it, as confidently as if she hadn't seen it was there at all. She had the tickets all engaged now; she'd already talked to Mrs. Oakley; she practically had her sleeves rolled up all ready to go to work packing them both up. It was all neat and shipshape and perfectly under control. But Madge was not going; she knew that now. The resistance of yesterday had stiffened up in her again, until it was taut and rigid inside her. She couldn't have loosened it at that moment, no matter what her reason might have told her. All she could do was to make her voice very mild.

"I'm sorry, dear," she said. "Sorry you went ahead with those things without speaking to me again. Because I've decided not to go just yet."

Margaret's mouth looked rather stiff now, as she spoke.

"I do think you're being very foolish, Mother."

"Maybe I am. I often am, I guess. But of course it's not a hard and fast decision. We can change it any time, when or if we decide it's wiser to go away."

"And very unreasonable," Margaret went on in a harder voice, as if Madge hadn't said anything. "Here I am now, and can help you. You've never liked making decisions; you've always liked me to arrange things for you, and now when I've done both for you—you choose to act like this. After all, it isn't as if I had tried to make a snap decision for someone I didn't know like a book. There's no use pretending we don't know each other after all these years."

Well, that was true, up to a point. And one of the things Madge had always known was that Margaret wanted her own way, had been very overbearing about it even when she was a child. Madge shouldn't blame her for it now, because after all it was her own fault for having let Margaret do this sort of thing to her for so long. Why did one's own children act as if their parents were *their* children, after they reached a certain age? It seemed to grow on them as time went on, too.

"You know too much, my dear—and too little," Madge said.

"I'm sure I don't know what you mean by that! You're just being evasive, Mother. You *know* I'm right about this. You haven't once been able to say I wasn't."

"Maybe you are," Madge conceded, but there was a finality in the way she said it which expressed opposition, not agreement. That was it, she thought. That was why Margaret had tried to make her come back with her: because she had made up her mind that it was the right thing for her to do, not because she *wanted* her there, not because she was really worried about her mother's safety or wanted her close by. She just wanted to propitiate her own conscience and satisfy her sense of responsibility. And once she had decided what was right, she was bound to carry it out, in her quietly capable way. In her sweetly ruthless, self-righteous way. Whether it was what anybody else wanted was beside the mark. How did anyone ever become so sure of his own judgment, Madge wondered, and then—briefly—was Clay up against the same thing? And if so, how did a man stand it? How had she stood it herself for so many years? Except, of course, that she'd been conditioned, gradually and inexorably. By Hugo. And why she should suddenly rebel against it now, of all times, when she had less solid reason on her side than ever before . . . when Margaret was unquestionably right, and they would probably still have to follow the course she had laid out for them—tardily and with bad

grace . . . she didn't know. She threw one look at Emmy, but Emmy
was knitting steadily and gazing a long way off, now, out of the
window.

"I'll probably come along, after a while," Madge said quietly.
"But not—just yet, I think."

"Well, I must say—" Margaret drew a long breath. She was trying very hard to control the anger which was plainly there in her;
trying to keep the poise on which she prided herself. "After my giving
up everything at home to come to you, just dropping all my work and
inconveniencing everybody! Traveling all the way out here—"

"You shouldn't have, dear, and I'm very sorry."

"I'm sorry too," Margaret said with great restraint, and after a
moment's blank silence, which had grown up suddenly in the room,
"I'd better try to get my own reservation for tonight then—if I can,"
she said.

"I wish you could stay over," Madge murmured emptily. But
Margaret didn't answer that. She turned and left the room. And
Madge continued to stand, with her hand on the back of a rocking
chair, her fingers sliding back and forth over the smooth wood. She
looked over at Emmy, and Emmy finally looked up to meet her eyes.

"Oh Emmy," she said miserably, "I must be crazy."

"No," the other said. "You have to work those things out sometimes."

"But not such small—such personal things—at a time like this."

"Well, we remain persons, don't we? No matter what goes on
around us."

"I was going to say yes, you know. That I'd go, I mean. Before
she came in."

"I know." Emmy nodded and looked back at her knitting.

"Oh my dear, *is* it all right with you, this way?"

"Perfectly all right. I meant what I said, Madge. I'm not sorry
at all. I think I'm rather glad. Maybe we've each got a challenge
to meet, one way or another."

"But you don't really mind? You're sure you don't care?" Madge
said anxiously.

"Listen to me, Madge—and don't ever forget I said this. The
only thing I care about—is not getting in the way. That's *my* challenge, do you understand? I've been ill so much, and so long, and I
couldn't be any use, so I could only try not to be a bother. I don't
want to be extra trouble to anybody, in case of an emergency. I don't

want to stand—or lie—in anybody's way, whether anything happens or not."

Madge stood listening to her words even after they had stopped. She was looking at Emmy, who looked so frail always, and had had to fight such great odds, for such a long time. Madge had a swelling feeling inside her, of admiration—but of fondness even more. She was really very, *very* fond of Emmy, she thought, with a sort of gratefulness to the friend who made that warmth of feeling possible.

* * *

It was hard to have Margaret go, after that. Madge kept wanting to make amends for her own obstinate perversity, but of course there was nothing she could do, unless she gave in altogether. They didn't refer to their disagreement at all after that morning. Margaret's manner was dignified and a little hurt, but she was being forbearing again, after her first flare of exasperation, and when it came time for her to leave, she kissed her mother gently and Madge clung to her for a moment, almost forlornly.

It was only when Margaret had left that Madge seemed to come back abruptly from her personal problems, to the real and sober ones which everyone around her was facing. All in all, people were busier and less jittery as the days went on, settling down to discount the wilder local rumors, focusing more clearly on the actual war overseas and less confusedly on their own imaginary beachheads. You didn't hear any more stories of families taking to the hills with a supply of canned goods to see them through some problematical siege. But at the same time, everybody was much more earnest and conscientious about the defense precautions which had been set up.

At Oak Lea, Mr. Wells made himself useful in getting the blackout arrangements for the house into more workable shape. He got a roll of black building paper and made ingenious blinds to supplement the window draperies which Mrs. Oakley had now dyed a deep purple. (Better than black, anyway, she said, regarding her once bright rooms morosely.) She had a jealous pride about that house, and about keeping it up to the standards of her leisured guests, a curious pride which was a sort of luxury—Mollie Oakley's only luxury, perhaps—and which was in fact oddly at variance with her private and somewhat antagonistic opinion of those same guests. But she was too harried now by the mere physical strain of keeping the house running and the guests fed, to care too much about such things as gay chintz curtains.

Connie, the little half-trained maid, had departed for the aircraft plant on the same day the Smiths had left for the Middle West. Mrs. Oakley had once remarked that her house was just like a bus stop for these half-baked girls anyway, on their way from high school to the aircraft plant, and she grimly got in one more of them. Eunice it was this time, who was even more slack and scatterbrained than Connie. Mrs. Oakley herself was doing all the cooking by this time, and with only the one incompetent girl for the housework and a woman in from outside to do regular cleaning, there was always something left undone. But even so, she refused rather stiffly Mrs. Fairlie's diffident offer to make her own bed. Even with a bit of half-concealed contempt, Madge suspected, as if she doubted that Mrs. Fairlie could make a bed.

So Mrs. Fairlie continued going to the Red Cross to fold little squares of gauze, while Mrs. Spencer calmly took a daily shift at a plane spotting station near by, and Madge looked at her in renewed awe, as though that were a difficult and dangerous job. (She would have been afraid she'd make a mistake, herself; wouldn't see a plane in time, or would get mixed up in reporting it.) Meantime, a young married woman moved into the room the Smiths had had, though she doubtless wouldn't be there long; only while her husband was at the airfield, and he expected to be sent off any time. They came in and out together sometimes, very much together, and remote in their deep personal preoccupation, as though disconnected from the other people living around them.

But the rest of the guests had drawn closer together. One thing Madge observed with interest was that they all stayed around together in the evenings now, instead of going off early to their separate rooms. Mrs. Spencer talked a little about some of the places where she had been, names which were being mentioned more and more often in the war news. And Mr. Wells matched places with her now and then, or even so far unbent as to mention the work he had done during the first World War, when he'd been a dollar-a-year man in Washington. His manner was a trifle less shy and jerky now than it had been before, and Mrs. Spencer was less critically detached. They were all friendlier, that was it. Even Ella Holcomb and her self-dramatizations were granted a little more tolerance, if not exactly sympathy.

The talk followed the news constantly, of course, in installments, as each day's catastrophes were added to the ones before. Though the papers were careful to play up every faintly hopeful item, like the sinking of a Jap troopship, or any report that a battleship had been bombed by the Americans or the English, whether or not it had been surely destroyed. One week there were four Japanese transports reported sunk. And the stand those little garrisons were making at Wake and Midway was magnificent. But as the weeks went on, the real attack on the Philippines started again in grim earnest, and the Japs began landing in force on Mindanao. (There were several submarine attacks on oil tankers right off the California coast, too, and that seemed very close to home.) Then again, out there, communications with Wake had broken off . . . and by the first of the year General MacArthur had moved to Corregidor . . . and the British battle down the Malay peninsula moved slowly toward Singapore. It was like watching, at a great distance, some grisly procession of events —unrolling always backward, instead of forward. (But it was the rumor near at hand—the arrest of a Japanese farmer near San Diego, perhaps—another blackout in San Francisco or Los Angeles, with that ominous note "unidentified planes" sounding again and again, which made the far-off course of the war seem real.)

One day some high official would firmly announce that there was no possible danger of the coast cities being bombed. . . . And then a few days later someone else—equally official—would say grimly that an attack on the coast was almost certain to come, and that people must take it seriously and tighten up all their organizations for defense. And Madge and Emmy asked each other the question which no doubt everyone else in the United States had asked himself at some time or another, which was . . . *if* air raids should begin there, could they (they personally—and they as a people) stand up under them as well as the English had?

"How can one ever know, ahead of time?" Madge asked.

"We can't," Emmy said soberly. "We can only hope. And that's what insecurity really is, isn't it? Not being *sure* what one can—or cannot—take."

"Well, I'm practically sure, myself," Madge said.

"Sure of what you'd do and feel if we had an air raid right here?" Emmy looked at her curiously, and a bit skeptically.

"Yes, I am. Sure that I'd be—terrified out of my wits," said Madge.

"But that isn't the point," Emmy objected. "They say everybody's frightened when it comes right down to it, and it's only a pose pretending they're not. It isn't whether you're frightened or not, but what you'd do about it."

"Get under the bed, most likely," said Madge, and they both laughed as if it were only a joke after all.

And so they stayed on into February, and the weather grew warmer and the country moved its clocks up an hour, to Standard War Time, and just after the middle of the month Singapore fell to the Japanese. (And a week later, an enemy submarine shelled an oil field near Santa Barbara. The first shot fired on American soil, the paper said dramatically.)

"Whew! It's getting warmer," Madge said to Emmy with a wry little smile which was almost a copy of Emmy's own. "D'you think we'd better plan to go the first of March, instead of waiting until April? No use in being just plain foolhardy, I suppose."

"I don't know," Emmy said, looking out of her window into the unbroken distance over the ocean, "I don't know—but I have a feeling that it won't really—make much difference now. . . ."

* * *

And then a few days later they had another alarm in the middle of the night. Afterward, there would be questions and arguments about what really happened that Tuesday night: why the anti-aircraft guns around Los Angeles had gone into action, what had actually been seen, to spread the alert all up and down the coast, and make that alarm the realest one that the ordinary citizen was to experience out that way. All Madge knew—and the first she knew, coming out of a deep sleep—was that she was sitting straight up in bed, gripping the blankets and staring in front of her. That horrible wailing, howling siren again, running up and down one's spine . . . She wished it would stop; no matter what else was going to happen, she wished that insane noise would *stop!*

She must have wakened with its first shriek, and now she began wondering hastily and stupidly what she should do. She wanted, unreasonably, to turn on the light and look at the clock, but of course she couldn't, because the window was wide open. Anyway, she didn't know just what comfort it would be to find out what time it was. She sat there with her knees drawn up, a fistful of blanket clutched in each hand, staring straight ahead of her into the darkness of the room as if trying to see through it. And then she turned her head, rather stiffly, to look out of the window, in the instinctive searching reaction which was half fearful and half exploratory. And there her gaze stopped again and fastened itself, doubting what it saw.

It was still dusk, but no longer solid dark. And through it a light was shining out there, bright and daring, just over the sea. Surely that light had never been there before. Quite far out, it must be, but there was no doubt about its being there. Not very high; it might be on a ship—or a plane, flying low. Or would it be what they called a flare? It was rather red; no, more pink perhaps, but it was so clear and strong that Madge was hypnotized almost as much as she was alarmed by it. The night was fading all the time, but this light stood out like a deliberate beacon, unearthly, beautiful, but at that moment rather terrifying. *Because it shouldn't be there,* Madge felt sure. Lights weren't allowed on shore or off shore, and an enemy must be insane (or boldly confident) to show one like that, whether it was a signal or whatever it was. It might be fire of course; it had a glow that was like a fire.

The siren had stopped. It had been going all the while she had been holding her breath and staring out that window from where she still sat, rigid, in bed. And now in the sudden silence there was another sound much closer, and equally sudden. The sound of a loud but muffled thump. Something falling—in the house, it seemed to be. Or could it possibly be . . . they said they sounded like giant thumps, at a distance. . . . (Though this reminded one rather more of somebody falling downstairs.) At any rate, between that light outside and that sound in the house—if it was in the house—Madge wasn't staying in bed, not this time. She wasn't going to stay alone here to meet whatever was going to happen, or had already happened, maybe. She must find somebody.

She got out swiftly and shuffled for her slippers and wrapped her robe hastily around her. Probably she should take something with her, she thought distractedly: money, or a flashlight, or her fur coat . . . but she couldn't remember at the moment just what she was supposed to take. She opened the door and went out in the hall, cautiously, because it was darker out there. With a feeling of exquisite relief she saw someone right there, only a few feet away, and coming toward her. It was Mrs. Spencer, judging by the height and thinness of the long draped shape.

"What—on earth—was that?" breathed Madge.

"Well, it was the air raid siren, to begin with," Mrs. Spencer said dryly.

"Yes, I know—I know, but that other—awful thud? Was it in the house?"

"I don't know. Certainly sounded like it. We'd better find out," said Mrs. Spencer. She had a flashlight which she put on for just long enough to show them the head of the stairs, and they felt their way in that direction. But when they reached there and started down, Mrs. Spencer in the lead, there was another sound which they began to hear below them, a moaning, whimpering noise.

"Good heavens!" Madge whispered. "Do you suppose something really has—?"

"I can't imagine," the other woman said impatiently, and they continued down, slowly and carefully, and closer to the sound. The living room below was unbelievably dark; no pale light from outside could possibly come in through those purple curtains. There was another moan, and the sound, simultaneously, of a door opening from the lower hall. Mrs. Spencer turned on her flashlight again, and it showed a figure hunched up, half sitting and half lying at the foot of the stairs.

"Good Lord!" she said involuntarily, really startled for the first time, apparently.

"What *is* it?" Madge asked, trying to peer around her. It seemed to be a woman. Meantime, whoever it was coming from below (Mrs. Oakley of course, Madge thought) had turned on another flash, and the two circles of light converged on the crouching figure, so that its face leaped out in sudden grotesque familiarity. It was Ella Holcomb lying there, really crying now, not just moaning.

"Why, Mrs. Holcomb!" Mrs. Oakley's voice came puffing and alarmed out of the dark space above her flashlight. "Whatever happened to you?"

"I fell," Ella moaned. "Oh, I fell—all the way down, I think!"

"Down the stairs?"

"Yes—oh dear—oh dear, it hurts so!"

"Where?" Mrs. Spencer asked practically.

"My arm—my wrist, I think. I must have sprained it. Broken it, maybe," she said tragically.

"Land sakes. . ." Mrs. Oakley breathed, a sound which was strangely pregnant with exasperation and relief, and a sort of wonder at the things which people could do—and did—to make life more hideous than it already was. But Mrs. Spencer said quite calmly, "We'd better get her over on the couch. If it's her arm, I guess she can walk."

So they helped her over, the three of them, avoiding the hand which she was tenderly nursing, one holding the flashlight as they moved across the room, a witch-like huddle of dark figures.

"These curtains are all drawn," Mrs. Oakley muttered. "We'd better turn on some lights. Reckon we'll have to do something about bandaging that wrist, even if it is just a sprain." She put on one reading lamp and crossed back to where the other two were standing over Ella. The latter had subsided in a plump crumpled mess in the corner of the couch. She was still holding her wrist with her other hand, and still sobbing, more like a lost child than like an injured woman.

"Poor Ella," Madge murmured. "I'm so sorry, dear."

"Can't you tell us what happened?" Mrs. Spencer asked, crisply but not unsympathetically, as though reserving judgment.

"Oh I don't know, I don't know! I rushed out into the hall and I couldn't see anything—only that awful noise was going—and I felt for the bannister and started down, but I missed a step and I guess I hadn't fastened my kimona. . . ." She gave an ineffectual pluck at the latter, which was in fact spread wide around her, not covering her blue flowered nightgown. "Are the planes coming?" she asked fearfully now, seeming to recollect all at once the cause of her terrified descent.

"Oh good Lord," Mrs. Spencer said abruptly.

"We wouldn't know, dearie," Mrs. Oakley said, but she sounded as irritated now as Mrs. Spencer was disgusted. "They don't tell *us* anything either, you know. Just wake us up in the middle of the night with that infernal yowling when we all need our sleep. At least some of us do," she added darkly, and then almost in the same breath, "I'll go and get a bandage for that wrist."

"You'll need hot water," Mrs. Spencer said.

"One of you better put a kettle on then," said Mrs. Oakley, and gave only a brief glance at the stairway as another step was heard there. "So you're up too," she said noncommitally to Mr. Wells, as she turned away toward the kitchen. "Everybody's up now," she added glumly, "except the young ones, if they're in at all. . . ."

"And Emmy! Oh dear—" Madge exclaimed, suddenly and contritely, "I'd better go and speak to her. She'll be wondering what all this moving about means."

"I wouldn't do that," Mrs. Spencer said quickly.

"You wouldn't?" Madge looked at her in surprise and doubt.

"She may not have wakened at all. She's often said she doesn't even hear the siren if her good ear is down on the pillow, you know. Much better not to alarm her."

"Well—" Madge hesitated. "Maybe you're right." She looked from one to the other, and Mr. Wells nodded officially.

"No use disturbing and worrying her," he said. "No use at all.

She would have called, or even come out, if she'd heard us and been at all worried."

"We—ell," Madge said again, rather forlornly. They all seemed to pause for a second, as though to listen for a call from Emmy.

"Of course, she's *your* friend, Mrs. Fairlie," Mrs. Spencer said, "And it's not for me to tell you what to do. But after all, it is too bad to make something out of nothing."

"Yes," Madge said meekly. "Of course you're right. Though maybe I might just glance in the room and see if she's awake . . ."

But as she turned, Ella caught at her arm. "Harry," she said tremulously, as if she'd heard nothing of what they'd been saying. "*Where's* Harry? Doesn't he know I need him?" And Madge stood still, immobilized as much by that plaintive query as by the hand on her arm.

"Why I—don't know, dear—" She looked up at Mr. Wells who had come over to them now as Mrs. Spencer went out to the kitchen, but his own look of slightly shocked surprise gave her no answer to offer Ella. "We'll help you to get that arm fixed up. You're all right, dear," she hurried on persuasively. "There's nothing to be frightened of." (Or was there? she reminded herself. She was a fine one to be reassuring anybody else.) But the others were impatient and annoyed with Ella, or judging by Mr. Wells' face, even a little scandalized. Well, the poor thing was sort of repellent, somehow; huddled there, half put together in that exotic colored kimona, with her much curled hair down around her face and her blue eyes watery and wandering. She was hysterical of course, but she was pitiable too, and Madge was sorry for her. The one prop she'd always depended on was gone and she was still quite lost without it, had no one to turn to, in bed or elsewhere, when a terrifying noise awakened her.

"It's all right," Madge said again, and tried to pull the edge of Ella's kimona farther over her knees, protectively, aware that Mr. Wells did not quite approve of such deshabille, even in an air raid. He himself had a long wool dressing gown cinched tightly around him with its long fringed belt, though his sparse gray hair was standing up in peaks.

"She fell on the stairs and hurt her wrist," Madge explained a little defensively, just as Mrs. Oakley came irritably bustling back, her hands full of bandages.

They got Ella's wrist bound up, at any rate, Mrs. Spencer being certain that it wasn't broken, only sprained. But after that, there was a moment of anticlimax, a vague sense of not knowing what to do next, as they looked around at each other. Realizing that the whole

thing had just been another false alarm, after all. Mrs. Oakley offered
to get them some coffee, but was plainly thankful when Mrs. Spencer
said they'd much better go back to bed again. So Mr. Wells assisted
the still limp Ella upstairs again, with Mrs. Spencer following after.
And Madge, who had offered to stay with Ella if she was still nervous,
turned aside for a moment, to go to Emmy's door. She opened it very
softly, and listened, but there was no sound. The curtains were pulled
almost together so that there was only the faintest light in the room,
but she could just see the quiet figure on the bed.

"Emmy?" she said, her voice very light, and there was no answer.
So she shut the door again and went back to the living room where
Mrs. Oakley had put out the lights and was pulling open the blackout
curtains. Madge went to help her. It was quite light outside now, a
lovely pearl gray where sea and sky ran together. And looking out, she
remembered with a sudden sense of delayed shock, that light which
she had seen out there, and actually forgotten for a while. There
wasn't a sign of it now. She wondered if she should mention it, if it
were something which could possibly have gone unobserved by others.
She pulled another curtain, and stood looking anxiously into the unbroken silvery mist. No, not a thing. But still . . . one shouldn't let
anything go unquestioned these days. That's what they said.

"Your room looks out toward the sea, doesn't it?" she asked Mrs.
Oakley, hesitantly, after a moment.

"Yes, sure it does," the other agreed, glancing at Madge. "Just
below this, it is. The house being on a side hill this way gives me
two rooms down there."

"Yes," Madge said. "Yes, I know. But what I was wondering was
. . . Did you notice the light out there a while ago?" she asked lightly,
as if it were of no consequence really. "Just after the siren began?"

"Light? Offshore?"

"Yes. Right out there." Madge pointed. "Not very high. It could
have been on either a plane or a ship, I suppose," she said, non-
chalantly. "But it was very bright—and pink. Almost like a fire. It
just made me wonder, rather . . ."

Mrs. Oakley was looking at her fixedly, an odd expression on her
round face.

"You mean the big star?" she inquired bluntly.

"The—big—" Madge returned her gaze with utter blankness.

"Yeah. That's where you see the Dog Star this time of year. It's got
another name, too, but I forget it. I guess you never got up early
enough to see it before," said Mrs. Oakley.

"Well, no," Madge admitted, her face very warm. "I guess—not." She turned to look out the window again, trying to imagine what she had seen as it really was. Imagination . . . imagination; it did such extraordinary things to a person, led one so far out of bounds sometimes. . . . Then she turned back to Mrs. Oakley, apologetically. "That *was* silly of me, wasn't it?" she said. Somehow it seemed to be the finishing touch to the farcical performance they had all just taken part in. Taking the star Sirius for a Japanese plane! She was even more of a fool than Ella. Why couldn't she ever have learned to be sensible and practical like Mrs. Oakley? Self-contained like Mrs. Spencer? Or calm and peaceful like Emmy, sleeping quietly through all the fuss. She wished she could have gone in to talk to Emmy now, despite what the others said. Well, she'd tell her all about it in the morning, and Emmy would laugh her wry little laugh, both with her and at her. Maybe she'd even be sorry she'd missed all the excitement. . . .

* * *

It was the new girl, Eunice, who found her. She had gone in with the breakfast tray as usual, a little later than usual in fact, on account of Mrs. Oakley having overslept. The fact that there was no answer to her knock didn't bother the girl, for Miss Burns didn't always hear her; she generally just knocked and went on in anyway. But when she had gone halfway across the room that morning, Eunice had given one look toward the bed, and then one sharp stifled cry, and come rushing out again with the tray still in her hands, the china jiggling on it as she almost ran through the dining room to the kitchen. And Mrs. Oakley had had to go back to that bedroom alone, her plump face dropped into sagging lines of apprehension.

Miss Burns was lying on the bed, fully dressed even to her shoes, though she had carefully spread a newspaper at the foot of the bed to protect the blanket cover. But the quilt was half thrown back, and it seemed as if she must have started, or at least tried, to get up. She might have sat up, perhaps, and reached in the dark for her medicine, and knocked it off the table, which was crowded with books. There was a pill box on the floor, the lid fallen back and several small pills strewn mutely beside it. Then—possibly—she had groped for her cane, but it had slipped away from her and fallen on the floor too. Of course, she might have reached for the cane first, in alarm, and the medicine afterward, feeling the dreaded stricture in her heart coming on. They would never know which it had been. And it didn't really matter now. Later that morning, at the breakfast table, Madge sat without appetite, listening to the others discussing it, wishing vainly that they wouldn't, no matter how kindly.

"Why she didn't *call* us," Mrs. Spencer said repeatedly, "I can't understand it. We surely would have heard her after the siren stopped, out there in the sitting room, right outside her door, almost. Unless it was the siren itself that was too much of a shock waking her up that way."

"She'd heard that siren in the night before," Mrs. Oakley said, grimly. "More likely it was the other noise—well, I mean to say, all that row with the lot of us running around . . ." She broke off short with a look at Ella Holcomb, who was sitting there looking solemn and big-eyed, her wrist still done up in the bulky bandage they had put on the night before. Madge looked at her too and then glanced away quickly, wondering if Ella realized what the others were thinking, that it was the crash and commotion *she'd* caused which had probably frightened Emmy so much as to bring on the heart attack. But it wasn't Ella's fault that Emmy had stayed on there, at Oak Lea, where such things could happen. . . .

"What I can't understand," Ella herself remarked plaintively, "is why she was all dressed."

"Eunice says she always was dressed when she came in in the morning. Lately, that is. She didn't use to do that, but—"

"You mean to say," Mrs. Spencer took her up slowly, and there was no contempt or impatience in her tone now, Madge noted apathetically, only stark pity, "that she has slept with her clothes on all these weeks—ever since we got into the war?"

There was a short silence, as if nobody could bear to answer that question. And then Madge herself spoke, quite low.

"I think . . . she felt awfully helpless, not being able to move quickly, and with her hands so stiff, too. She needed help sometimes, with—hooks or zippers. I knew she had taken to bathing and changing her clothes in the middle of the day, lately, but I didn't realize why."

"But if she'd only called out, last night! That's what I cannot get through my head, or if she did, why we didn't hear her." Mrs. Spencer kept coming back to that one practical point, as though in futile argument with the woman who was dead; or it might have been in debate with herself, of course, because she had stopped Madge from going in there the night before.

"She didn't call," Madge said then, so quietly but definitely that they all looked at her. "She—didn't want to give any one else any bother. She dreaded being in the way because she was ill. Or making any extra trouble during an emergency. She said that to me, once. Of course she couldn't have known last night what was really happening. She must have just heard the siren, waking her up suddenly—and then all of us running around . . . and lain there waiting . . ." Oh Lord, Madge added, not aloud but to herself—if I'd *only* gone in there to see if she needed anything—not listened to anybody else. Did she think I'd gone and left her?

She got up quickly and excused herself. There was a silence in the room behind her as if the others had realized their lack of tact. But she couldn't eat, and she couldn't go on sitting there. She went up to her room, and when she got there she stood in the middle of it, as if she hardly knew what she had come for. Then she sat down slowly on a straight chair and stared in front of her, and after a while two difficult tears squeezed themselves from her eyes and ran down her cheeks. This hurt so terribly. Realizing now what Emmy had never let her know before: that she must have been apprehensive every minute, never taking her clothes off at night, never letting her guard down by day, trying always to be ready—sartorially and spiritually both—for whatever might happen.

And nothing had really happened—that was the strange, strange thing. An imaginary war, Madge thought again. . . . And yet Emmy was a casualty just the same, just as much as if it had been a real one. She must have been so frightened in there alone last night, helpless to get up, not knowing what was going on or what was still to come. And yet she'd had the courage to lie there quietly and not even call out, just because she thought that was the thing to do. What was it she'd said? That everybody was frightened when it came and it was only how you took it that mattered. Maybe Emmy had wanted to meet that challenge, had even wanted to stay on at Oak Lea to meet it. Madge wondered about that, and tried to find a little comfort in it.

She sat staring at her own unmade bed for a long time, until finally she became aware of it, and of her own passive futility in sitting there, and after another while of hopeless looking at the bed, she got up and carefully and methodically made it, just to have something to do. And when she got through she took a half-soiled handkerchief and carefully dusted everything in the room, listening with another sort of care to the casual noises downstairs. When those—other people —came, she would have to go down again. . . . But when she had finished her dusting she thought suddenly that Ella wouldn't be able to make her own bed with that lame wrist, and maybe Eunice was still too upset and shaken to do her upstairs work.

She went along the hall quietly to Ella's room and found it empty and the bed unmade as she'd expected, so she started on that, thankful to have something to concentrate on for a few minutes longer. It was while she was working there that there was a short knock and Mollie Oakley came in. She was well into the room before she saw Madge, and then she stopped short with a frown of surprise, as if suddenly not sure what room she had come into. Involuntarily, Madge began to apologize.

"I'm sorry, Mrs. Oakley, but I thought maybe Eunice was still—"

"Eunice has quit," Mrs. Oakley said flatly.

"Oh . . ." said Madge.

"She said, what with the war and all, she was too nervous to work where people were dying in the night and throwing 'emselves downstairs too." Madge recoiled sharply, but as the two women looked at each other, they both seemed forced to consider this viewpoint, which Mrs. Oakley had brought in with her like a soiled piece of clothing, and thrown down on the floor between them.

"I'm sorry about that," Madge said finally. "You are having an awful time."

"Oh, I'll get somebody else," the other said harshly, but she didn't look as if she believed it just then—and she did look about all in, Madge thought.

"Why don't you let me help you?" Madge said suddenly. "Just until you do get someone. Let me help with the beds and upstairs work anyway." She hadn't meant to make that offer again, after Mrs. Oakley had brushed it off so brusquely the first time, but now she found herself doing so, as if she couldn't help it, and she didn't know whether it was because she needed something herself—or because Mrs. Oakley really needed the help. The other woman looked at her, not quite suspiciously, but with a doubtful sort of speculation.

"I don't hold with the guests helping around a place like this," she said shortly.

"Well—I only meant, it might save you that much, just for the present—while you have your hands so full."

"I'll say I have," the other sighed, and then she allowed, half reluctantly, "I guess it's decent of you to offer. Not many would, at that. I don't mean to sound ungrateful."

"I didn't want you to be grateful," Madge said, and knew she sounded irritable herself. "I'm not good for much," she added, a little defiantly. "But I *can* make a bed!"

Mrs. Oakley's glance went beyond her for a moment, as if to appraise the half-made bed.

"Yes. I guess you can," she admitted grudgingly. "The thing is, though," she broke out suddenly, with that queer note of truculence which was so apt to break through her otherwise self-confident surface, "it's *my* house, and I want things done my way. It's got to be that way, or I don't know where things are at, that's all. And you're a guest, see, and used to giving orders—"

"I'll do whatever you say," Madge said more meekly now, but wondering why—why she was doing this.

"I suppose you'd want a cut in your room rate, or something?"

"No," Madge replied. "I didn't mean that." And Mrs. Oakley had the grace to look abashed that time.

"Well, I didn't know. I didn't know if you'd be staying, even," she muttered. Madge looked at her steadily. "Yes, I'll be staying," she said. She couldn't go now, if she had wanted to. She couldn't run away, after Emmy had stuck it out. She would have to stay—to the full limit of the time they had planned—without Emmy, and no matter how much she missed her. "I'll be staying—for some time yet," she repeated. "And if I can be any use while I'm here—I'd be glad," she ended rather forlornly.

"Oh go ahead, if you want to," Mrs. Oakley said abruptly. "God knows I need the help."

Part Three

Chapter Eleven

MADGE HAD STAYED ON RIGHT UP TO THE END OF APRIL. SHE STUCK IT out while the early local hysteria gradually died down and sober real-ization of the real war Out There came to take its place. She stayed on at Oak Lea, working for her landlady in an ambiguous kind of way, and thought more than once that it was a funny kind of war work. She was a little chagrined too to find how tired she got over it, and that she couldn't put in as many hours at the Red Cross when she'd already done a morning's housework. But there was a compulsion in her to keep going, not to stop and think—about Emmy or anything else. And her efforts did seem to be a little helpful to Mrs. Oakley after all, for Eunice had not been replaced for some time. Even Mollie Oakley herself, skeptical, defensive and blunt as she was, had finally accepted Madge. She'd broken down at last and reluctantly admitted (in the intimacy of dishwashing one night) that she didn't know what she'd have done without her.

For Madge had gradually widened her field, even to helping Mollie with the dinner dishes occasionally. She didn't always know what the other guests thought about it, though sometimes that was fairly ob-vious. There was a family named Foster (a father, mother and grown-up daughter) who had come for a while after Ella Holcomb and the young flyer and his wife had gone, and Mrs. Foster made it very plain that she suspected Mrs. Fairlie's "altruism" of being strictly menial. She's dying to know whether I'm being paid or not, Madge thought, half resentfully—and half enjoying the other woman's dis-comfiture, because she couldn't decide just how to act toward Madge.

It was an anomalous position; Madge had to concede that ruefully to herself at times. But still, in some strange way she felt that she was discharging some obligation—to Emmy perhaps, more than to Mrs.

221

Oakley and the war. So she stayed on obstinately, to see the Fosters come and go, to see Ella and Mr. Wells depart and others come in their places, until only Mrs. Spencer and she were left of the ones who had been there all that winter. And when the time finally came for her to go, Mrs. Oakley said to her, with her moist warm hand enclosing Madge's firmly, "Come back sometime, won't you?" and there was a simple yet urgent sincerity in her tone.

"Oh, I will!" Madge said quickly, and had a stronge impulse to lean over and kiss the other woman; in fact the only reason she didn't was because she didn't think the undemonstrative Mollie would have liked it, or even considered it fitting. "I will," she said again, and let it go at that.

But when Madge went home that time, in April of 1942, she knew that she would not be going away again for a long while. It was a simple, personal conviction, not wholly due to the war's compulsions, but the years piled up to prove it. Five of them, before she even contemplated moving on again. And even the manner of her arrival at home was characteristic of what would follow along afterward. She hadn't planned at all, as she should have, just how she would get the house opened up and put in running order. She knew, in an indifferent sort of way, that this was the first time she had ever gone back to the House with no one waiting for her; there weren't even any maids this time. But halfway across the continent she began to think that maybe she'd better go to a hotel first, after all, until she found someone to go in and clean the place up. Then she remembered that There Was a War On, and you couldn't get into any hotels at the last minute.

She had trouble enough, even getting a taxi, and had to share one when she did. But finally, after dropping the others on the long way up town, she saw that the cab was circling slowly around Elephant Square, while the man searched for the right number . . . and that was when she began to feel the old sinking within her, like an elevator going clear down to the basement. This couldn't still be real. It really couldn't. Trees all out in leaf again (but the wading pool was empty), the old-fashioned street lamps just coming on (no dim-out here), people walking through the Square back from work, home to dinner . . . Oh, it was fantastic, foolish, like a play that went on and on, year after year, with nobody even watching it. And the House, as they drove up to it, looked just the same too, except that it was completely dark, and the curving steps were very dirty, with bits of paper and dead leaves which had caught in odd corners against the railing.

The taxi man put two of her bags out on the steps and went back for the other two, but when she had the front door open and asked him if he would mind bringing them in for her, he shook his head with a sort of lordly contempt.

"This is as far as I go, lady," he said shortly, and told her the fare.

"Oh . . ." Madge said. She paid him and watched him go down the steps almost wistfully. Then she stooped to pick up the two smaller bags as he drove off, and took them through the vestibule and put them down. She made two trips for the larger ones, just managing to drag them over the sill and through the two doorways to a spot just inside the big hall. Then she closed the heavy outer door, shutting out the Square with its strangely warm, dark radiance, and felt for the hall light switch which was in the vestibule. As the lights flared up she stood in the doorway beside the clump of suitcases, and blinked a little as she looked around, and shivered at the damp cold which met her like a wall.

Just the same. The oriental rugs were in storage, of course, so the floor was bare, but out here there was no furniture to be covered, so it looked much as usual—the chest beside the stairs, the two Jacobean chairs, the long table empty of flowers, naturally, no card tray and no cards or messages. . . . Madge turned to the left and walked slowly into the drawing room, feeling automatically for the switch, turning on the lights, and stopping to look around. The furniture was swathed in dust covers in here, queer bulbous shapes in tan linen, the floor bare and dim with dust, the inlaid table with a film over it, dulling its delicate pattern. She left the lights on and turned back into the hall, went through the archway into the library, turned on the lights there and looked down the length of the room toward the cold fireplace. This room had lived more than the drawing room, and so now it seemed more dead, more wholly deserted than the rest. But she stood there longer, as though unable to move again. It was like breaking something she could almost touch, like strings or cobwebs, when she did turn back to the hall once more. But she moved more quickly now, with a determined briskness, as she crossed the hall, lighted up the dining room, glanced over the bare dimmed surfaces of table and sideboard, empty of silver, and went on through the swing door with its little diamond-shaped pane of glass, into the pantry and the kitchen.

She went over the whole house, except for the cellar and the attic, lighting the lights in every room and leaving them on, until it was ablaze, as it had been when the Hugo Fairlies had been giving one of their big parties. It was a cold blaze now, reflecting back the bareness and chill of the house itself. It was the end of April, and outside the evening had seemed warm and muggy after an indecisive shower, but the feel of winter had been closed in here. Madge thought absently about the furnace, but she didn't know how to start it; she'd have to see about a man to do that. Maybe she could find a little kindling to start a fire in her own bedroom fireplace, though.

When she came to the stairs, she noticed her bags again, and paused to pick up one of the small ones and take it along with her. And when she came into her own bedroom, she put it on a chair and went swiftly over to the bed and jerked off the cover to expose the hump of blankets and pillows neatly piled there. And then she took a slightly soiled handkerchief from her handbag and carefully wiped off the top of her dressing table, and took off her hat and laid it down there with her gloves and bag. She didn't know why she did that; the place was hopeless . . . there was nothing, no small ineffectual gesture which could make it seem faintly livable or lived in. But in some way, that particular gesture was a defiant announcement to herself, at long last, that that was where she belonged—and that was where she meant to stay.

When she had been through all the second-floor rooms, she started downstairs again, not quite knowing what she was going to do next. And then she reached the landing and faced Hugo's portrait, and stopped and switched on the small horizontal light over the painting. Certainly, Hugo should have his light also, she thought gravely, and stood regarding him. She was quite calm and detached about it at first. It was a good portrait still: that same cold gleam in the eye—the look of solid bony structure behind the forehead, along the jaw—the mouth, with its weakness half-concealed by the neat mustache. Oh dear God, thought Madge suddenly, not praying, not even thinking really. It was just a picture, after all . . . but it had been a person. A man. And as the picture still dominated the hall, so the man . . . No, Madge cried out inside herself—*no!* He's nothing any more.

But he still hung over the place. And he still hung over her, because she was his handiwork, in great part—for better or worse. She hadn't been able to make another life or become another person even after all this time. It couldn't have been so, of course, if she had been a strong person to begin with. But even the weak were supposed to grow stronger through experience, she thought—even the weak—if they didn't go under altogether.

Madge stepped back on the landing, slowly, as if backing away from him, feeling instinctively for the balustrade beside her. But her hand hadn't yet found it, and her feet had almost reached the stairs behind her, when suddenly the doorbell began to ring. It rang loudly through the house once, while Madge whirled around and stood still with alarm and amazement. But she was facing the hall now and as the bell began to ring a second time she almost ran down those three stairs and across to the front door. When she opened it, she saw a tall, very thin figure standing there, and it wasn't until she noticed the little goatee, not quite as trim and pointed as it used to be, that she recognized the man.

"Why—Mr. Delephant!" she said softly, in wonder and relief. He peered at her.

"Mrs. Fairlie? It *is* you, then?"

"Yes," she said, almost happily. "It's me. But how in the world did you know I was here?"

"I didn't, Mrs. Fairlie. I had no idea you were back. That's why I was disturbed when I saw your house all lighted up. It looked as if every light in it was on, as I came across the Square just now."

Madge laughed, with what she herself felt was an almost hysterical abandon. (It felt *good* to laugh, just then.)

"I've been going all around the house," she said. "I just got back, you see, and I suppose I did turn on every light in the place. It never occurred to me that anyone would notice it and worry. . . ."

"Well," Mr. Delephant said, relieved, but a trifle embarrassed now, too. "I had no thought of being officious, you know—"

"Why of course not! I think it was sweet of you to take an interest and stop and inquire."

"I just didn't quite like to pass by without making some inquiry," he said carefully.

"But it was so nice of you—and it's so nice to see you."

"It's delightful to have you back," he said formally. "Mrs. Delephant will be so pleased to know that you are here again."

"Do remember me to her, won't you? How is she?"

"Oh quite well, quite well," Mr. Delephant said hurriedly. He seemed to want to go now, having done his duty. "I must be getting back. It must be—nearly dinner time—and she'll be wondering . . ."

"Yes, of course," Madge said. But he hesitated for a second longer, glancing past her through the vestibule, yet seeming not to look very far.

"You're all right here?" he asked. "You—have what you need— and someone to help you. . . ?"

"Oh yes," Madge said quickly. "Quite all right."

"Well, in that case . . ."

"It was awfully kind of you to stop."

"Not at all. Not at all. Good night then, Mrs. Fairlie."

"Good night," Madge said softly, and closed the door.

It was better, when she came back into the hall. The house was just as empty as it had been before, once their voices had stopped echoing through it. But it was *not* so cold. She began to feel hungry, reminded by Mr. Delephant's mention of getting home to dinner. But she was afraid there wasn't a thing to eat in this whole cavernous place. She went out to the kitchen again and looked through a couple of cupboards, but the last cook had cleaned out everything. What a fool she'd been not to have had her dinner while she was still downtown; she just hadn't thought, that was all; she seemed to have come back here in a sort of trance, not even watching one step ahead of her. Well, she was too tired to go back now. And the only other thing to do was to go to bed.

She began turning off lights, going from room to room again, reversing her previous course. In the library she stopped and dug into the cold fireplace for a half-charred log, which had not been cleaned out, and picked up two small pieces of wood which had been lying lonely in the wood basket these last six months. With a bit of newspaper around them, she carried them upstairs in one arm, and took her other small suitcase in her other hand. There were no matches upstairs though, so she came down again. No matches in the library either, or the drawing room, and she didn't know where they were kept in the kitchen. She gave it up shortly, because she was suddenly just too exhausted to go on looking. But as she came back into the hall she stopped to tackle another of her bags, one of the big ones. She dragged it across the bare floor to the stairs, hoisted it up one step and then another. It was a brute of a thing, she thought pettishly; she'd never get it up all the way. But it had her only warm wrapper in it. So she got it up to the landing and laid it flat and then, sitting groveling on the steps, she opened it and took out the wrapper and a blouse for the morning—handling them gingerly, because her hands were so dirty. They really were filthy, she thought—from traveling, and from everything she'd touched in the dusty house, and now from that half-burned log. A hot bath was what she wanted more than anything; she'd have that just as soon as she got the bed made. She'd get warm and clean, and then just go off to sleep. . . .

Upstairs again, she went into the bathroom and turned on the tap in the wash basin; turned it back and forth several times and stared at it stupidly. No water? Frozen pipe or something? And then she remembered. Oh, of course, of course. The water was always turned off when she went away. She didn't seem to have *any* sense left, none at all. Oh dear, thought Madge, oh dear . . .

Well, she couldn't make up a clean bed with those hands; it wasn't worth while anyway, if she couldn't have a bath. Or worth while even to take her clothes off; she'd only be that much colder. So she went back into the bedroom and took the blankets off the bed and dumped them on the chaise longue. Then she opened the window looking out on the Square—it was really warmer outside than it was indoors any-way—and went back and with her coat still on, lay down on the small couch and pulled the blankets up around her. But she didn't go to sleep right away, after all. She lay there listening to the sounds which came up from the Square . . . the same old sounds, that she never thought of till she came back to them again. Same old Square; same old circle she'd gone around once more and fetched up at the same old place. Well, she was home again anyway, she thought. Home for a good long spell this time. Mrs. Hugo Fairlie—At Home . . . And all at once, Madge began to giggle weakly into the warm blankets tucked up around her chin. If Hugo could see her now, she thought. . . .

* * *

It was probably just as well that Madge had had that initiation on her return home, because after that the house could never again seem quite so cold or empty or forbidding as it had then. Even when it took her days to get the plumber—any plumber—to come out and turn on the water and fix the leaks. (She went over to Mona's to get a bath during those days though she stubbornly declined to stay at Mona's house.) Even when she discovered that the cleaning woman she had had to help out last year—together with all other potential clean-ing women—was doing welding now . . . Even when she had to de-pend on the druggist's thirteen-year-old boy to start the furnace and he sometimes woke up too late to come around before school . . . She was often dazed and discouraged, but not surprised by anything, any more.

There was no possibility of getting maids, of course. She even felt obscurely that no matter how muddling her efforts were, if she managed to keep that big house going, without diverting other people from their larger problems, she would in some measure be doing what was expected of her these days. Though she did not for some time figure out just who expected it of her—or why. It was as though the House simply sat there, across her path, large and unyielding as if to say: it was her job, and that was that. But this was very different from doing a few beds and dishes at Oak Lea. Madge had never learned the mechanics of housekeeping from the ground up, and she did things the hard way, and made innumerable mistakes. The mere *steps* there were to take in that house she had never quite realized before. And when she was at the farthest end of the drawing room the telephone would be sure to ring and she would have to go at a dog trot out to the kitchen or the den to answer it before it stopped ringing. And when she was up in Ronnie's old room, say (she cleaned two or three rooms thoroughly each day and then began over again after each round), then that would be the very moment when the doorbell would peal out and she would go racing down again, to be met with that oft-repeated question, "Do you have any rooms or apartments to rent here?" from some harassed looking woman or wistful young couple. Madge was shocked by that query at first (she could just imagine what Hugo would have said!), and then she felt a little distressed to think that people should have to go from house to house to find a place to live, but she got used to it after a while; just answered politely, concealing her annoyance at being called away from her work once more. For it took most of her hours and most of her days, just to keep the place reasonably clean. She seldom saw any of her old friends; they were all busy anyway.

She still went down one day a week to the Red Cross, to sew, or to work on surgical dressings. Because that was the only place where she seemed to come, not quite in touch maybe, but at least within earshot of the war and the rest of the world. She knew that she was getting walled in again, somehow. It was like the Depression, in a way—when she had realized so often that she had money and everybody else had none. Only now it was the War, when everybody else had one boy, or two—or three, at camp or already overseas, and she had none. She realized once more how invulnerable—how immune —she must look from the outside, protected in her sealed-up vacuum from all large brutal events, and every small harsh reality as well. But it was a strange thing to realize that the only personal emotion she was entitled to in connection with the war was to be thankful that Ronnie was dead. She could be glad, now, that he had not lived to grow up. There had been no reason that she could ever find, before, through all those years—until now. And there it was. But that was a strange dead end to come to in life, to realize that only the dead were safe. One of the women sitting beside her at the Red Cross one day turned to her and asked, "Have you got a boy?" and Madge said quietly, "I did have. . . ."

"I sort of thought you had," the woman went on comfortably, her hands working rapidly, "though I didn't think I'd ever heard you say—" Then suddenly the sense of Madge's answer came through to her, and her hands paused and she glanced sidewise.

"You mean—he was killed?" she said in an abruptly hushed voice, apprehensive and apologetic for her question.

"Yes," Madge said, not thinking what the other was thinking.

"Oh Lord, I'm sorry. I didn't mean to—" There was a little silence between them in the middle of the voices all around them, and then, as though in some compulsion of sympathy the other woman said hesitantly, "He must have been one of the first, wasn't he? How long ago—was it?"

"Twenty-two years ago," Madge said, thinking back, year after year, to that time. And then from the way the woman's eyes stayed riveted on her, second after second, as though they couldn't move, she realized finally what she had thought—what she had thought Madge meant. And Madge couldn't look up to meet her eyes, somehow. She could feel it when her glance moved away finally, as certainly as if a light had been shifted away from her face. And still the woman didn't speak, just went on with folding her two-by-two's, pad after pad. She thinks I'm crazy, Madge thought. Thinks I was trying to dramatize myself maybe; identify myself with what they're going through now, trying to break in somewhere where I don't belong, where I've got no business at all. Why don't people ever know that you don't have to have the same kind of pain—in exactly the same place—to know what pain is?

But she felt cut off again, as though she had no part in this life all around her. (And why she should want any part in other peoples' suffering she didn't know!) And she felt uncomfortable all the rest of that afternoon, with that woman sitting beside her. When she left finally, she almost felt as if she didn't want to come back there again. She would, of course—but she didn't want to, because she didn't seem to belong. She must be getting a little queer, she thought.

The buses were crowded, of course, when she started home. They were always crowded nowadays, but taxis were even harder to get. Madge waited while three buses went by, bursting at their seams, before she succeeded in prying herself into one. Time was, at the beginning of the war, when she had felt riding on a bus was a mild adventure, and had rather enjoyed it; thought she was being One of the People and all that. But not any more. Now she simply stood and swayed with the rest of the sticky mass, enduring it, and wishing only that the woman in front of her, whom she was pressed against, had washed more recently. Thankful only when she could get off and start across the Square . . . on the same diagonal cross walk where she had once wheeled Margaret in her baby coach. Past the baby elephant where she had watched Ronnie climbing up and sliding off, with shouts of "Watch me, Mummie! Now watch me this time!" Where she had walked Brute, without a leash . . . when Ronnie was gone. Where she had sat on a bench and talked to a strange woman the dreary day of Hugo's funeral. Where she had crossed so many times since, with nothing to mark them in her memory, any more . . . And it all seemed so pointless.

She unlocked her front door, reflecting as she did so, with some pride and some irony as well, that she didn't dare forget her key nowadays, because there wouldn't be anybody inside to let her in. She turned back for a second to look in the mail box, but there wasn't anything; nothing from Margaret. Well, she hadn't really thought there would be. She went on through the vestibule, which was dark, but she didn't bother to snap on the switch there since it was still broad daylight outside. She went on up the stairs slowly but without pausing. She'd have to come down again presently and get herself some dinner, but she didn't even want to think about it yet. She'd change her dress first—anything would feel cooler, just the change itself. But she wouldn't cook anything tonight . . . wasn't worth it.

She had pulled off her dress and washed her face and neck and arms in the cool running water. She had come back to the bedroom and crossed to the closet door, and taken a half-mussed cotton dress off the hook there, when the door bell rang, a long, definite, even rather defiant sound in the still house.

"Oh damn!" Madge said aloud. It never failed, did it? No, never— not when she got up here, and had half her clothes off. And it would only be the paper boy, probably, coming around to collect for last week. But she jerked the dress over her head as she crossed the room, and buttoned it as she hurried through the hall. Then as she started down the stairs the bell rang again, once—not so long—like a voice not quite so sure of itself after all, and Madge put her hands up to smooth her hair as she went the rest of the way, still muttering to herself.

It wasn't the paper boy; it was a girl. About twenty, with long light brown hair which hung dispiritedly around her neck. She was fairly pretty, but her face was white and she looked tired—and just as cross as Madge felt. As Madge began to focus her eyes against the light outside so that she could see her more distinctly, she noted that her cheap dress was getting tight across the abdomen, and she knew what the girl wanted before she spoke.

"Do you have any apartments to rent here?" she asked.

"No, I'm sorry." Madge gave her her usual polite smile, restraining her own exasperation.

"Not even any rooms?"

"No. You see, this is a private residence . . . I'm sorry," Madge said again.

"Well, I'm sure sorry too," the girl said on a note of flat dejection. Her eyes glanced to the right and then to the left, just a quick inclusive flicker, and Madge didn't know whether it was making an ironic estimate of the size of the house, or was only the reflex of someone looking . . . looking for some sort of refuge, or escape, perhaps. "I've been all over," she said, starting to turn away, as Madge in turn started to push the door closed. "You don't know any place, do you?" the girl said, looking back. Madge shook her head, stopping the door at the three-quarter angle.

"No I—no, I don't," she said. "I guess it is—pretty hard to find a place."

"You're telling *me?*" the girl gave a short laugh. "Say, I've been to every first, second and third class dump in this town. I don't even pay any attention to the No Vacancy signs. And now I've started asking where there aren't any signs out, at all."

"Where *are* you staying?" Madge asked, though she didn't know why she asked it, since she certainly didn't feel like making conversation.

"Oh, at a motel. First one, then another. We came three weeks ago, nearly. My husband's out at that big plant—you know, the Fairlie Company? Making good money, too. But they won't keep you—the motels, I mean."

"They won't?"

"Five days!" said the girl grimly. "And then—" she made a gesture with her thumb over her shoulder—"*out!* Some kind of ruling—government, or the places 'emselves—*I* don't know which."

"I guess you'd better come in," Madge said.

"What?"

"I said—you'd better come in." Madge had opened the door full width again, but the girl stood and stared at her for a minute, as Madge herself looked back at her. It was as though they were both equally surprised.

"Good gosh, do you *mean* it?" the girl demanded.

"Well—I never took anyone in before—" Madge said, rather unhappily. "But I don't know why I shouldn't . . . After all . . ." She knew she wasn't being gracious about it, but she couldn't help it. She was too apathetic to be gracious about anything. She just didn't care, that was all. "There are quite a lot of rooms," she finished flatly.

* * *

Afterward, she didn't know why she'd done it. Whether it was the mood of deep isolation in which she had come home that day, or whether the sheer uselessness of the big house had at last piled up on her past bearing—she didn't know. But Mona Cressley thought she had taken leave of her senses.

"Good heavens, Madge," she said, when she heard about it. "I didn't mean you ought to take in *boarders* when I was talking about the fuel for such a big house the other day."

"Not boarders," Madge objected. "I'm not trying to feed them."

"Well, roomers, then—either way—you're just not the landlady type! Madge dear, you don't know what you're getting into. Get rid of the house—turn it over to this government agency, whatever it is, that makes them into apartments—and just keep one yourself if you want to. But don't try to run it and look after it all, yourself. You'll kill yourself, in the first place—"

"Oh, I guess not," Madge said mildly. Mona regarded her with a long and puzzled look.

"Honestly, Madge Fairlie," she sighed at length. "You are the most unpredictable person I ever met. I've known you half a lifetime—but I'll admit you can still surprise me."

"Can I?" Madge said, a tired note in her voice but a glint of amusement in her hazel eyes. (She remembered—years ago—Hugo's saying to her that she had no surprises left for him; none at all.)

Anyway, she thought, no matter who was surprised and who wasn't, you couldn't really satisfy anybody. But she had put the young Borins into Margaret's old room, and there they were—to stay, as far as she was concerned, until Dick Borin was reclassified—or until the baby came, if Gwen wanted to stay on when he had to go. She was a nice girl, and Madge knew she was lucky in having stumbled on her. She might, after all, have stubbed her toe on any one of a dozen applicants before Gwen came along. She had no idea, even then, that the young Borins were to be only the first of a long, changing succession. But it wasn't long after they came before Gwen was telling her about another couple they knew who were trying desperately to find a place to be together whenever the boy could get in from the artillery camp outside of town. So the upshot of that was that Madge put them in the yellow room on the opposite side of the hall. . . . And then presently Dick Borin told her, very casually, about a fellow named Hocker, in the engineering department where he worked, who'd been knocking around from one lousy room to another for the past eight months— and it wasn't as if he'd be here today and gone tomorrow either, not like Dick himself, just temporarily deferred. He had a bad heart and would have to stick right here. He was a nice guy, and it was tough, not being able to find a decent place . . . That was the way it had gone, once it started.

She didn't tell Margaret about these people staying in the House. She was going to at first, but when she sat down to write it out, she began to doubt how Margaret would take it. She might approve, be glad that her mother had at last found something useful to do. But on the other hand, she might hate the very thought of strangers in her old home. And she'd probably start worrying about her mother getting involved with dubious people who would take advantage of her. She might even come hurrying up here to do something about it— and Madge wasn't going to have *that*. So she didn't mention it for a month, and by that time it seemed harder still to bring up: to explain now why she hadn't spoken of it before. And then as time went on, there didn't seem to be any use in writing all about a lot of people who would only be there a short while anyway. For she found them changing . . . always changing.

It was the people, coming and going, that seemed so strange at first. Just to have them around at all—when she had begun to get used to the everlasting silence of the big house. And then just as she was getting rather fond of somebody, like Dick and Gwen, for instance, Dick was reclassified, and all of a sudden it seemed, he had been inducted and sent off to a southern camp. And Gwen had followed shortly after. But of course there were other young friends of theirs begging to take their places. Each time somebody left, Madge was firmly sure that she wouldn't let anyone else come in—but she always did. It became a queer, shifting pattern which had fallen into place around her almost while she wasn't looking. While she'd been up doing Hocker's room, maybe, or down in the kitchen mopping the floor which got so amazingly dirty since she'd been fool enough to tell those youngsters they could get their own breakfasts there. She couldn't think how else she'd gotten herself into this surprising and confusing mess—though the fact was, she hadn't time to think any more and maybe that was a good thing. She was too tired to think. She trotted doggedly from one end of the house to the other, upstairs and down again, and it was like a race in which she was always a lap behind.

She often thought of Mollie Oakley, and would have written to her if she'd had more time; she did manage to write her a long letter at Christmas, and had a card in return, which said very little, but cheered Madge strangely nevertheless. She wondered whether Mollie had any help at all now. . . . She herself found that some of the young people were much more helpful than others. Gwen had been sweet about helping Madge in the house; Hocker made a frightful mess of his room for such a restrained-looking young man, but he did eventually take on the care of the furnace, night and morning. And Tommy Wahlberg had been good about mending electrical things.

Things did get knocked about, somehow, with people coming and going so much, and there were always so many repairs to be made, especially in an old house. (If you could get anybody to make them.) Madge found that the expense of keeping the house going was much higher now than when she'd been alone. Even with fuel limited, the price was higher, and the light bills went way up, and the gas also. The laundry was terrible, and her good sheets and towels were showing the wear and tear from having to send them out, once the old washing machine had broken down beyond repairing. And this thing called Rent Control didn't allow people to pay much for rooms like hers, Madge had found. But after all, she had never thought of making the house *pay;* that wasn't why she had started doing this, and it certainly wasn't why she kept on.

There was one night when she had seen Dick and Gwen at the foot of the stairs, only a few days before he'd gone off to camp, that was. He was just going back to do some extra work at the plant that night. Madge had remembered that she'd meant to defrost the refrigerator, and she had started to come downstairs again, but they hadn't seen her at all. Gwen had been standing on the first step, and he on the lower floor; he'd lifted her off and was holding her against him, with her head just above his as she kissed him, her arms around his neck and her feet just barely touching the stairs. Madge stopped short far above them and looked away, waiting a minute until he should go. But when he did, it was very suddenly, banging out the door, as if he'd remembered it was late. And Gwen had turned slowly and come up the two stairs to the landing and stopped there, and leaned her arms on the high square newel post, and buried her face in them. She had stood there with her shoulders stiff, as though holding them so, rigidly braced against the thing which racked her, and Madge had continued to stand still up above, hesitating whether to come down to her or not. Finally she had turned and gone very softly back to her own room, to wait with her door closed until Gwen had gone past.

Maybe that was why Madge kept on—that, and the fact that she'd gotten into it, of course, and didn't know how to get out. She was the last person in the world who should have been sentimental about young love, she told herself. But if people ever did find anything so rare and so wonderful, she was also the last to want to take it from them. And if some of these young couples were able to be together for a while who couldn't have been, without her house to live in—maybe that was something, no matter what came later. Dick Borin had been killed on Tarawa, just one year and four months later, when the baby was still less than a year old. And Tommy Wahlberg was in the Italian campaign and had both feet blown off by a land mine. On the other hand, there was that cheerful red-headed boy—a flier, he was, and he was to go through all the rest of the war, out in the Pacific area, without a scratch. . . . But he and his little Marcia had just been married before they came to Elephant Square, and she stayed on when he left—and he hadn't been gone three weeks when Madge discovered, sickly unbelieving at first, that something was going on between Marcia and Hocker. That was when she had to get rid of Hocker and start looking after the furnace herself. . . . And after that she took no men or girls alone, only couples.

That was the way Madge saw the war, from the heart of Elephant Square. From the farthest, safest sidelines, where only the echoes reached her. Yet she did know some of the names and faces now, had seen some of them going by before they disappeared in the distance —Dick, and Tommy and Bud . . . Gwen, Mary—and Lou of course, always Lou, very far off but still there in one part of her consciousness. In the area marked "England" in her mind . . . where those dreadful rocket bombs had started falling now, on top of everything else.

And then, quite out of proportion to those bigger things, Madge had a small and very personal scare in the spring of 1944, when Margaret began writing about coming up for a short visit with her that summer. She felt all at once as if she had been concealing a criminal past which Margaret would discover if she came. She began looking around the house, with Margaret's eyes, realizing how much it was showing all the wear and tear of the last two years. Things she had grown used to too gradually to notice, like the parquet floor of the front hall which needed refinishing and waxing so badly. And the linoleum in the kitchen which was worn almost through in two or three places. Even the chair covers in the drawing room, which she had weakly let the young people use for a meeting place, looked positively greasy. And of course the white paint upstairs . . . Well, Madge defended herself, to herself, all houses looked run-down nowadays, especially old ones. Still, she wouldn't know how to prepare Margaret for what she would see. She didn't know how to begin.

But Margaret didn't come after all. It was D-Day that saved Madge; it seemed that with the invasion of France, and everybody's thoughts turned intently that way, Margaret must have put her own thought of relaxation behind her once more, and decided she couldn't get away. Madge was relieved. Though on second thought, she was much more relieved about Lou, because now those flying bombs wouldn't keep on much longer. Of course Lou and Thomas were practically out in the country, but even so . . . The war had been going on forever, and Lou had almost admitted to being tired, lately. Now at last it seemed as though it might be over—not right away perhaps, but sometime.

The summer was hot and tiresome at home, and Madge had three couples staying there now; she would never take more than three. And gradually the summer wore itself almost out—and so did she. But as time went on, so did the Allies, until late in August Florence was finally liberated. (It was the milkman who told Madge more about Italy than she'd ever learned in the papers, because he'd been invalided home from there; a nice intelligent young fellow he was, too, but with one stiff leg.) And then only three days later, it was Paris . . . Paris was free again—and people said everywhere that It Wouldn't Be Long Now. It couldn't be.

The first week in September came, still hot and dusty, and Elephant Square had a tired and wilted look. The milkman was very

late in arriving one morning, and Madge was doing the lower back
stairs, but she came in to speak to him as she always did, to be sure
she had the tickets right. She saw then that he seemed to be puttering, absent-mindedly, over the bottles and tickets both.

"Good morning, Jack," she said. "It's hot again, isn't it?"

"Sure is," he agreed, without looking up. He looked a bit wilted
himself today, his smile not quite so ready. His leg probably bothered
him, Madge thought. Poor boy.

"I'd better put those bottles in the icebox right away," she said.
"Things don't keep very well, these muggy days." It had been almost
an idle remark, just to say something, but he looked up at her so
strangely that it startled her.

"What is it?" she asked, but he dropped his gaze and stuck two
fingers into the empty bottles he was about to pick up.

"Nothing," he said. And then, not quite casually enough, "You
hear about those old folks across the Square?"

"Old folks? No," Madge said, surprised, but uneasily arrested,
somehow. "I don't know practically anyone who lives around the
Square any more."

"Well these two must've been here a long time. Same name as the
Square—real name, I mean to say."

"You don't mean—Delephant?"

"That's right. Lived over on the west side. Old lady, and her
husband. She—uh—died," said the milkman, in a tone of some
restraint.

"Oh no!" Madge exclaimed in quick distress. "Oh, I'm sorry. Poor
old soul—I didn't even know she was ill."

"Guess nobody else did either."

"Oh dear, I should have gone in to see them," Madge said. "I
was always meaning to . . . isn't it dreadful, when one puts things
off? I haven't laid eyes on them for—I don't know how long it is
now."

"Quite some time, I guess. Nobody'd seen them." It struck Madge
that the man's tone was very queer, and he was still twiddling with
those bottles, looking down at them but not picking them up.

"What do you mean?" she asked slowly. "Was there anything—
that is—out of the way?"

"Well yes, there was, Ma'am. You see . . . Well, she starved to
death, I guess," he said bluntly, and yet unwillingly, as if a person
hated even to say such a thing. Madge stared at him in gathering
horror, not altogether taking it in. "*I* don't know, of course," he

said, picking up the bottles at last, "but that's what the doc said when he got there. Called it malnutrition. Sort of an understatement at that," he added grimly.

"You mean they—both—" Madge spoke so faintly he could hardly hear her, but he seemed to know what she was trying to say.

"The people two houses down got to wondering about 'em. Hadn't seen anybody around outside for so long. Tried ringing the doorbell and couldn't get any answer. Got to talking to me about it this morning, so I got the cop and we broke in."

"Oh no—no," Madge said softly, moving her head from side to side, not knowing she was doing it.

"They were both upstairs," said the milkman. "He was sitting there in a big chair alongside the bed. Seemed like he was just waiting . . . She'd been dead since—well, I don't know," he said abruptly, and then went on again as if he couldn't help it. "House was like a barn—hardly any furniture in it, even. I don't know when they'd last had any food."

He was shaking his head too, now. He looked rather shaken himself, for such a husky young man. But when he saw the stricken look of horror which seemed to have hardened on Madge's face he added awkwardly, "I guess maybe I shouldn't 've told you, Mrs. Fairlie. I didn't know you knew them. But you'd have heard about 'em anyway —from somebody else."

"Oh yes," Madge said, almost impatiently. "Of course I would. But if I'd only known sooner. How can we know so little about other people?" she demanded of him, remembering the other time when she had thought so nearly the same thing, about Emmy, down there at Oak Lea.

"Sort of gets you, doesn't it?" the young man said. "Funny thing— I've seen plenty of dead people by now." He jerked his head as if to indicate a place not too far away. "Plenty, even, that—" He broke off. "But you know—war's one thing. Nobody likes it and nobody expects it to be pretty. But my God, you don't expect to find things like this—right here—when you start out on the morning's route—"

"No," Madge said. "No. You don't." He was on his way to the door now, as if reminded of his milk route, when she asked, "Where is—*he*, now?"

"The old man? Over there still, I guess. The doc wanted to take him to the hospital, but he didn't want to go. He—he's awful weak, of course, and he don't seem to know what's happened. He's kind of half there, I guess."

But Madge said quickly, "Oh no . . . No, they mustn't do that. I'll go over. Right now."

She wasn't really aware of walking the block between her own house and the Delephants'. She went out and closed the front door without even thinking of the key, that time. (She had left the back door open, fortunately, just as it was when the milkman went out.) She was thinking only that things like that just didn't happen, right next door, to people you knew. That's why they had these pensions and welfare associations and so on, wasn't it? But of course the Delephants hadn't approved of such things. And they'd be too proud to go to them for help—for themselves. They would hate to give up their pride, but even more they'd hate to give up their privacy, by letting other people know that they were destitute. That was it.

But she found their front door open now, open to all the rest of the world. She walked right into the high dark hall she remembered so well, and the doctor heard her and came to the big double hall doors to see who it was. He was not the Delephants' old physician, she knew that. He was a little man she'd never seen before, and he looked harassed and unreceptive when she first spoke to him. But when he found out what she had come for he seemed relieved, in a doubtful way.

"Well, I don't know," he said. "He ought to go to the hospital. He's very weak and he'll need nursing. But I'm damned if I know if I could get him in right now, they're so crowded."

"And they always hated hospitals," said Madge. "That is, they thought they were too public," she explained apologetically.

"You don't say?" said the doctor, giving her an odd look. "Well, I don't know," he said again. "It'd be a ward, if I could get him in at all . . . but I don't want to make the shock worse in his condition, and he doesn't quite get what's happened yet. . . . We've got to do something with him," he muttered, looking at her gloomily. "Maybe I can get a nurse for you. I've been waiting here till after they took *her* away. But now he just says he'd rather not leave, thank you. . . . He's so very polite about it!" The doctor seemed for the moment to be nonplused by this phenomenon which was not quite a medical symptom.

And when Madge went with him into the room where Henry Delephant was lying, half propped up on a very old couch which was the only piece of furniture in the room, the old man was still very polite.

"Forgive—not getting up," he said in a faint voice, raising one hand a little way toward her and dropping it back again. She was relieved to see that at least he seemed to know her, or rather just simply to accept her as she came over to him. She picked up the bony hand and held it, and said gently, "Mr. Delephant, I want you to come over to stay at my house for—a few days? Will you do that?"

He looked at her, his eyes very pale and vague, yet seeming to search hers for understanding, as if she might help him toward something he couldn't understand himself.

"Very—good of you," he whispered, and his eyelids fell shut for a moment. Then they opened again and he continued to look at her as though the mere recognition of her face was steadying to him. "Not sure," he said—"just now." There was a pause while he reached for a little more breath. "We—haven't been—visiting lately . . ."

"Oh, but you will come," Madge said very softly. "Very—informally of course. You won't have to—make any effort at all. I would like so much to have you."

His eyes fell closed again, but there was a faint inclination of the head at the same time, and Madge knew that he had accepted her invitation. She looked up and saw the doctor nodding also, but with that same peculiar look in his small narrowed eyes, as if in all his experience of human beings, he had never run across this particular species before. And after a minute she slipped away to go back and make things ready. The doctor would bring him over presently, and tell her what to do until he could get a nurse for her. She almost ran the little distance back to her own house, as though to keep ahead of her own thoughts, not to let them catch up with her. She found the front door closed, of course, and looked at it in sick consternation for a minute, vainly pushing at it and turning the door knob back and forth. Then as she had a sudden remembrance of that open back door, and turned away to go around the house, she saw that there were a couple of letters in the box. She barely looked at them as she hurried around the corner to the narrow back alley; only a bill— and an air mail from England.

Not from Lou, though. She didn't even register that fact until just as she was going in the kitchen door, and then she looked at it again. From Thomas, she thought, with one small distracted fragment of her mind. Odd, because Thomas never wrote her except at Christmas time. . . . Well, she couldn't stop to see why he was writing now. She must go upstairs and get out clean linen. She dropped both envelopes on the splash board by the sink, and then halfway across the kitchen she turned back. Lou—Lou might be ill, or something; that thought had only partially gotten through to her even now. But she picked up the letter again, tore it open hastily, and read it all the way through standing by the sink.

She didn't sit down; she didn't even lean on the board there to steady herself; just read it to the end (it wasn't long) and stood there looking straight ahead of her then, knowing she must go upstairs to fix a bed. . . . But Lou was gone. Lou was *gone*—when it was almost over. . . . Why, it was only yesterday, wasn't it—or was it the day before?—that the paper said London had announced that those robot bombs had ended, finally, after eighty days. . . . But of course this letter was written some days ago—even with the air mail. Madge turned it over to look at the date, mechanically. That was so like Thomas, she thought—and he had written so typically, so restrainedly. He had gone out, he explained carefully, in the middle of the morning, just into the village. The bomb had come over while he was away, and no one in the village was sure just where it had struck, at first. But he had come back, and found his house was gone. It was a very small house, Madge thought absently; quite easy to demolish . . . it wouldn't even have needed one of those things to do it. Thomas himself sounded as if he didn't quite believe what he was writing. Poor old Thomas.

And Lou. Poor—dear—old Lou; the big sister who'd always told her what to do, as far back as she could remember . . . Lou, who was so practical always, who had married over there, for security. There was something, some vague connection between these two things, Lou's death and Mrs. Delephant's, though they seemed so far apart; and it wasn't just that Madge herself had learned of them on this same day. No, that wasn't it, and it wasn't the war either. The war was blind and irrelevant. It was only an accidental part of something else. There was some thread, though, fine and invisible, which tied those two things together in her mind; she kept feeling for it as she walked on through the house, more slowly now. But she didn't have time to think it through now, because she had to go upstairs. She didn't even have time to weep for Lou. Not just then.

Chapter Twelve

MARGARET HAD COME HOME AFTER A SIX-YEAR INTERVAL, AND THERE was no one to meet her at the station. After one long look around she carried her own bag over to the cab stand and got into a taxi there, giving the driver the old address on Elephant Square. There was no flurry of the unmet, disappointed visitor about her; it was all done with her usual unperturbed efficiency. And yet as she settled back in the seat with an air of bodily relaxation, there was no relaxation in her eyes. She seemed to be watching attentively—yet not seeing at all—the familiar corners they passed, the crowded sidewalks (which had never been so packed before the war), the many uniforms which were still to be seen on the streets, almost a year after the war ended.

Margaret was trim and even smart in her five-year-old suit, but she herself was faded, if the suit was not. She was still pretty, in a clearly molded yet colorless way, like a Della Robbia which has lost the delicate tints that once gave it a special life of its own; but there was a look of strain somewhere behind that immobile face— a faint tenseness around her mouth and a crease between her brows, which was never quite erased now, no matter how calmly she appeared to look out on the world.

No one was watching her; the driver slewed carelessly around the corner into the Square, his attention on the street in front of him. But anyone who had been with her must surely have had an impression of fine-drawn concentration, that focusing of the returned traveler who has been long away . . . of someone returning home, and anxious—almost unbearably anxious—to get there. As if she might have been carrying an invisible load for a long distance and finally saw the point ahead where she would be able to put it down. But

when the cab stopped, she lifted her one bag out on the curb herself, before the driver could come around the car, and unlike her
mother on that other arrival four years earlier, Margaret paid the man
and motioned him absently to leave the suitcase on the sidewalk
where it was.

"Never mind," she said, as though she wanted him to go away.
"I can easily carry it in myself."

She went up the steps and was about to ring the bell when, on
an afterthought, she drew back her hand and tentatively tried the
door knob. It gave easily and she walked in through the vestibule,
and stood looking around the hall, still holding the bag. There were
no rugs in the hall, and the bare floor had a dull, almost bruised
look in the afternoon light which streamed down on it from the high
front window. There were no flowers on the hall table either; there
had always been a big bowl there, a gem of color against the dark
wood. . . . And this was June. Margaret's expression was puzzled as
she moved over to the drawing-room door and glanced in. She stopped
involuntarily when she saw that someone was there; a youngish
woman with no hat and rather untidy hair, who was sitting comfortably on the couch reading a magazine. She looked up for an instant's
incurious glance.

"How do you do?" Margaret said, on a courteous but questioning
note, responding to the old instinct of belonging to this place, being
in some sense responsible to and for it.

"Hello," the girl said carelessly and her eyes went back promptly
to her story.

"Were you—waiting for someone?" Margaret suggested politely.

"Me? No," said the girl. "Not particularly. Just waiting till my
husband gets home."

Home . . . Margaret gazed at her, and the girl's look in return
was more curious now. But there was a sound of the front door opening, and Margaret turned her head and body slightly, almost carefully, to see who was coming in behind her. The figure which emerged
from the vestibule was familiar, and her quick intake of breath was
almost like a gasp of recognition. But that figure was greatly changed
since she had last seen it, with bent shoulders and gaunt old head,
with a short untidy beard instead of the neat goatee, and with long,
thin wavering legs which moved slowly across the corner of the big
square hall. Margaret's lips opened automatically to say Mr. Delephant's name, but he didn't see her and she didn't speak after all. He
kept moving steadily toward the foot of the stairs, like a figure pulled

on a track, and once there he put one bony hand on the rail and began climbing up, step by step. Margaret's lips remained slightly open, watching him while the faint crease in her forehead deepened in a sort of anxious bewilderment. It was like watching the ghost go stalking across the stage in Hamlet . . . or like a railroad station, perhaps, with strange people waiting there, or going by unseeingly.

Margaret turned back to the girl in the drawing room.

"Can you tell me—that is—" she paused, and then brought it out. "Does Mrs. Fairlie still live here?" she asked, with strained quietness.

"Oh yes. Sure, she lives here. She runs the place."

"She . . . Oh, I see."

"You're new, aren't you?" the girl inquired.

"I—well yes. I seem to be."

"Going to stay?"

"I—hope so," Margaret said, almost inaudibly. And then, as if forcing herself to speak up, "Have you any idea where I could find Mrs. Fairlie now?"

"Out in the kitchen, I expect. She's generally there this time of day, getting the old guy's supper. You go through the hall and take the door over at the back—on the right, that is . . ."

But Margaret had already turned back. She put down her suitcase at last, by the foot of the stairs, as if she'd just remembered that it was in her hand. And as she crossed the hall she heard the front door open again, and slam, and long footsteps starting upstairs at a run, and that voice from the drawing room calling out sharply, "Hi, Joe! I'm in here—" but she didn't turn around to look this time.

She went almost blindly through the dark back vestibule where the old wall telephone still was, with a high stool just beneath it, and pushed open the swing door into the kitchen, and when she saw her mother standing at the sink with an apron over a mussy cotton dress, she spoke faintly but with an immensity of relief in her voice.

"Mother!" she said, and Madge turned around.

"Margaret . . . Margaret *darling!* How did you ever—"

"I sent you an air mail . . . I decided—rather suddenly."

"It hasn't come," Madge said wonderingly, trying to get her bearings. "Oh my dear, I wouldn't have had you come this way for the world! After all this time—with no one to meet you—and the house the way it is now—"

"Well I did think—for a couple of minutes—that you must have sold the house, and moved away without telling me," Margaret said, and there was a strange catch in her voice. They had their arms around each other now, as though they had just found each other. And Madge was patting Margaret's shoulder, as if to reassure her, and reassure herself at the same moment that the child was really there.

"Margaret darling," she said again. "It's so *good* to see you! But I never meant to let you come into it this way. I'm always such a blunderer . . . I should have told you—but I got myself into letting these different people stay here, almost without knowing it—and it got so complicated. I'll tell you all about them."

"It doesn't matter," Margaret said with a long sigh. "As long as you're still *here*."

It was the last thing Madge had ever expected Margaret to say when she finally found out about the House. She felt a load of compunction roll off her mind, which she must have been carrying there all these years without ever realizing what a heavy lump it had been. But it was a strange way to have Margaret come home, after six years—alone—with one suitcase—and without any warning at all. She didn't really explain much either; just said again that she had decided rather suddenly to come.

"It just seemed the best time," she said. "The Tremaines invited Joan to spend two months out at their ranch, and Fairlie was dying to go to the Scout camp—so I put him in it—and came. After all, I'd been talking about a visit for long enough . . ."

"Oh *yes*," Madge said, "I can hardly believe my luck, that's all. And Clay—won't be too forlorn, will he?" she added conscientiously.

"I guess not," Margaret said.

"Is he still doing that same work—at an aircraft plant, wasn't it—that he was doing during the war?" Madge asked the question tentatively, and Margaret answered it carelessly.

"Oh no. He's out of that now. He's looking around for something more permanent. Taking his time you know, so as to be sure to find the right line. And now—tell me about you."

It was only natural for Madge to do the larger share of the explaining, after all. She told Margaret just how she had first started taking in those young couples during the war; she went way back to that day when Gwen Borin had come to the door, and then she came down through the different names, and what they were like, and what had become of the ones who had written back to her.

And Margaret accepted it all, nodding gravely and listening with the same far-off attentive look she had had coming out in the cab the day she arrived. For Madge's story took some days to tell, off and on, between settling Margaret in Ronnie's old room (her own being occupied) and introducing her to the others who came and went at odd hours—and of course, carrying on the same round of chores in the house which had become second nature to her now. She told Margaret about Mr. Delephant too, and how she had come to take him in, though she could never quite describe the elusive horror of that day. There was something about it which even the stark facts could not express for Madge.

"Of course," she said, "I didn't expect him to *stay*. . . . A few days or a couple of weeks, maybe, till he was stronger, and—less dazed, poor soul. But you see he's never been quite clear about things ever since. He seems almost to realize, sometimes—but then he's more troubled. And I hate to see that sort of groping, painful look in his eyes. Most of the time he just accepts me, and the house, and all the rest. . . . And he's very gentle and appreciative and polite, just as if he were paying a short visit. He could go to a home, I suppose—but as long as I'm here, and there's so much room . . . He's very little trouble."

"What happened to their own house?" Margaret asked, and Madge lifted her shoulders and dropped them, quite simply.

"It went to the mortgage company, I think—or whatever they do about those things. Foreclosure, isn't it? Anyway, I know it was mortgaged as high as it could be. There wasn't a thing left—not anything, Margaret. It's hard to believe, isn't it?" Her eyes sought Margaret's with a wide questioning look, as if asking *her* to explain such a thing, and Margaret looked away.

"Yes," she agreed, after a moment. "And when you think they owned the whole Square down here once . . ."

"They'd even sold all their furniture, little by little. Just to be able to *eat*," Madge said, in a low tone as if someone—or something—might overhear her. "Or maybe they burnt up some of it—nobody knows. I don't know if they had any other fuel in that house all the winter before. While the rest of us thought we were doing pretty well, keeping our rooms between sixty and sixty-five . . ." And then after a minute she began explaining how she had happened to give Mr. Delephant her own big room. "It was the one I'd cleaned last," she said naively, "that was all. And I thought he'd be more comfortable there anyway. It was always more of a man's room, I guess—I never really felt much at home there by myself. It was too big . . ."

But even that didn't seem to shock Margaret too much now. She accepted without comment the fact that Madge had elected to move up to the third story and use two small maids' rooms and bathroom for herself. She listened passively to the whole story, giving a rather absent nod sometimes. Madge had a feeling of almost uneasy surprise that Margaret had not begun at once to advise her about the running of the house, to point out where she had made mistakes. It was only when Madge said finally, with a touch of apology, "Of course I wouldn't have kept on this way, once the war was over, except for the housing shortage. When this last couple finds a regular apartment, I won't be taking in any more . . ." It was only then that Margaret took her up with something of her old air of authority.

"No. I should think not. You'll want to have the house fixed up properly again, and have it to yourself again, incidentally. Some of these days there even ought to be some maids looking for work. After all, it isn't everybody who can find a job—even now."

"Yes," Madge said. "Yes, I suppose so."

But she didn't tell Margaret that she had had a man out that spring to go over the house and give her an estimate on all the things which needed doing, and that the figure he'd quoted had frightened her. She hadn't fully realized how badly the place had run down, how many things about it were shabby or out of repair. Paint and plumbing and floors—not to mention the condition of her linen and curtains and even the upholstery on the chairs. It was really appalling, and all the time taxes had been going up—and prices. Prices of everything. Everybody said they would go higher once they took off the things called controls. And yet her income was less, steadily less. She didn't quite understand about it, though Mr. Purcell still dwelt on the frightful mistake she'd made to sell the Fairlie stock when she had. At the bottom, he said glumly. For it seemed that during the war that kind of company had had an enormous boom. And then of course she'd put so much of that money into the Trust Fund Mr. Hawley had advised, and that had all been invested in bonds . . . She understood dimly that bonds brought a small Yield anyway, and that somehow they were always being Called —and put into others with still smaller Yields. What Mr. Purcell called Governments.

"Any fool can invest in Governments," he had said, for it seemed that he wasn't one who believed in Trust Funds and the way they were managed. "You see," he had told her, "there hasn't been too much that we could do with what you had left here." They all seemed to have some different idea, Madge thought. She wondered sometimes what Clay's theories were, but that was one of the things she never asked about lest he might think she was interfering with what she had given them outright. She was still glad that she'd done that when she had, so she could know they were provided for, at least. And she didn't want Margaret to guess now that her own income had shrunk so badly, or Margaret would start feeling concerned about her, in turn.

After all, she still had a reasonable amount for her own needs, with the small steady trickle from the Trust, and the few stocks outside it. She had enough, she kept telling herself, as long as she was living this way, and didn't stop to look at the amazing gap between this—and what she had once had. As long as she didn't consider starting to repair the house . . . So she avoided that subject with Margaret, and stayed on safer things, and let herself just enjoy having her there and near her again. And she didn't ask her how long she could stay; just hoped that Clay would be generous, and that the children would stay on at their respective camps and ranches—all summer, perhaps. She thought Margaret was trying to renew herself in the old house, the way she used to, coming back to it as a source of reassurance and refreshment, and she hoped its shabbiness didn't spoil any of that for her. Like a slightly polluted spring . . .

She urged her to look up more of her old friends and go out with them, since she really couldn't get away much nowadays herself. And Margaret did go out every day somewhere, though often without saying where she was going or whom she was seeing; she never had liked to confide in her mother about what she was doing, after all. There were certain things which never changed, in people or between them. And Madge no longer rebelled against that; she had beaten her head long enough against what she now admitted as an implacable fact. The relationship between them had been fixed by the kind of persons they each were, and the day would never come now, Madge thought, when the shape or quality of that relationship would change. She was even thinking that thought, quietly and without any more of the old longing or inner mutiny, while she was working around the house, as that very day moved up on her, like someone already coming down the street whom she hadn't yet seen through the window.

*　　*　　*

Margaret had been there nearly three weeks. Madge noticed that she wasn't really looking very refreshed or rested yet, but then of course it was getting warm, and the heat had always wilted Margaret a little. She had gone out one afternoon, as usual; in fact she had gone out before lunch, and Madge expected that she would probably be away until late. It was about three o'clock when she herself went upstairs—first one flight, and then the next—to try to get a little rest, because she was pretty tired that day. It grew hotter as she went up higher, and she began to wonder, as she had before, whether she could really stand the summer up here again. Except for the hot weather, she liked it even if the rooms were small, because it gave her more privacy. She thought now that she might have rested better if she'd stopped to lie down in Margaret's room, but she really wanted to take her clothes off.

She ran some cool water into the old-fashioned tub, which had feet and a narrow flange around the top. And then after she'd had her bath she put on just a slip and a thin old chiffon negligee—quite inappropriate to the cook's old room on the third story which she had made into a sort of sitting room for herself. She lay down on the couch just under the side window and gave a sigh as her tired back muscles found a sort of solace against the hard cushion. She had only been there a few minutes when she heard the front door close, far below. She had left her own door open, and the one on the second floor too—from the back stairs out to the front hall—so she could hear anyone coming in, and she frowned now, listening intently. Oh dear, she didn't want to have to get up and go down . . . her back really ached today. But she didn't see who it could be; Agnes never got back from work until after five and Joe still later; and Mrs. Morrison stayed over at the hospital with her son until the evening now, generally. It might be Mr. Delephant, but he always sat out in the Square until late, when it was nice weather, watching the children play around the little bronze elephant. . . . And she didn't think Margaret would be coming back this early, either.

But it was Margaret. Leaning up on one elbow and listening, Madge heard whoever it was coming upstairs, and she was sure that was Margaret's step, the closer it came. She lay down again in relief, not bothering to call, just wanting to be quiet for a while longer. But in a second she heard Margaret's voice at the door below.

"Mother . . . You up there?"

"Yes, dear. Just resting." That was probably all Margaret wanted —just to know where she was. She'd done that when she was a child, coming home from school. But she'd never wanted to talk, or do anything else with her then; just to locate her. Madge was somewhat surprised now when she heard her steps coming up the last flight, rather slowly, as if Margaret were tired too.

"Hello," she said, appearing at the door.

"Hello darling. I didn't think you'd be back so early."

"Oh, it's too hot to keep mooching around." Margaret pulled off her small hat and threw it on the table with her white bag. Madge didn't know just what she meant by mooching around, so she kept quiet. "Hot up here too," Margaret said, going over to the front dormer window to gaze out over the trees in the Square. "I should think you'd go downstairs, where it's more comfortable."

"Well . . ." Madge said, "I know. But I wanted to get a bath and have my clothes off for a while."

Margaret turned back and looked at her and smiled with a faint derision. "You do look incongruous—up here on the third floor front, and wearing that old Hattie Carnegie negligee . . . Or was it Hattie?"

"Lanvin," Madge said lazily. "I got it the last time I was over . . . Ten years ago." The last time she had gone over to visit Lou and Thomas—but she didn't add that.

Margaret sat down in the low rocking chair, and ran her fingers through the hair at the side of her temples, which looked flat and moist.

"You know I really think it's sort of silly, you staying up here, even if it is more private. You could just as well take over two of the rooms on the northeast corner and shut yourself away there. You ought to begin trying to get rid of these people, anyway."

"I know," Madge said. She didn't want to be bothered talking about it then, but Margaret persisted.

"As a matter of fact, it's going to take quite a while to get things put in shape again, and you ought to do it in the summer. It's getting possible to get workmen again, but they'll be slow and you'll have to allow for a lot of time. The painting itself . . ."

Madge sighed. "It's going to be a big job, I'm afraid. An awfully expensive one . . ."

"Well, you just have to expect that, these days—and after all the punishment the poor old house has taken. I don't think you realize how badly it looks, Mother, to someone coming in from outside."

"Yes," Madge said submissively, "I know it's gotten pretty worn." (But why Margaret had to get started on that *now*, of all times . . .)

"It's not just worn—it looks down at heel—sort of disreputable.

I keep seeing new things that—well—" Margaret got up again, as though too restless to stay seated. She sounded edgy and irritable, and Madge watched her worriedly as she picked up her bag and got a cigarette out and lighted it.

"I'm sorry, darling. I know you've always had a sort of pride as well as fondness for the place. But—everybody's house has gotten run down during the war. . . ."

"I know," Margaret said, more quietly, obviously trying to be reasonable. "There was a reason for it then. But now—something ought to be done about it, that's all I mean."

"I'll try to do something—gradually," Madge said. Margaret was pacing back and forth across the small room, and she turned to look at her mother.

"Why gradually? If the jobs have to be done—"

"Well, I mean I'd rather not pay for it all at once," Madge said mildly. "Take on one thing at a time . . ."

"Oh nonsense, Mother—that's just procrastinating, and you know it. You don't want to be upset, and you've always put things off. But after all you might as well be really upset all at once, and get it over."

"You don't understand," Madge said slowly. *Why* did she have to start all this now? Why couldn't she let her alone—to work things out herself? She'd had to do it for quite a while now. And it was too bad for them to get into one of these arguments again; she didn't want to fight Margaret, and Margaret just didn't know how things were with her now. But Margaret stood looking down at her, smiling— knowingly and indulgently, as sure as she had always been that she knew all about it.

"Don't I?" she said.

"No, you don't. I don't have as much money to spend on things as I used to—"

"Of course not," Margaret said lightly. "None of us does. But you can make out, can't you, darling?" She was still smiling, teasing her, rather as an older person might a younger one.

"Yes," Madge said, looking back at her quite calmly from the cushion where she was leaning. "I can make out. But I think I'd better work it out myself, and take my time. I don't know why you're suddenly trying to get me stirred up—get this done, get that done—"

"I just want to be sure you will start," Margaret said abruptly, turning away to find something to put her ashes in. "I'd like to be sure, before I go, that you *are* going to do something." She said the last words with her back to Madge, who slowly sat up.

"Are you—do you have to go soon?" she asked wistfully, forgetting the argument.

"Fairlie's month at camp will be up in a little over a week," Margaret said. "And I'll have to do something about the house, too. I can't leave it standing empty—and go on paying the rent."

Madge knew that they had sold that other house where she'd visited, some years before, but she'd always supposed that they owned the one they'd been in ever since. She tried to take that in, at the same time she was trying to grasp the other implication—of an unoccupied house, but it was the last that she spoke of first.

"But Clay—" she said. "You mean he's staying at the club?"

"Clay is away, at the moment," Margaret said crisply. "But naturally, I can't just leave all my responsibilities for weeks on end. You know I have to go back, Mother."

"Oh, of course, dear . . . I wasn't thinking. It just seemed to come suddenly because you hadn't spoken of your plans before. I guess I had a feeling of hurry—because you were trying to hurry me!" And she laughed a little to smooth it all over.

"Well, I do want you to get started," Margaret said, still obdurate. Madge looked at the floor.

"I will," she said gently. "I will."

"When?"

"Oh my dear, don't sound like that. Let me run my own house—and you run yours." She smiled to soften it, looking up at Margaret, an odd figure of appeal, with her gray hair soft and unruly, and the once expensive negligee falling aside from her plain tight little slip. But Margaret looked back at her with her gray eyes dark and stormy and her fine mouth grim.

"It may have to be mine again," she said. "My home, I mean. That's why I want it to be decent—to bring my children back to. I don't want them to have to live in a run-down boardinghouse—yet. And it isn't as if you *had* to . . . I know you did it for the war at the beginning—I *know* all that. But now it's either pose or procrastination—I don't know which—it seems like sort of an *act* to me, this little landlady-living-on-the-top-floor business—but that's all beside the point. . . ." She stooped to stub out her cigarette, jabbing it down into Madge's empty cloisonné stamp box. Madge had been staring at her with wide, frightened eyes, as the words rushed on, but now she said, very softly, "The point is—Clay. Is that it?"

"Yes," Margaret said, straightening up her back again—very straight indeed. "That's right. Clay."

"Why didn't you tell me, darling, all these weeks?"

"Because I thought maybe I could find him," Margaret said in a hard voice. "That's why I came up here. To look for him." The hard voice crumbled a little.

"To look for him?" Madge said, aghast. "Don't you know—where he is?"

"No. I don't. Not now. He left, about a month ago. Said he might come up here to get a job—that was all. He didn't want me to know where he was. He just wanted to drop out. . . . But I thought maybe I could find him . . . if I looked, and inquired carefully from a couple of people that he used to know and might look up. If I didn't—scare him away." Margaret's voice was miserable now, with humiliation. But Madge felt more at sea than ever.

"You mean—it isn't—a woman, he's after—but a job?" she asked almost timidly.

"That's it—that's what it's always been—a job!" Margaret said passionately. "Oh he's no good, Mother—he never has been. No-account—just what Father tried to tell me. He's all talk—theory—self-deception. He gets jobs and won't or can't keep them. Sometimes he can't even get them. And he's ashamed about it, and defensive, and then sometimes he blames it all on me. And now he's just—walked out. That's all. Now you *know.*"

And suddenly Margaret had picked up the hat and bag she'd thrown on the low table, and turned and fled across the room, and out, and down the stairs.

* * *

Madge started after her, but Margaret paid no attention to her pleading call, and she suddenly realized that she couldn't go down on the lower floor that way; it was getting late and people would be coming in. So she gathered up her silly loose draperies and went back and began hastily putting her clothes on. She wasn't thinking coherently as she picked up her flimsy girdle and pulled it on, and then her wartime rayon stockings. She had scarcely begun to take in any of it, only to feel a sense of deep shock—only to recognize the passionate hurt which Margaret was suffering and to know that somehow she must try to help her. Even the shock was not of surprise, because it was like something long delayed, which she had expected years ago and then gradually forgotten to watch for. She must always have known that there was something wrong with Margaret's marriage . . . And now, it was as if there were large pieces of the whole picture lying close to her hand which she could reach out and put into place—in just a minute.

But consciously she was thinking only, as she pulled a thin dress on over her head, no wonder . . . No wonder that the girl had looked so tired and strained, and preoccupied; even haunted sometimes. Or that she'd had that frightened look when she first came back and thought the House—her only refuge, was going to fail her. And no wonder at all that, just now, when she'd reached the end of her rope, her nerves and temper too had frayed out to the breaking point. Perhaps it was kinder after all, to let her have this few minutes to pull herself together before they tried to talk any more. Her mother knew that Margaret wouldn't have told her anything even now, except that she had come to some definite ending and had to have some place to turn for haven. The House, again . . .

Madge went quickly and quietly down the back stairs, avoiding the place that creaked, quite without knowing she was doing so. She went down the front upper hall to the door of Ronnie's old room, which was closed, and for a sharp second felt that old constriction of the heart for fear Margaret wouldn't open it, even now. But at her one soft knock Margaret's voice spoke evenly and promptly from the other side.

"Come in," she said, as if she were expecting her, and when Madge went in Margaret said without turning around from the dressing table where she stood, "I'm sorry, Mother. I didn't mean to go into such a tailspin. I shouldn't have taken it out on you." She had taken off her own dress now, and washed her face, which was still flushed, but had regained its usual lines of composure.

"Oh, my dear," Madge said, going over to her. She touched her bare arm gently, but she didn't try to kiss her or caress her further. "Why didn't you tell me when you came—or long ago?"

Margaret shook her head, as though to relieve it of a dull pain.

"I couldn't, Mother. First one reason and then another, I guess. It's gone on so long. . . ."

"How long?" Madge said. "Tell me." It would be better if she could talk about it quietly now. She sat down in a chair near by, and Margaret followed her example, submissively it seemed, and sat on the small bench before the dressing table, and put one elbow on the latter, and rested her head in that hand.

"I don't know," she said dully. "It began back in the depression, I guess. The first depression, while you were abroad. It was the first time I ever realized what it meant not to have all the money one wanted—for anything. Clay was let out of the bond firm, of course; he tried to get other things, and I tried to keep him from getting too discouraged. But it was a bad time. It was only the allowance you gave me that kept us going, when the baby came—and for months after."

"If you'd only let me know," Madge said, sadly.

"I couldn't, Mother. Clay's pride was so raw—don't you see? You hadn't approved of him, or our marriage in the first place—"

"Margaret dear, I don't think you ever quite understood—" Madge began, but then she stopped. She had been going to say that it was more Hugo who had disapproved than she, but what was the use? And Margaret was going on as if she hadn't spoken anyway.

"So it made it that much worse when everything went wrong. And when you came home, so innocent and unconscious about what was going on in the world—well, that got him on the raw too."

"I see," said Madge quietly.

"It even did me, at times," Margaret admitted. "But then when you turned that money over to us, I thought everything would be all right, and that Clay would have his real chance. He *had* been studying investing and market cycles and all that kind of thing. And of course I didn't know then that he was just a theorist . . . Just a —tycoon in his own head. I really believed in him. At least I tried to . . . Most of the time."

She seemed to be finding it harder to go on.

"But he did do very well in managing things, didn't he?" Madge said encouragingly. "All those years you've been in Salt Lake, I thought . . ."

Margaret didn't take that up at once. There was a silence, which grew longer, second by second. Finally she said with difficulty, "Yes— he did all right, as long as the market was with him. Up through the middle thirties. Until the next break came along."

"Was there—?" Madge asked uncertainly, and Margaret raised her head to smile across at her, half in pity.

"Oh yes. You wouldn't know about that, darling—but there was a bad break in the market in 1937 and '38. That was what they called the Recession. That was when Clay lost practically everything you had given me."

Madge looked at her uncomprehendingly.

"You don't mean—everything?" she said.

"Practically everything," Margaret repeated. "I don't pretend to understand it, but we know those things do happen. When people don't really know what they're doing in the market—sometimes even when they do," she acknowledged, as if trying to be fair. "World events don't choose much, I guess—between the just—and the unjust." Her voice was very bitter now. "We had the house left, anyway, for which we had paid too much, incidentally. But we got a mortgage on it, and rode along there for a couple of years more. We were still there when you came to visit last, in 1940, weren't we?"

"Yes," Madge agreed quietly.

"Well, after that we sold it for what we had left in it—not much, I may say . . . And then of course there was defense work and war work from then on—plenty of it—and of course patriotism bolstered up Clay's pride all through that period so that he didn't feel ashamed to do any kind of factory work." Madge shivered a little at the coldness in Margaret's voice. "But it was that time," she went on relentlessly, "1938—and the couple of years after, that had really done something to Clay that he never got over. And to me too, I guess." Margaret got up suddenly, and walked across the room aimlessly. But she turned around there and looked straight across at Madge. "I had to admit to myself then, you see, what I'd really known all along and just tried to conceal from both of us—I guess, that Father was right, and Clay didn't amount to anything. And never would."

"But you still loved him?" Madge asked anxiously.

"Yes. I still loved him. But I didn't respect him, Mother. I couldn't. He was too full of—excuses. He rationalized everything. He blamed the world—and the system—and the other fellow—for his own lack of —Oh, I don't know, for things that were really his own fault. He has brains, in a way. He could have done something maybe, but he was always a little ahead of himself, impractical or egotistical—or something. Wanted to be his own boss, for one thing. Couldn't bear to feel that he was *under* anyone, inferior to anyone. Don't you remember the way he used to try to patronize Father? It was that same thing. He has an inferiority complex, of course," Margaret said coldly. "He admits that, himself."

She stood there, tall and straight, a little like a statue of something symbolic, Madge thought; justice, perhaps. Only justice would not be taking sides; justice would not be accusing, and Margaret was. Madge found herself looking across at her with a clearness she had never had before when looking at Margaret; it had always been clouded before by some sort of feeling: resentment, or yearning, or her own frustration. But now there was something she was beginning to see.

"Don't you think," she said, gropingly, "that he may have felt—your lack of belief in him—and that made it harder for him to find his feet again?"

"But I did everything," Margaret said evenly, "to try to help him, in those first years. To try to believe in him, actually. But you can't keep that up in the face of—disintegration, Mother. You can't respect a sham, day after day. And you can't even pretend respect when the sham breaks up in pieces before you. Can you imagine what it would be," Margaret said, coming over closer to her again, and looking down into her mother's eyes, "to see a grown man sitting slumped in his chair with his hands over his eyes—and tears trickling through his fingers? To have him put his arms around your knees—and sob—that he was no good—that you were too good for him and never should have married him? It's—demeaning—" Margaret said, in a tight strained voice, "to both of you."

But Madge had lowered her eyes from Margaret's, as if ashamed; and more ashamed for Margaret's having told her that, than for Clay. Poor Clay, she thought. Poor Clay. Because he was right, in a way. He never should have married Margaret; only a strong man could have stood up to what she was—and what she expected, perhaps. She was too strong herself, too far above him. It would make the contrast between them too great, and almost too hard to bear. Madge knew what that feeling was.

"It seems so pitiful," she said softly. "I feel so very sorry for him. And you must have too, dear."

"Yes, I felt sorry for him. Terribly sorry, sometimes. But you can't go on being sorry year after year. You get sick of it—hopeless about it—and impatient too."

"But if you loved him—and you say you did still—"

"I still do," Margaret said, slowly, but in a tone which said that she hated herself for it.

"But wouldn't that be the one thing that would keep you going? That would make you merciful—and make you keep on trying to help him? You don't always love people you respect," Madge said very quietly. "I don't know why, but that's the way it is, sometimes."

Margaret glanced at her briefly. "I'm afraid that's something you wouldn't know about, Mother, so I couldn't expect you to understand. But of course it did keep me going, in a way. Looking after him, just as I was looking after the children. Accepting him—and being patient.

God, how I have had to learn to be *patient*," she said. "That's what I've done for years." There was an underflow of passion beginning to rise in her again. "But that isn't enough for *him* now! Oh no—he blames it on *me*. Says I live on too high a plane for him—I'm just too noble, or some such infantile stuff. Says he's had enough, that's all. . . ."

She dropped down on the side of the bed as if exhausted, and sat there, putting her slim hands up to cover her face, and Madge, watching her with compassion and the same old helpless yearning, yet found herself watching too—to see whether the tears would trickle through *her* fingers. She was appalled at herself, and got up and came over to put her hand on Margaret's head, and fondle it tenderly.

"My poor child," she said softly. "I'm so sorry. So terribly sorry. And it seems so—terribly unnecessary. If you love him so much, why can't you just let him *know* that, and rest on it?"

"He does know it!" Margaret burst out, as if she furiously resented even that fact.

"But why do you—why *must* you look up to him so? If he's good and decent, it seems to me that matters so much more than anything else. Can't you accept the fact that he is just one of the smaller people of the world—like so many of the rest of us—and that it isn't an evil, or a deliberate fault, and he can't really help it? Maybe he wouldn't be so proud in his way, if you weren't, in yours."

"Well, if I'm proud," Margaret said, lifting her head suddenly as though reminded of it, "I suppose it's because I'm my father's daughter —and I have a lot to be proud of!" Yes, Madge thought clearly, that was it, that had always been it. Margaret's admiration of Hugo—and perhaps the abilities she had inherited from him too—had built a sort of high, impregnable foundation under her, from which she had always looked down on the world around her. She would be the worst woman in the world, probably, for a man who didn't have much self-confidence of his own. But she was going on now, insistently, raising her voice a trifle. "I can't throw that away, Mother, don't you see? It's part of me, that pride—and I have a right to it, because my father was as fine and big as he was. And I've always tried to live up to it, too!"

Margaret got up from the bed and went over to the closet and began putting on a dress, as if to pick up that business of living again —and properly clothed—and Madge's eyes followed her. "One thing that you naturally don't think of," Margaret went on wearily now, "is what I've had to cope with, in keeping a house going, and feeding and dressing a family on an inadequate and always *irregular* amount, because my husband can't make a steady living. That's the thing—never knowing what you can count on from one month to the next, and one year to another. Something you've never even had to consider, you see. It's all very well to be sympathetic, but nobody can eat sympathy, I can tell you! It's making do with this and making do with that—and all the time keeping up appearances so as to save *his* face. I've done it all, Mother—I tell you I've done *everything* to protect him—"

"But not from yourself," said Madge, in a very low tone. Those four words stopped Margaret short. She looked at her mother with a sort of astonishment and hurt unbelief.

"How can you say such a thing to me, Mother? Why are *you* turning on me, and now, of all times?"

"Oh my child, I'm not turning on you—ever. It's only that there's something that you don't see, about yourself. And it could be so important, if I could just show you."

"You don't think the financial facts of life are important, do you?" Margaret said coldly.

"Yes," Madge said, "of course I do."

"But you don't really know anything about it, do you? You've always been so completely safe yourself. So protected. I'm thankful that it's been that way for you—I don't mean I'm not—but you see, it doesn't even occur to you what I'm up against right now: that with Clay gone I have nothing to live on except a couple of war bonds left over from what we got from the house. That I have two school-age children that I can't look after properly and at the same time earn a living for them and myself, too. Though God knows I could do it better than Clay!"

"You'll come back here, of course," Madge said simply, with a sort of unshaken dignity. "I haven't as much income as I had before—I told you that. But we do have the house, and we can certainly all manage, even if there are some things we'll have to do without."

"You're very generous, Mother. You always have been—and I sound as if I'd never appreciated it, I suppose. Well, I have, and I'm sorry to have to call on you again. I'm sorry to be the one to make you do without things now. I'm afraid you don't know what that means, Mother. You've never done without anything in your whole life, have you, darling?" Margaret's tone was quietly and sadly satirical. Even the endearment, in its suggestion of indulgence, was ironic. But the question itself was rhetorical, not looking for a reply, and it was like an explosion out of utter stillness when Madge drew a long, unsteady breath, and answered it.

"Yes," she said. "I have. I've done without love, for a great many years. And that's something *you* have had all your life."

She hadn't really meant to say it. And she hardly knew what she would say now to follow it up, to answer the blank arrested look on Margaret's face. But she had heard that one remark just one time too many. And besides, there was something she must do now—something she had started blunderingly to do at long last, and it was like a road which she felt rather than saw ahead of her, yet knew she must follow once she had started down it. There was a compulsion in her, greater than any she had ever known before. But Margaret was only looking at her in that puzzled way as if she didn't think she could have heard her mother correctly.

"You don't mean—you think *I* don't love you?" she said gently, a little deprecatingly, as though to suggest that people didn't really say those things, no matter what disagreements they might have. Madge smiled back at her with complete forgiveness.

"You don't, really, dear. It isn't your fault—or mine either, perhaps, though I always used to feel it must be mine. It's just one of those things that happen in some families. You gave your love so wholeheartedly to your father and took his point of view so completely—there just wasn't very much left for me. Those things *do* happen you know. Just as Ronnie gave me more, I think, than he could ever have given his father . . . But Ronnie has been gone a great many years now," Madge said reflectively. Margaret was still looking at her as if she really didn't know what her mother was talking about.

"But Mother, what a peculiar—what an *absurd* thing for you to say! As if Father hadn't been here with you for years and years after Ronnie—"

"Your father didn't love me, darling. Didn't you know that?" Madge looked straight back at her.

"Why, of course he did! I don't know what you mean." (It was like someone throwing up her hands instinctively, refusing to look at anything so preposterous.)

"Oh no," Madge said, with quiet ruthlessness (pulling those hands down, gently but firmly). "Not after the first six months or so. Not quite that long, I guess."

"Whatever has made you think such things?" The girl was shocked now, righteously shocked; perhaps even a little doubtful of her mother's mental—or say rather her emotional—balance.

"Well," Madge smiled sensibly, but with a touch of wryness, "there was a good deal of evidence to prove it."

"What do you *mean*, Mother?"

"Can't you guess?" Madge asked.

"Guess! Why, I can only think you've taken leave of your senses— I don't even know what's come over you."

"Just a realization that I've got to tell you what I never meant to," said Madge.

"You mean," Margaret said, her words coming stiffly, "you are trying to tell me that my father was the sort to—have any dealings with other women . . . *My father!*"

"There were a great many of them," Madge said inexorably, "from shortly before you were born, right up to the time of his death."

"Oh Mother, how can you say anything so foul!"

"You don't believe me, do you?" Madge's hazel eyes were wide with old suffering, but very dry.

"Well, what earthly proof have you of such a statement? Whatever made you believe anything so fantastic of a man like Father?"

"He told me so himself, a number of times," Madge replied, in a tone which sounded quite matter of fact.

"Oh Mother, now—you can't—"

"He rather gloried in it. He was what people nowadays call sadistic, I guess. He liked to hurt me. He didn't care what sort of situation he put me in. Do you remember," Madge went on slowly, but with an effect of suddenness somehow, which seemed to arrest Margaret's impatient disbelief once more, "a girl named—Nellie— that we had as an upstairs maid that last spring and summer before he died? Rather a pretty girl, with red hair?"

"Why—yes," Margaret admitted, though almost unwillingly. "Yes, I remember, vaguely. She had a very white skin, didn't she—and brown eyes?" The picture seemed to be coming back to her in spite of herself. Her mother nodded.

"She slept in the little back room on the second floor. The sewing room it was—later. Right in my own house," Madge said simply. Margaret was looking away from her, frowning, toward the window, but she seemed to be still recollecting . . . remembering.

"She left very suddenly," she said thoughtfully. "I'm trying to think what it was that happened—in the front hall, it seems to me . . . You and I had come in together—I was upset—about not hearing from Clay, that was it, and she was impertinent. And then she went off into a regular torrent of abuse, and started to follow you up the stairs. I didn't know what she was talking about—something about rich people and the way they treated girls like her, wasn't that it? I thought she was crazy. . . . But you sort of parried her some way—" Margaret broke off and looked slowly back at her mother, a gathering wonder in her eyes. "And then . . ." She stopped again, and there was a space of silence while Margaret went on remembering. "And then," she repeated finally, in a tone which had altered in a curious way, "Father came in the front door, very urbane—as he always was. . . . And she sort of glared at him like some kind of a wounded animal —and then suddenly caved in, with tears in her eyes, and went off to the back of the house. And she—left right after that, didn't she?"

"Yes," Madge said quietly, as Margaret finally stopped. "He was through with her then."

"I didn't know I even remembered all that," Margaret said in a strange, dazed voice. "But I do now. I remember the way she looked —at him. . . ." It was that recollection of her own which had convinced her. Unavoidably. After a moment she gave Madge a look which was almost pitiful, and said, "My—father . . ." and Madge went over to her and put her hands on Margaret's shoulders.

"My darling—I'm sorry. I didn't mean you ever to know, if I could help it. But that was the way he was. He had many fine qualities, you know. Those were real. You mustn't think now that they weren't. He had tremendous ability, and vision—everybody said so— and great intelligence. And I've always understood that he had great integrity too—in business."

"Do you really mean—that he had many—affairs? Not just something that he lost his balance about once, maybe?" The girl asked the question painfully, as if she had to know, and Madge made the answer as simple as possible.

"There was always someone, I think. Now one, and now another. I don't know just how many different ones there were, in twenty-two years."

"And I thought . . ." Margaret said. "I believed in him so utterly. I thought he was above everybody else, in just about every way."

"I know. I know. That's why I always tried to keep it from you. It seemed too cruel to destroy such worship, or such an ideal. I thought it was better for you to have that. But I was wrong. You built him up too high—and yourself with him, somehow—on a foundation that wasn't quite real."

"My whole foundation," Margaret said in a curious tone. "And it was rotten at the base. Oh Mother—Mother—did other people know?"

"I suppose so," Madge said. "But I was never quite sure, because I wouldn't talk about it myself. They say one's family is the last to hear of those things. But your father was rather a careful man in many ways. . . ."

"How you ever did it," Margaret said, "how you ever lived that way . . ." She put her arms around her in some belated instinct of protection. She was beginning to think of Madge at last.

"I should have left him," her mother said, meeting her eyes. "But I didn't. I didn't have the courage to go out—on my own."

"Oh darling," Margaret murmured. "I've been so—so—I never even began to realize. And here, all the time, what I thought *I* was living up to was . . ." Suddenly she stopped, as though some new unpleasant implication had struck her hard, off guard, and she caught her breath sharply, and Madge saw that she was flushing slowly and painfully from her neck up to her hair. "Oh, he was *low*," she cried out then. "He was unspeakable!"

"He was weak—in that way," Madge said simply. "I suppose we're all weak in one way or another. *I* don't know which ways are the worst, sometimes. Try to remember that, dear. Don't make it harder for yourself than it has to be."

"But do you know what he did—to me and *my* love?" Margaret said, very low. "When I was first in love with Clay . . . Father made me feel that it was the wrong kind of attraction between us, that it was too much of the physical and nothing else. He made me ashamed of my feelings, and he played on that shame, until he got that promise from me, not to see Clay for a while. That's what he did! I'll never forget that afternoon, and the flood of guilt he made me feel—and the time I went through all those weeks afterward. And then the way I felt after I'd run away with Clay—and Father was dead, not knowing what I'd done." She had put her hands up over her face again, and Madge tried to pull them down, in reality this time.

"Oh my dear," she said.

"He even left me with a feeling that's come back to me at times all through my life—that I shouldn't have cared for Clay in quite the way I do. Maybe I shouldn't—I don't know. Maybe that's *him* in me all this time, my inheritance from a man who was—so rotten . . ."

"Oh darling, darling—*no!*" Madge said. "You mustn't feel that way, ever—or I shall know I made a worse mistake when I told you about him. What makes it right for you, and holds you to Clay, is that you can and do love him in every way."

"Yes. I do." The words came out, half smothered. "I still love him! I can't help it. I never could help it, Mother—and to look down on him in some ways, as I have—felt contempt when maybe I should have felt only pity—it's almost torn me apart. And yet I miss him so when he's gone, I feel like half a person. And I don't know what I'll *do* if he doesn't come back. If I can't find him . . . So we can begin again . . ."

"I'll find him for you, dear," Madge said quietly. She was a mother comforting her child, reaching for any promise to quiet the pain in that voice, not knowing she was going to make it until she heard the words, not knowing how she would fulfill it then. But there was a certain grimness underlying her soft voice, and she added, almost more to herself than to Margaret—"I did it once before. . . ."

Chapter Thirteen

LATER THAT NIGHT, AND IN THE WEEKS TO COME, MADGE REALIZED how foolish that promise was. In a city of that size, to expect to find a man who had no known address; no job; who was not looking up his old friends—who didn't want to be found . . . It was absurd, after all. And she was no F.B.I. In fact, she couldn't imagine why she had said even to herself that she had found Clay that other time, considering that Margaret herself must sooner or later have run across him, just as she had first met him, among her own young friends. But it was just a wandering bit of conviction which had come to her inexplicably, something she seemed to know without being told. And it gave her the only support she could find for believing her own ingenuous promise to Margaret now.

For of course Margaret herself did not believe that Madge, or anyone else, would find Clay for her. She was deeply shaken, and her former solid belief in her own deserving right to happiness had been entirely undermined in one afternoon. They didn't go on talking about it after that day, for it was much too painful. Once or twice she asked her mother another question about Hugo Fairlie, and then went off to nurse the answer in silence. But for the most part they talked practically of what must be done next, and what they could plan together about the house and for the children.

It was decided that Margaret would leave the following week. Fairlie would be coming back from camp then, and she would arrange to give up the house there and start packing up. Fortunately their lease would expire on the first of September. By the time Joan came back also, from her visit at the ranch, Margaret would be ready to move, and by the middle of August or very soon after, she would bring both children back home to Elephant Square. Meantime Madge would expain to Agnes and Joe that her daughter's family were coming back to live with her and she would have to have their rooms. Mrs. Morrison could stay on a while longer if necessary, until the time her boy was released from the veteran's hospital, and they would be going home anyway. Mr. Delephant would be there still, of course: a permanent visitor—a vague old gentleman without any home, whom the children must be taught to accept and be kind to.

"And maybe," Madge said, in a worried way, "I can have a few things done around the house while you're gone, so it won't look so badly to them." She didn't dare promise to get into too much expense, now especially—when the whole family might have to depend on her for a while.

But the day after Margaret left she called up the man about the floors; she could have that much done, at any rate, she told herself cautiously. He promised glibly to come out in two weeks; not before that—no ma'am. So she started looking for slip-cover material—and faces, always faces. Not that she expected to find Clay in the bargain basement at Sears or Penny's, or in the drapery departments of the higher-priced stores either, but she was looking everywhere, on the streets, in the elevators, in the restaurants. Some day, surely, she'd see him somewhere, if he were in the city at all. She looked around searchingly whenever she had her lunch downtown in some restaurant, and then—more practically and economically—she thought of lunch counters, and she began doing what she had never in her life done before: dropping into one or another of those places for a cup of coffee at different hours of the day.

She would go shopping day after day—without buying anything— and stop for coffee whenever her spirit flagged. There were a lot of shops, fortunately. But there were a lot of lunch counters, too. And after a while Madge was drinking so much coffee during the day that she wasn't sleeping very well at night. Though as July went on, that could just as easily be blamed on the heat, instead of the coffee; or on her worry and remorse about Margaret. For she kept asking herself what earthly good she had done by destroying the thing which had meant most to the child—taking her confidence along with it— if Clay was gone anyway?

The floor man didn't come when he said he would, of course; was evasive and offhand when she called him again. So she telephoned the man who had given her the estimate on painting the upstairs woodwork—and found to her consternation that he had raised his price by almost a third. So she put that off once more. And she hadn't found any decent, inexpensive slip-cover material either. She wasn't, in fact, getting anywhere. And she wasn't finding Clay, no matter how she rode the buses and tramped the hot, slightly softened pavements. She remembered what Margaret had said about his spending his time at the library when he had no job, so she went there several times and sat in the reference room, reading the newspaper right down to the want ads, covertly watching anyone who came in. At least it was cooler in there, and it was pleasant to get off her poor feet too. Finally she inquired at the desk one day whether anyone answering Clay's description had been in lately, but the woman shook her head in a puzzled way. . . .

Agnes and Joe left on the first of August, and Madge started cleaning their rooms. And then gradually she washed all the upstairs windows and the curtains, shabby and thin as they were. She was getting awfully tired again, but she couldn't stop; she had to be ready for the children; and she couldn't stop looking for Clay either, for that would be to admit defeat. But this business of not sleeping until one or two in the morning made it seem rather useless to go to bed early, whether she was tired or not. Oh well, people said you slept less and less as you got older, so she might as well get used to it. Madge was getting close to another birthday now, and trying not to remember it. It was a bad one—the worst one yet. Her sixtieth.

One night she'd gone upstairs meaning to take off her clothes and try to read for a while, but it was so hot up there that she went to the window to see if there was even a breath coming in. She stood there looking out on the round, cushiony tree tops, still and unruffled in the quiet dusk. She had been meaning all summer to move down from these top-story rooms—and hadn't done anything about it. But tonight it was just too hot up here. She'd get her book and go downstairs again, to the library; maybe she'd even go out and sit on a bench in the Square for a while . . .

She went down one flight and softly past Mr. Delephant's door, and on down the lower stairs into the empty hall. She unbolted the front door again and stood looking across at the Square for a couple of minutes; then she felt in the pocket of her house dress to be sure she had the key tied in the corner of her handkerchief. Going out, like this, alone (at night—on foot) was a thing she couldn't have brought herself to do, even a couple of years ago. But now she closed the door firmly, and moved on down the steps and across the street. The Square had always seemed rather dreamlike to her at night, and she wondered whether that was because she had actually dreamed about it so often. She didn't know why, but it was a familiar background, like a stage setting, for many different dreams, always with the same peculiar half light—neither moonlight, nor sunlight, nor lamplight. Sort of twilight, really, but through which one could see quite clearly.

Madge passed several couples . . . walking past her on the wide asphalt path, sitting on benches, or lying on the dry, moth-eaten grass. She didn't look at them carefully; people in pairs didn't interest her at present; besides, all she was looking for just then was an empty bench. But then she saw one where a man was sitting alone, and she left the path and started toward it, just the way you would in a dream, without stopping to think about it at all. It couldn't be, of course—and she was going to be awfully embarrassed in another moment, walking right up to a strange man, and then having to turn away again. But there was something about the set of the heavy shoulders, something about the position, with his hands in his pockets, and his feet thrust out in front of him . . .

She paused ten feet away and drew in a long breath, and then let it out softly, almost cautiously, so as not to blow away this image in front of her.

"Hello, Clay," she said quietly, and he looked back at her steadily without the least change of expression.

"Hello—Madge," he said.

He'd never called her that before. There was a sort of heavy irony, even a vague truculence, in the way he said it. But Madge, in the light of all she'd learned about him lately, realized quite clearly that this was only another blind stab at protecting himself. A rejection of civility, lest it make him appear to be asking for anyone's favor . . . just as he was deliberately sitting there on the bench without moving, without making any attempt to rise. Why, his whole manner to her had never been anything but a defense, Madge thought, with a sudden quickening of sympathetic surprise. While all the time she'd thought he was looking down on *her*—was feeling contempt, if not dislike, for her. What pitiful and ridiculous things people were, she thought, as she sat down beside him, quite as if he'd asked her to, quite as though they often met this way in the Square, of a summer evening.

"I've been looking for you," she said in a matter-of-fact way.

"The hell you have." It was a completely noncommittal statement. Neither the words nor the tone told her anything.

"The trouble was, I didn't know where to look!" And she smiled at him sidewise, with a certain appeal, as if inviting his amusement over such a manifestly foolish situation. But he declined to be amused.

He said heavily, "I often come over here to sit for a while. Seems a logical place to come, to try to figure things out," he added, with some undertone of sarcasm which she didn't quite get. "I don't come in the daytime though. I didn't know you came out at night." He seemed bent on being just as rude as possible, and she sighed. Finally he said, abruptly, "I s'pose Peg's told you that I've quit."

Madge hesitated. It was a part of her own inconsistency, she supposed, that she had never really thought out what she would say to him if she found him. Her aim had been focused so entirely on the primary objective. She realized now that she must have intended just to turn him over to Margaret. But that was not so simple, under the circumstances, and probably wouldn't have done any good, even if Margaret had been here.

"Margaret was back here for a while," she said finally. "Did you know?"

"Peg—here?" He turned his head. "I wouldn't have come within five miles of this place, if I had known."

But Madge ignored that and went on quietly, "She was paying me a visit. It was a long time since she'd been back, you know. Before the war . . ."

"Yeah. I know, I know all about that. Well then, you know all about us, I guess."

"I know about her," Madge said. "I don't think I've ever known all about you, Clay."

"You knew I was no damn good right from the start, didn't you? Must be quite a satisfaction to be able to say I told you so, and so forth, and so forth."

"But I never told her so, Clay," Madge said steadily. "And I never disliked you, whatever you may have thought. It was her father who tried to keep her from marrying you."

"Well, you believed whatever he told you, didn't you?" Clay said rudely. He was looking, not at her, but ahead of him, indifferently, down at his outstretched feet, but Madge was facing toward him on the bench and gazing at him with such a steady, concentrated intensity that finally he was compelled to turn his head toward her. Then she spoke.

"You—really—think that I believed—everything that Hugo Fairlie told me, for a matter of some twenty-two years?"

"Didn't you?" he said.

"What a fool you always thought me, Clay," she said simply. "That was the ironic part of it, really. Because while you were always disliking me, resenting me—whatever it was—I always rather liked you. Right from the first, remember? We'd have been friends—if *you'd* been willing."

He seemed unable to answer that at once, and there was a silence between them while he continued to look at her, as if to see if she could possibly be telling the truth. Finally he looked away.

"Well, you never said so," he said grumpily. "You never stood up for me, that I could see, against the old man. And later on, you always seemed to be serenely sitting up there on top of your pile of dough, without a glimmering of what went on down below, or what even your own daughter was up against, for instance, during the depression."

"I know," Madge admitted humbly. "I never had the—guts—to stand up to Hugo. About anything. And I was very dumb about money, I know that too now. Lots of us are weak—and not very bright, in this world, Clay."

"You can say that again!" Clay said abruptly, and then after a second he added, "Only I never thought I'd live to hear you say it."

"But you never stopped to think how I felt, did you, Clay? You never saw me as a person at all, just as a sort of symbol—of the idle rich, didn't you?"

"Well, weren't you?" Clay said bluntly, and they faced each other eye to eye with a new and curious frankness.

"I don't think—any human being is *just* a symbol of anything," Madge said, softly and slowly now, feeling her way. "I think maybe that's one big trouble with the way we all look at things. The Rich —the Poor—the Capitalist—the Working Man—why, they're just big blown-up words that have grown into cartoons, Clay. Caricatures, I guess I mean. They're just not real pictures of real people—but we go right on acting as if they were."

"They were drawn from real people to begin with," Clay reminded her dryly. "They didn't grow up out of thin air, you know."

"No—o," Madge said uncertainly. "But that doesn't mean that the same picture fits everybody else in the same—well, the same income bracket, I suppose you'd call it. For instance, you've always taken me as a horrible example of the Rich Widow—haven't you?— and maybe I have been—a horrible example, I mean. But that doesn't mean that I'm a sample of all Rich Widows. If you really knew me at all, or even put your mind on it for a couple of minutes, you'd know very well that I'm not typical of anything!"

He was beginning to grin at her, even if it was unwillingly; at her earnestness perhaps, or perhaps it was just at *her*.

"This is the damnedest conversation," he remarked.

"Yes, isn't it?" she agreed, in some surprise, but she ignored the hint of levity in his voice. She sounded puzzled herself. She had been thinking with that part of her mind which always hung a little aloof, that it was very peculiar for her and Clay to be sitting talking this way, and the most peculiar part of it was that it was she who was doing so much of the talking. No, perhaps the most peculiar thing of all was that she knew now—so surely—not exactly the words, but the heart of what she had to say to him. Somewhere, she thought, in still more surprise, she must have learned more than she'd realized at the time. This wasn't quite what she wanted to say to him even yet, of course. But it seemed as if these things were in the way between them, and would have to be cleared out before they could rach the point. She sighed. "I guess I just mean you've got some kind of a—cartoon—stuck in your mind about anybody who has any money, Clay. You think the Rich are dishonest—and rotten . . . and useless, of course, just because they're rich, because they couldn't possibly have made any money except dishonestly. And I just think that's rather silly and stupid," Madge ended with sudden definiteness.

"Oh you do, do you?" Clay asked rather dourly, but as if he couldn't quite decide whether to take her seriously or not.

"Yes, I do . . . Curiously enough," she added, in an odd detached little voice, "even my husband was considered absolutely straight—in business."

That was the thing that made him really stare at her, soberly now, and almost as if he wondered whether he had ever seen this little woman before.

"*Even* your husband?" he repeated.

"Well, have you ever heard anything to the contrary?" she asked politely.

"No."

"I didn't think so," she remarked in the same detached way. And then added, a trifle dryly, "As a matter of fact, even the people who have looked after my affairs since Hugo's death, seem to have been quite honest. That's surprising, isn't it, considering all the pictures that have been drawn about the investment business? And you know how a widow with money is supposed to be easy game for anybody who—who wants to pull a fast one on her . . ." She smiled a little; she didn't know why she was falling into Clay's own vernacular this way. But he didn't smile back now. His face, which had undergone a number of changes during these past few minutes, had gone suddenly very grim.

"I suppose Peg has told you," he said brusquely, "about the money you turned over to her?" and Madge gave a quick exclamation of distress.

"Oh Clay!" she said. "I didn't mean that—I wasn't even thinking—"

"You know, though?"

"Yes, but—"

"That I tried to manage and invest it for her, and—"

"Yes," Madge broke in gently, trying to stop him, "I know."

"And lost practically all of it," he said, rubbing it in, like salt, in his own wound.

"I know, Clay—but I don't blame you—not for one minute. I just don't think anybody really knows as much about those things as—we think they do, maybe. Everybody who's advised me has had some different theory, quite honestly, as I said, but I can't see that *any* of them have been right—all the time."

"Maybe so," Clay said grimly. "But that doesn't make a fellow feel any better about it. You *feel* like a crook, even when you know you aren't one." He leaned forward, with his elbows on his knees, and ran his fingers through the mat of his hair; he seemed to be pulling at it, as if to get hold of something he could hang on to. "God, if I could only have made it up," he said, on a sort of groan. "You don't know what it does to a guy to fail—and fail—and fail—"

"Oh Clay—my dear boy," Madge said. "I ought to, if anyone does—" But he hadn't quite taken in what she said; his head was too far under the black wave which had broken over him once more.

"You don't know," he said doggedly, "what it does to a man to know he's failed his wife and kids, over and over again. The way I've failed Peg."

"I'm not sure," Madge said quietly, "that you did fail her—entirely."

"Well, I'm not going back," he said. "I'm through."

"That's not what I meant," Madge said very distinctly, as if he were a little deaf. "I mean I think she's failed you, too, Clay." It was hard for her to say, even now, about her own child, but she knew it had to be said for that was the point: that was the thing they'd been coming to by all this roundabout route. That was what she had come out to the Square to tell him tonight, though she hadn't known he was there when she started. It was the very thing she'd been looking for him for, for weeks, to tell him. And when she'd gotten it out, he sat there, quiet, for a minute, so she knew it had gotten through to him at last.

Finally he said, "Oh Lord, Madge, I don't know. I don't know. Sometimes I've wondered . . . I tried, believe it or not. And I did have some bad breaks, any way you look at it. But everything that went wrong got me more and more with my back up to the wall, and feeling that anybody else would have had the sense to do it differently. Peg would've done it differently herself. She wouldn't tell me so, you understand, not in so many words . . . She was always so goddamned patient and long suffering!" he broke out suddenly, and Madge said softly, "Yes . . . I know."

"But everything *she* took on—the house and the kids, and the women's stuff she did outside—they all went like silk. People were always telling me how efficient my wife was, what a good business head she had . . . And what a big help *that* was—to me, if you see what I mean! *I* knew she was a swell person, but it's hard to take from all sides. I've had a bellyful, that's all."

"Margaret is efficient, like her father," Madge said quietly, "and she inherited his confidence and assurance too, I guess. But she sapped yours, didn't she, Clay?" She was looking at him with infinite sympathy, as he sat forward with his elbows still on his knees, and his hands hanging down between them. He shook his head like a dazed dog.

"I don't *know*, I tell you! But she did something to me. Sometimes I kind of thought she was trying to set herself up on top, just to make herself feel better in her own mind for having married such a poor dope. Just because she was ashamed of caring for me."

"Oh no, Clay," Madge protested.

"Oh yes," Clay said bitterly. "Sure—I know she was too good for me. We both knew it. I never ought to have married her, if I couldn't live up to her, and that's all there is to it."

"Not quite all, Clay," Madge began, but he wasn't listening again.

"Sometimes it was better," he said broodingly, "when I got a decent job and could hold my head up around the house, didn't feel she was trying to protect me—make excuses for me, even to my own kids. Maybe you don't think *that's* something to take! But now with the war over the whole thing was beginning all over again, and it's going to be worse from now on, for the guys like me—pushing fifty —with nothing much behind us and nothing at all ahead. Plenty of jobs—yeah, but it's the young fellows they want. People don't change," he said glumly. And that seemed to be the place Madge was waiting for.

"I think—Margaret has," she began almost timidly.

"I see." He was grimmer than ever. "Well, I wouldn't blame her much, at that."

"No, you don't see at all. I don't mean she's stopped caring for you. She misses you terribly, Clay. She needs you, don't you know that? It's the other way that she's changed. All that assurance and the illusion of her own rightness. Because that was sort of an illusion, Clay. Margaret wasn't invulnerable, the way she thought she was."

"I don't know what you mean." He sounded irritable again, impatient. "I don't know what you're driving at."

"I mean she sees things differently—sees herself differently, maybe. That part of her is changed. I . . . changed it, myself," Madge said faintly, more as a confession than with any pride of accomplishment. And Clay had turned to her with a look of instant, ready accusation in his eyes.

"What do you mean?" he demanded almost roughly. "What have you done to her?"

"I told her—about her father."

He continued to look at her, with suspicion changing into amazement, and the amazement into a sort of stern disapproval.

"You mean . . . you told her—what a heel he—"

"Yes," she said.

"My God," he said. "That's the one thing I never did—and never would have told her."

"You knew about him, then?"

"Well, hell, of course I knew. A fellow hears those things, even if the family doesn't . . . I thought *you* didn't," he said abruptly, "until just a few minutes ago."

Madge gave a faint sound, the whisper of a laugh.

"I told you—you thought I was a fool. But I don't believe any woman on earth is quite that stupid, Clay."

"Well Peg thought he was—well, he was the Angel Gabriel to her, just about," Clay said, and added fervently, "the bastard. And I don't mean Gabriel."

"I know," said Madge. "I did everything to keep it from her

for years. I thought that was the right way. But it's done something wrong to her, Clay—I don't know why—but it has. Maybe just because it was false. And she had to know, now, not to go on spoiling her own life, and yours."

"But what has it done to her, being told all that now?" Clay asked, his brows knotted, trying to figure the whole thing out, and Madge was silent for several seconds. That was hard to answer; it was even hard to know what the answer was, yet. Perhaps the answer itself would depend on Clay, finally.

"It's hurt her—pretty badly," she admitted at last. "It was cruel to do it—but I think I was right, this time. It's made her more human, or made her accept the fact that she's human, maybe. It may make her more compassionate toward others, in time. But it's made her need you right now, Clay. I think she needs you more than she ever did. . . . So *now* will you come back?" Madge ended suddenly.

He got up as if he couldn't go on sitting there any longer. He was facing away from her, but she could see that his fists must be balled up tight inside his coat pockets where he had jammed them. Finally he turned around and his voice was hard, as he looked down at her.

"And what makes you think it will work now, when it didn't before?"

"I don't know," Madge said, with utter candor. "How can I tell, for two other people? But I would like to see you both try it again. The way things are—now."

"I still haven't got a regular job," he said harshly. "I've only had a couple of temporary things since I've been back here. No reason to think I can support her any better than I ever did."

"There is more than one kind of support," Madge said.

"God, Madge, you don't know what you're asking. We've gone all through it—and called it quits, can't you understand that?"

"You don't love her any more, then?" she said. Their gaze had met and tangled almost as though they were wrestling with each other.

"There have been times when I've hated her," he said.

"I know that." She accepted it simply. "But that doesn't answer my question."

His heavy shoulders shifted slightly then; it might have been a shifting of weight; or something like a shrug—of final resignation possibly, and his fists in his coat pockets might have loosened up too, from the look of them from the outside.

"You're a stubborn little devil, aren't you?" he said. "I suppose

I do. Some things you can't uproot, even when you'd like to pull 'em out with your bare hands."

"I know," she said. "I—know." And then she got up slowly to stand beside him. "Will you walk over to the house with me?" she asked quietly, as if they had finished what they had to say between them now. And as they walked across the Square, she began telling him about what she had done with the house during the war. When they reached the street, he took her arm to cross it, and when they came up the steps he unlocked the door for her and would have left her there, but she told him to come into the hall for a minute.

"It looks so badly," she said. "Maybe you can tell me what I ought to do about it. I hate to have them all come back to it this way." And she turned on all the lights and they stood together inside the door, looking around the hall.

"Yeah, I see what you mean," he said.

"You wouldn't—help me yourself, would you, Clay?" she said in her most timid tone. "Just for a little while—until you find something you really want to do?"

"I might," he said.

"It would be the most enormous help. I just can't get anybody to fix the place up."

"Lot to do, all over the house, is there?"

"There certainly is." She sighed. "You don't know how I need somebody—just to take hold, and *begin*."

"You do, do you?" He was looking down at her now with a faint, knowing grin, seeing through her, but indulgent with her too. "Want me to move right in tomorrow, eh?"

"I certainly do," she said fervently, and he put his hand on her arm again and squeezed it a little.

"Thanks, Madge," he said.

She wondered if he was going to continue calling her that, and hoped he would; it seemed to make things better between them, somehow. She watched him as he stood there, his glance still traveling around the big square hall, pausing on various familiar points and moving on again, and as she watched she realized, in this light, how much older he looked than she'd remembered. Fifty, he'd said, and it surprised her. He was nearly ten years older than Margaret of course, and he showed it now, whereas he hadn't a few years ago. His face had deep lines for a man of his age, and his hair—that mat of springy, tight curly hair—was thoroughly grizzled now. Not unbecoming—but still—it was a great change. And his eyes, always such a light blue, looked even lighter; faded perhaps. Madge saw them pause rather longer on some object in the hall, and she glanced that way herself. Hugo's portrait, on the landing . . . It suddenly came to her that she might take that down now, some day . . . But Clay's eyes had dropped from that, and were smiling in a funny way.

"D'you know," he said suddenly, pointing at the stairs, "that that's where Peg and I sat, the first night I ever saw her?"

"Was it?" Madge said, smiling in return, without thinking just how that could have been.

"It was that awful stuffed-shirt party you had here, some kind of a musical affair."

"Oh—yes . . . Yes, I do remember that party. Very well. And you—I couldn't think who you were when you came in! I'm so bad at faces, and I was trying frantically to cover up, and make you feel at home."

"Well, you succeeded, didn't you?" he said, his grin broadening. "But you couldn't have remembered me—because you never saw me before. I crashed that party, Mrs. F.!"

"You *did?*" Madge said blankly. "Why, I always thought Margaret had asked you, or some of her friends had brought you along. Hadn't you met her somewhere else before?"

"Nope. That was the first time I ever saw her."

Madge looked at him and began to laugh.

"For heaven's sake, Clay Ferguson! And here I was racking my brains to place you . . ." But then she paused in a puzzled way. "You know," she said slowly, "Margaret never told me that."

"No," he agreed, and the smile vanished from his face. "Oh no. She wouldn't. She was ashamed of it. Of what you and her father would have thought of our meeting that way. Maybe that's one of the reasons why she's always been ashamed of me," he said.

Madge looked up at him steadily, and there was the beginning of a faint twinkle in her tired eyes. "But after all, I picked you up first, didn't I?" she said. "We'll have to tell her that some day."

*   *   *

There was, of course, the immediate question of whether Clay should go out to join Margaret and help her move out of the other house. But Madge withdrew herself from any discussion of that—withdrew carefully, just as she did when she suggested that he telephone Peg from Elephant Square the next morning, and then went out and left him in the den, closing the door behind her, just as soon as the telephone connection was put through. She had done her part, and now she must be very careful. Never let Clay feel again that he was not his own boss, not the head of his own family, or that he was in her house on sufferance. Heaven knew she wanted him to stay this time, as long as he would, and could be happy there. It was so wonderful to feel that he *liked* her at last; that he'd taken her in, accepted her as a friend. It had taken eighteen years. . . . She was puttering in the kitchen that next morning, happily dazed, not quite sure of what she was doing with her hands, when he gave a bellow for her from the den.

"Hey, *Madge!*" he yelled. "Where'd you get to, anyway? Come here, will you? Peg wants to say something . . ."

She came running, then. And Margaret's voice at the other end of the wire was low, and faintly tremulous, though you could tell that she was trying to keep it steady.

"I can't really say anything now, darling—not over the phone. But you must know how I feel. And Clay's going to stay up there and help you with odd jobs around the house till we get there . . . that's more sensible, don't you think so? And he wants Joan to finish her last term before high school down here, and I—I'm doing what he says. I can arrange for her to stay in town with the Tremaines for that long, I'm sure. But Fairlie and I will be along the end of next week, just as we planned. Only . . . Mother?"

"Yes, dear?"

"Only now—it'll be about the happiest homecoming I've ever had. I want you to know that."

Madge was crying foolishly when she put down the phone and turned away, and Clay put one arm around her shoulders and bent his head to kiss her cheek. Then he asked her rather hastily what she wanted him to begin on, and she swallowed—hastily too—and said, picking up the challenge, that she thought he'd better start on the front hall.

That hall floor was a major job in itself. He had to rent the equipment, and he didn't know how to use it—but then, Madge didn't either, and it became a matter of hilarity between them, to discover just how you went about scraping and cleaning and waxing a fine old floor. And of pride, and mutual congratulation too, when it was done. Madge had never before dreamed that she could have *fun* with her son-in-law; that she and Clay could actually enjoy working and planning together. But that was the way it was, in the following days. The rugs were brought out of storage next, and spread out and vacuumed, but they smelled overwhelmingly of moth crystals for several days, and that provided a cause for joint anxiety and merriment between them also. They were like a couple of irresponsible but earnest youngsters together, which was incongruous and even amazing to Madge. She wondered once, with an inexplicable twinge of guilt, whether perhaps Margaret had always been a little too serious for Clay, whether she had unwittingly blanketed that boyish, foolish side of him.

But it wasn't as though they weren't getting things accomplished between them, for they were. After the hall, Clay fell to work on the downstairs windows (the hall, the den, the dining room—and all the kitchen ones) which had been just too much for Madge to tackle alone. He did most of them now, but when he was nearly done, she would stand inside and they would gesticulate with their hands and make faces (until they broke down laughing at each other) from opposite sides of the glass—to indicate the spots which had been missed, and then both of them would polish vigorously away at them until one or the other would nod approval. He was not lazy, and Madge noted that with a sort of pride, as if she might have been the first to discover the fact. She reflected too upon how much more he seemed to enjoy doing these jobs around the house than he had ever seemed to enjoy being properly waited on there, or in his own home either. He kept looking ahead now, to one thing after another which needed doing, though of course it couldn't all be done before the others arrived.

"Why, hell," he said once, with a sort of relish, "you've got enough jobs around here to keep a handy man busy for six months!"

"I think I'd have to call him a building superintendent, though," Madge said, smiling.

"I might apply for that job," he said, with one eye cocked at her a little higher than the other.

"And I might hire you before you could get away!" Madge retorted. But then she added warmly, "Oh Clay, you don't know what it means to me, to have someone around whom I can depend on—who really gets things done! If you knew how helpless I've felt here, all these years . . ." But when he asked her once whether she had ever considered making the house over into regular apartments, she looked at him in consternation.

"Oh no!" she said.

"I don't mean this boardinghouse idea. That's no good for the long run. But dividing the whole place up into six or eight decent-sized flats, so you can make something out of it. Lord knows it's big enough, and there's still a howling demand for that kind of thing."

Madge's glance traveled in a worried way around the dining room where they were sitting only the night before Margaret was to arrive.

"Oh no," she said again. "That would be way beyond me. And . . . it would really change the house for good, then. I don't believe Margaret would like that—"

"Maybe not," Clay said briefly, and changed the subject.

And yet, when the others came, and took their places in the House, and some sort of family life began there again, the fact was that the house was not the same any more, and the family was not the same either. Madge and Clay between them had done much in one short week to give the place a welcoming shine, like a newly scrubbed face. But it couldn't be the same as it had once been, any more than an old woman could go back to being the spoiled and petted darling she had been as a girl. The drawing room and library were both closed off now, and Clay had moved a davenport into the cheerful bay window in the dining room, with a couple of big chairs to flank the fireplace there, to make it into a temporary living room. As for the upstairs, it all seemed a little like a railway station where assorted travelers had put down their baggage in little piles and were camping out each in a different corner.

Even the family itself was a new and somehow tentative thing. Except for young Fairlie, all their relationships with each other were slightly altered. He alone accepted everything without question, his hazel eyes sparkling with lively interest behind his big spectacles. Joan would not have taken it all so simply; she might have been critical of the changes in the old house, and she might well have been aware of some subtle change in or between her parents. Margaret looked the same outwardly, of course; the calm, the quiet surface, were still there, seemingly unbroken. But there was something—subdued, perhaps; some hint of uncertainty in her eyes now and again. And there was a lack of sureness in Clay also, along with that scarcely perceptible tension which had reappeared on the very day of her arrival. Having dropped his protective bluster, for the time at least, he didn't seem to know what to put in its place. Madge knew that they were both groping, both trying to find their way back to one another. And it must be harder, she thought, for two people to reach each other through all the snarl of things which the years had tangled up between them, than it would be when they didn't know each other at all. She tried not to notice, not even to look from one to another when they were all together—most of all not to put out a hand either to guide or to grope with them. Outwardly they were a couple, casually rejoined after a two months' absence from each other, and what went on in the immaterial region just behind that casual exterior was nobody else's business, any more than what went on behind their bedroom door.

As always, it was the routine of days, one piling up on another, which covered up the tensions, like the insulation wrapped around a wire. Fairlie started in at school. He was a trusting child, rather as Madge had been, and made friends easily—as she had too, at that age. He liked the new school, and he liked the old house, and he liked old Mr. Delephant, accepting him as a natural phenomenon in these new surroundings. Clay took on the laying of new linoleum in the kitchen as his next job, and planned to paint the woodwork after that, though he admitted, a little touchily (before anybody else could suggest it), that he probably ought to have gone about it the other way around. But Margaret was being careful not to make suggestions these days; she herself started to make slip covers for their own upstairs sitting room, out of some fine old curtain draperies—an undertaking which her mother regarded with some awe.

As for Madge, she adapted herself once more, slipping in and out between these new activities and those other more ghostly comings and goings which the House had been harboring before Clay and Margaret came. (Mrs. Morrison, that large plain silent woman, who made her own bed and tidied her own room, and then waited patiently between her trips to the hospital, until her son should be well enough to take home. . . And Mr. Delephant, who went slowly up and down the stairs, reading in his room, sitting in the Square, watching the children play around his baby elephant, where he and Fairlie often had polite and solemn talks together, quite detached from the grown-up world.) It was strange, Madge thought, the people who had—well in a way, put in to port here, in the old house. It was a sort of Harbor really; a refuge at the end of the world for Henry Delephant, a momentary stopover for some of those young couples, and now a sheltered spot for Clay and Margaret to make repairs, before they started out again, perhaps. Only she hoped they wouldn't start out, but would stay on, indefinitely.

She saw the reason at last for having kept the House all these years. There was some point in it now, some excuse and compensation as well, for all the lonely idle years at first, and then for all the blind, back-breaking work in it. The House had finally justified itself, and maybe it even justified her. She often hummed as she went about the countless daily chores in it now. She never used to do that, and she caught herself at it with a feeling of astonishment. For Madge Fairlie was happy. She didn't dare say it, even to herself. It all seemed a little too good to be true, this pattern of cooperation and peace—and company, at last.

The design wasn't finished yet of course. She knew that. Clay still had to have a real job; Joan would be coming to join them with her young, insistent and possibly disturbing personality; this new tolerance between Clay and Margaret might not last. They were both being so careful now, but one or both of them would give way some time, inevitably, when they got tired, or impatient. . . . Madge herself might so easily start irritating one or the other of them again. It was so pleasant now, but there were so many possible pitfalls. And the most likely one, of course, the most dangerous one, was that matter of a job for Clay.

She had been surprised at first, and then relieved, to find that he could put it aside this way, even for a little while. And then Madge saw that Clay was putting it off, not just as something to be taken up later on but rather as something that he couldn't face again just yet. He wanted to get the house all fixed up for her first, he said; it should be painted throughout before it would be decent again, and he thought he could even do that plastering job on the library ceiling where the pipe had burst two years before. . . . Madge was constantly and secretly amazed by his industry, for she had always believed it was very difficult (judging by her husband and her father) to get men to do odd jobs around a house. But she saw all at once that the House was a godsend to Clay, not only because it made him feel important and necessary, but because it gave him an excuse to push that other thing away from him. Her heart went out to him in sympathy once more, because she had so often procrastinated herself about things she didn't want to do.

"Oh, I'm not worrying," he said largely, one morning. "Not now, when we've all got our feet on the ground, here together, and know where we're *at*. There are still plenty of jobs around; the point is to find something worth staying in, from here on out. So once I get you fixed up here, I'll start really looking around again, really go to town for something permanent."

He sounded young and hopeful; the old Clay, just starting out again. But he didn't look young, Madge thought uneasily; he looked thoroughly middle-aged, and when they sat in the bright morning sunlight in the dining room, as they were doing that moment, he looked rather closer to his late than to his early fifties, even though his body was still young, and he seemed to be able to work tirelessly at these purely physical jobs. She didn't dare look at Margaret just then, so she kept watching him instead, smiling encouragement and agreement as he said those things. She watched him push back his chair then, and get up from the table and stand there for a second, throwing his shoulders back and lifting his chest in an exaggerated gesture of coming to attention, before he went around to Margaret's place to lean over and kiss her.

"Gotta get going," he muttered, as though confidentially, "or the woman boss down there will be firing me!"

And Margaret lifted her mouth to his, and Madge, not meaning to watch, did so. It wasn't long, but it wasn't one of those brief marital pecks either, which you generally saw husbands and wives give each other before other people. It was as if they both—no, not just enjoyed it, but took something life-giving from each other as they gave it. And for a second Madge had a most peculiar and disturbing pang of—it must be a sort of *envy,* she thought, quite shocked—before Clay straightened up with a pat which was more of a slap, on Margaret's back and shoulder. The girl's eyes followed him to the door, while Madge still watched her and saw the look in them—a look of hope and hopelessness combined, a look of love—and pity.

She must have felt Madge's gaze at last, because she dropped her own glance to the plate in front of her, as though to brace herself for a second before looking up to meet it. For of the three of them, it was Margaret who was most on the defensive these days, as if forced constantly to wonder whether the thing she couldn't help seeing in Clay, so clearly and critically, was partly her own fault after all. Madge saw it and understood it and it hurt her to watch, knowing that she in turn was responsible in some degree for what she saw in Margaret's face. What an endless, unpredictable chain it was, this responsibility of one person toward the next, and his or hers in turn upon another. Like the chain reaction people talked about now when they spoke of this awful atomic bomb that had ended the war. Madge had not the dimmest idea of what radioactivity was, but she wondered for a moment whether it actually was, or ever could be, more deadly or far-reaching than the effect of human beings, one upon another.

And then Margaret spoke quietly.

"You're wonderful with him, Mother."

"*I* am . . . Oh Margaret dear—"

"Yes, you are. You help him a lot. You give him confidence—that sense of his own importance that he needs so badly. Sometimes I think you can do more for him—than I ever can."

"Oh my dear . . . my dear. If I could only do something—*anything*—to help you both to work it all out and get on a firm base."

"You help me too," Margaret said simply. "I'm learning quite a lot from you, darling; that I was too—dense, shall I say?—to learn when I was younger."

Madge was speechless then. She could only bite her lips, and shake her head at Margaret, and smile a little watery smile at her. But later that day something began to come clear in her mind, as if it had been there all the time, but hadn't quite taken shape before. It was the sense of hurry in her which did it; she simply couldn't wait, that was it; she couldn't run the risk of waiting for something to happen and perhaps spoil what they already had here. For they were all happy now, or nearly happy; even Margaret would be, if she could feel that Clay would stay as he was now. Madge saw quite suddenly what she had to do, and that same night, after Fairlie had been sent off to bed, and in that lazy indecisive space while the other three sat on downstairs, she began.

"You know, Clay," she said. "I've been thinking about a suggestion you made to me a while ago. I don't suppose you've even thought of it since."

"Did I?" he said, with the tolerance any man is likely to show toward his own suggestion.

"It was just casual—an idea of what I might do with this place."

Margaret looked up slowly, a shade of apprehension darkening her eyes. But Clay grinned. He remembered, apparently.

"Yeah?" he said. "But you didn't go for it."

"Oh it scared me," Madge said, frankly. "Any new suggestion scares me! You ought to know that by this time. But I've been thinking it over some more . . ."

"Do you mind," Margaret asked, with a certain mild constraint, "just mentioning what it is you two are talking about—just the mere key to the code, you know. . . ."

Madge looked at her quickly, a little taken aback by her tone. "Why, Clay suggested that I might sometime like to make this house into regular apartments. Six or eight, you said, didn't you, Clay? There *is* an awful lot of house here—even for all of us—and it's a lot to take care of, this way, too. But if we could each have our own apartment just the way we want it—and then rent the others—without really feeling we've given up the house after all. . . ."

"Sure," Clay said, "it's a natural. Location—type of building—size—not too big or too small. And God knows there's a need for it." He spoke with decision and authority, but Margaret looked over at him, a struggling, inscrutable expression in her eyes.

"Well of course the thing that scared me was the thought of doing anything like that alone, or for myself. But if *you* . . ." Madge wavered a trifle as she looked at Clay now. (After all he might just think it was too small for him. . . . It might have been thrown off just as a theory, an academic suggestion.) "If you'd consider taking it on, Clay . . . I mean, plan it out and manage it—See if it was even practical to get—material and things. . .?" She made it sound just as tentative as she could, just as if she didn't—for once in her life—have a very clear idea of where she was going.

"Yeah, that's the hitch," Clay agreed. "Everybody goes crazy even trying to get a piece of pipe these days, let alone a bath tub."

"I wondered if we mightn't just—make a start with the living room and library," Madge suggested very timidly. "I mean, if they could just be painted up and the ceiling fixed—they're right next to the servants' dining room and lavatory—so if a door could be cut through—couldn't it be used almost as it is?"

"Say, I think you've got something there!" He was leaning forward, looking at her attentively, and enthusiasm was rising in his voice. "Why, I could almost do that single-handed—maybe one man to help me—and we ought to be able to get what we need for that much."

"Do you think so, Clay? Honestly?" Madge's eyes were beginning to shine. "And would you be willing to do it—I mean, put off looking for anything else for a while, and taking this on as a—as a sort of business agreement? If we could rent that one big apartment, why that would be a salary for you to start with—And then we could go on from there. . . ."

"Boy, would I like to do it!" Clay said, and then appeared to be thinking it over, ponderously as a business man should—perhaps to counteract the impulsiveness of that exclamation.

"Of course I suppose it would be too small for you to want to bother with indefinitely," Madge slid in quickly, "but if you could just get me started. And we could all live here, meantime. . . ."

But then for some reason, Madge and Clay both looked toward

Margaret at the same moment, both realizing that she hadn't said a word for some minutes. She was sitting alone on the couch, where she had put down her magazine beside her; her long hands were lying quietly on her lap in front of her.

"How do you feel about it, dear?" Madge asked softly. "The house—will come to you eventually." That was the question that she ought to have asked Margaret earlier—alone. But she had forgotten for a little while, what she had always known, that the House meant more to Margaret than to any of them. It was as though the spirit of the House belonged to her by some inalienable right, and she was the only one who could give title to it . . . to make it into a public thing, for good. "It's really up to you," Madge said, quietly questioning now. But Clay put his own question in before Margaret could answer, and it had a slight edge to it, so that it cut in easily between the other two.

"Yes, Peg, how do you feel about it?" he asked, and suddenly all the defensive tension, and belligerent challenge, the bitterness and irony which he had distilled out of many years of defeat, were back in his voice again. It was as if he knew ahead of time, and threw it at her before she could say it, the conviction that she would have no part of it—no faith in anything *he* had suggested . . . That only cold water could come down from that clear mountain stream.

Margaret raised her eyes slowly, to look in front of her, not at either one of them, but straight between.

"I think it's a very—good suggestion," she said in a still, muted voice. "I think it's a splendid idea, Clay." And then looking at her mother, almost pointedly, "When do we start, darling?"

* * *

There was more to it than that, of course. Actually, the real work on the house didn't begin until October, for they decided to make the more drastic alterations after all; not all at once, but gradually. Clay had gone out right away and talked to several people, and got bids and estimates on the time it would take to get materials. He even dickered with a man who had started to build a duplex and then given it up, for lack of hinges and doorknobs—and Clay came out of the dicker triumphantly with two small electric stoves and refrigerators which the other man had already lined up. After that, there was no holding him. Madge swallowed hard when he gave her the estimates, but she didn't waver even then, and felt rather proud of herself for the way she carried it off. An investment was what it was, she told herself firmly, and if she took the money out of some silly engraved piece of paper and just added it to what was already *in* the House, why that would be something that she could really see and understand, and even keep track of herself, if Clay should tire of it. She knew about renting rooms now, didn't she?

So she told Mr. Purcell that she would like to sell some stock and put the money into fixing up her own house for apartments, and Mr. Purcell didn't approve at all. He said that the market had taken a sharp drop lately, and she'd be sacrificing anything she sold now. Furthermore, he said, they'd probably seen the peak of these high prices on real estate and with labor as high as it was, it didn't seem to him a very good time to go into anything like that.

"But you see," Madge said simply, "it *is* a good time for me. In fact it's the only time . . ." But she didn't explain what she meant by that. For probably the first time in her life, she explained nothing. So Mr. Purcell rather gloomily sold two or three stocks to cover what she needed, and neither Margaret nor Clay knew nor inquired where the money came from. They still assumed that when Madge wished to make an investment of any kind, the funds were always there at her disposal. For Margaret had never taken seriously her mother's one reference to not having as much as she once had. In the first place, that was the sort of statement which well-to-do people had been making ever since 1929; in the second place, it was a generalization which applied to the whole world. Madge knew that she didn't have much left outside of the Trust Fund, but she was the one now who was determined to keep her affairs to herself. If the children had any idea that she was getting really low in her own resources, it would ruin everything. Clay would begin again to brood upon the sense of his own guilt, for having lost what she had given Margaret, and the whole new foundation they were trying to build upon together would be wrecked. She simply couldn't risk that.

So she told herself again that this was an Investment, and the work got under way, and the House began to echo with the noise of hammers and saws, and strange feet and voices. And the whole family took the most intense and personal interest in it, from Madge right down to Fairlie, who was delighted with everything. Even Mr. Delephant paused at the drawing room door to observe the wall being put up to divide it, and the sounds and smells of building seemed to bring a puzzled but reminiscent interest into his far-off gaze. Clay was full of himself and his new role as building supervisor and apartment manager combined; it was wonderful the way he seemed to know just what to do and how to go about it, Madge assured Margaret, happily, even rather proudly. And Margaret, who was being meticulously careful not to suggest anything, not to interfere, not to run anybody, would look back at her mother with serious eyes, and nod anxiously, and earnestly agree.

"Yes, he does seems to be good at this kind of thing. Maybe it's what he's always needed. . . . Oh Mother darling," and she came up to her, and took Madge's face between both her hands, and kissed her gently. "Thank you," she said.

"What for?" Madge came back quickly. "Don't you know that I'm happier right now, myself, than I've—almost ever been?"

And it was true. Here she was, sixty years old already, and except for the slight jar she had felt when she crossed over that dreaded dateline—it didn't even matter. Funny, she had thought once that by the time she was sixty, nothing would matter at all, that she wouldn't even feel anything by then. But now . . . Well, she thought perhaps the feeling people had about their ages, right up through the years, until they became actually ill or crippled, was only the old question of vanity. She had to admit that Clay had been quite a help to her when he'd looked across at her on the morning of her birthday, with that odd appraising stare of his—bold because it was so unconcealed perhaps—and said bluntly, "Hell, Madge, you don't look sixty any more than—well, than Fairlie here looks twenty!" That was very silly, she knew, but it was pleasant. And if Margaret thought it was silly too, she didn't say so, just smiled indulgently at them both, as if they both seemed rather young to her.

But Margaret's whole attitude now was one of conscious striving —toward tolerance for the others, and in that, perhaps, toward some reassurance for herself. She had grown in tenderness toward her mother as the enormity of what Madge had gone through with her father grew and took shape in Margaret's own consciousness. It was as if the only way she could retrieve some of the misplaced devotion she had given him was by giving a larger measure of it to her mother than she might ever have done otherwise.

It was a wonderful and heady period for Madge, a happy one for them all; and she hugged that certainty closer to her as the weeks went on. Nobody expected everything to run smoothly all the time. Materials did *not* always turn up when they had been promised, and the workmen were slow and indifferent, and didn't do things the way Clay wanted them to—and he got very irritated and impatient and grouchy with everybody at times, especially if he suspected that any lack of progress reflected on him. But that only served to keep the household human, Madge felt. And she was even beginning to take a little secret pride in the way she herself—his own mother-in-law!—was able to laugh him out of his irritability. (What a *fool* she'd been, she thought later on.) She would tell some ridiculous tale about the way she had tried to get something done during the war, when the furnace had broken down, for instance, and her own utter, impotent dependence on some great oaf of a mechanic who hardly knew the difference between a lump of coal and a lump of ice. . . . And Clay would begin to laugh at her, or with her, and it was rather fun to bring him around—to make him and the others all laugh together, even if it was at her own incompetence. She used to be so apologetic about her inadequacies, but she wasn't any more. She even suspected at times that Fairlie considered his grandmother a great wit. . . . Which was enough to go to any woman's head—and she did remember to caution herself about losing the latter.

What she did lose, however, was that sense of fearful caution which she had had for the first few weeks after the children had come back: the implicit fear, even in the midst of her happiness, that none of this could last. It *would* last now—because she had herself made the foundations of the House secure under them all; that was the difference. The big downstairs apartment should be ready to rent by the middle of November, and then they would fix up the den and dining room and kitchen for Madge's own apartment. And then the second floor, which would be the real transformation of the House. . . . But it was all going to work out now, and they would all go on having fun together, and all stop worrying about money, or anything else—and if people outside insisted upon harrowing themselves about inflation and the atom bomb and even another war—well, let them, she thought . . . let them.

She wondered afterward whether the moment when one feels safest is, in the very nature of life, the most dangerous one. Or whether it was only her perennial stupidity which had made her feel safe at all. Not that it mattered which it was, after the first insidious crack appeared beneath her. At least she was not too stupid to see it then—and she had seen it before anyone else had, thank God for that. She could comfort herself with that in the days and years to come.

It was an evening in the early part of November—but the weather didn't have anything to do with it. It was a Friday, too, and that had a little to do with it, though only incidentally, because Fairlie had wanted to go to a movie. He'd brought up the subject at the beginning of dinner, and followed it persistently all through the meal ("Can we go, Mom? Can we? Don't you want to go, Daddy?") until Clay and Margaret in self-defense had finally agreed to take him, since there was no school the next day. Margaret and Madge had hurried through the dishes together, even though Madge had declined to go. She didn't say so, but she thought it was nice for them all to go together without anybody else tagging on; she was rather careful about that sort of thing. So when Margaret went up to get her coat, Madge settled down in a chair by the dining-room fireplace with some darning in her lap. Clay had just thrown another log on the fire, and dropped into the other chair to look at the paper. Fairlie was already out in the hall somewhere, impatient to be starting, and Madge smiled as she heard him calling to his mother to hurry up. . . . She looked across at Clay and thought how much happier, and more relaxed he looked these days—and her own sense of content grew proportionately. If she were a cat, she'd be sitting there purring away as if she had a little gas engine inside her, she thought amusedly.

And then she heard Margaret coming down again, and almost spoke to Clay to get him started, and then purposely restrained herself, because that was another of the things she was careful about—not to interfere, not to prod any of them in any way. So Margaret came all the way across the hall and appeared in the doorway again.

"Come on, Clay," she said, with a touch of wifely impatience. Curiously enough, she was not nearly so patient—so *painfully* patient—as she used to be, but Madge thought it an improvement, because it made her more natural.

"What for?" Clay said, not looking up.

"Oh, don't be silly. You know you told us you'd take us to the movies."

"Did I?"

"Clay—darling, don't be exasperating. You know you did. We've been breaking our necks to get ready, and Fairlie's champing at the bit out here. Come *on*, dear."

"Oh gosh," Clay said lazily. "You go."

"Well, I like that! We both promised Fairlie. You're *not* going to back out on me now."

"Oh-h yes I am!" Clay grinned and slid lower in his chair, with his legs stretched out in front of him as if challenging anybody to move him. Madge looked studiously down at the sock she was darning, with her lips tucked in to keep from smiling, though she knew very well she would have wanted to shake him if she'd been his wife.

"Come on, Clay. Don't be mean," Margaret said, a little uncertain now and a little aggrieved.

"I'm not mean," he protested innocently. "I'm just damn comfortable, and I don't wanna go out. You and the kid go along, and I'll stay here and keep Madge company."

"I don't mind being alone, Clay," Madge said hastily. "I'm used to it . . . Please run along!"

But Margaret's gaze had moved from Clay over to her, slowly and gravely, where it rested for a long minute.

"I am *not* going, thank you," Clay said, beginning to sound stubborn about it. "Why the hell should I go chasing out to some moronic movie when I'm more comfortable right here? You don't have to go if you don't want to, Peg. And you've got company if you do want to—so why make a goat of me? I've got company right here, and a comfortable fireside, so why in heck I should—"

"Yes," Margaret said dryly, "I see you have."

"Come *on*, Mother! For gosh sakes"—Fairlie's shrill voice came suddenly echoing back from the front door.

"'Yes, dear, I'm coming. Well I'm certainly—not going to beg you," she said to Clay, quietly now. "Good night." The last was directed impartially to both Madge and Clay as she turned away, and then she was gone. Clay raised the newspaper again, and in another second they heard the front door close firmly. It didn't slam. Madge almost said, "That *was* sort of mean, Clay," or— "She was disappointed, you know, dear—" But no—*no!* It was still up to them. She would not say anything at all. It was one of those perfectly insignificant marital brushes, which meant nothing at all. The fact that she happened to have got caught between, involuntarily, meant nothing either. Clay and Margaret had weathered really serious differences together, and *that* was where she had been able to help, she reminded herself, trying—she hardly knew why—to justify herself in some way.

Clay went on reading, and she went on darning; nothing was said between them. It was not necessary to say anything. They had become so used, each one, to having the other one around. They might just as well have been a long settled married couple themselves, Madge thought, with the faint beginnings of amusement in her again—and then broke that thought off abruptly. The log in the fireplace broke too, and Clay grunted and got up to poke it together. Standing on the hearth, he began to feel his pockets for matches, and then stood there lighting a cigarette, looking down over it at Madge.

"Those my socks?" he asked idly.

"No," Madge said calmly. "They're Fairlie's. You didn't think your feet were that small, did you?"

He grunted again, and let himself down into the opposite chair, where he sat smoking for several minutes. Madge took a brief glance at him, and saw that he looked entirely comfortable and quite unremorseful; not even thoughtful. Presently he put out the cigarette and yawned, and picked up the paper again. If *he* didn't feel guilty about Margaret, she didn't know why on earth she should, Madge thought, almost resentfully. But the way Margaret had looked for a moment—that still bothered her. That quiet, reflective look she'd given her—her mother, not Clay. It was something behind that look that Madge was trying to see, something it reminded her of.

And then she suddenly remembered—another time. A Saturday afternoon, that was—a rainy one, several weeks ago. Margaret and Clay had been going to drop in at a cocktail party with some of their old friends. Madge had been busy all day, and had got herself a pot of tea and brought it into the dining room—right here, where she was sitting now. And Clay who had been fussing around in one of the rooms across the hall had come in for a minute and thrown himself down on the couch, and suddenly decided he'd have some of Madge's tea. So she'd brought him a cup, too, and then Margaret had called down from the stairs to say she was going up to dress and was he ready to go to the cocktail party? And Clay had said, "Cocktails, my eye! I'm a tired old man and I'm taking up tea. I'm not going to any cocktail party." There was a moment's silence from the stairs; then Margaret had acquiesced. "Okay, if that's the way you feel about it," she'd said carelessly, and gone off upstairs to do something else.

She hadn't made anything of it at all, and Madge hadn't thought she really wanted to go. But the incident came back to her now. And she realized that though she herself had not taken any part in either incident, she had been *there,* both times. And if she hadn't been there, Clay would have gone with Margaret. Clay didn't like to be alone. Madge remembered from the times she had stayed with them before, how restless he had been, almost aggrieved, if he had come home in the afternoon and found Margaret out. He was so dependent on her in so many ways. Unless . . . he was finding that he could often be dependent on Madge instead, relaxing in her company, finding amusement in her shortcomings, expanding in the confidence she gave him. Surely she needn't be deprived of that. . . .

Yet even as she protested to herself, she remembered Margaret's steady, questioning look, and it made her unhappy, not as though she had done anything wrong, but as though she had blundered again somehow. The point was—wasn't it?—that Madge had no right to help Clay, even to build up his own self-esteem, if she were getting in Margaret's way and making it harder for her to do the same thing herself. She had no right here—this minute, in this room—if by being here she had encouraged him to slight his own wife. Made him prefer, even involuntarily, her own company to Margaret's. What an odd, backhanded thing this relationship was becoming, Madge thought, bewildered. . . .

She finished a sock, and sat there with her hands quiet in her lap for a long moment. And then she began carefully putting away her needle and thimble, and tidying up her work basket. Maybe she shouldn't stay down here, and have Margaret come back in another hour or so and find them still sitting here—steeped in a sort of mutual content. It seemed foolish—but maybe it wasn't after all.

She put the basket on the small table beside her and got up, picking and brushing threads from her skirt, rather elaborately, so as not to seem in too much of a hurry. Clay lowered his paper, conscious of her movement.

"What'sa matter?" he said, surprised.

"Well, I think I'll go on up," she said, yawning slightly.

"Already?"

"Yes, I think so. I'm a bit tired tonight."

"Well, hey," he said. "That's a fine thing. Leaving me cold after the rest of the bunch has walked out."

"You should have gone with the others," she said smiling.

"The hell I should. I didn't want to go with the others. I was happier right here. Till you start to walk out on me—"

There was no personal undertone in the words; it was a simple statement of fact, and he made it almost lazily. "Well," Madge said lightly, "I guess you can still be happy right here till the rest get back." But now as she started to go past him, he had suddenly put out his arm so that it blocked her like a closed gate, and she stopped, looking down at him.

"Fine thing," he said again. "You going to bed at half-past eight, when you never went up before ten in your life before; go on back and sit down, and stay awhile," he said in the tone that sounded—

and no doubt made him feel—like the lord and master of the situation. Madge looked down at the arm barring her way . . . It was a low gate, she thought inconsequently, only about knee high—but she couldn't exactly step over it. At the same time it seemed perfectly ridiculous to go all the way around the dining-room table as she would have to, to avoid it, and so reach the door into the hall. After all, he certainly wasn't going to wrap that arm around her knees and hold her there. But she stood still, not wanting to move against it, and her glance shifted back to his face again, though he was not looking up at her now. He was just sitting there looking straight ahead of him quite confidently, with his arm stuck out, waiting for her to go back to her chair as he'd told her to. She looked down on the top of his head, at the tight curled mat of grizzled hair and for a second she had an impulse to put her hand on it and pat it—not so much the head, as the hair. It looked so springy, like moss, and yet soft too—like a poodle's wool maybe. She'd always wanted to feel it, though she'd never known it until that minute. She had even put her hand out a little way, and then drawn it back, shocked—not so much by the gesture itself as by the feeling that had prompted it.

"Come on, Clay," she said quickly. "Let me by, won't you?"

"Won't play, huh?" He dropped his arm, but he sounded a little hurt. And she in turn felt a quick distress, as if she'd really let him down. Yet the whole thing was so silly; it was silly that she even felt she ought to go. But she was more sure of it now than when she first got up.

"I'm just tired, that's all," she said, trying to pass over it easily and casually, trying to move along lightly toward the door. But just as she reached it he said, "Wait a minute," and turning, she saw that he'd gotten up out of the deep chair and was standing there frowning at her. Then he started to come over after her, and she had to hold herself to keep from running out into the hall, not because she was afraid of Clay—oh heavens, no!—but because everything was so confused, and complicated, and she didn't seem to know what it was all about.

"Look," he said, as he reached her. "Are you mad at me about something?"

"Goodness no! Of course not. I'm just tired, I told you."

"Well, I'd hate to have you get mad at me, you know—now we've finally gotten to be pals. I guess I sort of count on that now, Madge. Our being friends, I mean."

"Of course we are," Madge said quickly. "You can always count on that, Clay."

"That's good," he said, and then uncertainly, "well then—good night." He put his hands on her shoulders and kissed her cheek, as if to make it official.

"Good night, Clay dear," she said briskly, smiling at him, but his hands were still on her shoulders, keeping her there.

"You're a funny little piece, Madge," he said, still puzzled.

"Oh no, not very," she murmured. "Just an—old model, that's a little run down, maybe."

And then she broke away, gently and not—she hoped—too precipitately. As she went into the hall she heard him muttering something to the effect that, Hell's bells, he supposed he'd have to go to bed himself pretty soon, just for something to do. Maybe, she thought, hurriedly, this was all that was necessary. Just one evening where he found himself deserted . . . But she knew quite well that she was only stalling to gain time with herself, so that she wouldn't have to think it out while she climbed those stairs. There were so many of them, and now of course there was that extra flight, on up to the third floor—only now she had a feeling that when she got up there, there wasn't going to be any place for her to go—after that . . . even in her thoughts.

As a matter of fact, when she reached her attic sitting room, she turned on the light mechanically and went methodically across to the windows to pull down the shades, and then she sat down in the low rocking chair, with her back straight against its back, and her hands folded tightly in front of her. And then she started thinking—not quite so methodically—what she was going to do next. For something very queer and complicated was happening to them all, or was beginning to happen, unless she herself—by being very, very careful —could manage to avert it. It was something that she had never dreamed of, even in her careful precautions against all possible pitfalls. It was a combination of things, and that was what made it so complicated.

If it had been just a question of her getting in the way, she could have handled that. Just by leaving Clay alone, like this, or showing him that she wanted to be alone herself, when he showed signs of turning too readily to her for understanding or companionship. That was simple enough—almost elementary . . . if she could only do it without hurting his feelings. Without stirring up that old defensive sensitiveness of his, or this new personal element which had grown up between them without their even knowing it; she hardly knew what it was yet—that personal thing.

For she was *not* in love with her own son-in-law, or he with her, she told herself sternly. She had liked Clay always—certainly—even when she hadn't understood him, and now that her sympathy had built a bridge across that gap of misunderstandings, she had grown truly fond of him. More than that, some old loneliness in her must have begun to reach out toward him. She would have liked to rest her head on his shoulder tonight, just as she would have leaned on Ronnie, if Ronnie had grown up. Just to rest there, in assurance of some strength to depend on that wasn't her own.

But that was all. She knew it was. It had to be. And there again, if that was the only thing she had had to bother with, she could have done it: stuffed her childish longing for comfort and protection back into herself, where it belonged, and gone on as usual. But there was Clay himself to reckon with. There was something in his face tonight, something puzzled and searching as he had stood looking down on her, not understanding what had struck her. For Clay had grown fond of her too, in some way which had nothing to do with their formal relationship. It was fantastic, after all the generations of jokes about them, to think of anybody being *fond* of a mother-in-law, in even the most filial way. There were lots of fantastic situations in life, but this particular combination just wasn't in the book, so it must be only in her imagination. Why, she must seem an old lady to him, she reminded herself—even though she behaved so childishly sometimes. Maybe he even had that thing they liked to write about in books nowadays—some sort of mother complex. Madge shivered a little at the thought.

But still she did know that she had some special sympathy and some soothing humor to offer him, which Margaret hadn't. Maybe that was what he was aware of, but it was like something in a solution which was not yet crystallized, and might never crystallize if she were careful enough. On the other hand, it might . . . Some little change around them that she couldn't help or foresee, some shift in temperature—some heat—or cold . . .

Even cold might do it. She might try her best to be casual and withdraw a little and that in itself might set him wondering, as it had so quickly tonight. And if he ever realized—if his feeling did change ever so little more, and become conscious of itself, then—she didn't know whether she could handle it or not. When another person's emotions came into action, you couldn't tell just which way they would go; you couldn't even be sure what they would do . . . to your own. It was that same strange process of one human being reacting on another, and then that one back again—or on to someone else. That deadly, inexorable, unpredictable chain reaction which never stopped in the world, as long as people were alive in it.

And so . . . she might become too fond of Clay herself: that was what she was afraid of, wasn't it? That ultimate humiliation, after all these years of refusal to contemplate any sort of—attachment—because she had been too old, even at middle age! And *now,* when she was getting old, to have that old loneliness surge up in a new form and try to fasten itself on something which never could belong to her . . . Which belonged to her own daughter, in fact.

She had come closer to Margaret these past two months than she ever had before. The old barrier between them had been growing more immaterial all the time; there had been only the remembrance of it left, only a shadow of puzzlement between them now and again. Like that look Margaret had given her that evening. Oh, Margaret wasn't jealous of her own mother; Madge was sure of that. But envy was another thing perhaps, and could be just as devastating. And Margaret *was* aware now that her mother could make Clay's and her readjustment more difficult. That was the thing Madge had to face: that she was *in the way,* not as some mothers-in-law were, but in this new, preposterous, unorthodox fashion. As unpredictable a fashion as only she could have invented—not meaning to at all. More than that, if Margaret should ever guess for one instant what had come just to the edge of her mother's mind tonight . . . or if Clay himself should so much as wonder . . . Madge didn't think she could bear it.

She got up stiffly, and with her hands still locked in front of her, began walking softly up and down and across the small room. She heard a door close on the second floor, rather loudly and irritably. Oh Clay, Clay, she thought sadly, I didn't mean to hurt your poor tender feelings. I don't want to hurt you at all. But Margaret's marriage was the most important thing, after all. She and Clay had something deep and lasting between them; they loved each other still; and Madge would never forget the afternoon when Margaret had broken down and let her mother know how much she loved him. She—Madge Fairlie—couldn't risk jeopardizing that.

So where would they go? Clay with no job, even with jobs available; it would be the same thing all over again, and Madge didn't think the marriage could survive that same unhealthy swamp another time. Not so soon; not even with Margaret's clearer vision. Well, then that meant that they'd have to have the House, and Madge would have to go. That was the only other way out. She stopped in the middle of the floor, trying to think, clearly—and trying to stifle the mere apprehension of fright which had begun to rise in her. Where—could she go—herself? Not traveling any more. She didn't have the money to spend on travel nowadays. With what she had put into the apartments, there would be even less . . . Yes, less. Because Margaret and Clay would need the income from the apartments; that was the only way she could help them now, to give him the job of running the House, and whatever he could make from it as salary. And that would leave her only that little monthly dribble which still came in from the Trust Fund.

She couldn't get an apartment here in town; Clay and Margaret would never consent to that. And they mustn't know that she couldn't travel. So there was only—where? She thought slowly, of England— and Lou, who was gone. And Europe—where she might have lived more cheaply—but that was gone too, in another larger sense. And Florida—expensive, the only parts of it she knew. And California . . . Oak Lea, perhaps. Yes, she'd liked it there, but it wasn't cheap either. Maybe she could write to Mollie Oakley, though. Maybe Mollie—would give her a job. If worst came to worst, she could do that, couldn't she? And Margaret wouldn't know.

Perhaps she could wait just a bit and see. Maybe a few weeks would smooth things out if she were just terribly careful. But—if it didn't work, that meant that it would have gotten worse, and some damage would already have been done. No, she couldn't wait, this time, for events to make the decision and save her making up her own mind. She'd always done that before, procrastinated, like poor Clay. But *she wasn't going to do that now*.

She unlocked her fingers finally, which were stiff and white from gripping each other, and went over to her desk in the corner and sat down there, fumbling for a piece of paper. She would write Mollie now, tonight, and then she would take the letter downstairs, and out to the box across the Square, before she could possibly weaken. At least she wasn't afraid to go out in the Square at night any more, even in winter. (How fortunate! she thought, parenthetically.)

*   *   *

But when she woke up that next morning, she thought she must have been insane the night before. She didn't even think of it for a couple of minutes, and then the sense of something faintly remembered and—unpleasant, began to bother her, until all at once it came down on her again like an awful weight which had been mercifully relieved during the night. She *couldn't* actually have written that letter—and gone out and mailed it too. . . . It wasn't possible! She sat up suddenly, as though there might still be some way to stop it, but sitting there with her shoulders uncovered only made her realize the penetrating cold of the November morning and that she had to get up and get Mr. Delephant's breakfast. And just as Sarah had done in that same room years before, she went stumbling barefoot and almost blindly across the floor to close the window.

But as Sarah had not done, Madge stood at the window shivering for a moment, staring out of sleep-swollen eyes, down at the Square below which was just beginning to take shape in the thin morning light. No billowy green tree tops now, only bare branches through which one could see the whole Square laid out starkly like a map. Gray walks, faded brown turf, and the small blank square of dry wading pool out there in the center. But desolate as it looked—she *couldn't* leave this place, Madge thought. Miserable as it had been at times, it was all an inextricable part of her. It was the only home she had, and she was too old now, ever to take root in any other one.

She wondered if she could have dreamed that last evening, and the letter too. Mollie wouldn't consider it for one minute, of course, and so there was no use in saying anything to Margaret and Clay. But the trouble was that she had to wait for the answer to come, and that was a bad ten days for Madge, while she was waiting. She was living on two levels during all that time. Going about on the top level as though nothing at all had happened, or would happen; but down on that other, lower level of her mind, those other thoughts went on about their business—not subconsciously and not unrecognized, just with a sort of relentless deliberation, each little thing noted up there and hastily dismissed, more carefully considered down below. (Margaret's slight coolness to Clay for a day or two after the movie—and Clay's slightly sullen indifference in return. Except when he was with Madge, when he became more comradely than ever. The renewed discussion of how they would eventually divide up the second floor, with Madge's newly sensitive retreat from siding with either one of them . . . only to realize that they both felt she had let them down.)

And down there also, underlying everything else, marched that deeper fear, an almost hopeless sense of the inevitable moving slowly forward. It was a sort of no man's land that she was facing, empty and wide open to all the devastation which she had been hearing about all these years. It was that very wasteland which she'd been taught to dread anew each time someone had said (indulgently or enviously as the case might be), "Well, *you* don't have to worry anyway. You'll always have plenty . . ." or (knowingly), "My dear, you don't know how lucky you are. . . ." It was the thing people talked about almost in their sleep: INSECURITY. Uncertainty—dependence —real poverty, perhaps. Not yet, no; not quite yet. She had a little left, out of the great deal she had once had. But if she gave up the House and went out into the world with only the slim income she had left now, there would be no real bulwark left. After all, you couldn't practically force people to take on something, as she had here, and then after a while snatch it back from them. The House would be gone, to all intents and purposes, except to visit in occasionally, at long, tactful intervals.

And presently she would be old and sick on top of everything else; really old, in body and not just in imagination or in vanity. Like the Delephants . . . Madge felt her heart shrink up in terror when she thought of the Delephants. Oh no, she thought—she'd lived safely—and softly no doubt—for too long to go out into that wilderness deliberately now. She'd never pretended to herself that she had any sort of courage, and it was too late now. Clay and Margaret were younger, and tougher too, and they'd have to work it out somehow themselves.

And then Mollie's letter came, after ten long days, with a sensible, everyday three-cent stamp, as though Mollie had never heard of air mail. The letter was with the other mail which came at breakfast time, and it was brief and forthright, which was like Mollie also.

"I wouldn't care to try anything like this with anybody else," she had written. "But with you I don't know. Help is still hard to get the Lord only knows. Maybe we can make a go of it Mrs. Fairlie if you want to come and try it out. I can let you have one of the rooms downstairs, under the living room and board too but we will have to see how much you can do before I know what I can pay you outside of that." Madge read the letter through and laid it down by her place. She would take it up to her room with her presently, and think it over up there: what to do with it now that it had come; how to answer it. How to let herself and Mollie down together, for Mollie Oakley would never think much of her again, Madge thought sorrowfully. She didn't think much of herself, for she had been hoping against hope that Mollie would turn her down.

She sat with her finger hooked idly in the handle of her coffee cup, pretending to finish her breakfast, looking vaguely around the table, feeling rather like a ghost in her own house, as she observed with a supernatural detachment the temporary goings-on of these temporary tenants. Fairlie was dawdling, and Margaret was trying to hurry him along. Clay was reading the paper, but flapping it occasionally in subconscious irritation. Finally he put it down with a grumble of relief as Fairlie bounced out the door, and Margaret sighed and looked over at her mother, and let her glance linger on her in a puzzled way. Her mother didn't know whether she herself looked a little queer right now, or whether it was another of those reflective looks which Margaret kept turning on her nowadays. Madge picked up her coffee cup at last and took one cool sip of the dregs left there. . . . And then she put it down again so suddenly that it seemed almost to bounce in the saucer, and said—rather loudly, to her own ear—"You know, I've got rather a surprise for you two."

They both looked at her expectantly. Oh *dear,* she thought, they were all so frightfully optimistic these days! Their reactions weren't even normally suspicious. So then she tried to ease up to it more gently. "I hope—you're not going to think I'm a deserter," she said, and her voice from being too loud, was now almost too faint, like a wind that had dropped suddenly.

"Why on earth should we, darling?" Margaret replied easily.

"You don't mean you're going to welch on letting us use the kitchen until we get fixed up ourselves?" Clay said in his paliest tone, cocking his eyebrow at her, and Madge rushed headlong at that opening.

"Well, no, not exactly. But I am going to let you use that whole apartment, when it's done. I've decided to go to California."

They stared at her.

"Suffering cats!" Clay said blankly. "When did you get that idea?"

"Oh . . ." Madge looked away from him. "A while ago. I just didn't think I'd mention it till I was sure I could have a room at Oak Lea. You remember how lovely it was there, don't you, Margaret?" The tone was an appeal.

"Why—yes, of course," Margaret said slowly. "But I had no idea you wanted to go back again now."

"I liked it there," Madge said. "I guess I've—always meant to go back some day."

"But Mother, I don't understand. Why don't you wait and go later on in the winter? It's always worse here in January and February."

Clay said nothing; he was still staring at Madge, but frowning now. Madge looked down, fingering the edge of the table, nervously.

"I'm tired, I guess. I've been realizing that more and more, lately. I'd rather go soon," she added, a little pitifully as though to say, Oh *don't* stop me now . . . let me go—let me go.

"You've been doing too much," Margaret said.

"Maybe. Maybe—I just want a rest—in the sun," Madge said, and pressed her lips tight together for a moment.

"Well at least we can have your apartment all ready for you by the time you get back," Margaret began again.

"But I want you to rent it," Madge broke in quickly. "Just as soon as it's ready. And to go on fixing up the rest of the house just as you both think best. I—don't want to feel I *have* to come back by any definite—time, you see. There's just one thing—" She had almost stopped when she began again, hurriedly, before either of them could speak. "There's only one thing I want you to promise me—and that is to give Mr. Delephant a home here, for as long as he lives. . . ." Her voice slipped away from her then; but perhaps it was her saying that which brought home the finality of her intention to the other two.

"Why *Mother!*" Margaret said, in a protest so shocked and so amazed that it stopped in its own tracks, as if not knowing how to go on from there. And Clay said, roughly, almost in the same breath, "Look here Madge—you can't do that . . ." And that was only the beginning.

She hadn't realized how strongly they would oppose the whole idea. Maybe she ought to have expected that, though she hadn't really looked beyond the small anguished struggle within herself. But she found now that their opposition was stiffening her own feeble resolution, that resolution which had almost been still born. How long she could continue to hold out she didn't know . . . for that first morning's discussion was only the first installment of an argument which went on for days. Margaret came to her later that morning, when she was alone, and took her by the shoulders and looked into her eyes.

"Now tell me, darling, what it is? Why do you want to go and leave us?"

"I don't want to leave you!" Madge cried out quickly. "But I want to go back there—where it's warm—while I can, and your being here now gives me the chance."

"I never knew you to make so much of the climate before."

"But I'm getting older, dear—can't you understand? Older people don't *like* winter and cold rainy weather, Margaret."

"Then why don't you want to come back in the spring?"

"I may, dear—Oh I will of course, later on. But I don't want to *keep* moving around—"

"Is there anything wrong with you, Mother, that you haven't told me? Your health, I mean."

"No—no—oh, just a little arthritis maybe," Madge said, feeling badgered and looking for some way to turn. But of course that only started Margaret wanting her to consult a doctor and so that particular argument went chasing down a byway with Madge fleeing ahead of it, looking for escape.

And that afternoon Clay cornered her when she was working out in the kitchen.

"Well, Mrs. Fairlie, when are you leaving us?" he said cheerily, and Madge saw that he was going to try to kid her out of this foolish notion of hers. She lifted her chin an inch.

"Why—about—next Wednesday, I thought, if I can get a reservation," she said gamely.

"Gosh, can't you get off before that?" said Clay. "I thought you were *really* in a hurry—" But he broke off suddenly. "What's the matter, Madge? It is me? Is that it, that you just can't stand having me around all the time?" The deep lines in his forehead were showing up. The haunted look in his eyes, and Madge turned to him quickly and put her hand on his arm—and knew, sick at heart, that she wanted to put her arms around him instead.

"Oh *no*, Clay—no! You know it isn't. I've loved having you here, having you all with me. You'll never know what it's meant to me. You must believe that."

"Then I just don't get it," Clay said flatly. "You're running out on us—that's what it is. This winter clime stuff doesn't fool me for a minute."

"Well," Madge said desperately, "maybe it isn't only the climate. Maybe I want to—get rid of the house."

"Get rid of it?" he repeated slowly.

"That's right. Can't you understand that? After all the years it's hung around my neck? Can't you see what a *relief* it is to have you to take it on this way? To have you and Margaret so interested and wanting to live here . . . You do want to live here now, don't you, Clay?" Her eyes searched his with intense anxiety and he nodded slowly.

"Yeah—yeah, I guess I do. Seems kind of like home now, at that. But with all the plans we've made together, I should think you'd want to stay and see it through."

"Well, I don't," Madge said, a trifle pettishly now. "I'm tired of seeing things through. And I wish you'd see about my reservation for me."

"Oh you do, do you? You think maybe I want to get rid of *you*, do you? Is *that* it?" He was scowling at her again.

"No, that's not it, Clay Ferguson, and you know it very well—and you're only trying to make it harder for me—and if you won't be decent and get my ticket, I'll get it for myself!" Madge's face was flushed and her eyes were bright and angry, and Clay moved up and put his arm across her shoulder.

"Okay," he said quickly, "O—kay! if that's the way you want it, Madge, I'll get it. Only I can't understand the whole deal, that's all."

Well, she thought, that was one way of getting her ticket, anyway . . . because she didn't think she could have walked in, in cold blood, and got it herself. She didn't know how she was ever going to go through with it all anyway. . . . But maybe if she bullied the lot of them as she had suddenly turned and bullied Clay, she would get all the little things done that she couldn't have brought herself to do. If she could just bully Margaret into packing for her—and Fairlie into running errands—and Mr. Purcell into arranging about the deed for the house . . .

For she had trouble with Mr. Purcell too.

"Mrs. Fairlie, I'm sorry to say so, but I think you're all wrong about this. You're already putting a lot of money into that house to make it an income-paying proposition. I understand that; we discussed it before and you made your own decision about it. But at least it was your property and you could live on it. Now you propose to put it in your daughter's name and have her husband run it, and you're stripping yourself of the one largest asset that you have left."

"Yes," Madge said. "I suppose I am." She sounded almost indifferent about it, and Mr. Purcell ran one hand through his thinning hair and got up to pace around his office. "I understand your feeling about your children," he said carefully, "wanting to provide for them and all that. And I've no doubt that what you say is true, that Mr. Ferguson is better fitted to supervise and manage the house as an apartment house than you are. But why not make him your agent if you prefer, and keep it in your name."

"It will be simpler," Madge said stubbornly, "if I decide to stay on out in California, to have them the actual owners."

She couldn't say, My son-in-law has always hated working under someone else. She couldn't say, I don't want him to feel, one of these days, that I am his boss after all . . . that I turned out to be just another one of those interfering, managing mothers-in-law. . . .

Mr. Purcell stared at her helplessly.

"Very well," he said after a moment, finally conceding that helplessness. "I'll have them go ahead with the title policy, if that's what you wish."

But when she went out of his office a few moments later, he threw up his hands and then dropped them heavily at his sides. "For this have we wives and mothers!" he muttered aloud as he turned back into the room. "For this do we sweat our guts out, to provide for their comfort and old age! For this, God damn it, do we put over half the wealth of the country into women's hands—to have them throw it away as if it were so much garbage. . . ."

He probably didn't realize that Madge could hear what he had said, fuming to himself in a kind of monumental frustration; he certainly didn't know that she had stopped short outside, thinking at first that he was speaking to her. But then she started on again, walking with that curious little rolling gait of hers, which was always unconsciously exaggerated when she was trying to be independent.

She was a great trial to Margaret too, she knew, for Margaret was definitely troubled about her mother now, had even begun to inquire at last whether Madge still had plenty to live on, and was plainly unable to tell whether her mother's vagueness on the subject was deliberate, or only the same old ingenuous ignorance. And when she learned about the house, she was deeply distressed.

"Oh no, Mother! I don't *want* you to do that," she protested. "You've given us too much already. . . ."

"I'd rather have it that way," Madge said with the same gentle obstinacy she had shown to poor Mr. Purcell. "It will be better all around—and the house would be yours some day, anyway. I shall feel freer. . . ."

But even so, Margaret kept worrying—worrying about her, and *at* her too; uneasily aware that there was something behind that bland obduracy, yet quite unsure of what it was. They were all either puzzled—or annoyed—or hurt by her walking out on them, as Clay called it, and Madge had to fight them all, singly or together by day, and then fight herself all over again at night. For though the outward gestures were being made, the preparations for departure moving up on her relentlessly as though she had not set them in motion herself, she still had no real conviction that she would go. She was trying to go; but maybe that was only to be able to tell herself that she *had* tried, later on. It was a wavering, swaying battle, and she herself knew that it wasn't yet won, not by any means. And the night when Fairlie looked at her plaintively and said, "Gosh, Gran, I don't see what you want to go away for just when we've all been having so much fun here! I don't see why you want to go and spoil everything . . ." that night Madge went up to her rooms at the top of the house and cried—broke down and cried, with a bitterness and abandon which she had not known, or had not given way to, since the day Brute was run over, nearly twenty years ago.

Why do they make it so hard, she asked, of someone—who never answered. As if it wasn't bad enough already! Why didn't she go down again, right now, and tell them she wasn't going and never had intended to go? Just give in. She would have to do it sooner or later —tomorrow or the next day—or even Wednesday, which was the day she was supposed to go.

But Wednesday came, and still she hadn't told them. She woke at four that morning and lay there, numb, but wide awake in the darkness, wondering just when she would break down that day. At breakfast?—but that would delay Fairlie getting to school—or later in the morning, when the man came for her trunk? Or would she hold out right up to the evening, and then crumble, like a panic-stricken child, at the very last minute, with the dark coming on . . . If Margaret should put her arms around her just once more and say, "Mother, it still isn't too late, and we don't want you to go. . . . We won't know how to get along without you. . . ."

But that was fantasy, Madge thought wearily. Or was the getting up to put a few last things in the open trunk—the looking out of the window for a brief last-morning glance at the wintry Square—was that the fantasy, after all? A last momentary deceiving of herself into thinking that she could ever do anything so heroic as merely leaving home again—but this time for good?

The day began slowly but picked up speed as it went along. The trunk went off at one, Madge watching it down the narrow stairs stonily—and silently. And in the afternoon she went over to say good-by to Mona. Mona had wanted to come to her, but for some tenuous reason, Madge felt she'd rather go to the Cressley house instead, so that she could leave when she wanted to. She seemed to be trying to leave herself an exit now, an escape at every step along the way. But Mona didn't ask any questions. She must have guessed something by this time, about Madge's circumstances, or about her giving up the House to Margaret and Clay, but all she said, when Madge got up to go, was a quiet, "You know, you're quite a person, Madge Fairlie. I've always known you had a lot more courage stowed away than *you* ever thought you had."

"Oh no," Madge said, looking back into her eyes rather sadly. "Oh no!" And then she blurted out, "I may not get off even now, and that's the plain truth, if you want to know it."

"You mean—you're trying to bluff everybody, for some mysterious reason of your own?" Mona said, a little puzzled now.

"Yes," Madge answered. "Everybody but myself." And that was when she made her escape, thankful that she could get away. But she turned at the door to look back with her little deprecatory smile. "I'll call you in the morning," she said matter-of-factly, "if I don't get off after all."

So that was the opening crack, she told herself, going home in the taxi; she had known it would come, any moment. But it was getting late by the time she got home, and Margaret was beginning to get Mr. Delephant's supper, as though she'd already taken on that part of her new job. Madge, with a somewhat frustrated feeling, went on upstairs to her own rooms, where everything was all picked up and tidy and ready for departure. Well, she would get her bath before dinner, she thought, and put on the fresh things she had laid out there, anyway. . . . As she was dressing again, the strap on her slip broke, and she exclaimed in annoyance, then laid it aside and got another one out of the suitcase. And when she was dressed she picked up the offending garment and took it downstairs to mend. The lights were on in the dining room but no one was there; Margaret was still out in the kitchen, and she had heard Fairlie playing and humming to himself on the second floor as she came down. The rest of the House was pleasantly quiet, now that the workmen had gone home. She didn't know where Clay was.

But as she was threading her needle, she heard him come out of the apartment across the hall and in a minute he appeared in the dining-room doorway and stopped and stood regarding her from there.

"Hi," he said gravely, and she looked up at him smiling and said "Hi!" like a gentle but satiric echo, in return. She was sitting at one end of the couch and he came across and sat down beside her, looking fixedly at the work in her hands.

"All ready to take off, are you?" he asked after a minute.

"I—guess so," she said, uncertainly. This was the time then, she thought, this minute—to start backing out . . . but she felt too weak to go backward, or forward either.

She clipped the thread and started to lay down the needle and scissors on the table at her end of the couch. He was still watching her hands, rather dully, without expression. But then he shifted his body slightly, swung his feet up on the other end of the couch, and lay down flat with his head in her lap.

"For heaven's sake, Clay!" She sounded almost as much alarmed as surprised, and pulled anxiously at the slip she'd just mended to get it out from under his head—as though that was the thing she was trying to protect. She had to hold herself firmly in check to keep from struggling up and dumping him off on the floor. Really, she thought, this was a little too much! He had closed his eyes with a comfortable grunt, and she looked down at his face, with an unreasonable feeling of being utterly trapped there.

"Golly, but I'm tired," he sighed. "And here you are going off and leaving the whole damn shebang on my hands." His voice was a mixture of complaint and complacency. He was put upon, it seemed to say—but of course he was the guy who could Take It. But still, he wanted you to *know* he was put upon. And then he opened those disconcerting pale blue eyes, always a shade lighter than you remembered them, and looked straight up at her. "Why do you do it, Madge?" he asked directly. "Why do you go, anyway? You don't want to—I know you don't; and you know we're going to miss you like hell."

"Because I know a good way out when I see one!" Madge retorted, with a touch of grimness now, and a new touch of alarm too, for she heard the swish of the swing door from the kitchen, and that was Margaret's step in the pantry. "For heaven's sake, Clay," she said again, quite sharply. "Get *up*, will you! D'you think you're a lap dog, or what?"

The door from the pantry swung open briskly, but Margaret must certainly have heard her mother's tone of genuine annoyance. And as she came into the room Madge was struggling to free herself of Clay's heavy head and shoulders, lifting and pushing them away a little, and slithering out from under as she got to her feet.

"Your husband thinks he's a lap dog, or something!" she exclaimed again, with so much irritation that Margaret could only laugh as she stood there surveying them.

"Just like all Saint Bernards and Airedales," she remarked.

But Clay had recovered himself and his balance and was sitting up with his feet on the floor again, rubbing his head.

"I was trying," he said in a tone of injured dignity, "to tell the little woman here that we were going to miss her—trying, in my simple way, to anchor her." And then he got up abruptly. "I mean that, too," he said, as if to set the record straight before them all. "And I'm not speaking for Peg or any polite family business either. I personally am going to miss you like the devil, Madge, and that's the God-bitten truth."

"I guess she knows that," Margaret said, after a second, very softly. "She knows we'll both—miss her terribly." And she and her mother looked at each other across the dining room table; it was a long, steady look, and Madge knew finally, in that moment, that Margaret really loved her. It was worth it, she thought—to go anywhere on earth, or beyond it—just to be able to take that knowledge with her at last.

And by that she knew thankfully, that Margaret had seen nothing beyond the fact that Madge felt herself too much implicated in Clay's rehabilitation—and knew that it was best to leave Margaret's own job to Margaret. That was all there had been to see. And after that they began to move around quickly, setting the table, and calling Fairlie downstairs, and the minutes began to go by very fast indeed. Dinner was gay, and not dreary and strained as Madge had feared it would be, and by the time it was over and the dishes cleared and washed, there wasn't much time left, as Madge's train was due to leave at nine and it would take twenty minutes or more to drive down.

"I want to get on a little ahead," she said, "so I can get myself stowed away before the train starts lurching around."

"You'll be going right to bed anyway, won't you?" Margaret said.

"I wish you didn't have that horrid early arrival in Chicago. I do hope you'll sleep."

"Oh no, I never do the first night. I'll probably lie awake for hours!" Madge replied lightly, but her tone already had an odd, sleep-walking quality in it.

And then she went upstairs for the last time, to get her things on, and Margaret followed after her only a moment later, and stood watching her wordlessly as she put her hat on carefully, and then she went over and put her arms tight around her mother, and knocked the hat a little askew again.

"Oh Mother," she said. "Mother darling."

But that was all. Clay's step was on the stairs now too, coming up to get her bags, and when he'd picked them up, Madge looked around hastily to see if she'd left anything, and her glance brushed past the window. She'd meant to go and have a last long look down into the Square, but she couldn't now, with the others standing right there. So they went down in a procession, and Mr. Delephant came out of his room to say good-by, in his most punctilious, courtly fashion, wishing her a pleasant trip (as though he were the host after all, and she only a weekend guest). And then, down on the lower landing, standing—was it providentially?—in front of Hugo's portrait, was Fairlie, who didn't want to see her go, but didn't want to be kissed either. Madge kissed him anyway and he grinned at her and backed away, embarrassed.

The taxi was waiting, so they didn't linger, and it took only the briefest seconds to stow the bags in the back before they were off, and Madge didn't even have a chance to look up the curving steps to the front door, which had always appeared so heavily imposing to her. Then finally, as they turned the corner to circle the Square, she did take one hasty look back and across at the House, which seemed very foursquare and safe and solid, standing there in the dark.

Though it had never been very safe for her, she thought absently, and caught at the idea in a sort of surprise, as it almost went by her. Why no, there never had been any real safety there, had there? Shelter yes, and protection of a sort—from the weather, say. But you couldn't be protected, in any house, from the things which were already inside it. And this thing called safety—this security they talked so much about—what was it, after all? Was there—any such thing in the world? Not against old age, there wasn't. Or against illness. Or war. And certainly not against these newer things they were all dreading now. Atomic bombs. And more wars to end war . . . and homes, and families, and all civilization along with them. So why should people dwell so heavily on the security which went with money—if it even did that? Why should they think so much more of it than of any other kind of safety? Why should they even expect it?

Margaret had one of her mother's hands in her own, and was talking away, lightly and deliberately in that same old way that she used to keep the conversation going at a party, and Madge was nodding her head in a preoccupied way, even putting in a vague word now and then. But she was thinking, quite irrelevantly . . . of her younger sister Judy, who had died of cancer before she was forty. Of Lou who had married in England—for security. Of Emmy Burns . . . and Mrs. Delephant . . . And Clay and Margaret—and everybody she knew. Even of herself and her own—sheltered?—life.

They had reached the station almost before she knew it, and gone through the business of checking tickets and collecting bags, and filing through the gates and down the long runway beside the train, with the engine sighing loudly to itself. There wasn't very much time left now, and Madge asked them, rather urgently, please—not to wait. So Margaret kissed her and Clay kissed her and she waved her hand at them from the steps; Margaret (calm, self-possessed Margaret) was crying openly, but Clay had his arm around her, and kept it there, holding her close against his side as they turned finally and walked away together. And Madge retreated numbly into the car again, along between the still green curtains to her own lower berth. (No drawing room this time; no more private compartments!) And with people passing by occasionally, brushing against the curtains, exchanging brief laughter or abrupt sentences out there, she unfastened her night case, and absent-mindedly took out a few things she would need, and presently, while she was still arranging herself, she felt the train under her moving, moving slowly and with an exquisite smoothness. She looked up for a moment, her lips open and her hands still, and thought quite peacefully, but a little surprised, So I did go, after all.

She had brushed her teeth at home, so she wouldn't have to go into the dressing room, and as the train gathered speed and began to rock her around in its usual brusque fashion, she undressed and tucked her bag and clothes out of the way, so that she could slide into the bed and stretch out. She lay there for a couple of minutes then, looking up at her reflection in the polished lower side of the upper berth which faced her. It was a dull reflection which softened her white hair, and lines, and generally old look—but Madge wasn't deceived. She was old enough, and rapidly getting older, and what was worse, she was a little old fool, going out to face all kinds of things of which she had no real and practical conception. But she didn't deceive herself about that either. She knew nothing at all of hardship. All she had learned was a little endurance, perhaps—which might help her to endure a little more. Life was largely a matter of endurance, wasn't it?—now of one kind, now another. (Like that old saying about the man who learned to carry a cow by starting in when it was just a calf, Madge thought inconsequently. . . .)

But it was a very curious thing: lying there, racketing along in a train—which she had always loathed anyway—knowing less than ever of where she was going, she felt safer than she had in many, many years. Just because she knew there was no safety anywhere, and it was foolish to look for it or count on it. You never knew, that was all—from one moment to the next, and no matter where you were. But you had to go along anyway . . . and you *could* go along anyway, that was the wonderful, incredible thing that Madge knew now. She reached up and snapped off the small reading lamp, and lay in the humming, clanking darkness with her eyes closed. It was as though she were swinging out into space. She had stepped off the hard earth and there was nothing below her—nothing at all. And yet she was swinging there, easily, at the far free end of some long, fine cable which she could neither see nor feel. So of course—she thought drowsily—if you couldn't hang on to it, it couldn't break either. Extraordinary thought . . . extraordinary feeling. . . And within ten minutes of turning out the light, Madge was asleep.